THE MARQUISE OF O——
[*AND OTHER STORIES*]

HEINRICH VON KLEIST

The Marquise of O—

AND OTHER STORIES

Translated and with an Introduction
by Martin Greenberg

Preface by Thomas Mann

FREDERICK UNGAR PUBLISHING CO.
NEW YORK

Republished 1973
by arrangement with the original publisher,
Criterion Books

Copyright © 1960 by Martin Greenberg
and Criterion Books

Manufactured in the United States of America
Library of Congress Catalog Card Number: 73-8744-1
ISBN 0-8044-2478-0 (Cloth)
0-8044-6365-4 (Paperback)

Fourth Printing, 1979

KLEIST AND HIS STORIES
by Thomas Mann

Heinrich von Kleist was descended from a family of squires and officers, residents of Mark Brandenburg. There was little about this baby-faced young man to predispose people in his favor. In society he appeared sullen, melancholy, tongue-tied—a disability stemming in part from a speech defect, which made his sporadic contributions sound unpleasantly severe. He seemed unusually liable to fits of sudden embarrassment, stammered or blushed, and altogether impressed his associates by his neurotically forced and tense manner. To infer from such a strange habitus the presence of surpassing genius, weighed down by a sense of mission and tormented by vast issues, would certainly be rash. Yet it is quite true that in Kleist's case such a conjecture would have been borne out by fact. He was one of the greatest, boldest, and most ambitious poets Germany has produced; a playwright and storyteller of the very first order; a man unique in every respect, whose achievement and career seemed to violate all known codes and patterns. Kleist dedicated himself to his extravagant themes with a passion little short of frenzy, and the demands he made upon himself could not fail to destroy his system, never very strong and pitched to hysteria from the very first. Trying to force what cannot be forced, and undermined by psychogenic ailments, this poet was clearly destined for an early death: at the age of thirty-five he killed himself and a woman who was incurably ill, whom he did not love, and with whom he had nothing in common but a powerful death wish. "I am going," he said, "since there is nothing left for me either to learn or to gain in this life." Kleist died because he was weary of his incompleteness and eager to return his botched self to the universal flux—hoping, perhaps, that some day it would arise in a more perfect shape.

Within the short span of thirty-five years Kleist flung forth (the term will hardly do considering how painfully this writer worked over his manuscripts, and yet it seems to fit very well once we attend to the extreme, frightening vehemence of his productions) an *oeuvre* imposing in its proportions: eight plays, one of which—*Robert Guiscard*—remained a mighty torso; an equal number of stories; a novel, scheduled to appear in two volumes, which has never been found; a series of essays, including that brilliant piece of philosophical discourse called "On the Puppet Theatre"; a group of marvelously wrought anecdotes and, finally, several pieces of topical journalism which share the violence, amounting almost to fury, of his central works. All this was accomplished by a young writer whose brief career was further curtailed by his profound and protracted ignorance of himself, who could never make up his mind whether he was destined to be a poet and nothing but a poet, and who worked spasmodically, not calmly and steadily. The only genre hardly cultivated by Kleist is the lyric—and we may well ask why he chose to bypass it, why this extraordinary master of poetic rhetoric, whose plays abound in magnificent flights of poetry, could never get himself to speak directly and freely *in propria persona*. What was it, we ask, that pushed him constantly toward more objective modes of communication, toward the vehement yet at the same time quite impersonal manner of his stories? And then we are reminded of his inability to converse freely with other human beings, of the speech defect referred to earlier. True, Kleist reveled in dionysiac oratory; yet the confessional mode of which Goethe was so prodigal (remember that Goethe would have labeled all his literary productions "parts of one great confession") remained forever closed to him. The final secret of Kleist's tormented life went into the grave with the dying man, who shortly before had written to his devoted sister: "The fact of the matter is that there was no help for me on this earth."

Kleist was born in Frankfurt on the Oder, the son of a retired major, Joachim Freidrich von Kleist. At the age of fifteen the delicate, sensitive boy was placed, according to custom, in a regiment of guards stationed in Potsdam, where (also according to custom) the common soldiers were beaten and the officers were illiterate wastrels. While still an ensign he was sent to the Army of the Rhine, took part in the siege of Mayence and two hot skirmishes. "May God give us peace to enable us to make up, by more humane deeds, for the time we kill here so unethically." This hardly sounds like enthusiasm for the soldier's profession. Kleist's distaste for the profession did not diminish but on the contrary grew steadily, even after his return to garrison life in Potsdam. The young lieutenant, just turned twenty-one, asked for his release. After seven years of service, every one of which he cursed, the release was granted him and he was free to matriculate as a student in the university of his native city. The next few years were to be dedicated to a study of the sciences, mathematics, philosophy, and a project entitled "The Encyclopaedia of Literature."

It is obvious that literature did not mean at first to the young Kleist what it came to mean later: intensive production, passion, tragedy, destiny. At that stage literature implied principally erudition, enlightenment, moral perfection, sound scholarship. The profession of a university teacher seemed the right one for him. Whatever he assimilated he put to immediate use by lecturing privately to young girls of his own class. It was moral pedagogy, not love, that prompted his engagement to a certain Wilhelmina Zenge, whom he had previously instructed in German grammar and now made to write essays on the subject of the true aims and satisfactions of married life.

But a moment arrived when Kleist dimly perceived that all this, his engagement first and foremost, was sheer nonsense; that science and mathematics, scholarship and philosophical speculation, even moral perfection, were really no concern of his; that this whole realm of abstraction with which he was mortifying himself (as in other ways he mortified himself as a high-minded bridegroom) was a waste of his nervous energy and his vital powers. The crisis occurred in the summer of 1800 when Kleist suddenly undertook a journey— the first in a long series of restless peregrinations. This first trip, incidentally, was made for medical reasons, though exactly what those reasons were is not known. He went to a hospital in Würtzburg for the "removal of an impediment to marriage." The phrase may have referred to a nervous ailment or, as one biographer states, to a minor physical malformation. There is also some mention of adolescent "confusions" into which Kleist was afraid of relapsing.

In his letters, Kleist wrote about his stay at the clinic in terms at once enigmatic and emphatic, using phrases like "incredible sacrifices" and "tremendous stakes." But he returned triumphant, calling out to his bride, "You were born for motherhood!" and "Girl, how happy you will be!" Yet a short time later he was writing: "I have often wondered whether it is not my duty to leave you." And in fact he left her, with the strange words: "There is one term in the German language most women will never understand. That is the term *ambition*." And later in the same letter: "Don't write to me again. My only wish is to die."

This combination of ambition and desire for annihilation is difficult to comprehend. As Kleist himself put it: "Everything is tangled in my mind like the fibres on a distaff." His whole nature rebelled against the notion of accepting some nondescript position, such as would have been necessary if he were to marry Wilhelmina. His scientific ambition, his quest for truth, had suffered a shock through the study of Kant's philosophy, which overthrew all his moral and intellectual notions. It had suddenly dawned upon him that truth and perfection are not within our reach, and that all our knowledge is conditioned by the peculiar nature of our ratiocination. This insight overwhelmed him. "My one supreme goal has vanished, and I am bereft." For a while he simply drifted, idle, vacant, unmoored. And yet not entirely unmoored. For in the interim, without quite knowing or wanting it, he had started to write. After brief stays at Göttingen, Berlin, Strasbourg, Berne, Köningsberg, Dresden, he came for a while to Paris, bringing with him two barely begun plays, *The Schroffenstein Family,* and *Robert Guiscard, Duke of Normandy.* The first he was eventually to complete: it turned out to be a bombastic and picaresque play, full of absurdities yet not without flashes of genuis. Kleist himself soon labeled it a "wretched piece of trash." The figure of Guiscard, on the other hand, became a figure of destiny for Kleist. Having set out to conquer Byzantium, that Norman duke persisted in his design against all odds, although his army was decimated by the plague and he himself tainted with it. A figure of destiny and at the same time a poetic task that was never to be completed, which Kleist attacked again and again: a symbol of the ambition we have heard him allude to earlier. And yet there is a grotesque element to this ambition, which refers only indirectly to the world, fame, literary accomplishment but directly to his Prussian ancestry and his family, before whom he wished to justify his existence in a desperate see-saw between pride and inferiority. *Guiscard* was to be the proof that he, although *déclassé,* was worthy to bear the name of Kleist. All who read the fragment of *Guiscard* were full of admiration. For a while the project was referred to as "the crown of immortality." But eventually the poet had to admit defeat. "I have spent half a thousand days, including many nights, trying to add another crown to those already won by our family. But now our patron saint calls out that I have done enough. She kisses the sweat on my brow and comforts me by telling me that if every one of her sons had worked as hard as I, our name would not be missing from the constellations . . ." Greater nonsense has never been uttered. If this name has a place among the constellations it is he and he alone who has put it there.* I do not know, and doubt whether anyone else knows, what honors have accrued to Brandenburg through the deeds of the majors and generals von Kleist. But I do know that there is only one Kleist in all the world, and that is the one who wrote *Penthesilea, Michael Kohlhaas,* and the one tremendous act of *Robert Guiscard,* which is so superb that is is impossible to imagine its continuation. Without our poet the name of Kleist would be nothing, yet he opines that his inspired labors are done only for the glorification of his family, every sign of disapprobation on whose part he feels as a stab.

What confusion and childishness must have reigned in this mind! And yet there are elements in this crazy "ambition" which are more consonant with the serious cast of the term, though even they are tainted with the dismal and the soul-destroying. Kleist's ambition was in its very essence damaged by *hubris,* jealousy and envy, always overreaching itself, the passion of one pretending to a crown that is not rightfully his and which must be torn from the head of its true owner, in this case the most great, most richly blest Goethe.

Kleist's ambivalent attitude to Goethe, forever oscillating between humility and hatred, admiration and fierce jealousy, and leading finally to a personal clash, contributed greatly to the bitterness of his life. And yet his extravagant dream of deposing that sovereign of letters from his throne was not altogether absurd. Kleist was

* One of Kleist's forebears, Ewald von Kleist (1715–1759), was a poet, but I am not familiar with his work, nor do I greatly regret my ignorance.

shy and taciturn as a rule. But one day in Ossmannstädt he told
Wieland, then an old man, who knew how to get him to talk, the
plan of his *Guiscard* and recited some passages from memory. The
aged arbiter of letters was fascinated. He exclaimed that here was
a force capable of filling a gap in German dramatic literature which
even Goethe and Schiller had been unable to fill. After Kleist had left,
Wieland sent after him the following note: "Nothing is beyond the
grasp of your genius. You must complete your *Guiscard,* though
Caucasus and Atlas together were on your shoulders." Small wonder
that Kleist's opinion of himself rose extraordinarily. But not for
long. Shortly after, he burned the manuscript, sparing, however, a
few pages from which he was later to reconstruct the fragment.

Goethe once wrote: "A man who is unable to despair has no need
to be alive." Kleist's tempestuous temperament was only too prone
to despair. But even during his fits of anguish his gaze remained
fixed on the crown of the Olympian Goethe. For Kleist knew deep
down that there was something in him which might, eventually,
enable him to outdistance Goethe and Schiller, those favorites of
the gods—something pre-Olympian, titanic, barbaric; something
elementally dramatic, having nothing to do with erudition,
humanitas, the golden mean, Winckelmann's brand of Hellenism,
or any moralizing poetry of ideas; something ecstatic and enthusi-
astic, generating excesses of expression down to the smallest details
of a brutally frank style.

After the wild ferment of their early works, Goethe and Schiller
had reached the harbor of a high-minded and noble classicism, of
ideal beauty. It is this stage which represents the apogee of our
literary culture. There is nothing else in our literature as loftily beautiful as Goethe's *Iphigenia.* There could be no more successful
formal experiment than Schiller's imitation of classical drama in
The Bride of Messina. Nevertheless, it is Kleist's plays alone, lacking
as they are in harmonious proportion and decorum, that give us

the archaic shudder of myth the way Sophocles and Aeschylus do. This is especially true of the one work he was unable to finish, the *Guiscard* fragment.

I thoroughly understand—I even share—Goethe's unsympathetic reaction to this genius who was too wild and elemental ever to conform to any aesthetic convention. There can be no doubt that what Kleist was after was a "confusion of affects." This holds true even of his most charming and delightful version of Molière's *Amphitryon,* where Goethe found a certain obscurantism in Kleist's interpretation of *le partage avec Jupiter* as a Christian overshadowing by the holy spirit. It is also true that Kleist was painfully hypochondriac, could never come to terms with life, that his taste ran to pathological subjects such as somnambulism and hysteria, that he had an oppressive concern with legalistic involvements, apparent even in his last and most mature play, *The Prince of Homburg.* There is something ghastly about the perverse eroticism and cannibalism of his *Penthesilea,* which he dedicated to Goethe "on the knees of his heart" and which the latter coldly rejected. Even more ghastly is the berserk nationalism (Rome standing for France and Napoleon) of *The Battle of Arminius,* whose blue-eyed protagonist acts more deviously than any Punic leader—a perfectly realistic trait, though it rather warns against than idealizes the German character. Nor is the extravagant naiveté, the near-parody of popular style of *Kätchen von Heilbronn* to everybody's taste: a drama of knighthood which pushes romanticism to the brink of absurdity, full of somnambulism, *Doppelgänger,* angels leading people through fire and water. Goethe, who had earlier ruined Kleist's broad farce in the Dutch manner, *The Broken Pitcher,* by staging it in three acts (Kleist wanted to challenge him to a duel), instead of putting on *Kätchen von Heilbronn* burned the manuscript in his stove on account of its "damnable perversity." Later he wrote in a review, "With the best will in the world toward this poet, I have always been moved to horror and disgust by something in his works, as though here were a body well-planned by nature, tainted with an incurable disease."

This image stays with the reader because it rests on a true perception, and some of Kleist's own statements seem to bear it out. "You must realize that my heart is sick." And yet, quite apart from the fact that the man who had written *Werther* and *Tasso* was hardly in a position to pronounce so haughtily on the subject of morbidity, it can be claimed that in the case of Kleist abnormality has resulted in an increase of poetic power, rather than its opposite. Regardless of the elements of sickness in his genius or the recurrence of illness in a life overburdened by a sense of the highest responsibility, this was not a sick man. In his first play the following lines occur: "A man doesn't have to support calmly every stroke of fortune. When God strikes it is permitted to sink down and to sigh as well, for equanimity is a virtue only to athletes. As human beings we take our falls neither for money nor for show. And yet we should always get up again with dignity." Kleist always rose from his collapses and fits of despair with dignity, and moreover the relation between health and its opposite is too complicated for anyone to deny vitality rashly to a man of this sort. His physical illnesses bear a strong resemblance to the fainting fits which occur over and over in his writings—so that we may look upon them as recoveries through a profound return to the unconscious, to the sources of life; and his stubbornness and will to maturity is such that is puts all robustness to shame. In a single year, 1808, after the ecstatic labors of the *Penthesilea,* he wrote not only the overly sweet *Kätchen von Heilbronn,* but also the entire, savage *Battle of Arminius* and four of his most powerful stories, including the magnificent *Michael Kohlhaas.* Is this not vitality? And in 1810, one year before his death, he gave the world his most successful and, for all its oppressive features, most serene play, *The Prince of Homburg.* Then his painful life came to a close. Nor did it lack completeness. A life need not last for eighty years in order to be fully sustained and victorious.

Without laying any claim to minute accuracy in biographical matters, I have ventured these few remarks on the subject of Kleist's personality and literary career. I have done this on the assumption that Anglo-American readers of the stories presented here may wish to learn something about the extraordinary artist who fashioned them. The original publisher of Kleist's fiction (Georg Reimer in Berlin) must have been a man of unusual courage; yet the courage, not to say the temerity, of Criterion Books, Inc. deserves equal admiration. Not having seen the English version I can, of course, form no clear conception of how the translator went about his business. I am confident though, that he was thoroughly familiar with the rigors of his task, and that he has acquitted himself well. Even if his version were only half successful, he would still command our respect—for I honestly believe that no more arduous job of translation can be imagined.

Kleist's narrative is something altogether unique. To account for it by the cliché of "historical perspective" won't do: even in his own time Kleist's singularity stood out; no other contemporary writer resembled him in the least. His method of storytelling is as eccentric as his plots, and with every few exceptions—among whom Ludwig Tieck was the most notable—Kleist's contemporaries found his fiction intolerably mannered, unpalatable in fact. And yet how is it possible to accuse a writer of affectation who proves on every page that he has looked at life closely and rendered it responsibly? We are faced with a style hard as steel yet impetuous, totally matter-of-fact yet contorted, twisted, surcharged with matter; a style full of involutions, periodic and complex, running to constructions like "in such a manner . . . that," which make for a syntax that is at once closely reasoned and breathless in its intensity. Kleist succeeds in developing an indirect discourse over twenty-five lines without resorting to a single full stop: in this discourse we find no less than thirteen dependent clauses introduced by *that* and, at the end, a "briefly, in such a manner that . . ."—which, however, fails to pull the sentence up short, but instead gives rise to yet another *that* clause! The first sentence of *The Earthquake in Chile* has long been famous as a masterpiece of succinct exposition: everything the reader needs to know has been compressed into a very few words, and the narrative, as sober as it is beautifully articulated, betrays at once the hand of a master: "In Santiago, the capital of the kingdom of Chile, at the very moment of the great earthquake of 1647 in which many thousands of lives were lost, a young Spaniard by the name of Jeronimo Rugera, who had been locked up on a criminal charge, was standing against a prison pillar, about to hang himself."

All Kleist's stories are told in this unusual style, and none of them fails of extraordinary effect. I have called the American publisher of Kleist's fiction a courageous man; all the same, I think the man knows what he is doing, and I can scarcely imagine his enterprise falling flat. The present collection should find a large and responsive public, for everything in it is exciting, amazing, not to say sensational. Being an extremist, Kleist delights in out-of-the-way subjects and psychological borderline cases, and he can be brutal at times.

Kleist's stories range in length from the full-fledged novella to the terse anecdote: from *Michael Kohlhaas,* the story of a man whose outraged sense of justice turns him into an outlaw and incendiary, to such pieces as *The Beggarwoman of Locarno,* a ghost story dear to E. T. A. Hoffmann, in which the guilty lord of the manor, exacerbated with horror, finally sets fire to his house. "Exacerbated with horror": let the reader ponder the phrase; it is thoroughly characteristic of Kleist. As regards *Kohlhaas,* I need hardly emphasize the pre-eminence of this story (perhaps the strongest of all German stories) in this collection. Allowing for certain poetic liberties, the writer follows the facts of an old chronicle. A certain Kohlhaas, named Hans instead of Michael, actually lived. This man, prompted by a sense of justice that was accurate as a precision scale, and a passion for right which could not brook the brittleness of worldly institutions, allowed himself to be swept into those deeds of violence which Luther condemned and which we cannot wholly condemn—though we admit with Kohlhaas that his head is justly forfeit, *after* the satisfaction of his legal claim, which was sacred to him, however lawlessly pursued. This Kohlhaas, whose story Kleist relates to us without batting an eyelash or raising his voice, while all along working powerfully on our emotions, appears almost insane at times in his zeal to reform the world by terroristic methods—especially when we see him issuing "Kohlhaasian manifestoes" from the "seat of his provisional world government"; and Goethe thought that it was "not possible for a mature intelligence to enter into such forced and extravagant motivations with any degree of pleasure." He granted that the story was "prettily told and put together with much ingenuity" (as though prettiness or ingenuity had anything to do with this powerful piece), yet felt it necessary to add that it took a rather perverse kind of writer, and one deeply dyed in hypochondria to present such a "singular" case as having universal value and significance. Here we have Goethe, true to form, while in Kohlhaas it is Kleist—the whole Kleist—who is addressing us and who may have some value too. To put it quite bluntly: this writer was not the man to shield knavery from "perverse criticism" simply because it happened to be in the saddle; and neither was Rudolf von Ihering, one of the greatest lawyers Germany has produced, who around 1870 published his famous book, *A Fight for Justice.* In that work Ihering speaks with great enthusiasm of Kleist's law-obsessed hero, who turned criminal from motives of which his corrupt enemies could have no conception, since those motives were rooted in an absolute belief in the sanctity of the law, to which all else must be subordinated. "Kohlhaas' criminal acts," writes Ihering, "rebound with double force onto the prince and his counselors and judges, who had all tried hard to push Kohlhaas out of the path of justice and into injustice. . . . Judicial murder is the law's one unpardonable sin. . . . The victim of a justice characterized by partiality and venality is apt to take the law into his own hands and, as like as not, may exceed his immediate goal in his pursuit of redress; he may become a declared enemy of society, a criminal, and, when he is finally punished for his excesses, a martyr in the cause of justice."

I believe that the Anglo-Saxon reader will react to Kleist's tragic novella in the spirit of these words. *Kohlhaas* seems to me to have a peculiar relevance to the present time, when apathy toward the law, callousness toward injustice, a limp acceptance of "the way things are" exercise a paralyzing influence all over the world. Kleist shows us, incidentally, with a superb, mordant humor, the predicament into which a society accustomed to constant abuse of the law is thrown by a man who refuses to put up with such abuse; how his associates gradually withdraw from the doltish robber baron who created the whole mess—with whom they would have continued to get along easily had it not been for the unpleasant consequences of his insolent act. Dishonored and abandoned by everyone, the young knight "falls from one swoon into another."

There is much evidence of "confusion of the affects" in the uncanny, gripping story of *The Foundling*. I am tempted to rank it with *Kohlhaas* because of its moral depth and finesse. The writer portrays Elvira Piachi's adulterous psychological communion with the knight who once saved her life; her romantic and morally not quite acceptable erotic cult is discovered by her adopted son, a rogue, who proceeds criminally to impersonate the vanished lover. Kleist's delineation of Nicolo, the sinister and rather charming young villain, is superb, beginning with the first description of his strangely frozen physiognomy. Nicolo's vague physical resemblance to the dead lover, which facilitates his outrageous imposition, the anagrammatic relationship of the two names, Nicolo and Colino—these things introduce disturbing psychological overtones into the story by giving to Elvira's responses to her foster son a touch of obliquity, though she remains innocent to the point of indifference as far as her consciousness is concerned. Outrageous legal chicanery, fostered in this case by the clergy, also plays a part in this tale. The good Piachi is driven to extreme measures by these legal machinations. As usual Kleist pushes the logic of the story to a point of extravagant violence. Not content to make Piachi dash out Nicolo's brains against the wall and ram the unjust decree down his throat, he must also have him raving mad like Kohlhaas, refusing absolution before his execution, because the sedate merchant does not want to go to heaven (which has nothing to offer him) but prefers to go to the lowest pit of hell in hopes of "laying hands on the villain once more." In the end the Pope allows Piachi to be hanged without absolution. There is something both raw and redundant about this ending. Yet the story would lack something without the grim gesture with which Piachi, on the gallows ladder, raises his hands, cursing the *inhuman* law that denied him his place in hell.

This may be the place to say a word or two about Kleist's ambivalent attitude toward the Catholic Church. There are several passages in his letters betraying the North German Protestant's regret over his inhibitions, which prevent his return to a popular religion having so much to offer to the senses and the artistic sensibility. As a fiction writer, Kleist's attitude in this matter is changeable and contradictory. In *The Foundling* it is purely negative and hostile, likewise in *The Earthquake in Chile,* a superb story, in which all happiness and charity, purification and human fellow-feeling, issuing like a lovely flower from a common visitation, a terrible natural catastrophe, are changed by the fanaticism of a Dominican priest into an orgy of retribution and punishment. Again, in the case of Nicolo, Kleist is careful to point out that from an early age the rascal had shown a double inclination toward voluptuousness and bigotry. He had been a constant frequenter of the cells of the Carmelite monks, where, at the age of fourteen, he had lost his virginity to the concubine of the bishop, who shielded his later knaveries as a reward for marrying the slattern, of whom the bishop had wearied.

These invectives against priesthood and Catholic morality are too crass for us not to be astonished at the intensity with which the same writer, in his miraculous tale *Saint Cecilia, or the Power of Music,* opens himself to the seraphic charm of Catholic ritual and at the same time portrays the terrible force of its magic, capable of utterly confounding the menacing iconoclasts. Poets are versatile creatures. In *Don Carlos* Schiller has placed a terrible Grand Inquisitor on the boards; yet in his *Mary Stuart* he throws out all his liberalism when he makes Mortimer, in love with the beautiful captive Mary, intone a veritable blank-verse aria in praise of the magnificence of Catholic ritual. In *Saint Cecilia* Kleist is as pious as in other places he is full of northern austerity with respect to Catholicism. But it is certainly true that his piety is directed principally toward that art whose patron saint miraculously intervenes in the story—music. Music is at the same time the enchantment and the supremely sinister power—an attitude illustrated by a casual yet significant remark of the poet concerning "the feminine gender of this mysterious art." Dreadful in the extreme are the ravages which music, through the agency of its divine patroness, works in the minds of those who came to disrupt the service. Their conversion takes the form of an incurable religious mania that bellows to heaven with a ghastly voice. The like of this has never been told. It needed Kleist to send shiver after shiver down our spines by telling, in language which only his extremism could command, how these four blasphemers are compelled to bellow out to utter exhaustion the *Gloria in excelsis,* in voices having no longer any human quality, until the curious crowd which has gathered disperses in complete terror. Kleist once employed the phrase, "the full horror of music." When I read this I thought of the description of Tolstoi's face when he listened to great music: an expression of *horror* came into it.

In reading these stories, one experiences constantly feelings of shock, excitement, anxiety, ambivalence. *The Marquise of O——* is Kleist's earliest story. He wrote it at the age of twenty-eight, during the period when he held a small post in the Office of Domains at Königsberg, shortly after he had published anonymously his *Schrof-*

fenstein Family. The subject is ancient and has been treated many times. Maybe Kleist derived it from some French story cycle, or from Cervantes, or from Montaigne; maybe it came to him from real life. In any case, his way of treating it bears the most personal stamp, unmistakably Kleistian. It would be impossible to treat a scabrous theme with more seriousness and dignity. All to no avail, for the story was very ill-received. "Even to summarize the plot" wrote a journal which, ironically, was called *Der Freimütige* ("The Plain Dealer"), "is to ostracize oneself from polite society. The Marquise is pregnant, no one knows how or by whom. Is this the kind of subject that deserves a place in a journal dedicated to art? You can imagine what details are necessitated by such a plot and how they must jar on chaste ears." The chaste ears, for instance, of the lady who wrote the following to the editor: "No woman can read his story of the Marquise of O—— without blushing. Where will writing like this take us?" To be sure, the writer had principally the women against him. But even men like Friedrich von Gentz, otherwise a great admirer of Kleist's, were shocked, and their judgment faltered before a daring masterpiece which has since been assigned the high place accorded it even then by a few exceptional critics, such as the Austrian political scientist Adam Müller who called it "a marvelous story, of great moral dignity, equally perfect in style and in construction."

Adam Müller, by the way, happened to be a politician of romantic leanings, and a Catholic convert. So it is quite conceivable that his verdict (albeit upheld by time) may have been influenced by certain slight mystical allusions which the man who was soon to write *Amphitryon* could not keep out of this crassly realistic story. These references deserve pointing out. When the Marquise, beside herself over her incomprehensible condition, inquires of the midwife whether unconscious or immaculate conception were within the realm of nature, she receives the answer that "Apart from the holy Virgin, this had never happened to any woman on earth." This sounds matter-of-fact enough. But when the innocently outcast woman decides, at the time of her highest spiritual exaltation, to submit to the incomprehensible and withdraw into herself, devoting herself entirely to the education of her two children, and "to foster with maternal care that *gift that God had given her in the shape of the third*" she reasons about that ambiguous gift that, being of more *mysterious* origin, it must by the same token be more *divine* than other human beings. Or, rather, it is Kleist who inspires these thoughts in her, a poet always ready to explain a scandal by reference to some supreme mystery.

So much about this story which was once the most generally decried of Kleist's productions and which today is, perhaps, his most famous. I want to add just a few remarks about the remaining two stories in this volume. In *The Engagement in Santo Domingo* tumultuous, dangerous, murderous things happen, blow upon blow; at the end, suicide is brought in as the crowning disaster. The story turns on a misunderstanding between two lovers and its fatal consequences. The time is about 1800, the period when the Negro population of Haiti first revolted against their white overlords. Kleist's choice of plot was clearly dictated by his taste for the horrible, and wholly in keeping with that taste is his treatment of the climactic event of the story. Gustav von der Ried, a Swiss, who was saved earlier by the lovely mestizo Toni, imagines himself betrayed by the girl and shoots her. When the enormity of his deed dawns on him he puts a bullet through his head by placing the pistol in his mouth; and his skull, utterly crushed, "bespatters the wall in bits and fragments." Here, once more, we have the true Kleistian touch. And yet this tale of a faith tested and proving unequal to the test is deeply affecting. Such, apparently, was also Theodor Körner's opinion, who read the piece in the Viennese periodical *Der Sammler* ("The Collector"), and promptly decided to turn it into a play. The play, shallow and sentimental, appealed greatly to Goethe who had taken no notice whatever of Kleist's story. He even gave a public reading of

Köorner's adaptation at the Weimar court and drew sketches of a Negro hut to be used in the stage set during production. It is most annoying, and at the same time quite comical, to see a man of Goethe's stature bestow his favor time and again on rank mediocrity.

Lastly, there is yet another capital story, *The Duel,* which turns on the confusion issuing from a medieval trial by combat. This tale resembles *The Marquise of O——* in certain respects, since here, too, a woman seemingly guilty yet actually pure is trying without avail to convince the world of her innocence. But poor Littegarde is in a much worse predicament than was the Marquise, for Heaven itself being called upon according to custom to determine the issue, decides publicly against her and in favor of her accusers. She is driven to distraction almost, for her faith and her reason—the woman *knows* that she is innocent—seem hopelessly at odds. And not only is her own faith—that faith which shortly before could utter the proud words, "Should my knight enter the lists without helmet and armor, God and his angels will surely protect him!"—now proved hollow, but also the faith of her knight, Friedrich von Trota, who had been convinced both of her innocence and of the infallibility of God's arbitrament; while the faith of the villain, Count Jacob the Redbeard (a murderer, true, but in this particular issue a *bona fide* slanderer and dupe), is equally shattered in the end. The short work is full of theological implications and shows what duress is imposed on the human mind when God, the "wholly other," enters the scene. Everything turns out contrary to expectation: the champion of innocence is unseated, the "infallible" arms proclaim the liar true, and the accused woman is proved guilty not only of sexual trespass but of the additional fault of having inexcusably sent the knight who blindly trusted her to his destruction; proved guilty not only before the forum of Emperor and Empire but before the tribunal of her own sorely divided mind as well. "God is veracious and infallible!" He is indeed, but not the way we mortals like to imagine. Her champion, who was victimized in the joust, recovers miraculously from what appeared to be a mortal wound, while the heaven-sponsored victor, whose skin had been but slightly grazed, rots away slowly and irreparably. The words with which von Trota had questioned, in the moment of greatest emergency, the basis of the whole trial: "What obliges God's wisdom to make the truth manifest when we call upon him to reveal it?" prove justified after all. The Emperor in his turn decrees that the statutes covering the sacrosanct trial by combat be revised; after the traditional sentence declaring that the outcome of the duel will patently show which of the parties was the offender, a phrase is now to be inserted reading, "If God wills it so." This short phrase spells the approaching end of a chivalrous institution and a determination, somewhat shamefaced as yet, to abandon the consecrated duel as a means of ascertaining the truth. . . .

The idea of suspense is closely bound up with the idea of fiction. This is as it should be; to tell a story is to create suspense, and the art of the storyteller resides in this ability to make dull subjects sound entertaining and plots whose solution everyone knows in advance, exciting. Kleist, however, creates a very different kind of suspense. His tales conform closely to the Italian archetype—the *novella*—and *novella* means news. What he tells us so coldly and dispassionately is news of the most extraordinary kind, and the suspense his stories create has a specificity, a concreteness, that is positively alarming. We are filled with anxiety and terror, shudder in the face of mystery, doubt in the powers of reason and, indeed, in the power of God himself—all our "affects are confounded." Kleist knows how to put us on the rack and—such is his triumph as an artist—succeeds in making us thank him for that torture.

Translated by Francis Golffing

[CONTENTS]

The first time I read anything by Heinrich von Kleist was some thirteen years ago. Till then I knew his name vaguely as that of a German dramatist of the early 19th century, one of those obscure classic writers whom nobody reads or seems to know much about outside his own country. Kafka first drew my attention to Kleist. In his diaries, on which I was working at the time as an editor and translator, Kafka notes parallels to his own anguished life in that of the Prussian poet—their being bachelors who despaired of ever marrying, their families' contempt for their literary ambitions—and I was curious to see what sort of writer it was with whom the strange, rather unearthly Prague Jew had discovered an affinity. The work of Kleist's that I picked up to read was the long *novella Michael Kohlhaas,* a story that Kafka liked to recite aloud to his friends and from which he once gave a public reading in Prague. Its effect on me was immediate and overwhelming. Here was the work of a direct literary antecedent of the author of *The Castle;* the modern writer, original as he was, had not after all sprung out of nowhere. More important, here was a writer supremely interesting in his own right; a writer of world stature who for some reason was not known to the world. Soon I conceived the idea of translating all of Kleist's stories and making them available to English readers. And at last it has been possible to carry out that idea.

Kleist remained unknown to the world for so many years, and even his own countrymen ignored him for almost a century, because of those very qualities which today create an atmosphere of breathless excitement in his work. What makes him exciting is his modernity. Like Stendhal, like Georg Büchner, Kleist was an avant-garde writer in the true sense of the term; he was not only ahead of the literary fashions of his time, he was not only ahead of his generation, he was ahead of his age. Another century, and a new age, needed to roll around for him to come into his own.

What is this modern quality of his? It is possible to describe it in various ways, and from various points of view. The German critic Friedrich Gundolf, in a work on Kleist that appeared in 1922, saw him as the prototype of the lonely modern genius cut off from any community that might give him sustenance and support. "He ushers in the long line of those solitaries who in the 19th century led the struggle, as creators or as sufferers, against the bourgeois style and spirit—Büchner, Hebbel, Nietzsche in Germany, Stendhal, Flaubert, Baudelaire, Mallarmé in France." Georg Lukacs in 1937 dwelt on the despairing isolation, in the world of Kleist, of each from all, on the solipsistic immurement of his characters in their own passions and the characteristic *mistrust* that they consequently feel toward one another. "The fact that all of Kleist's works are filled with a burning yet unrealizable longing to burst the barriers of this isolation, to overcome this mistrust, only accentuates this situation the more, since the longing is inevitably doomed to disappointment." He calls

Kleist the great forerunner of modern drama "in the narrower sense of the term," wherein the psychology of individuals becomes their fate. Since drama for Lukacs is the social form of literary art *par excellence,* Kleist, because he initiates its "privatization," is a decadent playwright, a manifestation of the "period of decline of bourgeois literature." He is a decadent writer in general, reflecting the isolation and despair of modern life. The only work of Kleist's that he exempts from this stricture is *Michael Kohlhaas:* "Kohlhaas' passion—just because its roots are social rather than purely individual—is from the outset rational in the spirit of great tragedy." Lukacs' doctrinaire notions of what is decadent and what is progressive hardly weaken the force of these penetrating observations.

Elsewhere in his essay Lukacs speaks of Kleist's "radical nihilism." Nihilism is the wrong word—it betrays the bias and uneasiness of the ideologist who cannot admit the existence of real doubt and ambiguity—but it points in the right direction. It points to just the quality of Kleist that makes his work so startlingly modern: the *questionableness* at the heart of his world, the almost diabolical ambiguity of its atmosphere, the way things tremble and shift and make one wonder if they are what they seem. This is a characteristic of the modern age in the most literal sense: the world seemed flat but it turns out to be round, seemed fixed but it moves—nevertheless it moves, and when we have learned to appreciate, with Galileo and Freud, that things are not what they seem, we are into modern times. What Kleist does, in a way that is as radical as it is subtle, is to question the traditional, apparently self-evident moral, psychological, sexual and political conceptions. He subverts the solid, rational, customary foundations of the world order; suddenly everything begins to sway and we are in fear of falling. Kleist *frightens* one. That is why he wrote *novelle,* which are accounts of extraordinary happenings, tales of horror, rather than the regular sort of short stories or novels—to frighten one. But the fear inspired by his horror stories is not the delicious, half-nonsensical shudder of Romantic sensationalism; it is a metaphysical fear, as it were, a fear of what is revealed by the glimpse he gives one into the deepest interior and heart of things.

In the explosively short "Beggarwoman of Locarno," the Marquis is guilty of peevishly ordering the sick old woman to get up out of the corner of the room in which he keeps his shotgun and find herself a place behind the stove. In a matter of paragraphs he has set fire, in terror, despair, and weariness of life, to his chateau, and soon nothing remains of him but a heap of bones resting in the corner of the room from which he had ordered the beggarwoman of Locarno to get up. The narrative, which rushes along with the speed of an express train, makes one morally dizzy: one irritable action and the Marquis is utterly destroyed! A ghost story, it is not the ghost that scares you but the implied statement that the moral order is not rational and just, but cruel, impatient and insensate. It does not argue the point, it embodies it; the story fires itself off like a gun, leaving you not to reflect on it but to recover from it.

Michael Kohlhaas calls the political order into question, or rather the superb body of the story does; the concluding section, which ostensibly resolves the issues of Kohlhaas' "case," only does so formally; it does not really answer the radical doubts raised in the course of the narrative, and seems to me, with its fairytale supernaturalism, a good deal less forceful and serious. What Kleist does is evoke a powerful sense of dread and dismay which is never adequately accounted for just by the story of what happens to Kohlhaas, with the result that the accumulated feelings of terror remain undispelled when the story itself comes to an end. Or to put it another way, the horse dealer's agony becomes a metaphor for what Kleist calls the imperfect state of the world, the fundamental irreconcilability of the social order with justice and decency; the formal justice done Kohlhaas at the end of the *novella* does nothing to allay the feelings of anxious dread inspired all along by his fate. As first a toll is demanded of Kohlhaas and then his pair of black horses, as his man Herse is beaten and driven out of Tronka Castle, as his efforts to get justice for himself end in failure and the death of his wife, as favoritism, cowardice, and indifference interpose themselves mockingly whichever way he turns, human society begins to appear in a sinister, uncanny light. Law seems a series of malign impediments, justice an ever-receding gleam, and all authority arbitrary, clownish, and corrupt. I call the doubt that Kleist casts upon the social order radical because he is not just throwing up his hands and exclaiming over the wickedness of the world, which is still to accept society as given, he is questioning it right down to the ground. The castle that Kohlhaas sees near the toll gate, its battlements glittering above the field with a suggestion of mysterious separation from humankind and its purposes, is not too far removed from that other one which K. dimly perceives through the snow and the fog; it is only a step from Kohlhaas' struggle against official blandness and contumely to the doom of K.'s eternal efforts to prevail an inch against the impenetrability of the Castle.

Nevertheless a century separates Kleist from Kafka. A possibility exists for Kohlhaas which K. cannot even imagine. The horse dealer, taking justice into his own hands, falls on Tronka Castle with his small troop and burns it to the ground. That is, he becomes a revolutionist. Kleist calls him a brigand—"one of the most upright and at the same time one of the most terrible men of his age," whose "sense of justice turned him into a brigand and a murderer." But this kind of antithetical characterization, which Kleist with an inveterate Hegelianism is fond of making in all his writings, does not seem to me to succeed in the case of Kohlhaas. The horse dealer is an upright man, indeed he impresses one as being a kind of saint, but he does not impress one as being a terrible man too. The man we see is scrupulous and fairminded, and tries to restrain his leaping virile anger for fear of deviating even a hairsbreadth into injustice; in the scene in which he interrogates Herse about what happened at Tronka Castle, an extraordinary bit of writing and an example of

Kleist's supreme dramatic gift, all these qualities are vividly portrayed. It is true that this same man burns and kills; but our feeling for the horse dealer is not only one of sympathy but allegiance, and we are ready to accept these deeds as revolutionary acts, part of a just warfare against an immoral order. No brigand but a revolutionist, he publishes manifestoes calling on the people to join him in overthrowing the established authority and in building a "better order of things." Of course, such an ambition must seem close to madness under the circumstances, and for a little while the horse dealer is represented in the story as an obsessed creature with messianic delusions about wielding the sword of righteousness of his namesake the Archangel Michael. But this half-demented figure hardly accords with the Kohlhaas who is a man of sober judgment and experienced understanding, driven to take up arms only when he has been outrageously provoked, and who lays them down soon enough when Luther appeals to him to do so.

Kleist needed the "terrible" Kohlhaas to balance against the "upright" one so as to justify a resolution of the moral-legal issue in which justice is indeed done the horse dealer and all his demands are satisfied, but in which he on his side must satisfy the Emperor for breach of the peace of the realm by submitting his neck to the executioner's ax. But the realm whose peace the horse dealer is convicted of breaking is the same political order about which Kleist insinuates so many doubts in the body of the story; we cannot agree, after Kleist has called its justice so radically into question, after we have been shown its imperfection in such concrete detail, that it has the right to pass sentence on Kohlhaas.

Until the final section, when the gypsywoman of Jüterbock appears on the scene and the *novella* suddenly veers into a shadowy Gothic fantasticness serving to obscure its unsatisfactory conclusion, *Michael Kohlhaas* is a masterpiece of realism. It is written in a German that is extraordinarily compact, complicated, yet impetuous; peremptory to the point of ruthlessness, abrupt in its manner and its transitions, dry and impersonal, it is deliberately anti-literary. Friedrich Gundolf makes the illuminating observaton that Kleist's style, with its Roman harshness, goes back to the legal and official German of the Baroque period following the Reformation. It is a kind of prosaic, bureacratic style employed with telling antithetical effect to express mystery, violence, and terror (which again recalls Kafka). Discarding literary language as affected and used up, it tries to set down extraordinary things in plain, bare, matter-of-fact words. Kleist's style expresses a revulsion against the artifice and "lies" of literature, and the search for new truth.

The imperfect state of the world is considered from an altogether different side, and with an altogether different attitude, in the marvellous story *The Marquise of O——*. If *Michael Kohlhaas* hints at a rejection of the social and political order because of all its radical faults and imperfections. *The Marquise of O——* hints at contradictions of the soul and hidden antagonistic movements of the affections which it embraces in a sweeping affirmation of life. Opening in characteristic thunder clap fashion (a style Kafka imitated, notably in "The Metamorphosis,") it announces its antithetical theme right off: the widowed Marquise, whose reputation has never suffered a single stain, nevertheless must advertise in the newspapers for the unknown father of the child she is going to bear to come forward and marry her. Kleist then casts back to the beginning of the action and tells the story of a woman whose reason almost cracks under the strain of finding that she is pregnant without having the slightest idea of how it might have come about. One needs to risk the ludicrous to achieve the sublime. But the explanation of the Marquise's pregnancy proves more baffling and dismaying to her than the original mystery: the man who comes forward to reveal himself as the rapist who got her with child is none other than the Russian count who had come to her rescue like an angel (it seemed to her) and saved her from being raped by his own soldiers. This is too much for the Marquise: "Go away! Go away! Go away! I was

ready for some villain of a fellow, but not—not—not the devil!"
The Marquise cannot understand how a man who had shown himself to be brave and tender and an ardent suitor could have also
been her violator. He had seemed an angel in her eyes; now he was
the devil. And that of course is Kleist's point: Count F—— is both
angel *and* devil—or rather neither, but only human.

One should not mistake this point. Kleist is not saying that Count
F—— is a good man guilty of an inexplicable lapse, and that the
Marquise needs to understand that such lapses are human; he is
not a commonplace writer. What he is doing is questioning the foundations of the traditional, rationalist conception of love and virtue.
Kleist is deliberately suggestiong that the Count's impulse in possessing the Marquise while she lay unconscious was a manifestation
of that same impetuous, ardent quality which makes him so attractive
when we come to know him better in the story—indeed that the
rape was in its way an act of tenderness, even of virtue. For it rescues
the Marquise from retirement and celibacy, from the isolation and
death-in-life in which she had arrived following the death of her
husband the Marquis, from her state of what the world calls "virtue."
The hearty good sense of her mother knows this, which is why she
calls her daughter a goose when the latter becomes outraged on
discovering that the father of her child is the man she loves. The
Count with his unthinking vitality knows this, which is why he
presses his suit with appealing apologetic ardor. Kleist's story is about
how we try to do ourselves in with our own ideas—how our self-
consciousness as human beings can be the enemy of our life.

Elsewhere in the *novella* Kleist does not hesitate to tamper with
equally sacred conceptions. In the intense, supercharged scene in
which the Marquise is reconciled with her father the Commandant,
Kleist describes them as two lovers; there is an explicit suggestion
of incestuous feeling. But again, Kleist's motive is not the commonplace one of wishing simply to shock. This astonishing writer who
dwelt almost exclusively on themes of violence and horror in his

plays and stories, of fanaticism, murder, lynching, rape, and canni-balism, had a deep and unafraid understanding of love and sex. The sexual, incestuous element in the feeling between father and daugh-ter does not throw a lurid light on the scene and make their emotion questionable; it is rather an expression and intensification of their tenderness for one another. Kleist understood how false our distinc-tions often are; he understood the unity in life of what our fearful consciousness tries to separate.

The Marquise of O—— is not the only heroine of Kleist's who needs to be shocked back out of virtuous retirement into life. Lady Littegarde in *The Duel* has renounced her suitor, Sir Friedrich von Trota, and is about to becomes the abbess of a convent when Count Jacob the Redbeard's false accusation against her sets in train the events which lead to the duel and her marriage to Sir Friedrich. Here again, because Count Jacob is not entirely without appeal, and because he swears what he thinks is the truth, there is an oblique suggestion of extenuation for his degrading Lady Litte-garde—her isolation and retirement are an affront against life, her virtue is wrong, it invites a vulgar hand to be laid on it.

In *The Foundling,* an outrageous, extravagant story. Elvira is another one of these women of Kleist's who, having renounced life, in her case by marrying the old man Antonio Piachi after the death of the young nobleman who rescued her from the fire, invites some shocking retaliation. This story mutters all sorts of secret things under its breath. The passions which are its content threaten to burst the ostensible moral categories in which they are contained and pour out in an anarchic flood. The story trembles on the point of saying that Elvira returns her foster son's semi-incestuous passion for her, with-out knowing it, and that the old man's rage against Nicolo is really jealousy. Life has been denied too much, and feeling and morality are so out of accord that catastrophe is inevitable. At the end perfidy triumphs with staggering completeness.

In his early youth Kleist was a student of the Enlightenment and a devotee of reason. Then he read Kant's philosophy, he reports, and underwent a profound crisis of the spirit. Reason, he thought, was dethroned; the way was opened to him to pass from the pieties of his 18th century education to the turbulence and contrarieties—the livingness and truth—of life as he experienced it. The way was opened to him to become a modern writer, to question the traditional and the rational, the traditions and the reasons of civilization. As a lonely, neurotic outsider—a poet sprung inexplicably from a long line of Prussian army officers—he was situated so that he could do this. With Rousseauistic fervor, Kleist exalted spontaneity. He wrote in a letter once: "Every first inclination, whatever is involuntary, is beautiful; but everything is distorted and displaced as soon as it understands itself." Kleist's fiction is part of the revolution of modern times; it is an effort to uncover—and recover—the knowledge of what we really feel, our own actual feelings, which morality, religion and civilization have obscured. Büchner, Stendhal, Nietzsche, Freud, Lawrence, Kafka—he is one of that company, a hero of the modern spirit.

How well he puts it himself in the essay "On the Puppet Theater"! Meeting in a public garden in M—— the premier dancer of the opera, Herr C., Kleist says how surprised he was at having seen him at the puppet theater several times. Herr C. replies that there is a lot a dancer can learn from puppets; indeed they are more capable of expressing grace and beauty than human dancers because their motions obey mechanical principles and cannot be falsified or distorted—unlike the affected contortions of the ballerina P——, for instance, when she dances Daphne, or the young F—— when he dances the part of Paris. Mistakes like theirs "are inevitable ever since we ate of the tree of knowledge. But Paradise is barred and the angel stands behind us; we have to go all the way around the world and see if it might not be open again somewhere in the back." Kleist laughs; but it is hard for him to believe that a mechanical doll can possess more grace than the human body. Why, says Herr C., it is impossible for a human being to come anywhere near a puppet; only a god could match matter in this field; and this is the point where the two ends of the round world meet—I can see, Herr C. observes, that you haven't read the third chapter of the book of Exodus very carefully. I know very well, Kleist answers, what disorder consciousness introduced into the natural grace of human beings. And he tells an anecdote illustrating this, to which Herr C. replies with one of his own. Gracefulness, Herr C. concludes, is displayed at its purest in those human frames which possess either no consciousness at all or which possess an infinite one, i.e. in a puppet or in God. " 'In that case,' I said without really thinking, 'must we eat of the tree of knowledge a second time in order to fall back into the state of innocence?' 'Exactly,' he replied, 'and that is the last chapter of the history of the world.' "

To rediscover innocence through increased consciousness has been the aim of almost every modern movement; it exactly describes the aim of psychoanalysis.

Kleist was morbid, shy, and solitary; he suffered from a speech impediment and could hardly speak in company; he revised his writing endlessly—is it really surprising that he should have exalted spontaneity and impulsiveness? As Thomas Mann remarks, "he could never get himself to speak directly and freely *in propria persona*." He wrote plays, that is, he could represent the speech of others, and he wrote stories marked by their sternly impersonal style, but it was almost impossible for this great poet to say "I." His mind dwelt on dreams and death, fits and swoons, emotional raptures that swept away all barriers and impediments. He struggled to possess his self, his "I," by some supreme exertion, by subterfuge, by circumventing the shamed stammering self he wished to cast off. Kafka wrote as if in a dream, and fooled his self that way; afterwards his inhibition left instructions for the manuscripts to be destroyed. In yearning to express his own humanness with spontaneous freedom, Kleist possessed the genius to express something of the world's yearning to be spontaneously human. That is why his stories are not merely bizarre.

A Note on the Translation. I have taken the liberty of breaking up the patches of dialogue in the stories into paragraphs rather than running them together as in the German. This does more justice, I believe, to their dramatic quality. I have used the title "Marquise," a foreignism, rather than the English "Marchioness," which I think sounds more foreign, at least to an American ear. I was helped by F. H. King's spirited if inaccurate translation of *Michael Kohlhaas* and Henry Roche's version of *The Marquise of O——*. I have tried to put Kleist into a more or less natural modern English; I have not tried to imitate any period quality of his German.

—MARTIN GREENBERG

New York City
June 1960

The Marquise of O—

*I*N M——, a large town in northern Italy, the widowed Marquise of O——, a lady of unblemished reputation and the mother of several well-bred children, published the following notice in the newspapers: that, without her knowing how, she was in the family way; that she would like the father of the child she was going to bear to report himself; and that her mind was made up, out of consideration for her people, to marry him. The lady whom unalterable circumstances forced to take this unusual step, which she did so bravely in the face of the derision it was bound to excite in the world, was the daughter of Colonel G——, Commandant of the citadel of M——. Three years or so previously, her husband, the Marquis of O——, to whom she had been devoted heart and soul, had died during a trip to Paris on family business. After his death, yielding to the wishes of Madam

41

G——, her worthy mother, she left the estate near V—— where she had lived until then and returned to the Commandant's house with her two children. There she spent the following years in strict seclusion, occupying her time with painting, reading, educating her children, and caring for her parents: until the ———— War suddenly filled the neighborhood with troops of nearly all the powers, including those of Russia. Colonel G——, who was under orders to defend the fortress, urged his wife and daughter to retire to the latter's estate near V—— or to his son's place. But before the ladies could make up their minds as between the hardships of a siege or the horrors they might be exposed to in the open country, the citadel was invested by Russian troops and commanded to surrender. Announcing to his family that he would carry on as if they were not there, the Colonel retorted with shot and shell. The enemy in turn bombarded the fortress. He set the magazines ablaze, captured an outworks, and, when the Colonel delayed to answer a second summons to surrender, ordered a night assault and carried the fort by storm.

Just as the Russian troops, supported by a violent cannonade, were breaking into the citadel, the left wing of the Commandant's residence caught fire and the women were forced to flee. The Colonel's wife panted after her daughter, who was flying down the stairs with her children, and shouted for them all to keep together and take refuge in the cellars; but a shell exploding in the house at that very moment made the confusion there complete. The Marquise, flinging open a door, found herself in the citadel square, where the flashing of the cannon in violent action lit up the night and drove her, helpless to know where she should turn, back inside the burning building. Here, unluckily, just as she was about to escape by the back door, she ran into a troop of enemy sharpshooters who fell silent the instant they laid eyes on her, slung their muskets, and, gesturing obscenely, marched her off with them. In vain the Marquise screamed for help to her terror-stricken women fleeing through the back gate as she was flung back and forth among the horrible gang of quarreling soldiers. They dragged her to the rear castle yard, where she was on the point of collapsing to the ground under the filthy abuse inflicted on her when a Russian officer, hearing her screams, came running up and began to lay about him with furious strokes, scattering the dogs panting after their prey. To the Marquise he seemed a very angel from heaven. He smashed the last of the murderous brutes, whose arms were wound about her slender figure, in the face with the hilt of his sword and made him reel back with the blood gushing from his mouth; then, saluting her courteously in French, he offered her his arm and led her, speechless from all she had gone through, to the other wing of the residence, which had not caught fire yet, where she fainted dead away. A little while after, when her terrified women appeared, he told them to call a doctor; promised them, as he put his hat on, that she would soon recover; and returned to the fray.

In a short time the square was entirely in the hands of the Russians, and the Commandant, who kept up a resistance only because no quarter was offered him, was just falling back with his dwindling force on the entrance door to the residence when the Russian officer, with a heated face, came out of that very door and called on him to surrender. The Commandant answered that that was just what he had been waiting for, handed him his sword, and asked permission to go into the castle and look for his family. The Russian officer who, judging by his actions, was one of the leaders of the assault, granted his request on condition that he was accompanied by a guard; he placed himself hurriedly at the head of a detachment, threw his force into the fighting wherever it was still in doubt, and posted men as fast as possible at all the strong points of the fort. No sooner was this done than he ran back to the drill square and ordered his men to battle the roaring flames which were threatening to spread in every direction, himself performing prodigies of exertion when his orders were not carried out with the necessary zeal. One minute he was scrambling among the burning gables, hose in hand, aiming the stream of water at the flames, the next minute he had darted into the magazines and, striking terror to the souls of his fellow Asiatics, was rolling out powder kegs and live grenades. Meanwhile the Commandant had passed inside the house and was horrified to learn about the misfortune that had befallen his daughter. The Marquise, however, who had entirely recovered without the help of any doctor, just as the Russian officer said she would, and who was overjoyed to find all her people safe and sound and stayed in bed only to allay their extreme anxiety about her, assured him that her one wish was to get up and tell her rescuer how grateful she was to him. She already knew that he was Count F——, Lieutenant-Colonel of the T——th Rifle Corps and Knight of the Order of Merit and of several others. She asked her father to beg him not to leave the citadel before he had made an appearance, if only for a minute or so, at the residence. The Commandant, who respected his daughter's feeling, returned without delay to the fort, where he found the Count on the ramparts, going up and down among his battered troops and issuing an uninterrupted stream of orders; and, no better opportunity offering, he then and there conveyed his grateful daughter's wish to him. The Count promised him that he was only waiting to snatch a moment from his duties to pay her his respects. He had been anxious all along to hear how the Marquise was, but the reports of some of his officers had drawn him back into the thick of the fighting.

At daybreak the Commanding General of the Russian forces arrived to inspect the fort. He paid his respects to the Commandant, regretted that his bravery had not been helped by better luck, and gave him leave to go wherever he liked on his parole. The Commandant thanked him earnestly and said how much this day had put him in debt to the Russians in general and to the young Count F——, Lieutenant-Colonel of the T——th Rifle Corps, in particular. The General asked what had happened; when he was told the

story of the criminal attack on the Commandant's daughter, he became furious. Calling the Count forward by name, he praised his
noble-spirited conduct in a short speech, which caused the officer to
blush furiously, and ended his words by ordering the villains who
hàd dishonored the Czar's name to be shot; would he tell him who
they were? Count F—— gave a confused reply, in which he
said that he could not give the General their names because it
had been impossible to recognize their faces by the feeble glimmer of the castle-yard lamps. The General, who had heard that
the castle was already in flames at the time of the episode, looked
surprised; it was possible, he remarked, to recognize people one
knew well by their voices in the dark; and ordered him, when the
Count shrugged his shoulders with an embarrassed air, to investigate the matter at once. But just then somebody pressed forward
from the back of the circle and reported that one of the villains whom
the Count had wounded had fallen in the corridor and that the
Commandant's people had lugged him into a closet where he still
was. The General sent a guard to fetch the man; questioned him
briefly; and, when he had revealed the names of the others, had the
whole crew, five all told, shot. When this was done, the General
posted a small garrison in the fort and issued marching orders to
the rest of his troops; the officers scattered on the double to their
different corps; the Count made his way through the crowd of hurrying soldiers to the Commandant and said how very sorry he was,
but under the cricumstances he could only send his warmest regards
to the Marquise; and in less than an hour the entire fort was clear
of Russians again.

The family now began to think how they might find some occasion
in the future to tell the Count how grateful they felt toward him;
imagine their horror, then, when they learned that he had been
killed in a skirmish on the very same day that he had marched
away from the fort. The messenger who brought this news to M——
had with his own eyes seen him carried off, mortally wounded in

the chest, toward P——, where he had died, according to a reliable report, at the very moment when the bearers were lifting him from their shoulders. The Commandant went in person to the posthouse to see if he could learn anything more about the Russian's death. He discovered that when the Count was hit on the battlefield he had cried out, "Julietta, with this shot you are avenged!" and after that had never opened his lips again. The Marquise was inconsolable for having let the chance slip to throw herself at his feet. She made the most violent accusations against herself for not having gone to him in the fort when he declined (probably, as she thought, from modesty) to come to her in the castle; pitied the unfortunate lady, with the same name as her own, whom he had been thinking about even as he was dying; tried in vain to learn her whereabouts so as to tell her the unhappy news; and could not get the thought of him out of her own mind until several months had passed.

At this time the family were obliged to move out of the Commandant's residence to make room for the Russian commander. At first they thought of going to Colonel G——'s estate, which was very much the Marquise's inclination; but as the Colonel had no liking for country life, they ended by taking a house in town and fixing it up to live there permanently. Their life now flowed back into its accustomed channels. The Marquise had resumed the long-interrupted education of her children, and in her leisure hours turned to her easel and her books, when, quite unaccountably for someone who had always been a paragon of good heath, she found herself troubled by a persistent indisposition that made it impossible for her to see anyone for weeks on end. She suffered from nausea, dizziness, and fainting spells, and was at a loss to explain her strange condition. One morning, as the family sat at tea and her father had gone out of the room for a moment, the Marquise, rousing herself from a lengthy fit of abstraction, said to her mother, "If a woman were to tell me that she felt the way I did just now when I picked up

the cup, I should certainly think to myself that she was pregnant."
Madam G—— said she didn't know what her daughter meant. The
Marquise explained that she had just felt the same sort of twinge
she had had when she was carrying her second child. Madam G——
said it was perhaps the spirit of fantasy that her daughter was going
to be delivered of, and laughed. Yes, the Marquise replied in the
same humorous spirit, and Morpheus was the father or one of his
attendant dreams. But then the Colonel came back, the conversation
was interrupted, and when the Marquise recovered a few days later
the whole thing was forgotten.

Not long after this, just when the Commandant's son, who was
Forest Warden, happened to be at home, the family were frightened
out of their wits to hear a servant enter the room and announce that
Count F—— was there. "Count F——!" gasped father and daughter
together, and they all fell speechless. The servant swore that his
eyes and ears had not deceived him and that the visitor was already
waiting in the anteroom. The Commandant immediately jumped up
to open the door himself, and the Count entered, handsome as a
young god, even if his face was rather pale. After they had gotten
over their surprise and the Count had assured the parents—who
said no, it couldn't be, he must be dead—that he was very much
alive, he turned, with an expression of great tenderness on his face,
to the daughter; and the very first thing he asked her was, how did
she feel? Very well, the Marquise said, she only wanted to know
how he had come back from the dead. But he would not let his
question drop and said she was not telling him the truth; her face
showed signs of unusual fatigue; unless he was much mistaken, she
was feeling ill. The Marquise, softened by the warmth with which
he spoke, replied: very well, her fatigue, since he would have it so,
was perhaps the last trace of an indisposition that had troubled her
several weeks ago; she did not think that anything more would
come of it. To which he replied, with an outburst of delight: nor did
he!—and he asked her if she would marry him. The Marquise

did not know what to make of such behavior. Blushing deeply, she looked at her mother who, in turn, was staring in embarrassment at her husband and son; whereupon the Count went up to the Marquise and, taking her hand as if to kiss it, asked her if she had understood him. The Commandant inquired if he would not like to sit down; and with elaborate courtesy, touched nevertheless with some solemnity, he drew a chair up for the Count.

"Indeed," said the Colonel's wife, "we shall go on thinking you are a ghost until you've told us how you rose up out of the grave in which they buried you at P——." Letting go the lady's hand, the Count sat down and said that he was forced to be very brief: he had been wounded mortally in the breast and carried to P——; for months there he had despaired of his life; during this time his only thoughts had been for the Marquise; he could not describe the pleasure and the pain that coupled together in his image of her; after his recovery, he had returned to the army, where he had felt a terrible restlessness; more than once he had reached for a pen to pour his heart out to the Colonel and the Marquise; but unexpectedly he was sent to Naples with dispatches; he could not be sure that he wouldn't be sent from there to Constantinople—he might even have to go to St. Petersburg; meanwhile it was impossible for him to go on living any longer without a clear understanding about something that was absolutely necessary for his soul's peace; he had not been able to resist taking a few steps in that direction while passing through M——; in short, he cherished the hope of obtaining the Marquise's hand, and he implored them as earnestly as he knew how to give his suit an immediate answer.

After a long pause, the Commandant replied that the offer, if seriously intended, as he did not doubt it was, was a very flattering one. But his daughter had made up her mind, after the death of her husband, the Marquis of O——, never to marry again. However, as the Count had recently laid so great an obligation on her, it was not impossible that this should sway her from her resolution; he asked him to allow her a little time to think the matter over quietly. The Count assured him that his friendly answer was a great encouragement to his hopes; that in other circumstances it would have made him perfectly content; that he appreciated fully how boorish it seemed for him to ask for more; but that compelling reasons, into which it was impossible for him to go, made a definite answer extremely desirable; that the horses which were to take him to Naples were already hitched to his carriage; and that he implored them with all his heart and soul, if there was anybody in that house to take his part—here he shot a look at the Marquise—not to let him ride away without a more favorable reply. The Colonel, rather taken aback by such insistence, said that although the gratitude his daughter felt for him justified his assuming a great deal, it did not justify his assuming so much; she could not take a step on which the happiness of her life depended without giving it prudent consideration beforehand. It was absolutely necessary for his daughter to enjoy the pleasure of his closer acquaintance before declaring herself. He invited him to return to M—— after his trip was done and be their guest for a while. If after that—but not before—the Marquise thought that she could find her happiness with him, he would be only too happy to hear that she had given him the answer he wanted. The Count blushed and said that during the whole trip he had foreseen that his impatient desires would meet with this fate; that he looked forward to being utterly miserable during the interim period; that although he could hardly like the unhappy part he was now compelled to play, he would not deny that a closer acquaintance was all to the good; that he believed he could answer for his reputation, although it was a question whether any consideration should be given to that most deceptive of all things; that the only dishonorable act he had ever committed was a secret from the world and he was already on the way to making it good—in short, that he was an honorable man, and he begged the Commandant to accept his assurance of the truthfulness of all he said. The Commandant smiled

faintly, though without a trace of irony, and said that he quite agreed
with everything the Count had said. He had never come across a
young man who in so short a time had revealed so many superior
traits of character. He was pretty well convinced that a brief period
of reflection would overcome all present hesitation; but before he
talked things over with his own family as well as with the Count's, no
other course was possible. At this, the Count announced that his
parents were dead and he was his own master. His uncle was General
K——, on whose assent to the marriage he could rely. He added
that he possessed considerable means and would be able to make
Italy his home.

The Commandant bowed politely, explained his wishes once
again, and requested him not to press his suit any further until he
returned from his trip. The Count, after a short pause in which he
showed every sign of extreme uneasiness, turned to the Marquise's
mother and said that he had done everything possible to get out of
having to make the trip; that he had gone as far as he dared in im-
portuning the Commanding General and General K——, his uncle,
to be relieved of the mission, but that they hoped that the journey
would rouse him out of the melancholy still weighing on him from
his illness; and that, for this reason, he was now completely miserable.

The family did not know what to say to this. The Count rubbed
his forehead and went on, saying that if there were any hope of his
coming nearer the goal he sought, he would put off his departure
for a day or even more. And he looked in turn at the Commandant,
the Marquise, and her mother. The Commandant stared at the
floor with an expression of displeasure and did not speak. His wife
said, "Go along, why don't you, and make your trip to Naples; then
come back to M—— and give us the pleasure of your company
for a while; we'll see about everything else after that."

The Count sat where he was for a minute and seemed to be
trying to decide what he should do. Then, getting up and putting

his chair aside, he said that since he was forced to recognize that the hopes with which he had entered their house were premature, and since the family insisted on a closer acquaintance, which he was far from blaming them for, he would send his dispatches back to the headquarters at Z——, for them to be forwarded by some other means, and accept their kind invitation to be a guest in their house for a few weeks. Then he paused for a moment, standing by the wall with his hand on the chair, and gazed at the Commandant. The latter replied that he would feel extremely sorry if the passion that the Count seemed to cherish for his daughter should get him into serious trouble; right now the Count must know what he absolutely had to do and what he didn't, and whether he could send the dispatches back and occupy the room they had for him. At these words they saw the Count change color; he kissed Madam G——'s hand, bowed to the others, and withdrew.

The family did not know what to make of such behavior. The mother said that surely it was not possible that he should think of sending the dispatches he was carrying to Naples back to Z—— simply because he had not been able, on his way through M——, during a five minutes' conversation, to persuade a lady whom he did not know at all to consent to his proposal of marriage. The Forest Warden exclaimed that such reckless behavior would certainly be punished by nothing less than imprisonment in a fortress! And such a man would be dismissed into the bargain, added the Commandant. However, the latter continued, there was no danger of that. The Count had only been talking wildly; he would think twice before returning the dispatches. But the mother, when she learned about this danger, was extremely apprehensive that he would send them back. His headstrong, single-minded nature, she thought, was capable of just such a deed. She begged her son to run after him and dissuade him from a step that promised nothing but disaster. The Forest Warden replied that his interfering in that way would have the opposite effect and only encourage the Count to hope that he could gain his purpose by this stratagem. The Marquise thought the same thing, although she was convinced that, unless her brother did something, the Count would certainly send the dispatches back; he would rather bring disaster on himself than show himself up for an empty talker. All were agreed that his behavior was extraordinary and that he seemed accustomed to capturing ladies' hearts, like fortresses, by storm.

At this moment the Commandant noticed that the Count's coach was standing ready before the door. He called his family to the window and asked a servant, who came into the room just then, whether the Count was still in the house. The servant said that he was below in the servants' hall, in the company of an adjutant, writing letters and sealing packets. The Commandant, repressing his dismay, hurried downstairs with his son and asked the Count, whom he found conducting his business at a most unsuitable table, if he didn't care to step into his own room, and if there was not anything else he might do for him. The Count's pen continued to dash across the paper as he said no, thank you, his business was already done; he asked the Commandant what the time was as he sealed the letter, and, after giving the adjutant the whole portfolio, wished the latter a pleasant journey. The Commandant, who could not believe his eyes, said to the Count, as the adjutant left the house, "Sir, unless you have very weighty reasons——"

"The most compelling reasons," the Count interrupted, and walked with the adjutant to the carriage and opened the door for him.

"In that case," the Commandant continued, "I would at least send along the dispatches——"

"Impossible," the Count retorted as he helped the adjutant to his seat. "The dispatches wouldn't do any good in Naples without me. I thought of that too. Drive on!"

"And your uncle's letters?" called the adjutant, leaning out of the coach door.

"They can reach me," replied the Count, "at M——."

"Drive on!" the adjutant called, and away went the carriage.

Count F—— now turned to the Commandant and asked him if he would be good enough to have somebody show him to his room. He would have the honor of doing that himself, the disconcerted Colonel replied; he called to the Count's servants and his own to look after the luggage, and conducted him to the guest room; after which he stiffly said good day. The Count dressed; left the house to report to the military governor of the place; and for the rest of the day was nowhere to be seen, only returning to the house just before dinner.

Meanwhile the family were feeling extremely upset. The Forest Warden described how peremptorily the Count had answered the Commandant's questions; said his returning the dispatches looked to him quite deliberately done; and asked what on earth could be the reason for wooing at a post-horse gallop. The Commandant said that he could not make head or tail of the business and ordered his family not to mention it again in his presence. The mother kept peering out of the window from one minute to the next to see if the Count had not come back regretting his hasty decision and wanting to undo it. Finally when it got dark she sat down next to the Marquise, who was working busily at a table and seemed to shun conversation, and asked her in an undertone, while the father was pacing up and down the room, what she made of the whole thing. Looking hesitantly toward the Commandant, the Marquise said that if her father had prevailed on him to go to Naples, everything would have been all right. "To Naples!" exclaimed the Commandant, who had overheard what she said. "Should I have had the priest sent for? Or should I have had him locked up and sent to Naples under guard?"

"No, no," the Marquise said. "But a real effort to remonstrate with him would have had an effect." And she bent down, a trifle unwillingly, over her work again.

At last, toward evening, the Count appeared. They were only waiting for the matter to come up again, after the first greetings were over, so as to attack him with their combined force and get him to retrieve what he had done, if that was still possible. But they waited in vain. During the entire dinner he carefully skirted everything that might have touched on the subject and talked instead to the Commandant about the war and to the Forest Warden about hunting. When he happened to mention the skirmish at P—— in which he had been wounded, the mother drew him into an account of his illness, asking him how it had been in the little town and if he had had everything he needed there. In the course of this conversation he told them a number of things that were interesting for what they revealed about his passion for the Marquise: how she had seemed always to be at his bedside during his illness; how in his feverish delirium he kept confusing her image with that of a swan that he had seen as a boy on his uncle's estate; how he was especially moved by the recollection of a time when he had spattered the swan with mud and it had dived silently under the water to rise up pure and shining again; how the Marquise, in the shape of the swan, was always swimming about on a flaming flood and he had called out Thinka, which was the name of the swan from his boyhood, but had not been able to make her come to him, for all her pleasure lay in gliding up and down and haughtily puffing out her breast—suddenly he said, with a deep blush, that he was terribly in love with her; looked down at his plate again, and was silent. At last it was time to get up from the table; the Count, after a few words with the mother, bowed to the company and retired to his room, leaving them standing there in complete perplexity again. The Commandant thought that they should let matters take their course. In doing what he did, the Count was probably counting on the influence of his relatives, for otherwise he would be ignominiously dismissed. Madam G—— asked her daughter what she thought of him after all this, and whether she could find it in her to say something to him that would avert a catastrophe. "Mother dear," replied the Marquise, "I am afraid I can't. I am sorry that my gratitude should be put to such a hard test. But I had made up my mind not to remarry; I really shouldn't want to put my happiness at stake a second time, and certainly not without giving the whole matter a lot of thought." The Forest Warden said that if that was her firm resolve, it would be a help to the Count, even so, to know it; it seemed evident to him that he needed to be given some sort of definite answer. The Colonel's wife replied that since this young man, who was the possessor of so many unusual qualities, had said that he was willing to live in Italy, she thought it was only fair to give his offer some consideration and to test the Marquise's determination not to remarry. The Forest Warden dropped into a chair next to his sister and asked her if she liked the way the Count looked. The Marquise answered with some embarrassment, "I like him and I don't like him," and appealed to the way the others felt.

"Supposing," said Madam G——, "that nothing that we are able to learn about him while he is away in Naples contradicts the general impression you have of him now, and supposing he renews his offer on his return, what answer would you give him then?"

"In that case," replied the Marquise, "since in fact his desire to marry me seems so strong—" she hesitated at this point and her eyes glistened—"in that case I would be ready to satisfy it for the sake of what I owe him."

Her mother, who had always wished her daughter to remarry, was hard put to it to conceal the joy this declaration gave her, and wondered what it would lead to. The Forest Warden got up restlessly from his chair and said that if the Marquise thought there was any possibility of her favoring the Count with her hand, then something ought to be said to him right away which would make it possible to avert the consequences of the crazy thing he had done. His mother thought so too. After all, she said, with a man like that there was no great risk, since one need hardly fear that the rest of his life would not be in keeping with all those superior qualities he had demonstrated on the night the Russians stormed the fortress. The Marquise looked down at the ground with a tense and nervous expression. "Perhaps he might be told," her mother went on, as she took her hand, "something to the effect that until he returns from Naples, you won't enter into any other engagement."

"I can promise him that," the Marquise said. "Only I am afraid that it won't be enough for him and will get us all embroiled."

"Let me worry about that!" her mother said with elation, and turned her head to look for the Commandant. "Lorenzo," she asked, "what do you think?" and she began to rise from her chair. The Commandant, who had heard everything, continued standing at the window and looking out into the street without saying anything. The Forest Warden promised them that with this harmless assurance he would guarantee to get the Count out of the house.

"Well, go ahead and do it! Do it right now!" his father exclaimed, turning away from the window. "Here I am, surrendering to this Russian a second time!"

His wife jumped up at these words, kissed him and her daughter, and, while her husband smiled at her bustling energy, wanted to know how they could tell the Count about it right away. It was decided, at the Forest Warden's suggestion, to ask him if he would not care to join the family for a moment if he were still dressed. The Count sent back the answer that he would be honored to join them at once, and hardly had the valet returned with this message than he himself burst into the room, with great strides of joy, and threw himself down at the Marquise's feet in a state of intense emotion. The Commandant was about to speak when the Count, springing to his feet, said that he knew everything that he needed to know, kissed his hand and that of his wife, hugged the Marquise's brother, and asked them if they would do him the favor of helping him to find a traveling coach. The Marquise, though her feelings had been stirred by this scene, said, "I really am afraid, Count F——, lest your impetuous hopes——"

"Not at all! Not at all!" replied the Count. "You've agreed to nothing, if the reports you get about me should clash with the feeling that moved you to call me back into this room." On hearing this, the Commandant gave him a hearty hug, the Forest Warden offered him his own carriage on the spot, a soldier was sent running to the posthouse to hire horses, and, all in all, his leaving occasioned more rejoicing than ever they had known at anybody's coming. He hoped, said the Count, to overtake the adjutant with the dispatches at B——, from where he would go on to Naples by a shorter way than through M——; in Naples he would do everything possible to get out of having to make the trip to Constantinople; and since his mind was made up, if the worst came to worst, to sham illness, he promised them that, unless he ran into unavoidable delays, he would be back in M—— without fail in about four to six weeks. Just then his orderly reported that the horses were harnessed and everything was ready for his departure. The Count picked up his hat, went up to the Marquise, and took her hand. "Well, Julietta," he said, "I feel a great deal easier now,"—and he put his hand in hers—"although it was my dearest wish to marry you before I left."

"Marry her!" they all exclaimed.

"Marry her," the Count reiterated, kissed the Marquise's hand, and assured her, when she asked him if he had taken leave of his senses, that a day would come when she would understand his meaning. The family were ready to get angry; but he immediately bade goodbye to them all very warmly, begged them not to bother their heads about what he had just said, and took his departure.

Several weeks passed, during which the family anxiously awaited, with very different feelings, the outcome of this strange affair. The Commandant received a polite letter from General K——, the Count's uncle; the Count himself wrote from Naples; the answers the family received to their inquiries spoke quite well of him; in short, the engagement seemed as good as concluded when the Marquise's indisposition came back again stronger than ever. And for the first time she noticed an inexplicable change in her figure. She spoke frankly to her mother about her condition and said she did not know what to make of it. Her mother, who felt very anxious about her daughter's health because of these strange attacks, wanted her to call a doctor in for consultation. But the Marquise was against the idea and hoped that her natural vigor would prevail; she suffered the sharpest pains for several days without following her mother's advice, until recurrent sensations of so unusual a kind filled her with such alarm that she had the doctor called; he was a man who enjoyed her father's fullest confidence. Inviting him to sit down on the divan—her mother was away just then—after a brief introduction she told him jokingly what her condition looked like to her. The doctor gave her a searching look; deliberated a while after he had finished his careful examination; and then said, with an expression of great earnestness, that the Marquise's diagnosis was perfectly correct. When she asked him what he meant and he had explained himself quite clearly, observing with a smile he was unable to repress that she was in perfect health and needed no physician, the Marquise tugged the bell cord while she looked at him very hard from the side, and asked him to leave. Speaking under her breath as if he were not worth bothering about, she muttered that it was no pleasure for her to joke with him about such things. The doctor testily replied that he wished she had always been as little inclined to joking as she was now, took his hat and stick, and got up to go. The Marquise promised him that she would report his insults to her father. The physician retorted that he would swear to his opinion in a court of law, opened the door, bowed, and began to leave the room. As he stooped to pick up a glove that he had dropped, the Marquise asked, "But how is it possible, Doctor?" The doctor said he didn't really see any need for him to tell her about the ultimate causes of things, bowed once more, and left.

The Marquise stood there as if thunderstruck. Then she pulled herself together and was about to run to her father when she recalled the intensely serious manner of the man who she thought had insulted her, and her limbs were paralyzed. She threw herself down on the couch in a state of violent agitation. Mistrusting herself, she reviewed every minute of the past year, and decided she had gone mad when she thought about what had just happened. At last her mother came in; when she asked her in alarm why she was so upset, her daughter told her what the physician had said. Madam G—— unhesitatingly called him a shameless, frivolous quack and encouraged her daughter in her determination to tell her father how the doctor had insulted her. The Marquise assured her that the doctor had spoken in deadly earnest and that he seemed perfectly prepared to repeat his mad opinion to her father's face. Madam G——, now more than a little frightened, wanted to know if she thought there was any possibility of her being in such a condition.

"Graves would start to teem first," the Marquise said, "and the womb of a corpse give birth!"

"You are a strange child," her mother said, giving her a tight hug. "Why are you so upset then? If you *know* that it isn't so, why should a doctor's opinion, even the opinion of a whole panel of doctors, bother you? He either made a mistake or he was being malicious, but what difference does it make to you? I think, however, that the right thing for us to do is to tell your father."

"Oh my God!" exclaimed the Marquise, with a convulsive start. "How can I feel calm about it? Don't my own internal sensations, which I am only too familiar with, argue against me? If I knew that somebody else had these symptoms, wouldn't I myself think that she was pregnant?"

"Oh, how awful!" the Colonel's wife replied.

"Malice or mistake!" the Marquise continued. "Why should a man who seemed to deserve our respect until today try to hurt me in such a mean and wanton way? Me, who never once offended him? Who received him with absolute confidence, anticipating in advance the gratitude I would feel toward him? And whose own wish, as his first words showed, seemed an honest and straightforward one to help, not to cause me greater pain than I have ever felt before? But if, since a choice has to be made," she went on, while her mother steadily regarded her, "I conclude that he made a mistake, how is it possible for me to believe that a physician, even a mediocre one, could err in such a matter?"

Her mother said, with a touch of sharpness, "And yet it has to be one or the other."

"Yes indeed, Mother dear," the Marquise replied, her face reddening with an expression of injured innocence as she kissed her hand, "so it does. Although my condition is such an enigma that you must allow me to have my doubts. I swear, for such an assurance is needed, that I am as innocent as my own children; your own conscience cannot be clearer, more honorable. Nevertheless, I must ask you to send for a midwife; I need to convince myself about the way things really are with me and, whatever the result, find some peace of mind."

"A midwife!" Madam G—— cried in a shocked voice. "A clear conscience and a midwife!" And she was unable to speak.

"A midwife, Mother dear," the Marquise repeated, falling on her knees before her, "and this very instant, or I'll go mad."

"Very well," the Colonel's wife replied. "But please make sure you don't have the confinement under my roof." And she got up to leave the room. The Marquise, following her with outstretched arms, prostrated herself on the ground and embraced her knees. "If a life against which it was impossible to level one reproach," she cried with the eloquence of grief, "a life that followed your example, gives me a right to your respect, if any maternal feeling still pleads for me in your heart as long as my guilt is still not absolutely clear, please don't forsake me at this terrible time!"

"Please tell me why you are so upset," her mother said. "Is it just because of what the doctor said? Just because of those internal sensations you have?"

"Yes, Mother," the Marquise said, with her hand on her heart. "There is no other reason."

"No other, Julietta?" her mother asked. "Think a moment. A misstep, as unspeakably painful as it would be to me, does, well, sometimes happen, and in the end I should have to forgive you; but if you went and invented some fairy tale about a revolution in nature in order to escape your mother's censure, and piled one blasphemous oath on another so as to impose on a heart that is only too ready to believe everything you say, that would be more shameful than I know how to say; I could never love you again."

"May the kingdom of heaven lie as open to me some day as my heart is open to you now," cried the Marquise. "I have concealed nothing from you, Mother."

This exclamation, which was uttered with so much pathos, shook her mother deeply. "Oh heavens!" she cried. "My darling child, how sorry I am for you!" And she raised her daughter up, kissed her, and held her in her arms. "What in the world are you afraid of, then? Come, you look quite ill to me." And she wanted to take her to her bed. But the Marquise, whose tears were flowing copious and fast, protested that she was very well and that there was nothing wrong with her except for that strange and inexplicable condition.

"Condition!" her mother burst out again. "What condition? If you are so sure about your memory, isn't it madness to be so terribly afraid? Can't these vague internal sensations of yours have deceived you?"

"No, no!" the Marquise said. "I haven't deceived myself! If you'll just call the midwife in, you will see that this dreadful thing which is destroying me is true."

"Come, my darling," said Madam G——, who was beginning to fear for her reason. "Come along with me and lie down. Whatever was it that you think the doctor told you? How flushed your face is! All your limbs are trembling! What could the doctor have told you?"—and now completely skeptical of what the Marquise said had passed between her and the doctor, she drew her daughter away with her.

"Dear, best Mother!" the Marquise said, smiling through her tears. "I've not gone out of my mind. The doctor told me that I was pregnant. Send for the midwife and, the instant she says it isn't so, I'll feel easy again."

"Good, fine," the Colonel's wife said, stifling her fear. "She'll come right away; since you are absolutely set on having her laugh in your face, I'll get her in right away so she can tell you what a dreamer you are, and not quite right in the head." And she pulled the bell cord and immediately sent one of her people to fetch the midwife.

The Marquise was still lying in her mother's arms, her breast heaving apprehensively, when the woman appeared and heard Madam G——'s explanation of the strange idea that was making her daughter ill: the Marquise swore that her behavior had always been virtuous and yet, deluded by some kind of mysterious sensations, she insisted on being examined by an experienced woman. The midwife, as she probed the Marquise, gabbled about young blood and the cunning of the world; when she finished, she said she had had to do with similar cases in the past; all the young widows who found themselves in her predicament would absolutely have it that they had been living on a desert island; at the same time she spoke soothingly to the Marquise and promised her that the light-hearted buccaneer who had landed in the night would soon come back to her. When the Marquise heard this, she fainted dead away. The Colonel's wife could not subdue her motherly feelings and, with the help of the midwife, labored to revive her; but her anger got the better of her when her daughter came to. "Julietta!" she cried, in accents of intense suffering, "Won't you please, please tell me the truth and say who the father is?" She still seemed ready to forgive her. But when the Marquise said she would lose her mind, her mother got up from the couch and shouted, "Go on, then! You are a contemptible creature! I curse the hour I bore you!" and she ran out of the room.

The Marquise, who was about to swoon again, drew the midwife down to her and laid her violently trembling head on her breast. In a faltering voice she asked her how inflexible the laws of nature were: was it possible to conceive without one's knowing it? The midwife smiled, undid the Marquise's dress, and said that that was not the present case. No, no, of course not, the Marquise hastened to say, she had known when she conceived, she only wanted to know in general whether such an occurrence was possible in nature. The midwife answered that, with the exception of the Holy Virgin, no such thing had ever happened to any woman on this earth. The Marquise trembled more and more violently. Fearing that she was going to give birth any minute, she clutched the midwife in terror and begged her not to leave her. The woman tried to reassure her, telling her that her confinement was still a long way off, advising her how in such cases one could escape the cackling of the world, and promising her that everything would turn out all right. But as these words, which were meant to comfort her, only pierced her bosom like so many knife thrusts, the Marquise managed to get a grip on herself, announced that she was feeling better, and asked her companion to leave.

Hardly was the midwife out of the room when the Marquise received a note from her mother that read as follows: "It is Colonel G——'s wish that in view of the existing circumstances the Marquise should leave his house. He sends her herewith all the papers concerning her property, and trusts that God will spare him the misery of ever seeing her again."

The letter, however, was wet with tears and in one corner a word —"dictated"—had been erased. The Marquise burst into tears.

Weeping over her parents' mistake and the injustice into which these good people were led, she stumbled to her mother's apartment. Madam G—— was with her father, she was told; she tottered to her father's apartment. When she found the door shut against her, she sank to the ground in front of it and in a pitiable voice called all the saints to witness that she was innocent. She must have been there for several minutes or so before the Forest Warden came out and, with an inflamed face, said that the Commandant refused to see her. The Marquise, sobbing brokenly, exclaimed, "Dear brother!" pushed against him into the room, cried, "My beloved father!" and stretched her arms out to the Commandant. He turned his back on her and hurried into his bedroom. When she followed him there he shouted, "Go away!" and tried to slam the door; but she wailed and pleaded and would not let him do it, until he suddenly gave up and retreated, pursued by the Marquise, to the far wall of the room, where he stood with his back to her. Just as she threw herself at his feet and hugged his knees in her trembling arms, a pistol that he had snatched from the wall went off and the shot crashed into the ceiling.

"Dear God!" cried the Marquise, got up from her knees as white as a corpse, and ran from her father's apartment. "Order the carriage for me," she shouted as she came into her apartment; dropped into a chair deathly tired; dressed her children as fast as possible; and had her things packed. Just as she was holding her younger child between her knees and wrapping a last shawl around him before getting into the coach, the Forest Warden entered and said that her father had ordered her to leave the children behind in his care.

"My children!" she exclaimed, and stood up. "Go and tell that unnatural father of yours that he can come and put a pistol bullet through me, but that he won't take my children away from me!" And with all the pride of innocence she picked her two children up in her arms, carried them into the coach without her brother's daring to stop her, and drove away.

Having learned how strong she was through this courageous effort, she was suddenly able to raise herself, as if by her own bootstraps, out of the depths into which fate had cast her. The turmoil in her breast quieted as soon as she was on the open road, she kissed her children, the precious spoils of her struggle, over and over again, and felt quite pleased with herself when she thought about the victory she had won over her brother, thanks to the strength of her unspotted conscience. Her reason, which had been strong enough not to crack under the strain of her uncanny situation, now bowed before the great, holy and inscrutable scheme of things. She saw the impossibility of persuading her family of her innocence, understood that she must accept that fact if she did not want to be destroyed, and in a matter of days after her arrival at V—— her grief had given way to a heroic resolution to arm herself with pride against the onslaughts of the world. She decided to withdraw into herself entirely, to concentrate all her energies on the education of the two children she already possessed, and to lavish all her mother love on the third that God had made her a gift of. She made plans for restoring her beautiful estate, which, owing to her long absence, had fallen a little into disrepair, once she was over her confinement; sat in the summerhouse and knitted little caps and stockings for little limbs, while she thought about a comfortable arrangement of the rooms; and also which one she would fill with books and which would be best to put her easel in. And so, before the date of Count F——'s return from Naples arrived, she had become quite reconciled to living a life of ever greater seclusion. The porter was given orders to let nobody into the house. One thought only she could not endure, that the young being whom she had conceived in the purest innocence and whose origin seemed more divine to her than other people's just because it was more mysterious, should bear a stigma in society. An unusual means to discover its father occurred to her, a means that, when she first thought of it, made her start in pure terror and drop her knitting. Tossing restlessly through long sleepless nights, she kept turning the idea, which wounded her in her most sensitive feelings, over in her mind so as to accustom herself to it. Meanwhile she tried repeatedly to get in touch with the man who had deceived her so, even though she had made up her mind that he must belong beyond all redemption to the scum of his sex, and could only have sprung from the blackest and filthiest mire, whatever one might think of the place he now occupied in the world. But as her own feelings of independence grew stronger and stronger, and as she reflected that a gem keeps its value regardless of how it is mounted, she plucked up her courage, one morning when the new life stirred inside her, and had inserted in the newspapers of M—— that extraordinary appeal of which the reader was apprised at the beginning of this story.

Count F——, whom unavoidable business detained in Naples, had meanwhile written to the Marquise a second time to say that other circumstances might arise which would make it desirable for her to keep the tacit promise she had given him. As soon as he could get excused from making the trip to Constantinople, and his other obligations permitted, he left Naples and came right to M——, arriving only a few days after the time he had said he would. The Commandant received him with an embarrassed expression, said that urgent business called him away from the house, and asked the Forest Warden to entertain the guest in the meantime. The Forest Warden led him to his room and, after a brief exchange of greetings, inquired if he knew anything about what had occurred in the Commandant's house during his absence. The Count paled and answered, "No." Whereupon the Forest Warden told him about the shame that the Marquise had brought upon the family, recounting the whole story that our readers have just heard. The Count struck his forehead. "Why were so many obstacles put in my way!" he cried, forgetting himself. "If the marriage had taken place, we should have been spared all this shame and suffering!" The Forest Warden gaped at him and asked whether he was crazy enough to want to marry someone so contemptible. The Count retorted that she was worth more than the whole world that contemned her; that he had absolute confidence in her innocence, and that he would go to V—— today and renew his marriage proposal. At once he picked up his hat, said goodbye to the Forest Warden, who thought he had taken leave of his senses, and left.

Jumping on a horse, he galloped off to V——. When he dismounted at the gate and tried to enter the hall, the porter told him that the Marquise would not see anyone. The Count asked him whether this ban applied to a friend of the house as well as to strangers, to which the porter replied that there were no exceptions he knew of, and right after inquired with a doubtful air if he were not Count F——. "No," replied the Count, after looking at him sharply, and, turning to his servant and speaking loud enough for the porter to hear, he said that in that case they would stop at an inn and he would announce himself to the Marquise in writing. As soon as he was out of the porter's sight, he turned a corner and slipped along the wall of a great garden that stretched behind the house. Entering the garden through an open gate that he discovered, he walked up a path and was just about to climb the slope at the rear of the house when he caught sight, in a summerhouse off to one side, of the charming and mysterious figure of the Marquise, who was busily working at a small table. He walked silently toward her and stood in the entrance to the summerhouse before she noticed him, three short steps away from her.

"Count F——!" exclaimed the Marquise, looking up in surprise and blushing. The Count smiled, stood for a moment in the entrance without moving, then sat down next to her with such modest importunity that it was impossible for her to take alarm, and slipped his arm around her waist before she could think what to do. "Where did you come from, Count, how is it possible——?" the Marquise asked, and looked shyly at the ground.

"From M——," the Count replied, pressing her gently to him,

"through a back gate that I found standing open. I was sure you would forgive me if I came in."

"Didn't they say anything to you in M—— about ——?" she said, without moving in his arms, and stopped.

"They told me everything, dear Lady," replied the Count. "But as I am absolutely convinced of your innocence——"

"What!" exclaimed the Marquise, standing up and trying to free herself from his embrace. "In spite of that you are willing to come here——!"

"In spite of the world," he said, holding her fast, "in spite of your family, even in spite of your own lovely self," and he kissed her fervently on the breast.

"Please go away!" the Marquise cried.

"As convinced," he said, "my darling Julietta, as if I were omniscient, as if my own soul lived in your bosom."

"Let me go!" she cried.

"I've come here," he said—and he would not let her go—"to repeat my proposal and to receive my happiness from your hand if you will hear my suit."

"Let me go this instant! I order you to!" And she wrenched herself from his arms and started from the summerhouse.

"Darling! Paragon!" he whispered, getting up and reaching out to hold her.

"Did you hear me!" the Marquise panted, turning and eluding his grasp.

"Only let me whisper one secret to you!" begged the Count as he grabbed clumsily at the smooth arm slipping through his hands.

"I won't hear a word," the Marquise retorted, gave him a push against his chest, fled up the slope, and disappeared.

He was halfway up the slope in pursuit, determined to make her listen to him at whatever cost, when the door banged shut in front of him and he heard the bolt shoot home in rattling haste. He stopped short, not knowing what to do and wondering if he should

climb through an open window at the side of the house and keep
on until he reached his goal; but as hard as it was for him in every
way to give up, he saw no help for it now. Angry with himself for
letting her get away from him, he stole down the slope and left the
garden to look for his horses. He felt that his attempt to explain himself to her directly had irretrievably failed, and, going at a slow
walk back toward M——, he revolved in his mind the letter he now
saw himself condemned to write. But in the evening, when he was
in the blackest mood possible, whom should he run into at the
common table of an inn but the Forest Warden, who immediately
wanted to know if his suit had succeeded at V——. The Count answered with a short "No" and was tempted to say something nasty
and snubbing; but for the sake of courtesy, he added after a while
that he had decided to write to her and would shortly have the whole
thing cleared up. The Forest Warden said that he was sorry that
the Count's passion for the Marquise had robbed him of his senses.
He had to tell him, however, that she was already getting ready to
make another choice; he rang for the latest papers and handed the
Count the sheet that contained her appeal to the father of her child.
The blood rushed to his face as the Count read it through. His mood
changed abruptly. The Forest Warden asked him whether he
thought the man the Marquise was looking for would appear?
"Without a doubt!" the Count retorted as he bent over the paper
and greedily devoured what it said. Then, after going to the window
for a moment while folding up the paper, he said, "Now everything
is all right! Now I know what I have to do!" He turned around and
courteously asked the Forest Warden if he would see him again
soon; said goodbye, and went away fully reconciled to his fate.

Meanwhile some lively scenes had taken place at the Commandant's house. The Colonel's wife was very angry at her husband's
violent rage and at her own weakness in tamely submitting to the
tyrannical expulsion of her daughter from her home. When the
shot had sounded in the Commandant's bedroom and her daughter

had come rushing out, she had fainted away; true, she had recovered at once, but all the Commandant had said when she awoke was that he was sorry she had been frightened for nothing, and he had tossed the discharged pistol on a table. Later, when they were talking about demanding the children from the Marquise, she had timidly remarked that they had no right to take such a step; she pleaded, in a voice still weak and pathetic from the fainting fit, that there should be no more violent scenes in the house; but the Commandant had only turned to the Forest Warden and, livid with rage, had said, "Go and bring them here!" When Count F——'s second letter arrived, the Commandant ordered it sent to the Marquise at V——; she, as they learned later from the messenger, merely laid it aside and said thank you. The Colonel's wife, who was in the dark about so many things in the whole affair, and especially about her daughter's intention to enter into a new marriage for which she had not the slightest desire, vainly tried to bring the subject of the Count's proposal up again. But the Colonel always asked her, in a way that resembled an order more than a request, not to speak to him about it; on one such occasion, when he happened to be taking down a portrait of his daughter that still hung on the wall, he told his wife that he wanted to wipe the Marquise out of his memory completely, and that he no longer had a daughter. It was at this point that the Marquise's extraordinary appeal appeared in the newspapers. Madam G——, absolutely dazed by it, went holding the newspaper, which her husband had given her, into his room, where she found him working at a table, and asked him what in the world he thought about it all? The Commandant, without looking up from his writing, said, "Oh, of course, she's innocent."

"What!" Madam G—— burst out in complete astonishment; "Innocent?"

"She did it in her sleep," the Commandant said, without looking up.

"In her sleep!" Madam G—— replied; "Such a terrible thing could——?"

"Idiot!" shouted the Commandant, pushed his papers into a heap, and left the room.

The next time the newspapers appeared, the Colonel's wife read the following reply, the ink of which was still wet, in one of them, as she and her husband were sitting at breakfast: "If the Marquise of O—— will come to the house of her father, Colonel G——, at eleven o'clock in the morning on the 3rd of ——, the person whom she is looking for will appear there to throw himself at her feet."

Before she had read halfway through the announcement, the Colonel's wife was struck speechless; hastily glancing at the end, she handed the paper to the Commandant. The Colonel read it through three times, as if he could not believe his eyes. "Now for heaven's sake, Lorenzo," exclaimed his wife, "tell me what you think about it!"

"The vile creature!" replied the Commandant and stood up. "The cunning impostor! Ten times the shamelessness of a bitch joined to ten times the slyness of a fox would not equal hers! What a face! Did you ever see two such eyes? A cherub's look is no truer!" And he went on in this vein and could not calm himself.

"But if it is a trick," his wife asked, "what in the world can she hope to gain by it?"

"What does she hope to gain by it? She wants to carry her contemptible pretense to the bitter end," the Colonel replied. "She has already learned by heart the story that the two of them, he and she, intend to tell us here at eleven o'clock in the morning of the third. 'My dear little daughter,' I am supposed to say, 'I didn't realize that, who could have believed it, I beg your pardon, receive my blessing, all is forgiven.' But there is a bullet here for the man who crosses my threshold on the morning of the third! I think, therefore, that it would be better to have the servants put him out of the house."

After reading the newspaper notice over again, Madam G——
said that, if it were a choice between two incredibilities, she would
rather believe in some mysterious action of fate than in the infamy
of a daughter otherwise so excellent. But before she had a chance
to finish what she was saying, the Commandant shouted, "Do me
the favor of keeping still! I can't stand hearing one more word about
it!" and he left the room.

A few days later the Commandant received a letter from the
Marquise in which she asked him, with the most touching respect, to
have the goodness to send on to her at V——, since she was denied
the favor of being allowed to enter her father's house, the man who
would appear on the morning of the third. The Colonel's wife happened to be there when he received the letter; and, noticing the
confusion of feelings plainly reflected in his face—for if the whole
thing were a deception, what motive could he impute to his daughter
now that she did not seem to be asking for his forgiveness—she was
emboldened to propose a plan to him that she had been nursing
for some time in her troubled breast. While the Colonel continued
to stare vacuously at the newspaper, she said that a notion had occurred to her: would he allow her to visit V—— for a day or so? If
the Marquise really knew the man who had published the reply to
her appeal and he was only pretending to be a stranger to her, she
knew how to put her in a position where she would have to betray
herself even though she were the most cunning dissembler in the
world. The Commandant answered her by tearing the letter to bits
with sudden violence: she knew very well that he wanted to have
nothing to do with the Marquise, and he forbade her to communicate
with her in any way. He sealed the torn pieces in an envelope, addressed it to the Marquise, and gave it back to the messenger; that
was his answer. Hiding the exasperation she felt at his crazy obstinacy, which destroyed any possibility of getting to the bottom of
the business, his wife decided to carry out her plan in spite of him.
The following morning, taking one of the Commandant's soldiers

with her, she rode over to V—— while her husband was still in bed. When her carriage drew up before the gates of the estate, the porter told her that nobody was allowed to see the Marquise. Madam G—— said that she had been told that that was so, but asked him nevertheless to go in and announce that Madam G—— was there. He said it would not do any good, since there was not a person in the world that the Marquise would speak to. Madam G—— replied that the Marquise must certainly have mentioned her, as she was her mother, and that he was not to dawdle any longer but to do his duty. It was hardly a moment between the porter's going into the house on what he considered to be a useless errand and the Marquise's bursting out of the door, running toward the gate, and falling on her knees before the coach. Madam G—— got out of the carriage with the help of the soldier and, more than a little moved, lifted her daughter from the ground. Overcome with emotion, the Marquise bent over her mother's hand and, while the tears streamed down her face, she led her, with great deference, into the house.

"Dear, dear Mother," she said, after showing her to the couch but remaining standing herself and drying her eyes, "what happy chance must I thank for your coming to visit me?" Madam G—— gave her daughter an affectionate hug and said she simply had to come to see her to beg her pardon for the brutal way in which she had been turned out of her father's house.

"Pardon!" the Marquise broke in, and wanted to kiss her hands. But her mother would not let her and went on, "Not only did the answer that just appeared in the newspapers to your advertisement convince me as well as your father that you are innocent; I also have to tell you that the man himself appeared in person at the house, to our great and pleasant surprise."

"Who appeared——?" the Marquise exclaimed, sitting down beside her mother; "which man appeared in person?"—and her face was tense with expectation.

"The one who wrote that answer," Madam G—— replied, "the very man you addressed your appeal to, he himself in person."

"Then for goodness' sake," the Marquise said, her breast heaving violently, "who is he?" And again, "Who is he?"

"That," Madam G—— replied, "I would rather let you guess. Just imagine it—yesterday when we were having tea, right in the middle of our reading the answer in the newspaper, a man whom all of us know very well rushed into the room in wild despair and fell at your father's feet and, a moment after, at mine. We didn't know what to make of it all and asked him to explain himself. His conscience, he said, left him no peace, he was the scoundrel who had deceived the Marquise; he must know how his crime was judged and, if vengeance on him was demanded, he came himself to satisfy that demand."

"But who is he? Who? Who?" the Marquise cried.

"As I have said," continued Madam G——, "a young and otherwise well-bred man whom we should never have thought capable of such a despicable act. But I hope, my daughter, that you won't be horrified to learn that he is of humble station and lacks all those qualities which we should otherwise require of a husband for you."

"Just the same, Mother dear," the Marquise said, "he can't be entirely unworthy, since he threw himself at your feet before mine. But who is he, won't you please tell me who he is?"

"Well," her mother replied, "he is Leopardo, the chasseur, whom your father had come from the Tyrol not long ago and whom I have brought along with me, as you may have noticed, to introduce to you as your bridegroom."

"Leopardo, the chasseur!" cried the Marquise, clapping her hand to her forehead in despair.

"What are you afraid of?" the Colonel's wife asked. "Have you any reason to doubt he is the one?"

"How? Where? When?" the Marquise asked in bewilderment.

"He will only tell you that," she said. "Shame and love, he says, make it impossible for him to talk to anyone else but you. But, if you like, we can open the door to the anteroom where he is waiting with a beating heart, and while I go off somewhere you can see if you can get him to tell his secret."

"Oh, my God!" the Marquise exclaimed. "I once dozed off on the couch in the midday heat and when I woke up I saw him slinking away!" And she hid her shame-reddened face in her small hands.

Her mother dropped on her knees in front of her. "Oh my daughter!" she cried. "Oh my wonderful daughter!" and she threw her arms around her. "And oh your contemptible mother!" she said, burying her face in her daughter's lap.

"What's the matter, Mother?" the Marquise asked in dismay.

"I want you to know," her mother continued, "you who are purer than the angels, that there is not a word of truth in anything I said; that my soul is so corrupt that I could not believe in such radiant innocence as yours; and that I needed to play this shameful trick in order to convince myself."

"My darling mother," said the Marquise, and full of joy she bent down to lift her up.

"No," she said, "I won't budge from here, you marvelous, saintly girl, until you say you can forgive my vicious behavior."

"I forgive you, Mother, oh I do! Stand up," cried the Marquise. "Oh please do!"

"First tell me," said Madam G——, "if you can ever love and respect me as you used to."

"My adored mother!" the Marquise said, and also went down on her knees. "I never lost the reverence and love I feel for you. How could anybody have believed me when the circumstances were so queer? I am so happy that you don't blame me."

"From now on," Madam G—— said, getting to her feet with the help of her daughter, "I will wait upon you hand and foot, my darling child. You shall have your confinement in my house; if the circumstances were different and I were expecting you to present me with a young prince, I shouldn't take care of you with greater tenderness and consideration. I'll not budge from your side again the rest of my days. I defy the whole world; from now on your shame is the only glory I wish, if only you will think well of me again and forget the cruel way in which I repudiated you." The Marquise tried to comfort her with endless caresses and reassurances, but the evening came, and then midnight, before she succeeded. The following day, when the old lady's excitement, which gave her a fever during the night, had somewhat abated, mother, daughter, and grandchildren drove back to M——. The journey was like a triumph. They were as jolly as they could be and joked about Leopardo, the chasseur, who was sitting up front in the coachman's box; her mother said to the Marquise that she saw her blush every time she looked at his broad back. The Marquise responded to this with something between a sigh and a smile. "Who knows," she said, "who will finally show up at eleven o'clock on the morning of the third!"

Thereafter, the closer they drew to M——, the more serious they became, in anticipation of the fateful scene that was about to take place. When they alighted in front of the house, Madam G——, saying not a word about her plans, took her daughter to her old rooms, told her to make herself at home, and, declaring that she would be back shortly, slipped away. An hour later she returned, her face quite flushed. "Did you ever see such a fellow?" she said, secretly pleased nevertheless. "Such a doubting Thomas! It took me a whole hour to convince him, and now of course he is sitting there and crying!"

"Who?" the Marquise asked.

"Who else but the one who has the most reason to cry."

"You don't mean Father?" the Marquise said.

"Like a baby!" her mother said. "If I hadn't had to wipe the tears

out of my own eyes, I would have burst out laughing as soon as I was
out of the room."

"And all because of me?" the Marquise asked, getting up. "And
I sit here——?"

"Don't you budge!" Madam G—— exclaimed. "Why did he
dictate that letter to me? Let him come looking for you here if he
ever wants to see me again."

"Mother dear!" begged the Marquise.

"I won't relent!" her mother interrupted. "Why did he reach for
that pistol!"

"I implore you!"

"No, you won't," Madam G—— replied, pushing her daughter
back into her chair. "And if he doesn't come here by this evening,
you and I will go away tomorrow." The Marquise said it would be
cruel and unjust to do that. But her mother said: "Be quiet"—for
just then she heard a sound of sobbing drawing near; "Here he is
now!"

"Where?" the Marquise asked, and listened. "Can that be someone at the door, that terrible——?"

"Of course," Madam G—— replied. "He wants us to let him
in."

"Let me go!" cried the Marquise and jumped out of her chair.

"If you love me, Julietta," replied the Colonel's wife, "then stay
where you are." And at that very instant the Commandant entered,
holding his handkerchief to his eyes. Madam G—— took up a
position in front of her daughter, as if to protect her, and turned her
back to the Colonel.

"Dear, dear Father," cried the Marquise and stretched her arms
out to him.

"Don't you budge!" commanded her mother. "Do you hear?" The
Commandant stood in the middle of the room and wept. "Let him
apologize to you," continued Madam G——. "Why must he be
so violent! And why must he be so obstinate! I love him, but I love

you too; I honor him, but you too. And if I must make a choice, then I'll stay with you because you are the better one." The Commandant bent down until he was almost doubled over and roared so loudly that the walls rang.

"Oh my God!" exclaimed the Marquise, gave in to her mother all at once, reached for her handkerchief, and let her own tears flow.

Madam G—— said, "He can't even speak," and moved a little to one side. At which her daughter got up, put her arms around the Commandant, and begged him to calm himself. She herself was weeping furiously. She asked him if he would not sit down; she tried to persuade him to sit down; she pushed a chair toward him for him to sit on; but he would not say one word; there was no budging him from where he was, and yet he would not take a seat, just stood there in the center of the room, his head bowed to the ground, and cried. The Marquise turned halfway toward her mother as she held him up and said that he would get ill; even her mother seemed to waver in her firmness when she saw how convulsed he was. But when the Commandant yielded to the incessant pleadings of his daughter and finally sat down, and she crouched at his feet and caressed and comforted him incessantly, the mother started talking again, said that it served him right and that perhaps he would now come back to his senses, walked out of the room and left them alone.

Once outside, she wiped her own tears away, and wondered if the violent agitation of feeling to which she had exposed him might not be a danger to his health and if it were perhaps advisable to send for a doctor. For the evening meal, she prepared everything that she could think of that had a fortifying and soothing effect, turned back the coverlets of his bed and warmed the sheets so that she could tuck him in as soon as he appeared on his daughter's arm, and, when he still did not come and the table was already laid, tiptoed to the Marquise's room to hear what was going on. As she listened with her ear against the door, she heard a soft whisper that subsided into silence at that very moment; it seemed to have come from the Marquise; and as she was able to see through the keyhole, her daughter was sitting on the Commandant's lap, something he never in his life had allowed her to do. Finally she opened the door and peered in—and her heart leaped for joy: her daughter lay motionless in her father's arms, her head thrown back and her eyes closed, while he sat in the armchair, with tear-choked, glistening eyes, and pressed long, warm and avid kisses on her mouth: just as if he were her lover! Her daughter did not speak, her husband did not speak; he hung over her as if she were his first love and held her mouth and kissed it. The mother's delight was indescribable; standing unobserved behind the chair, she hesitated to disturb the joy of reconciliation that had come to her home. At last she moved nearer and, peering around one side of the chair, she saw her husband again take his daughter's face between his hands and with unspeakable delight bend down and press his lips against her mouth. On catching sight of her, the Commandant looked away with a frown and was about to say something; but calling out, "Oh, what a face!" she kissed him in her turn so that his frown went away, and with a joke dispelled the intense emotion filling the hushed room. She invited them both to supper, and they followed her to the table like a pair of newlyweds; the Commandant, to be sure, seemed quite cheerful during the meal, but he ate and spoke little, from time to time a sob escaped him, and he stared down at his plate and played with his daughter's hand.

Next day the great question was, who would appear at eleven o'clock of the following morning, for it was now the eve of the dreaded third. Father and mother, and the brother as well—for he too had made it up with his sister—were all agreed that, if the man were at all passable, the Marquise should marry him; everything that could possibly make the Marquise's position a happy one should be done. But if his circumstances were such that even with their help a marked discrepancy would still exist between his position and the Marquise's, then her parents were against the marriage; the

Marquise could stay with them as before and they would adopt the child. She, however, seemed inclined to stick to her promise, providing the man was not an out-and-out scoundrel, and to give her child a father at whatever cost to herself. In the evening the mother asked how they should receive the visitor. The Commandant thought the best thing would be to leave the Marquise alone around eleven o'clock. But the Marquise insisted that she wanted her two parents present, and her brother too, since she had no wish to share any kind of secrets with the person. Also she thought that their visitor's answer to her advertisement, in which he proposed the Commandant's house as the meeting place, suggested that he too wished to have her family present—a fact about the reply, she had to confess, that had won her good opinion. Madam G—— pointed out that her father and her brother would have very awkward parts indeed to play in the proceeding, and asked her daughter to excuse the men; but she was perfectly agreeable to being present herself. After a moment's reflection her daughter accepted this suggestion.

And finally, after a night of the most anxious suspense, the morning of the dreaded third arrived. As the clock struck eleven, the two women were sitting in the reception room, dressed as if for a betrothal; you could have heard the pounding of their hearts if the clatter of the morning had been hushed. The eleventh stroke was still shivering in the air when the door opened to admit Leopardo, the chasseur, whom their father had sent to the Tyrol for. The women paled when they saw him. "Count F——'s carriage," he announced, "is at the door and he begs to be received."

"Count F——!" the two exclaimed together, in utter consternation. The Marquise shouted, "Bolt the door! We are not at home to him," jumped up and was about to push the chasseur, who was standing in her way, out of the room and bar the door herself when the Count entered, wearing the same uniform, plus his decorations and sword, that he had worn during the capture of the fortress. The Marquise felt like sinking into the ground with confusion; she snatched up a handkerchief she had left on the chair and meant to fly into a neighboring room; but Madam G—— caught hold of her hand, cried, "Julietta!"—and as if choking on her own thoughts, her voice failed her. Riveting her eyes on the Count, Madam G—— repeated, "Julietta, please!" and tried to pull her daughter back. "After all, whom were we waiting for——?"

"Oh no, surely not for him!" she cried, suddenly turning around and shooting the Count a look that crackled like lightning while a deathlike pallor spread across her face. The Count went down on one knee to her; his right hand was pressed against his heart, his head hung down on his breast, and he stared with burning intensity in front of him, saying nothing.

"Whom else!" gasped the Colonel's wife. "We are such idiots— whom else but him——?"

The Marquise stood stiffly erect over him and said, "I am going out of my mind, Mother."

"You goose!" her mother retorted, pulled her to her and whispered something in her ear. The Marquise turned away and, hiding her face in her hands, went and fell on the sofa. "What's the matter with you!" her mother cried. "What has happened that you weren't expecting?" The Count did not move from the mother's side; still kneeling, he caught up the hem of her dress and kissed it. "Dear, kind, gracious lady!" he whispered and a tear rolled down his cheek.

"Get up, Count, please get up!" the Colonel's wife said. "Go over there and make her feel better; that way we shall all be reconciled and everything will be forgiven and forgotten." The Count stood up, crying. Getting down again before the Marquise, he took her hand as delicately as if it were made of gold that his slightest touch would tarnish. But she stood erect, crying, "Go away! Go away! Go away! I was ready for some villain of a fellow, but not—not—not the devil!" and, walking around him as if he had the plague, she opened the door and said, "Call the Colonel!"

"Julietta!" her mother panted. The Marquise looked with murderous fierceness first at the Count and then at her mother; her breast heaved, her eyes blazed; one of the Furies could not have looked more terrible. The Colonel and the Forest Warden entered. "Father," she called out before he had even come through the doorway, "I can't marry this man!" thrust her hand into a vessel of holy water fastened behind the door, with a sweep of her arm sprinkled her father, mother and brother with the water, and disappeared.

The Commandant looked surprised and asked what had happened; his face went white when he saw Count F—— in the room. The mother took the Count's hand and said, "Don't ask any questions. This young man is sincerely sorry for what he has done; give him your blessing, come, give it to him, and all will end well." The Count looked completely crushed. The Commandant laid his hand on him; his eyelids twitched, his lips were as white as chalk. "May God's curse avoid this head!" he cried. "When do you mean to get married?"

"Tomorrow," the mother answered for him, for he was absolutely speechless. "Tomorrow or today. Whatever you wish; the Count, who has shown such praiseworthy eagerness to redeem his offense, will certainly prefer the earliest possible date."

"Then I shall have the pleasure of meeting you tomorrow morning at eleven at St. Augustine's Church," the Commandant said, bowed to him, asked his wife and son to accompany him to the Marquise's room, and left the Count standing there.

They tried in vain to get the Marquise to explain her strange behavior; she was in a violent fever, would not hear of the marriage, and begged them to leave her alone. When they asked her why she had suddenly changed her mind and what made the Count more obnoxious to her than somebody else, she stared blankly at her father and did not answer. Madam G—— asked her if she had forgotten that she was going to be a mother; she said that in this case she had to think of herself more than of her child and, calling on all the angels and saints as witnesses, she swore again that she would never marry. Her father, seeing that she was extremely over-wrought, said that she must keep her word, left the room, and, after duly exchanging notes with the Count, gave all the necessary orders for the wedding. He also submitted a marriage contract to the Count in which the latter renounced all his rights as a husband, at the same time that he agreed to do anything and everything that might be required of him. The Count signed the paper and sent it back moistened with his tears. The next morning, when the Commandant brought the contract to the Marquise, he found her somewhat more composed. Sitting up in bed, she read it over several times, folded it up reflectively, unfolded it, and read it over again; and then announced that she would be at St. Augustine's Church at eleven o'clock.

She got up, dressed herself without a word, got into the coach with all her family when the hour sounded, and drove to the church.

The Count was not allowed to join them until they were at the church door. During the entire ceremony the Marquise stared straight ahead at the altar painting; she did not even vouchsafe the man with whom she exchanged rings a passing glance. After the service the Count gave her his arm; but as soon as they were out of the church the Countess bowed to him; the Commandant asked him if he might have the honor of seeing him occasionally in his daughter's apartment, to which the Count stammered something in reply that nobody could understand, pulled his hat off to the company, and went away. He took a place in M—— and several months went by without his so much as setting foot in the Commandant's house, where the Countess continued to stay.

Thanks only to the delicate, honorable, and exemplary way he behaved whenever he encountered the family, he was invited, after the Countess was duly delivered of a son, to the latter's baptism. The Countess, sitting up in bed with rugs around her shoulders, saw him only for a moment as he stood in the doorway and bowed respectfully to her from the distance. Into the cradle among the gifts with which the guests welcomed the newborn child he tossed two papers, one of which, as it turned out when he departed, was a gift of 20,000 rubles to the boy, the other a will making the mother, in case he died, the heiress of everything he owned. From that day on, thanks to Madam G———'s management, he was invited to the house more often; he was free to come and go, and soon no evening passed in which he did not appear there. When his feelings told him that everybody, seeing what an imperfect place the world in general was, had pardoned him, he began to court his wife the Countess anew. After a year she consented for the second time, and a second marriage was celebrated, happier than the first, after which the whole family moved to V———. A whole line of young Russians now followed the first; and when the Count once asked his wife, in a happy moment, why on that terrible third of the month, when she seemed ready to accept any villain of a fellow that came along, she had fled from him as if from the Devil, she threw her arms around his neck and said: he wouldn't have looked like a devil to her then if he had not seemed like an angel to her at his first appearance.

Michael Kohlhaas:

[*FROM AN OLD CHRONICLE*]

$\mathcal{T}$OWARD the middle of the sixteenth century, there lived on the banks of the Havel a horse dealer by the name of Michael Kohlhaas, the son of a schoolmaster, one of the most upright and at the same time one of the most terrible men of his day. Until his thirtieth year this extraordinary man would have been thought the very model of a good citizen. In a village that still bears his name, he owned a farm on which he quietly earned a living by his trade; the children with whom his wife presented him were brought up in the fear of God to be industrious and honest; there was not one of his neighbors who had not benefited from his benevolence or his fair-mindedness—the world, in short, would have had every reason to bless his memory, if he had not carried one virtue to excess. But his sense of justice turned him into a brigand and a murderer.

He rode abroad one day with a string of young horses, all fat and glossy-coated, and was turning over in his mind how he would use the profit he hoped to make on them at the fairs—part of it, like the good manager he was, to get new profits, but part, too, for present enjoyment—when he reached the Elbe, and near an imposing castle standing in Saxon territory he came upon a toll gate that he had never found on that road before. He halted his horses just when a heavy shower of rain was coming down and shouted for the tollkeeper, who after a while showed his surly face at the window. The horse dealer told him to open the gate. "What's been happening here?" he asked, when the tollkeeper, after a long interval, emerged from the house.

"Seignorial privilege," answered the latter as he opened the gate, "bestowed upon the Junker Wenzel von Tronka."

"So," said Kohlhaas; "the Junker's name is Wenzel?" and he gazed at the castle, which overlooked the field with its glittering battlements. "Is the old Junker dead then?"

"Died of a stroke," the tollkeeper said as he raised the toll bar.

"Oh! I'm sorry to hear that," Kohlhaas replied. "He was a decent old gentleman, who liked to see people come and go and helped along trade and traffic whenever he could; he once put down some cobblestones because a mare of mine broke her leg over there where the road goes into the village. Well, what do I owe you?" he asked, and had trouble getting out the groschen demanded by the keeper from beneath his cloak which was flapping in the wind. "All right, old fellow," he added, when the keeper muttered "Quick, quick!" and cursed the weather; "If they had left this tree standing in the forest it would have been better for both of us." And he gave him the money and started to ride on. He had hardly passed under the toll bar, however, when a new voice rang out from the tower behind him: "Hold up there, horse dealer!" and he saw the castellan slam a window shut and come hurrying down to him. "Now what?" wondered Kohlhaas and halted with his horses. Buttoning one waistcoat after another around his ample middle, the castellan came up to him and, leaning into the wind, asked for his pass.

"Pass?" said Kohlhaas, a little disconcerted. So far as he knew, he had none, was his answer, but if somebody would only tell him what in the name of God the thing was, he might just happen to have one in his pocket. The castellan eyed him obliquely and said that without a permit from the sovereign no dealer could bring horses across the border. The horse dealer assured him that he had already crossed the border seventeen times in his life without such a permit; that he knew every one of the regulations of his trade; that in all likelihood the whole thing would turn out to be a mistake, for which reason he wished to give it some thought; and that he would like it, since he had a long day's ride ahead of him, if he were not needlessly detained any longer. But the castellan answered that he was not going to slip through the eighteenth time, that the ordinance had recently been issued for just that reason, and that he must either get a permit for himself right now or go back to where he had come from. After a moment's reflection, the horse dealer, whom these illegal demands were beginning to exasperate, got down from his horse, handed the reins to a groom, and said that he would speak to the Junker von Tronka himself about the matter. He made straight for the castle, too; the castellan, muttering something about penny-pinching money-grubbers and what a good thing it was to squeeze them, followed him; and the two men, measuring each other with their glances, entered the hall. The Junker happened to be making merry with friends over wine, and they had all burst into uproarious laughter at a joke just as Kohlhaas approached with his complaint. The Junker asked him what he wanted; the knights, on catching sight of the stranger, fell silent; but no sooner did the latter launch into his request about the horses than the whole company cried out, "Horses! Where are they?" and ran to the window. Seeing the shiny-coated string below, they followed the suggestion of the Junker and trooped down into the courtyard; the rain had stopped; castellan, steward, and grooms gathered around them, and the entire yard looked the horses over. One knight praised the bay with the white blaze on his forehead, another liked the chestnut, a third patted the piebald with the tawny spot; and all thought that the horses were like deer and that no finer ones were raised in the country. Kohlhaas cheerfully replied that the horses were no better than the knights who were going to ride them, and invited them to buy. The Junker, who was very tempted by the big bay stallion, went so far as to ask its price; his steward urged him to buy a pair of blacks that he thought they could use in the fields, since they were short of horses; but when the horse dealer named his price, the knights thought it too dear, and the Junker said that Kohlhaas would have to ride to the Round Table and look for King Arthur if that was the kind of money he wanted for his stock. Kohlhaas, noticing the castellan and the steward whispering together while they shot meaningful looks at the blacks, and moved by a dark presentiment, did everything in his power to sell the horses. He said to the Junker, "Sir, I bought those blacks there six months ago for twenty-five gold gulden; give me thirty and they are yours." Two of the knights standing next to the Junker remarked quite audibly that the horses were probably worth that much; the Junker, however, felt that he might be willing to pay money for the bay but not for the blacks, and he got ready to go back into the castle; whereupon Kohlhaas said that the next time he came that way with his animals they might perhaps strike a bargain, took leave of the Junker, and, gathering up the reins of his horse, started to ride off. But just then the castellan stepped out of the crowd and said it was his understanding that he could not travel without a pass. Kohlhaas turned and asked the Junker if there actually were such a requirement, which would mean the ruin of his whole trade. The Junker, as he walked away, replied with an embarrassed air, "Yes, Kohlhaas, I'm afraid you must have a pass. Speak to the castellan about it and go on your way." Kohlhaas assured him that he had not the least intention of evading whatever regulations there might be for the export of horses; promised that when he went through Dresden he would take out a permit at the privy chancellery; and asked to be allowed to go through just this once since he had known nothing at all about the requirement. "Oh well," said the Junker as the wind began to blow again and whistled between his skinny legs, "let the poor wretch go on. Come!" he said to the knights, turned, and started toward the castle. The castellan, turning to the Junker, said that Kohlhaas at least should leave a pledge behind as security for his taking out the permit. The Junker stopped again inside the castle gate. Kohlhaas asked the amount of security, in money or in articles, that he would have to leave in pledge for the blacks. The steward muttered in his beard that he might just as well leave the blacks themselves. "Of course," said the castellan. "That's just the thing; as soon as he has the pass he can come and fetch his horses whenever he pleases." Taken aback by such a shameless demand, Kohlhaas told the Junker, who was wrapping the skirts of his doublet about his shivering body, that what he wanted to do was to sell the blacks; but just then a gust of wind blew a splatter of rain and hail through the gate and the Junker, to put an end to the business, called out, "If he won't give up the horses, just throw him back over the toll bar," and he went in. The horse dealer, seeing that he had no choice but to yield, decided to give in to the demand; stripping the blacks of their harness, he led them into a stable that the castellan pointed out to him. He left a groom behind with them, gave him some money, and warned him to take good care of the horses until his return; and, uncertain in his own mind whether such a law might not after all have been passed in Saxony to protect the infant occupation of horse breeding, Kohlhaas continued his journey to Leipzig, where he intended to visit the fair, with the rest of the string.

Arriving in Dresden, in one of whose suburbs he owned a house and stables that served him as headquarters for the business he did at the smaller fairs around the country, he went immediately to the

chancellery, where he learned from the councilors, some of whom
he knew personally, that, just as he had first suspected, the story
about the pass was a fable. Kohlhaas, whom the displeased councilors provided with the written certificate he asked of them, testify-
ing to the fact that there was no such regulation, smiled to himself
at the skinny Junker's joke, although he could not for the life of
him see what the point of it was; and a few weeks later, having satisfactorily disposed of his horses, he returned to Tronka Castle with
no more bitterness in his heart than was inspired by the ordinary
distress of the world.

The castellan made no comment on the certificate when Kohlhaas
showed it to him and told the horse dealer, who asked him if he could
now have his horses back, that he only needed to go down to the
stables and get them. But Kohlhaas learned with dismay, even while
crossing the yard, that his groom had been thrashed for his insolence,
as it was called, a few days after being left behind at the castle and
had been driven away. He asked the boy who gave him this news
what the groom had done, and who had taken care of the horses in
the meantime, but the boy said he did not know and, turning from
the horse dealer, whose heart was already swollen with misgivings,
he opened the stable door. Nevertheless, the horse dealer was
shocked when instead of his two sleek, well-fed blacks he saw a pair
of scrawny, worn-out nags: ribs like rails on which objects could
have been hung, manes and coats matted from lack of care and
attention—the very image of misery in the animal kingdom! Kohlhaas, at the sight of whom the beasts neighed and stirred feebly, was
beside himself, and demanded to know what had happened to his
animals. The boy answered that they had not suffered any harm and
that they had had proper feed, too, but since it had been harvest
time and there was a shortage of draft animals, they had been used a
bit in the fields. Kohlhaas cursed the shameful, deliberate outrage,
but, feeling how helpless he was, he stifled his fury and was getting
ready to leave the robbers' nest with his horses again—for there was

nothing else he could do—when the castellan, attracted by the sound of voices, appeared and asked him what the matter was.

"What's the matter!" Kohlhaas shot out. "Who gave the Junker von Tronka and his people permission to put the blacks I left here to work in the fields?" He asked if that was a decent thing to do, tried to rouse the exhausted beasts with a flick of his whip, and showed him that they did not move. The castellan, after looking at him contemptuously for a while, retorted, "Look at the brute! Shouldn't the clown thank God just to find his nags are still alive?" He asked who was expected to take care of them after the groom had run away, and if it was not right for the horses to pay for their feed by working in the fields. He ended by saying that Kohlhaas had better not try to start anything or he would call the dogs and restore order in the yard that way.

The horse dealer's heart thumped against his doublet. He wanted to pitch the good-for-nothing tub of guts into the mud and grind his heel into his copper-colored face. But his sense of justice, which was as delicate as a gold balance, still wavered; he could not be sure, before the bar of his own conscience, whether the man was really guilty of a crime; and so, swallowing his curses, he went over to the horses and silently weighed all the circumstances while unknotting their manes, then asked in a subdued voice: what was the reason for the groom's having been turned out of the castle? The castellan replied, "Because the rascal was insolent in the stable yard! Because he tried to stand in the way of a change we needed to make in the stabling and wanted us to put the mounts of two young gentlemen who came to the castle out on the high road overnight for the sake of his own two nags!" Kohlhaas would have given as much as the horses were worth to have had the groom right there so as to compare his account of things with that of the thick-lipped castellan. He was still standing there, combing the tangles out of the blacks' manes with his fingers and wondering what to do next, when the scene suddenly changed and the Junker Wenzel von Tronka, coming

home from coursing hares, galloped into the castle yard at the head
of a troop of knights, grooms, and dogs. The castellan, when the
Junker asked him what had happened, started right in, with the
dogs' howling murderously from one side on their catching sight of
the stranger and the knights' shouting them down from the other,
to give the Junker a viciously distorted account of the uproar the
horse dealer was making just because his pair of blacks had been ex-
ercised a bit. With a scornful laugh he said that the horse dealer
even refused to recognize the horses as his own. Kohlhaas cried out,
"Those are not my horses, your worship! Those are not the horses
which were worth thirty gold gulden! I want my well fed and healthy
horses back!"

The Junker, whose face paled for a moment, dismounted and
said, "If the son of a bitch won't take his horses back, he can let
things stay just as they are. Come, Günther!" he cried, "Hans, come!"
while he beat the dust from his breeches with his hand; as he passed
under the gate with the knights, he again cried, "Fetch some wine!"
and entered the castle. Kohlhaas said he would rather call the knacker
and have his horses thrown into the carrion pit than bring them back
the way they were to his stables at Kohlhaasenbrück. Turning his
back on the animals and leaving them where they were, he mounted
his bay and, swearing he would know how to get justice for himself,
rode away.

He was already galloping full tilt down the road to Dresden when
the thought of the groom and what they had accused him of at the
castle slowed him to a walk and, before he had gone a thousand
paces, he turned his horse around and headed for Kohlhaasenbrück,
intending, as seemed right and prudent to him, to hear the groom's
side of the story first. For in spite of the humiliations he had suffered,
a correct feeling, based on what he already knew about the imperfect
state of the world, made him inclined, in case the groom were at all
guilty, as the castellan claimed, to put up with the loss of his horses
as being after all a just consequence. But this was disputed by an

equally commendable feeling, which took deeper and deeper root the farther he rode and the more he heard at every stop about the injustices perpetrated daily against travelers at Tronka Castle, that, if the whole incident proved to have been premeditated, as seemed probable, it was his duty to the world to do everything in his power to get satisfaction for himself for the wrong done him, and a guarantee against future ones for his fellow citizens.

No sooner had he arrived at Kohlhaasenbrück, embraced his faithful wife Lisbeth, and kissed his children who were shouting with glee around his knees, than he asked after Herse the head groom: had anything been heard from him? "Oh yes, Michael dear," Lisbeth answered, "that Herse! Just imagine, the poor man turned up here about a fortnight ago, terribly beaten and bruised; so beaten, in fact, that he can't even draw a full breath. We put him to bed, where he kept coughing up blood, and after we asked him over and over again what had happened he told us a story that nobody understands. How you left him behind at Tronka Castle in charge of some horses they wouldn't let pass through there; how they had mistreated him shamefully and forced him to leave the castle; and how it had been impossible for him to bring the horses with him."

"So?" said Kohlhaas, taking off his cloak. "I suppose he is all recovered now?"

"Pretty well, except for his coughing blood. I wanted to send a groom to Tronka Castle right away to look after the horses until you got back there. Since Herse has always been an honest servant to us—in fact, more loyal than anybody else—I felt I had no right to doubt his story, especially when he had so many bruises to confirm it, and to suspect him of losing the horses in some other way. But he pleaded with me not to expect anybody to venture into that den of thieves, and to give the animals up if I didn't want to sacrifice a man's life for them."

"Is he still in bed?" asked Kohlhaas, taking off his neckerchief.

"He has been walking around the yard again," she said, "these last few days. But you will see for yourself," she went on, "that it's all quite true, and that it is another one of those outrages against strangers they have been allowing themselves lately up at Tronka Castle."

"Well, I'll have to investigate the business first," Kohlhaas replied. "Would you call him in here, Lisbeth, if he is up and around?" With these words he lowered himself into an armchair while his wife, who was delighted to see him taking things so calmly, went to fetch the groom.

"What have you been doing at Tronka Castle?" asked Kohlhaas when Herse followed Lisbeth into the room. "I can't say that I am too pleased with your conduct."

The groom's pale face showed spots of red at these words, and he was silent for a moment. Then he said, "You are quite right, sir. When I heard a child crying inside the castle, I threw a sulphur match into the Elbe that Providence had put in my pocket to burn down that robbers' nest I was chased out of, and I thought to myself: Let God lay it in ashes with one of his lightning bolts, I won't!"

Kohlhaas was taken aback. "But how did you manage to get yourself chased out of the castle?" he asked.

"They played me a nasty trick, sir," Herse replied, wiping the sweat from his forehead. "But what's done is done and can't be undone. I wouldn't let them work the horses to death in the fields, so I said they were still young and had never really been in harness."

Kohlhaas, trying to hide his confusion, replied that Herse had not told the exact truth, since the horses had been in harness for a little while at the beginning of the past spring. "As you were a sort of guest at the castle," he continued, "you really might have obliged them once or twice when they needed help to bring the harvest in faster."

"But I did do that, sir," Herse said. "I thought that, as long as they were giving me such nasty looks, it wouldn't, after all, lose me the blacks, and so on the third morning I hitched them up and brought in three wagonloads of grain."

Kohlhaas, whose heart began to swell, looked down at the ground and said, "They didn't say a word about that, Herse!"

Herse swore it was so. "How was I rude?—I didn't want to yoke the horses up again when they had hardly finished their midday feeding; and when the castellan and the steward offered me free fodder if I would do it, so I could put the money you had given me for feed in my own pocket, I told them I would do something they hadn't bargained for: I turned around and walked off."

"But surely you weren't driven away from the castle for that?" said Kohlhaas.

"Mercy, no," cried the groom. "For a very wicked crime indeed! That evening the mounts of two knights who came to Tronka Castle were led into the stable and my horses were tied to the stable door. When I took the blacks from the castellan, who was taking care of the quartering himself, and asked him where my animals were to go now, he pointed to a pigsty knocked together out of laths and boards that was leaning against the castle wall."

"You mean," interrupted Kohlhaas, "that it was such a sorry shelter for horses that it was more like a pigsty than a stable?"

"It was a pigsty, sir," Herse replied, "really and truly a pigsty, with pigs running in and out; I couldn't stand up straight in it."

"Perhaps there was no other shelter for the blacks," Kohlhaas said. "In a way, the knights' horses had first call."

"There wasn't much room," the groom answered, letting his voice sink. "All told, there were seven knights at the castle. If it had been you, you would have had the horses moved a little closer together. I said I would look for a stable to rent in the village; but the castellan replied that he had to keep the horses under his own eyes and that I wasn't to dare take them out of the yard."

"Hm!" said Kohlhaas. "What did you say to that?"

"Since the steward said the two visitors would only be staying overnight and would be riding on the next morning, I put the horses into the pigsty. But the next day came and went without their making a move; and on the third day I heard that the gentlemen were going to stay some weeks longer at the castle."

"Well, after all, Herse," said Kohlhaas, "it wasn't as bad in the pigsty as it seemed to you when you first poked your nose into it."

"That's true," the groom answered. "After I had swept the place out a little, it wasn't so bad. I gave the girl a groschen to put her pigs somewhere else. And by taking the roof boards off at dawn and laying them on again at night, I arranged it so that the horses could stand upright during the day. So there they stood, their heads poking out of the roof like geese in a coop, and looked around for Kohlhaasenbrück or wherever life was better."

"Well then," Kohlhaas said, "why in the world did they drive you away?"

"Sir, I'll tell you," the groom replied. "Because they wanted to get rid of me. Because, as long as I was there, they couldn't work the horses to death. In the yard, in the servants' hall, everywhere, they made ugly faces at me; and because I thought to myself, 'You can pull your jaws down till you dislocate them, for all I care,' they picked a quarrel and threw me out."

"But the pretext!" cried Kohlhaas. "They must have had some pretext!"

"Oh of course," answered Herse, "the best imaginable! The second day after we had moved into the pigsty, that evening I took the horses, which had got mucky in spite of everything, and started to ride them over to the horse pond. Just as I was passing through the castle gate and began to turn off, I heard the castellan and the steward clattering after me out of the servants' hall with men, dogs, and sticks, shouting, 'Stop thief! Catch the rogue!' as if they were possessed. The gatekeeper blocked my way; and when I asked him and the wild mob running after me, 'What the devil's the matter?'— 'What's the matter!' answered the castellan, and he caught my two blacks by the bridle. 'Where do you think you are going with those horses?' he asked, grabbing me by the front of my shirt. 'Where am I going?' I said. 'Thunder and lightning! I'm riding over to the horse pond. Did you think I——?'—'To the horse pond!' the castellan shouted. 'I'll teach you, you rogue, to go swimming along the high road to Kohlhaasenbrück!' And with a vicious jerk he and the steward, who had caught me by the leg, flung me down from the horse so that I measured my full length in the mud. 'Murder!' I cried. 'There are breast straps and blankets and a bundle of laundry belonging to me in the stable!' But while the steward led the horses away, he and the grooms jumped on me with feet and whips and clubs, leaving me half dead on the ground outside the castle gate. When I cried, 'The robbers! Where are they going with my horses?' and got to my feet, the castellan screamed, 'Out of the castle yard, you! Sick him, Caesar! Sick him, Hunter! Sick him, Spitz!' And a pack of more than twelve dogs rushed at me. Then I tore something from the fence, a picket maybe, I can't remember, and stretched out three dogs dead on the ground at my feet; but just when I had to fall back because of the terrible bites I had gotten, there was a shrill whistle: 'Whee—oo!' the dogs scurried back to the yard, the gate slammed shut, the bolt shot home, and I fell down unconscious on the road."

Kohlhaas, white in the face, said with forced shrewdness, "Didn't you really want to escape, Herse?" And when the latter, with a deep blush, stared at the ground, the horse dealer said, "Confess it! You didn't like it one bit in the pigsty; you thought to yourself how much better it was, after all, in the stable at Kohlhaasenbrück."

"Thunder!" cried Herse. "Breast strap and blankets I left behind in the pigsty, and a bundle of laundry, I tell you! Wouldn't I have taken along the three gulden I wrapped in a red silk neck cloth and hid behind the manger? Blazes, hell, and the devil! When you talk like that, I feel again like lighting that sulphur match I threw away!"

"All right, never mind," said the horse dealer. "There was no harm meant, really. Look, I believe every word you've told me; and if the matter ever comes up, I am ready to take holy communion myself on the truth of what you say. I am sorry things haven't gone better for you in my service. Go back to bed now, Herse, won't you, let them bring you a bottle of wine, and console yourself: justice shall be done you!" And he stood up, jotted down a list of the things the head groom had left behind in the pigsty, noted the value of each, also asked him what he estimated the cost of his doctoring at, and, after shaking hands with him once more, dismissed him.

Then he told Lisbeth, his wife, the full story of what had happened, explained its meaning, said his mind was made up to seek justice at the law, and had the satisfaction of seeing that she supported his purpose heart and soul. For she said that many other travelers, perhaps less patient ones than himself, would pass by that castle; that it was doing God's work to put a stop to such disorders; and that she would manage to get together the money he needed to pay the expenses of the lawsuit. Kohlhaas called her his brave wife, spent that day and the next very happily with her and the children and, as soon as his business permitted, set out for Dresden to lay his complaint before the court.

There, with the help of a lawyer he knew, he drew up a list of charges which described in detail the outrage the Junker Wenzel von Tronka had committed against him and his groom Herse, and which petitioned the court to punish the knight according to the law, to restore his, Kohlhaas', horses to him in their original condition, and to have him and his groom compensated for the damages they had sustained. His case seemed an open-and-shut one. The fact that his horses had been illegally detained pretty well decided everything else; and even if one supposed that they had taken sick by sheer accident, the horse dealer's demand that they should be returned to him in sound condition would still have been a just one. Nor did Kohlhaas, as he looked about the capital, lack for friends

who promised to give his case their active support; the large trade
he did in horses had made him acquainted with the most important
men of the country, and his honest dealing had won him their good
will. He dined cheerfully a number of times with his lawyer, who
was himself a man of consequence; left a sum of money with him
to defray the legal costs; and, fully reassured by the latter as to the
outcome of the suit, returned, in a few weeks' time, to his wife
Lisbeth in Kohlhaasenbrück. Yet months passed and the year was
nearing its close before he even received an official notice from
Saxony about the suit he had instituted there, let alone any final
decision. After he had petitioned the court several more times, he
sent a confidential letter to his lawyer asking what was responsible for
the excessive delay, and learned that the Dresden court, upon the
intervention of an influential person, had dismissed his suit out of
hand.

When the horse dealer wrote back in astonishment, asking what
the explanation for this was, the lawyer reported that the Junker
Wenzel von Tronka was related to two young noblemen, Hinz and
Kunz von Tronka, one of whom was Cupbearer to the sovereign's
person, and the other actually Chamberlain. He advised Kohlhaas
to waste no more time on the court, but to go to Tronka Castle
where the horses still were and try to get them back himself; gave
him to understand that the Junker, who was just then stopping in
the capital, had apparently left orders with his people to turn them
over to him; and closed with a request to be excused from acting
any further in the matter in case Kohlhaas was still not satisfied.

The horse dealer happened to be in Brandenburg at this time,
where the Governor of the city, Heinrich von Geusau, within whose
jurisdiction Kohlhaasenbrück lay, was just then occupied in setting
up a number of charitable institutions for the sick and the poor,
out of a considerable fund that had come to the city. He was especially concerned with roofing over and enclosing a mineral spring
for the use of invalids, which was located in one of the nearby vil-

lages and which was thought to have greater healing powers than it subsequently proved to possess; and as Kohlhaas had transacted a good deal of business with him during his stay at court and therefore was acquainted with him, the Governor allowed Herse, who ever since those unhappy days at Tronka Castle had suffered from pains in the chest when breathing, to try the curative effects of the little spring. It so happened that the Governor was present at the edge of the basin in which Kohlhaas had placed Herse, giving certain directions, just when a messenger from Lisbeth put into the horse dealer's hands the discouraging letter from his lawyer in Dresden. The Governor, while he was talking to the doctor, noticed Kohlhaas drop a tear on the letter he had received and read; he walked over to Kohlhaas with friendly sympathy and asked him what the bad news was; and when the horse dealer said nothing but handed him the letter, the worthy gentleman clapped him on the shoulder, for he knew the outrageous wrong done Kohlhaas at Tronka Castle as a result of which Herse lay sick right there, perhaps for the rest of his life, and told him not to be discouraged, he would help him to get satisfaction! That evening, when the horse dealer waited upon him in his castle as he had been bidden, he advised him that all he had to do was to draw up a petition to the Elector of Brandenburg briefly describing the incident, enclose the lawyer's letter, and solicit, on account of the violence done him on Saxon territory, the protection of the sovereign. He promised to include the petition in another packet that he was just sending to the Elector, who, if circumstances at all permitted, would unfailingly intervene on his behalf with the Elector of Saxony; and nothing more than this was needed to obtain justice for Kohlhaas from the Dresden court, in spite of all the tricks of the Junker and his henchmen. Overjoyed, Kohlhaas thanked the Governor earnestly for this fresh proof of his good will; said he was only sorry he had not begun proceedings in Berlin right off, without bothering with Dresden; and after duly drawing up the complaint at the chancellery of the municipal court and delivering it to the Governor, he returned to Kohlhaasenbrück feeling more confident than ever before about the outcome of his case. But only a few weeks later he was troubled to learn, from a magistrate who was going to Potsdam on business for the City Governor, that the Elector of Brandenburg had turned the petition over to his Chancelor, Count Kallheim, and the latter, instead of directly requesting the Dresden court to investigate the outrage and punish the culprits, as would have seemed the appropriate course, had first, as a preliminary step, applied to the Junker von Tronka for further information. The magistrate, who stopped in his carriage outside Kohlhaas' house, had apparently been instructed to deliver this message to the horse dealer, but he could not satisfactorily answer the latter's anxious question as to why such a procedure was being followed. He added only that the Governor sent Kohlhaas word to be patient; he seemed in a hurry to be on his way; and not until the very end of the short interview did the horse dealer gather from some remarks he let fall that Count Kallheim was connected by marriage with the house of Tronka.

Kohlhaas, who could no longer take any pleasure either in his horse breeding or his house and farm, hardly even in his wife and children, waited with gloomy forebodings for the new month; and, just as he had expected, Herse came back from Brandenburg at the end of this time, his health a little better for the baths, bringing a rather lengthy resolution accompanied by a letter from the City Governor that said: he was sorry he could do nothing about his case for him; he was sending along a resolution of the Chancery of State that was meant for Kohlhaas; and his advice to him was to go and fetch the horses he had left at Tronka Castle and forget about everything else. The resolution read as follows: that according to the Dresden court report, he was an idle, quarrelsome fellow; the Junker with whom he had left his horses was not keeping them from him in any way; let him send to the castle and take them away, or at least inform the Junker where to send them to him; in any case, he was not to trouble the Chancery of State with such petty quarrels. Kohlhaas, who cared nothing about the horses themselves—his pain would have been just as great if it had been a question of a pair of dogs—was consumed with rage when he received this letter. Every time he heard a noise in the yard, he looked toward the gate, with the unpleasantest feelings of anticipation that had ever stirred in his breast, to see whether the Junker's men had come to give him back, perhaps even with an apology, his starved and worn-out horses—the only instance in which his soul, well-disciplined though it was by the world, was utterly unprepared for something it fully expected to happen. A short time after, however, he learned from an acquaintance, who had traveled the high-road, that his animals were still being worked in the fields at Tronka Castle, now as before, just like the Junker's other horses; and through the pain he felt at seeing the world in such a state of monstrous disorder flashed a thrill of inward satisfaction at knowing that henceforth he would be at peace with himself.

He invited a bailiff, who was his neighbor and who for a long time had had the plan of enlarging his estate by buying property adjoining it, to come and see him and asked him, after the visitor was seated, how much he would give him for all the property Kohlhaas owned in Brandenburg and Saxony, house and farm, immovable or otherwise, the whole lot of it together. His wife, Lisbeth, turned pale at these words. Turning around and picking up her youngest child who was playing on the floor behind her, she shot a deathly glance past the red cheeks of the little boy, who was tugging at her neckerchief, at the horse dealer and the sheet of paper in his hand. The bailiff stared at him in surprise and asked what had put such a strange notion into his head all of a sudden; to which the horse dealer replied, with as much cheerfulness as he could muster: that the idea of selling his farm on the banks of the Havel was not, after all, an entirely new one; the two of them had often discussed the matter together in the past; his house in the outskirts of Dresden

was, in comparison with it, just something thrown in that they
could forget about; in short, if the bailiff would do as he wished
him to and take over both pieces of property, he was ready to close
the contract with him. He added, with rather forced humor, that
Kohlhaasenbrück was, after all, not the world; there might be purposes in life compared to which that of being a good father to his
family was an inferior and unworthy one; in short, he must tell him
that his soul aimed at great things, about which he would perhaps
be hearing shortly. The bailiff, reassured by these words, said jokingly to Kohlhaas' wife, who was kissing her child over and over
again, "Surely he won't insist on being paid right away!" laid his
hat and stick which he had been holding between his knees on the
table, and took the sheet of paper from the horse dealer's hand to
read it over. Kohlhaas, moving his chair closer to him, explained
that it was a contingent bill of sale that he had drawn up himself,
with a four-weeks' right of cancellation; showed him how nothing
was lacking but their signatures and the insertion of the actual purchase price, as well as the amount of forfeit Kohlhaas would agree
to pay in case he withdrew from the contract within the four-weeks'
period; and again urged the bailiff good-humoredly to make an offer, assuring him that he would be reasonable as to the amount and
easy as to the terms. His wife marched up and down the room, her
bosom heaving with such violence that the kerchief at which the
boy had been tugging threatened to come off her shoulders. The
bailiff observed that he really had no way of judging how much
the Dresden property was worth; whereupon Kohlhaas pushed
some letters over to him that he had exchanged with the seller at
the time of purchase, and answered that he put it at one hundred
gold gulden, though the letters would show that it had cost him almost half as much again. The bailiff reread the bill of sale and
found that it gave him the unusual right, as buyer, to withdraw
from the contract, too, and he said, with his mind already half made
up, that of course he would not have any use for the stud horses in

his stables; when Kohlhaas replied that he had no intention of parting with the horses, nor with some weapons hanging in the armory,
the bailiff hemmed and hawed and at last he repeated an offer—a
paltry one indeed, considering the value of the property—that he
had made him once before, half in jest and half in earnest, when
they were out walking together. Kohlhaas pushed pen and ink over
for him to sign. The bailiff, who could not believe his senses, again
asked him if he were serious; when the horse dealer answered, a
little testily: did he think he was only joking with him, the former,
with a very serious face, finally took up the pen and signed; however, he crossed out the clause concerning the forfeit payable by
the seller if he should withdraw from the bargain; promised to lend
Kohlhaas one hundred gold gulden against a mortgage on the Dresden property, which he absolutely refused to buy from him; and
said that Kohlhaas was perfectly free to change his mind at any
time within the next two months. The horse dealer, touched by his
behavior, warmly shook his hand; and after they had agreed to a
main stipulation, which was that a fourth part of the purchase
price should be paid immediately in cash and the balance into the
Hamburg bank in three months' time, Kohlhaas called for wine in
order to celebrate the happy conclusion of their bargain. When the
maidservant entered with the wine bottles, he asked her to tell
Sternbald, the groom, to saddle his chestnut horse; he meant, he
announced, to ride to the capital, where he had some business to
attend to; and he let it be understood that in a short time, after he
had returned, he would be able to talk more frankly about what, for
the present, he must keep to himself. Then, pouring out the wine,
he asked about the Poles and the Turks who were just then at war;
engaged the bailiff in all sorts of political conjectures on the subject; drank once more to the success of their business; and showed
the bailiff to the door.

When the bailiff had left the room, Lisbeth fell on her knees in
front of her husband. "If you have any affection for me," she cried,

"for me and for the children I have borne you, if you haven't already cast us out of your heart, for what reason I don't know, then tell me what the meaning of all this is!"

"Nothing, my dear wife," said Kohlhaas, "that you need to get upset about, as matters stand at present. I have received a resolution in which I am told that my complaint against the Junker Wenzel von Tronka is mere quarrelsomeness and mischief-making. And as there must be some misunderstanding here, I have decided to present my complaint again, in person, to the sovereign himself."

"But why do you want to sell your house?" she cried, rising with a gesture of despair.

The horse dealer took her gently in his arms and said, "Because, dearest Lisbeth, I will not go on living in a country where they won't protect me in my rights. I'd rather be a dog, if people are going to kick me, than a man! I am sure my wife thinks about this just as I do."

"How do you know," she asked him in a gentle voice, "that they won't protect you in your rights? If you go to the Elector humbly with your petition, as it is proper that you should, how do you know that it will be tossed aside or that his answer will be to refuse you a hearing?"

"Very well," Kohlhaas said, "if my fears are groundless, neither has my house been sold yet. The Elector himself, I know, is a just man; and if I can only slip past those around him and speak to his own person, I don't doubt that I shall get justice for myself and come happily home again to you and my old trade before the week is out. And then I should only want to stay with you," he added, kissing her, "till the end of my life! However," he continued, "it is best for me to be prepared for everything; and therefore I should like you, if possible, to go away for a while with the children and visit your aunt in Schwerin, whom you have been wanting to visit for some time anyhow."

"What!" exclaimed his wife. "I'm to go to Schwerin? Across the

border with the children to my aunt in Schwerin?" And terror made
the words stick in her throat.

"Certainly," Kohlhaas said. "And, if possible, right away, since
I don't want to be worrying about other things while I am busy
with the steps I mean to take in my case."

"Oh, now I understand you!" she exclaimed. "All you want now
are arms and horses, whoever wants the rest can have it!" And she
turned away from him, threw herself into a chair, and burst into
tears.

"Dearest Lisbeth," Kohlhaas said in surprise, "what are you
saying? I have been blessed by God with wife and children and
worldly goods; am I to wish it were otherwise for the first time
today?" He sat down next to her when she flushed at these words,
and she threw her arms around his neck. "Tell me," he said, smooth-
ing the hair away from her forehead, "what shall I do? Shall I give
up my suit? Shall I go over to Tronka Castle, beg the knight to give
me back my horses, and mount and ride them home to you?"

Lisbeth did not dare to say, "Yes! Yes! Yes!"—weeping, she
shook her head, hugged him fiercely to her, and covered his breast
with fervent kisses.

"Well then," Kohlhaas cried, "if you feel that justice must be
done me if I am to continue in my trade, then don't deny me the
freedom I need to get it!" And, standing up, he ordered the groom,
who had come to report that the chestnut was saddled and ready, to
see to it that the bays were harnessed the next day to take his wife
to Schwerin. Lisbeth said she had just thought of something. Rising
and wiping the tears from her eyes, she asked her husband, who had
sat down at his desk, if he would entrust the petition to her and let
her go to Berlin in his stead and hand it to the Elector. Kohlhaas,
moved by this change in her for more reasons than one, drew her
down on his lap and said, "My darling wife, that is hardly possible.
The sovereign is surrounded by a great many people, anybody coming near him is exposed to all sorts of annoyances."

Lisbeth replied that in nine cases out of ten it was easier for a woman to approach him than a man. "Give me the petition," she repeated, "and if all you want is an assurance that it will reach his hands, I guarantee he'll receive it!" Kohlhaas, who had had many proofs of her courage as well as her intelligence, asked her how she proposed to go about it; whereupon, looking shamefacedly at the ground, she answered that the castellan of the Elector's palace had courted her in earlier days, when he had served in Schwerin; that it was true he was married now and the father of several children, but that she was still not entirely forgotten—in short, let him leave it to her to make use of this as well as many other circumstances, which it would take too long to describe. Kohlhaas kissed her happily, said that her proposal was accepted, advised her that all she needed to do to speak to the sovereign inside the palace itself was to lodge with the wife of the castellan, gave her the petition, ordered the bays harnessed up, and, bundling her into the wagon, sent her off with his faithful groom, Sternbald.

But of all the unsuccessful steps that he had taken in his case, this journey was the most unfortunate. For only a few days later Sternbald entered the courtyard again, leading the wagon at a walk, inside of which the horse dealer's wife lay prostrate with a dangerous contusion of the chest. Kohlhaas, white-faced, came running over, but could get no coherent account of the cause of the accident. The castellan, according to the groom, had not been at home, so they had had to put up at an inn near the palace; Lisbeth had left the inn the next morning, ordering the groom to remain with the horses; and she had not returned until evening, in her present condition. Apparently she had pressed forward too boldly toward the sovereign's person and, through no fault of his, only because of the brutal zeal of a bodyguard, she had received a blow on the chest from a lance butt. At least that was what the people had said who brought her back unconscious to the inn toward evening; for she herself could hardly speak because of the blood flowing from her mouth.

Afterwards a knight came to get the petition from her. Sternbald said he had wanted to jump on a horse and gallop home immediately with the news of the accident; but in spite of all the remonstrances of the surgeon called in to attend her, she had insisted on being carried back to her husband at Kohlhaasenbrück without sending word ahead. Kohlhaas found her more dead than alive from the trip, and put her to bed where, gasping painfully for breath, she lived a few days longer. They tried in vain to bring her back to consciousness so as to get some light on what had happened; she lay in bed staring straight in front of her, her eyes already dim, and would not answer. Only just before her death did she recover consciousness. For when a minister of the Lutheran faith (which, following the example of her husband, she had embraced in what was then its infancy) was standing beside her bed, reading, in a loud voice which mixed pathos and solemnity, a chapter of the Bible, she suddenly looked darkly up at him, took the Bible from his hand as if there were no need to read to her from it, turned page after page, apparently looking for a passage; then her forefinger pointed out this verse to Kohlhaas, who was sitting at her bedside: "Forgive your enemies; do good to them that hate you." As she did so, she squeezed his hand with a look full of tender feeling, and died.

Kohlhaas thought: "May God never forgive me the way I forgive the Junker!" kissed her with the tears streaming down his cheeks, closed her eyes, and left the room. Taking the hundred gold gulden that the bailiff had already sent him for the stables in Dresden, he ordered such a funeral as became a princess better than a horse dealer's wife: an oak coffin with heavy brass mountings, cushions of silk with gold and silver tassels, and a grave eight ells deep, walled with fieldstone and mortar. He himself stood beside the tomb with his youngest child in his arms and looked on at the work. On the day of the funeral the corpse, white as snow, was laid out in a room that he had had hung with black cloth. The minister had just finished speaking with great feeling at the bier, when the sovereign's answer to the petition presented him by the dead woman was delivered to Kohlhaas: he was commanded to fetch the horses home from Tronka Castle and let the matter drop, on pain of imprisonment. Kohlhaas stuffed the letter in his pocket and had the coffin carried out to the wagon. As soon as the grave mound was raised, a cross planted on it, and the funeral guests gone, he flung himself down once more before his wife's now empty bed, then set about the business of his revenge. He sat down and drew up a decree that, by virtue of the authority inborn in him, commanded the Junker von Tronka, within three days of its receipt, to bring back to Kohlhaasenbrück the pair of blacks he had stolen from him and worked to death in the fields, and to fatten them with his own hands in Kohlhaas's stables. He sent the decree to the Junker by mounted messenger, instructing the man to turn around and come right back to Kohlhaasenbrück as soon as he had delivered it. When the three days passed without the horses being returned, Kohlhaas called over Herse; told him about his ordering the nobleman to fatten the blacks; and asked him two things: would he ride with him to Tronka Castle and fetch the Junker out; and would he be willing, after they had brought him to Kohlhaasenbrück, to apply the whip to him in the stables in case he should be slow about carrying out the terms of the decree? When Herse, as soon as he understood what was meant, shouted exultantly: "Sir, this very day!" and, throwing his hat in the air, promised that he would plait a thong with ten knots to teach the Junker how to currycomb, Kohlhaas sold the house and sent the children over the border in a wagon; when darkness fell, he called the other grooms together, seven in number, every one of them as true as gold; gave them arms and horses, and set out for Tronka Castle.

With this handful of men, at nightfall of the third day, he attacked the castle, riding down the tollkeeper and gateman as they stood in conversation in the gateway, and while Herse, amid the sudden bursting into flames of all the barracks in the castle yard, raced up

the winding stairs of the castle keep and with thrusts and blows fell
upon the castellan and the steward, who were sitting half undressed
over a game, Kohlhaas dashed into the castle in search of the Junker
Wenzel. In such fashion does the angel of judgment descend from
heaven. The Junker, who was in the middle of reading aloud the
decree sent him by the horse dealer, amid uproarious laughter, to
a crowd of young friends staying with him, had no sooner heard the
latter's voice in the castle yard than he turned pale as a corpse, cried
out, "Brothers, save yourselves!" and vanished. Kohlhaas, entering
the hall, grabbed hold of a Junker Hans von Tronka as the latter
came at him and flung him into a corner of the room with such force
that his brains splattered over the stone floor, and asked, as the other
knights, who had drawn their swords, were being routed and overpowered by his men: where was the Junker Wenzel von Tronka?
But, seeing that the stunned men knew nothing, he kicked open the
doors of the two rooms leading into the castle wings, searched up and
down the rambling structure and, finding no one, went down,
cursing, into the castle yard to post guards at the exits. In the meantime, dense clouds of smoke were billowing skywards from the
castle and its wings, which had caught fire from the barracks, and,
while Sternbald and three other men were busy heaping up everything that was not nailed down tight and heaving it out among the
horses for plunder, the corpses of the castellan and the steward, with
those of their wives and children, came hurtling out of the open
windows of the castle keep accompanied by Herse's exultant shouts.
Kohlhaas, as he descended the castle stairs, was met by the Junker's
gouty old housekeeper who threw herself at his feet; stopping on
the stair, he asked her where the Junker Wenzel von Tronka was; and
when she answered, in a faint and trembling voice, that she thought
he had taken refuge in the chapel, he called over two men with
torches, had the door broken down with crowbars and axes (since
the keys had vanished), turned altars and benches upside down, and
found again, to his furious disappointment, no trace of the Junker.

As Kohlhaas emerged from the chapel, he happened to meet a stable boy, one of the castle's servants, running to bring the Junker's chargers out of a large stone stable that was menaced by the flames. Kohlhaas, who that very instant spied his two blacks in a little thatched shed, asked the boy why he did not save them; and when the latter, sticking the key in the stable door, said the shed was already in flames, Kohlhaas snatched the key out of the lock, flung it over the wall, and, raining blows thick as hail on the boy with the flat of his sword, chased him into the burning shed, amid the terrible laughter of the men around him, to save the horses. But when the fellow reappeared, pale with fright, leading the horses in his hand a few moments before the shed collapsed behind him, he found that Kohlhaas had walked away; and when he went over to the grooms in the castle square and asked the horse dealer, who kept turning his back on him, what he should do with the animals now, Kohlhaas suddenly drew his foot back so menacingly that if he had delivered the kick it would have meant his end; mounted his bay without answering him, stationed himself in the castle gate, and in silence waited for daybreak while his men went on with what they were doing. Morning found everything except the walls of the castle burned to the ground, and not a soul left in it but Kohlhaas and his seven men. He dismounted from his horse and in the bright sunlight that bathed every nook and cranny of the castle yard he searched the place once more, and when he had to admit, hard as it was for him, that his attempt on the castle had failed, with a heart full of pain and grief he sent out Herse and some grooms to learn in which direction the Junker had fled. He was especially anxious about a rich nunnery called Erlabrunn that stood on the banks of the Mulde and whose Abbess, Antonia von Tronka, was known in the neighborhood for a pious, charitable, and saintly woman; for it seemed only too probable to the unhappy Kohlhaas that the Junker, lacking every necessity as he did, had taken refuge there, since the Abbess was his own aunt and had been his instructress in his early years. Kohlhaas, after informing himself about this circumstance, climbed the castle keep, inside of which a habitable room still remained, and drew up a so-called "Kohlhaas Manifesto," in which he called upon the country to give no aid or comfort to the Junker Wenzel von Tronka, against whom he was waging righteous war, but instead required every inhabitant, including relatives and friends, to hand him over forthwith, on pain of death and the certain destruction by fire of everything they called their own. He had this manifesto scattered throughout the countryside by travelers and strangers; he even gave a copy of it to his groom Waldmann, with exact orders about delivering it into Lady Antonia's hands at Erlabrunn. Then he had a talk with some of the Tronka Castle menials who were dissatisfied with the Junker's service and, drawn by the prospect of plunder, wished to enter his; armed them like foot soldiers with crossbows and daggers and taught them how to ride behind the mounted grooms; and, after turning all the spoils his men had collected into money and dividing it among them, he rested from his sorry labors for an hour or two inside the castle gate.

Toward midday Herse returned and confirmed what Kohlass' heart, always ready to expect the worst, had already told him: namely, that the Junker was to be found at the convent of Erlabrunn with the old Lady Antonia von Tronka, his aunt. Apparently he had escaped through a door in the castle's back wall and down a narrow, low-roofed stone stairway that led to some boats on the Elbe. At all events, reported Herse, he had turned up at midnight, in a skiff without rudder or oars, in a village on the Elbe—to the astonishment of the inhabitants, whom the burning of Tronka Castle had brought together out of their houses—and had gone on from there to Erlabrunn in a village cart.

Kohlhaas heaved a deep sigh on hearing this; he asked whether the horses had been fed and, on being told yes, he commanded his troop to mount up and in three hours' time stood before Erlabrunn. As he entered the cloister yard with his band, amid the mutterings of a distant storm along the horizon, holding aloft torches he had had lighted outside the place, and his groom Waldmann came up to report that the manifesto had been duly delivered, Kohlhaas perceived the Abbess and the Cloister Warden, in agitated conversation, come out under the portal of the convent; and while the latter, the Warden, a little old man with snow-white hair, shot fierce glances at Kohlhaas as his armor was being strapped on and called out bravely to the servants around him to ring the alarm bell, the former, the Canoness, white as a sheet and holding a silver image of the crucified Christ in her hand, came down the slope and prostrated herself with all her nuns before Kohlhaas' horse. Kohlhaas, as Herse and Sternbald overpowered the Warden, who had no sword, and were leading him off a prisoner among the horses, asked her where the Junker Wenzel von Tronka was, and, when she unfastened a great ring of keys from her girdle and said, "In Wittenberg, good Kohlhaas!" adding in a quavering voice, "Fear God and do no evil!" —the horse dealer, pitched back into the hell of his unslaked thirst for revenge, wheeled his horse and was about to cry, "Set the place on fire!" when a huge lightning bolt struck close beside him. Turning his horse back, Kohlhaas asked her if she had received his manifesto; the lady replied in a faint, barely audible voice, "Just a moment ago!"—"When?"—"Two hours after my nephew, the Junker, departed, so help me God!"—And when Waldmann, the groom, to whom Kohlhaas turned with a lowering glance, stuttered out a confirmation of this, saying that the Mulde's waters, swollen by the rains, had prevented his arriving until a few moments ago, Kohlhaas came to his senses; a sudden fierce downpour of rain, sweeping across the pavement of the yard and extinguishing the torches, loosened the knot of anguish in his unhappy breast; lifting his hat curtly to the Abbess, he wheeled his horse about, dug his spurs in, and crying, "Follow me, brothers, the Junker is in Wittenberg!" he galloped out of the cloister.

When night fell, he halted at an inn on the highroad, where he had to stop a day to rest his weary horses, and as it was clear to him that with a troop of ten—for that was his strength now—he could not challenge so large a place as Wittenberg, he composed a second manifesto, in which he briefly recounted what had happened to him and summoned "all good Christians," as he put it, to whom he "solemnly promised bounty money and other emoluments of war, to take sides with him against the Junker von Tronka as the common enemy of all Christians." In another manifesto, issued shortly after, he called himself "a free gentleman of the Empire and the world, owing allegiance to none but God"—a species of morbid and misdirected fanaticism, for which the clink of his money and the prospect of plunder nevertheless procured him a crowd of recruits from among the rabble whom the peace with Poland had turned out of service: and, in fact, he had some thirty-odd men behind him when he crossed back to the right side of the Elbe with the intention of burning Wittenberg to the ground. Horses and men camped under the roof of a tumble-down brick kiln, in the solitude of a dark woods then surrounding the place, and no sooner had he learned from Sternbald, whom Kohlhaas sent into the city in disguise with the manifesto, that it was already known to the people there, than he rode out with his band on the eve of Whitsuntide and set the city afire at different spots simultaneously while the townspeople lay fast asleep. While his men were plundering the suburbs, Kohlhaas stuck a notice up on the door post of the church saying that he, Kohlhaas, had set the city afire, and, if the Junker were not surrendered to him, he would raze the place so thoroughly that, as he put it, he would not have to hunt behind any walls to find him.

The terror of the Wittenbergians at this unheard-of outrage was indescribable; and no sooner had the fire, which luckily on that rather still summer night burned down no more than nineteen buildings (among them, however, one church) been partly extinguished toward morning, than the elderly Sheriff, Otto von Gorgas, dispatched a company of fifty men to capture the savage fellow. But the captain in command, whose name was Gerstenberg, managed things so badly that the whole expedition, instead of crushing Kohlhaas, only helped him to acquire a formidable military reputation: for when the captain split his force into squads so as to draw a ring around Kohlhaas and crush him, the latter, keeping his troop together, attacked his opponent at separate points and defeated him piecemeal, and by the evening of the following day not a man of the whole force on which the hopes of the country had been set stood against him in the field. Kohlhaas, who had lost a number of men in this encounter, again set fire to the city the next morning, his murderous efforts working so well this time that a great many houses and almost all the barns in Wittenberg's outskirts were burned to the ground. Posting his familiar manifesto again, indeed, on the corner walls of the City Hall itself, he appended to it an account of the utter defeat of Captain von Gerstenberg, whom the Sheriff had sent against him. The Sheriff was enraged by this display of defiance and placed himself with several knights at the head of a troop of one hundred and fifty men. At the Junker Wenzel von Tronka's written request, he gave the latter a guard to protect him against the violence of the people, who absolutely insisted on his being sent out of the city; and after he had posted sentinels in all the neighboring villages as well as on the city walls, to guard against a surprise attack, he sallied out himself on St. Jervis' Day to capture the dragon that was devastating the land. The horse dealer was sharp enough to give this force the slip; and after clever marching on his part, had drawn the Sheriff five leagues away from the city, where by various maneuvers Kohlhaas fooled him into thinking that he meant to withdraw into Brandenburg because of his opponent's superior force, he suddenly wheeled about at nightfall of the third day and made a forced march back to Wittenberg and set fire to the town a third time. Herse, who slipped into the city in disguise, was the one who carried out this terrible feat; and, because of the brisk north wind blowing, the fire spread so rapidly that in less than three hours' time forty-two houses, two churches, several convents and schools, and the Sheriff's own building were heaps of ashes. The Sheriff, who at daybreak believed that his adversary was in Brandenburg, marched back as fast as he could when he learned what had happened, to find the city in a general uproar; people by the thousands were besieging the Junker's house, which had been barricaded with heavy timbers and posts, and were shrieking at the top of their voices that he should be sent away. Two burgomasters named Jenkens and Otto, present in their official robes at the head of the assembled Town Council, tried in vain to presuade the crowd that they must wait for the return of a courier who had been dispatched to the President of the Chancery of State to seek permission for the Junker's removal to Dresden, where the knight himself had many reasons for wishing to go; but the unreasoning mob, armed with pikes and staves, paid no attention to their words and, after roughly handling some councilors who were demanding that vigorous measures should be taken, were on the point of storming the house and leveling it to the ground when the Sheriff, Otto von Gorgas, rode into the city at the head of his troop of horse. This worthy old knight, who was accustomed to inspiring the people to respectful obedience by his mere presence, had succeeded, by way of making up for the failure of the expedition from which he was returning, in taking prisoner, right in front of the city gates, three stray members of the incendiary's band; and while the fellows were put in chains before the eyes of the crowd, he made the Town Council a shrewd speech, assuring them that he was on Kohlhaas' track and that he thought he would soon be able to bring in the incendiary himself in chains: thanks to all these reassurances, he was able to disarm the fears of the crowd and get them to accept the Junker's presence until the return of the courier from Dresden. He dismounted from his horse and, after having the posts and palisades cleared away, he entered the house, accompanied by some knights, where he found the Junker falling from one fainting fit into another while two attending physicians tried to bring him around with aromatics and stimulants; and since Sir Otto felt that this was no time to bandy words with him about the conduct he had been guilty of, he merely told the Junker, with a look of quiet contempt, that he should get dressed and follow him, for his own safety, to the knights' prison. When he appeared in the street wearing a doublet and a helmet they had put on him, with his chest half exposed on account of the difficulty he had in breathing, leaning on the arm of the Sheriff and his brother-in-law the Count von Gerschau, a shower of terrible curses fell on him. The people, whom the lansquenets had great difficulty in restraining, called him a bloodsucker, a miserable public pest, and a tormentor of men, the curse of Wittenberg and the ruin of Saxony; and, after a sorry march through the devastated streets, during which the Junker's helmet fell off several times without his missing it and was clapped back on his head by the knight walking behind him, they reached the prison at last; protected by a strong guard, he disappeared into a tower dungeon. Meanwhile the return of the courier with the Elector's resolution aroused fresh alarm in the city. For the Saxon government, to whom the citizens of Dresden had appealed directly in an urgent petition, refused to hear of the Junker's staying in the capital before the incendiary had been captured; instead, it called on the Sheriff, with all the forces at his command, to protect the Junker where he was, since he had to be somewhere; at the same time, so as to quiet their fears, it told the good city of Wittenberg that a force of five hundred men under Prince Friedrich of Meissen was already on its way to guard them from any further molestation by Kohlhaas. The Sheriff saw clearly that such a decree would never pacify the people: for not only had several small victories, which the horse dealer won outside the city, given rise to extremely disquieting rumors about the size his band had grown to, but his way of waging war in the black of night, with ruffians in disguise and with pitch, straw, and sulphur, unheard of and quite unprecedented as it was, would have baffled an even larger force than the one advancing under the Prince of Meissen. After a moment's reflection, Sir Otto decided to suppress completely the decree he had received. He merely posted a letter from the Prince of Meissen at all the street corners, announcing the latter's coming; at daybreak a covered wagon rumbled out of the courtyard of the knights' prison and took the road to Leipzig, accompanied by four heavily armed troopers who let it be known, though not in so many words, that they were bound for the Pleissenburg; and the people having thus been satisfied concerning the disaster-breeding Junker, whose whole existence seemed involved with fire and sword, the Sheriff set out with three hundred men to join forces with the Prince of Meissen.

Meanwhile Kohlhaas' force, thanks to the strange position the horse dealer had won for himself in the world, had grown to one hundred and nine men; and since he had also managed to lay hands on a store of weapons in Jessen, with which he armed his band to the teeth, he decided, on learning about the two armies bearing down on him, to march against them with the speed of the wind before they could join forces to overwhelm him. Accordingly he attacked the Prince of Meissen the very next night, surprising him near Mühlberg; however, in this battle, to his great grief, he lost Herse, who was struck down at his side by the first volley; but, furious at this loss, he gave such a drubbing to the Prince, who was unable to form his men up in the town, that the several severe wounds the latter got in the three hours' battle and the utter disorder into which his troops were thrown forced him to retreat to Dresden. Foolhardy from his victory, Kohlhaas turned back to attack the Sheriff before he learned about it, fell upon him at midday in the open country near the village of Damerow, and fought him till nightfall, suffering murderous losses, to be sure, but winning corresponding success. The next morning he would certainly have renewed the battle with the remnant of his band if the Sheriff, who had taken up a position in the Damerow churchyard, had not learned

the news of the Prince's defeat at Mühlberg from scouts and therefore deemed it wiser to retreat, too, to Wittenberg, to await a more
favorable opportunity. Five days after routing these two forces,
Kohlhaas stood before the gates of Leipzig and set fire to the city
on three sides.

In the manifesto which he scattered abroad on this occasion, he
called himself "a viceroy of the Archangel Michael, come to punish
with fire and sword, for the wickedness into which the whole world
was sunk, all those who should take the side of the Junker in this
quarrel." And from the castle at Lützen, which he had taken by
surprise and in which he had established himself, he summoned the
people to join with him to build a better order of things. With a
kind of madness, the manifesto was signed: "Done at the Seat of
Our Provisional World Government, the Chief Castle at Lützen."
It was the good luck of the Leipzigers that a steady rain falling from
the skies kept the fire from spreading, and, thanks to the speedy
work of the fire stations, only a few small shops around the Pleissenburg went up in flames. Nevertheless, the presence of the desperate
incendiary, with his delusion that the Junker was in Leipzig, gave
rise to unspeakable dismay in the city, and when a troop of one
hundred and eighty horse that had been sent against him came
fleeing back in rout, nothing remained for the City Council, which
did not wish to jeopardize the wealth of Leipzig, but to bar the gates
completely and set the citizens to standing watch day and night outside the walls. It was useless for the Council to post notices in the
villages roundabout swearing the Junker was not in the Pleissenburg;
the horse dealer posted his own notices insisting that he was, and if
he was not in the Pleissenburg he, Kohlhaas, would anyhow act as
if he were until he was told where he was. The Elector, notified by
courier of Leipzig's peril, announced that he was assembling a force
of two thousand men, which he would lead himself to capture Kohlhaas. He sternly rebuked Otto von Gorgas for the ambiguous and
thoughtless stratagem he had used to divert the incendiary from the

neighborhood of Wittenberg. But it is impossible to describe the confusion that seized all Saxony, and especially its capital, when it was learned there that a notice addressed to Kohlhaas had been posted in all the villages around Leipzig, no one knew by whom, saying: "Wenzel the Junker is with his cousins Hinz and Kunz in Dresden."

It was in these circumstances that Doctor Martin Luther, relying on the authority that his position in the world gave him, tried to get Kohlhaas, by persuasion, to return within the confines of the social order; building upon an element of good in the incendiary's breast, he had a notice posted in all the cities and market towns of the Electorate which read as follows:

"Kohlhaas, you who say you are sent to wield the sword of justice, what are you doing, presumptuous man, in the madness of your blind fury, you who are yourself filled with injustice from head to foot? Because the sovereign to whom you owe obedience had denied you your rights, rights in a quarrel over a miserable possession, you rise up, wretch, with fire and sword and, like a wolf of the desert, descend on the peaceful community he protects. You who lead men astray with this declaration full of untruthfulness and cunning: sinner, do you think it will avail you anything before God on that day whose light shall beam into the recesses of every heart? How can you say your rights have been denied you, whose savage breast, lusting for a base private revenge, gave up all attempts to find justice after your first thoughtless efforts came to nothing? Is a bench of constables and beadles who suppress a petition that has been presented to them or withhold a judgment it is their duty to deliver—is this your supreme authority? And need I tell you, impious man, that your sovereign knows nothing about your case: what am I saying?—the sovereign you are rebelling against does not even know your name, so that one day when you come before the throne of God thinking to accuse him, he will be able to say with a serene face, 'I have done this man no wrong, Lord, for my soul is a stranger to his existence.' The sword you bear, I tell you, is the sword of brigandage and bloodthirstiness, you are a rebel and no soldier of the just God, and your goal on earth is the wheel and the gallows, and in the hereafter the doom that is decreed for crime and godlessness.

MARTIN LUTHER

Wittenberg, etc."

At the castle in Lützen, Kohlhaas was just turning over in his mind a new plan for burning Leipzig—for he gave no credence to the notices in the villages saying that the Junker was in Dresden, since they were not signed by anybody, let alone the City Council, as he had demanded—when Sternbald and Waldmann were unpleasantly surprised to notice Luther's placard, which had been posted on the castle gate during the night. For several days the two men hoped in vain that Kohlhaas would catch sight of it himself, since they did not want to have to tell him about it; but though he came out in the evening, it was only to give a few brief commands, he was too gloomy and preoccupied to notice anything, until finally on a morning when two of his men were to hang for violating orders and looting in the neighborhood, they decided to draw it to his attention. He was just returning from the place of execution, with the pomp that he had adopted since the proclamation of his latest manifesto—a large archangelic sword was borne before him on a red leather cushion ornamented with gold tassels, while twelve men with burning torches followed after—and the people were timidly making way for him on either side, when Sternbald and Waldmann, with their swords tucked under their arms, begun to march demonstratively around the pillar with the placard on it, in a way that could not fail to excite his wonder. With his hands clasped behind his back, lost in his own thoughts, Kohlhaas had reached the portal when he looked up and stopped short; perceiving the two men respectfully drawing back, he strode rapidly to the pillar with his eyes still fixed absent-mindedly on them. But who can describe the turmoil in his soul when he saw there the paper that accused him of injustice: signed by the dearest and most revered name he knew, the name of Martin Luther! A dark flush spread across his face. Taking off his helmet, he read the notice twice over from beginning to end; turned back among his men with an uncertain look as if he were about to say something, yet said nothing; took down the sheet from the pillar; read it through again; cried, "Waldmann, saddle my horse!" then, "Sternbald, follow me into the castle!" and disappeared inside. It needed no more than these few words to disarm him instantly, amid all the death and destruction in which he stood. He disguised himself as a Thuringian farmer; told Sternbald that very important business made it necessary for him to go to Wittenberg; turned over the command of the band in Lützen to him in the presence of the leading men; and, with a promise to be back within three days, during which time there was no fear of an attack, rode off.

In Wittenberg he put up at an inn under an assumed name, and at nightfall, wrapped in his cloak and armed with a brace of pistols picked up in the sack of Tronka Castle, he entered Luther's room. Luther, who was sitting at his desk surrounded by books and manuscripts, when he saw the stranger open the door and bolt it behind him, asked him who he was and what he wanted; and no sooner had the man, who held his hat respectfully in his hand, replied with diffident anticipation of the dread his name would arouse, that he was Michael Kohlhaas, the horse dealer, than Luther cried, "Get out of here!" and, rising from the desk and hurrying toward a bell, he added, "Your breath is pestilence, your presence ruination!" Without stirring from the spot, Kohlhaas drew his pistol and said, "Your Reverence, if you touch that bell this pistol will stretch me lifeless at your feet! Sit down and hear what I have to say; you are safer with me than you are among the angels whose psalms you are inscribing." Luther sat down and said, "What do you want?"

"To show you you are wrong to think I am an unjust man! In your notice you told me that my sovereign knows nothing about my case: very well, get me a safe-conduct and I will go to Dresden and lay it before him."

"Impious and terrible man!" cried Luther, puzzled and at the same time reassured by these words. "Who gives you the right to attack the Junker von Tronka on the authority of your own decree and, when you cannot find him in his castle, to punish the entire community that shelters him with fire and sword?"

Kohlhaas replied, "Your Reverence, nobody from now on! A report I got from Dresden deceived me, misled me! The war I am waging against society is a crime only as long as I have not been cast out of it, as you now assure me I have not been."

"Cast out of society!" exclaimed Luther, staring at him. "What kind of crazy ideas have got hold of you? How could anyone cast you out of the community of the state in which you live? Where, indeed, as long as states have existed has there ever been a case of anybody, no matter who, being cast out of society?"

"I call that man an outcast," Kohlhaas said, clenching his fist, "who is denied the protection of the laws! For I need this protection if my peaceful calling is to prosper; yes, it is for the protection that its laws afford me and mine that I seek shelter in the community; and whoever denies me it thrusts me out among the beasts of the wilderness; he is the one—how can you deny it?—who puts into my hand the club that I defend myself with."

"Who has denied you the protection of the laws?" cried Luther. "Didn't I write you that the sovereign to whom you addressed your complaint knows nothing about it? If state servants behind his back suppress lawsuits or otherwise make a mockery of his sacred name without his knowledge, who else but God has the right to call him to account for choosing such servants? Do you think, accursed and dreadful man, that you are entitled to judge him for it?"

"Very well," Kohlhaas replied, "if the sovereign has not cast me out of the community under his protection, I will return to it. Get me, I repeat, a safe-conduct to Dresden and I will disperse the band I have collected in the castle at Lützen and again lay my rejected complaint before the courts of the land." Luther, looking annoyed, shuffled the papers that were lying on his desk and made no reply. He was irritated by the defiant attitude this singular man took toward the state; and after thinking about the sentence Kohlhaas had passed on the Junker from Kohlhaasenbrück, he asked him what he wanted from the Dresden court. Kohlhaas answered, "Punishment of the Junker according to the law; restoration of my horses to their previous condition; and compensation for the damages that I as well as my man Herse, who fell at Mühlberg, suffered from the violence done us."

"Compensation for damages!" Luther cried. "You have borrowed by the thousands, from Jews and Christians, on notes and securities, to meet the expenses of your private revenge. Shall all that be counted in the final reckoning, too?"

"God forbid!" said Kohlhaas. "I don't ask back my house and farm and wealth, any more than the cost of my wife's funeral! Herse's old mother will present a bill for her son's medical costs, as well as a list of those things which he lost at Tronka Castle; and the government can have an expert estimate the loss I suffered by not selling the black horses."

Luther said, "Mad, incomprehensible, and terrible fellow!" and looked at him. "Now that your sword has taken the most ferocious revenge imaginable upon the Junker, what makes you insist on a judgment which, if it is finally pronounced, will weigh so lightly on him?"

Kohlhaas answered, as a tear rolled down his cheek, "Your Reverence, that judgment has cost me my wife; Kohlhaas means to show the world that she perished in no unrighteous quarrel. You yield to me in this point and let the court pronounce its judgment, and I will yield to you in all the other disputed points that come up."

Luther said, "Look here, what you are asking is only right, unless the circumstances are different from what the common report says they are; and if you had only managed to have your suit decided by the sovereign before you took your revenge in your own hands, I don't doubt that every one of your demands would have been granted. But all things considered, wouldn't you have done better to have pardoned the Junker for your Redeemer's sake, taken back the pair of blacks thin and worn out as they were, and mounted and ridden to Kohlhaasenbrück to fatten them in your own stable?"

"Perhaps so," Kohlhaas said, walking over to the window, "perhaps not, either! If I had known that it would need my dear wife's blood to put the horses back on their feet again, I might perhaps have done as your Reverence says and not made a business of a bushel of oats. But since they have cost me so dear now, let the thing run its course, say I; let judgment be pronounced as is my due, and let the Junker fatten my pair of blacks."

Luther took up his papers again, amid all sorts of thoughts, and said he would negotiate for Kohlhaas with the Elector. Meanwhile he would like him to stay quietly in the castle at Lützen; if the sovereign consented to grant him safe-conduct, he would be informed of it by the posting of a public notice. "Of course," he continued, as Kohlhaas bent to kiss his hand, "I don't know whether the Elector will choose mercy over justice, for I understand that he has got an army together and means to capture you in the castle at Lützen; but meanwhile, as I have already told you, there shan't be any lack of effort on my part." And he got up from the chair to dismiss him. Kohlhaas said that the fact that he was interceding for him put his mind completely at rest on that score; whereupon Luther waved him goodbye, but Kohlhaas, abruptly falling on one knee before him, said he had still another favor to ask. The fact was that at Pentecost, when it was his custom to receive Holy Communion, he had failed to go to church because of the military operations he was engaged in; would Luther have the goodness to hear his confession, without further preparation, and grant him in exchange the blessing of the Holy Sacrament? Luther, after a moment's thought in which he looked sharply at him, said, "All right, Kohlhaas, I'll do it. But the Lord Whose body you hunger to have forgave His enemy. Will you likewise," he said as the other looked at him in surprise, "forgive the Junker who has offended you? Will you go to Tronka Castle, mount your pair of blacks, and ride them back to Kohlhaasenbrück to fatten them there?"

"Your Reverence——" Kohlhaas said, flushing, and seized his hand.

"Well?"

"—even the Lord did not forgive all his enemies. I am ready to forgive my two lords the Electors, the castellan and the steward, the lords Hinz and Kunz, and whoever else has done me wrong in this affair: but, if at all possible, let me have the Junker fatten my two blacks for me."

At these words Luther turned his back on him with a displeased look and rang the bell. Kohlhaas, wiping his eyes, rose from his knees in confusion as a famulus entered the anteroom with a light, in response to the summons; and as the latter vainly rattled the bolted door, Luther meanwhile having sat down to his papers again, Kohlhaas drew the bolt and let the man in. Luther looked sideways for an instant at the stranger and said to the famulus, "Light him out," upon which the latter, surprised to see a visitor, took down the key to the house door from the wall and, returning to the half-opened door, waited for the stranger to leave. Kohlhaas, taking his hat nervously in both hands, said, "And so, your Reverence, I cannot have the comfort of the reconciliation I asked you for?"

Luther answered curtly, "With your Savior, no; with the sovereign—that depends on the effort I promised to make for you." And he motioned to his famulus to perform the service he had called him in for without further ado. Kohlhaas pressed both hands to his breast with an expression of painful emotion, followed the man who lighted him down the stair, and vanished.

The next morning Luther sent a message to the Elector of Saxony in which, after bitterly alluding to the lords Hinz and Kunz von Tronka, Chamberlain and Cupbearer to His Highness, who, as everybody knew, were the ones who had suppressed Kohlhaas' petition, he told him with characteristic candor that under these difficult circumstances there was nothing for it but to accept the horse dealer's proposal and grant him an amnesty so that he might be able to renew his suit. Public opinion, Luther remarked, was on his side to a very dangerous extent, so much so that even in Wittenberg, which had been set on fire three times by him, it was still possible to hear voices raised in his favor; and since Kohlhaas would undoubtedly let the people know about it if his proposal were refused, as well as make his own malicious commentary on the matter, the populace might easily be misled so far that the state would find itself powerless to act against him. He concluded that, in such an extraordinary case, any scruples about entering into negotiations with a subject who had taken up arms against the state must be set aside; that, as a matter of fact, the wrong done Kohlhaas had in a certain sense placed him outside the social union; and in short, so as to put an end to the matter, he should be regarded rather as a foreign power that had attacked the country (and since he was not a Saxon subject, he really might in a way be regarded as such) than as a rebel in revolt against the throne.

When the Elector received this letter, there were present in the palace Prince Christiern of Meissen, Commander-in-Chief of the Realm, uncle of the Prince Friedrich of Meissen who had been defeated at Mühlberg and was still laid up with his wounds; the Lord High Chancellor Count Wrede; Count Kallheim, President of the Chancery of State; and the two lords Hinz and Kunz von Tronka,

Cupbearer and Chamberlain, both intimate friends of the sovereign from his youth. The Chamberlain, Sir Kunz, who in his capacity of privy councilor attended to the private correspondence of his master and was authorized to use his name and seal, was the first to speak, and after again explaining in detail that he would never on his own authority have suppressed the complaint that the horse dealer brought against his cousin the Junker if it had not been for the fact that he had been misled by false statements into thinking it an unfounded and idle piece of mischief-making, he went on to consider the present state of affairs. He observed that neither divine nor human laws justified the horse dealer in taking such terrible vengeance as he had allowed himself for this mistake; dwelt on the renown that would fall on his accursed head if they treated with him as with a recognized military power; and the ignominy thus reflected upon the sacred person of the Elector seemed so intolerable to him that, carried away by his own eloquence, he said he would rather see the worst happen, which was for the mad rebel's sentence to be carried out and his cousin the Junker marched off to Kohlhaasenbrück to fatten his horses, than for Dr. Luther's proposal to be accepted.

The Lord Chancellor, Count Wrede, half turning toward Sir Kunz, expressed regret that his conduct at the start of this unquestionably awkward business had not been inspired with the same tender solicitude for the reputation of the sovereign as he now displayed in his proposal to settle it. He explained to the Elector the hesitation he felt about using the power of the state to enforce a manifest injustice; remarked, with a significant allusion to the followers the horse dealer was continually recruiting in the country, that the thread of the crime threatened to be spun out indefinitely, and declared that the only way to sever it and extricate the government from an ugly situation was to deal honestly with the man and make good, directly and without respect of person, the mistake they had been guilty of.

Prince Christiern of Meissen, when asked by the Elector to give his opinion, turned deferentially to the Lord Chancellor and said that the latter's reasoning naturally inspired him with the greatest respect; but in wishing to help Kohlhaas get justice for himself, the Chancellor overlooked the injury he did to the claims of Wittenberg, Leipzig, and all the country that the horse dealer had scourged in attempting to enforce his own rightful claim to compensation or at least punishment. The order of the state, as regards this man, was so disturbed that it needed more than an axiom borrowed from the science of jurisprudence to set it right. Therefore he agreed with the Chamberlain in favoring the use of the means appointed for such cases: they should get together a force large enough to capture or crush the horse dealer at Lützen.

The Chamberlain, bringing over two chairs from the wall and deferentially setting them down in the room for the Elector and the Prince, said that he was delighted to find a man of such integrity and acumen agreeing with him about the way to settle this puzzling business. The Prince took hold of the chair without sitting down and, looking him right in the face, assured him he had little reason to rejoice, since the first step such a course of action required was to issue a warrant for his, Sir Kunz's, arrest, followed by his trial on charges of misusing the sovereign's name. For though it was necessary to veil from the eyes of justice a series of crimes that led endlessly on to further crimes, for all of which there was not room enough before the throne of judgment, this was not the case with the original offense from which everything had sprung; and the very first thing the state must do was to try the Chamberlain for his life, if it was to own the authority to crush the horse dealer, whose grievance, as they well knew, was exceedingly just and into whose hands they themselves had put the sword he now wielded.

The Elector, toward whom the discomfited Chamberlain looked at these words, turned away, his whole face reddening, and went to the window. Count Kallheim, after an embarrassed silence on everyone's part, said that this was not the way to extricate themselves from the magic circle in which they were caught. With equal justice they might put his nephew Prince Friedrich on trial; for in the strange expedition that he had led against Kohlhaas he had overstepped his instructions in all sorts of ways, and if one were to draw up the long list of those responsible for the embarrassment in which they now found themselves, his name too would figure in it and he would have to be called to account by the sovereign for the events at Mühlberg.

As the Elector, with a perplexed look, walked over to his desk, the Cupbearer, Sir Hinz von Tronka, began to speak in his turn: he could not understand how the right course for the state to follow in this matter had escaped men as wise as those assembled here. The horse dealer, as he understood it, had promised to disband his company in return for a simple safe-conduct to Dresden and the renewal of the inquiry into his case. But it did not follow from this that he must be granted an amnesty for criminally taking his revenge into his own hands: these were two entirely separate matters, which Dr. Luther as well as the Council of State seemed to have confounded. "After," he continued, laying his finger alongside of his nose, "the Dresden court has pronounced judgment, whatever it may be, in the matter of the black horses, nothing prevents us from arresting Kohlhaas for his incendiarism and brigandage: a politic solution that unites the advantages of both statesmen's views and is certain to win the approbation of the world and of posterity." As the only reply both the Prince and the Lord Chancellor gave to the Cupbearer Sir Hinz's speech was a contemptuous look, and the discussion seemed at an end, the Elector said he would weigh in his mind, between now and the next sitting of the Council, the different opinions he had received.

Apparently the preliminary step contemplated by the Prince had killed all desire in the Elector, who was highly sensitive wherever friendship was concerned, to go ahead with the campaign against

Kohlhaas, for which all the preparations were made. At any rate he detained the Lord Chancellor Count Wrede, whose opinion seemed to him the likeliest one, and let the others go; and when the latter showed him letters indicating that the horse dealer's strength had actually grown to some four hundred men—indeed, considering the general discontent in the country owing to the highhanded actions of the Chamberlain, he might count on doubling or tripling that number in a short time—he decided without further ado to accept Dr. Luther's advice. The entire management of the Kohlhaas affair was therefore handed over to Count Wrede; and only a few days later a notice was posted, the gist of which we give as follows:

"We, etc., etc., Elector of Saxony, in especially gracious consideration of the intercession made to us by Dr. Martin Luther, do grant to Michael Kohlhaas, horse dealer of Brandenburg, safe-conduct to Dresden for the purpose of a renewed inquiry into his case, on condition that within three days after sight of this he lay down the arms which he has taken up; but it is understood that in the event that his complaint concerning the black horses is rejected by the court at Dresden, which is hardly likely, he shall be prosecuted with all the severity of the law for seeking to take justice into his own hands; in the contrary event, however, tempering our justice with mercy, we will grant him and all his band full amnesty for the acts of violence committed by him in Saxony."

Kohlhaas had no sooner received from Dr. Luther a copy of this notice which had been posted in every public square in the land, than he went ahead, in spite of the conditions it made, and disbanded his following, whom he sent away with gifts, expressions of his gratitude, and suitable admonitions. Whatever he had captured in the way of money, weapons, and military stores he deposited with the courts at Lützen as the property of the Elector; and after sending Waldmann and Sternbald off, the one to the bailiff at Kohlhaasenbrück with letters proposing to repurchase his farm, if that were possible, and the other to Schwerin to fetch his children whom he wished to have by his side again, he left the castle at Lützen and, carrying the remnant of his little property on his person in the form of notes, he made his way unrecognized to Dresden.

Day was just breaking and the whole city still lay asleep as he knocked at the door of the little dwelling in the suburb of Pirna which, thanks to the honesty of the bailiff, still belonged to him, and told his old servant Thomas, who looked after the place, when he opened the door and stared dumbfounded at him, to go to the Government House and report to the Prince of Meissen that Kohlhaas the horse dealer had arrived. The Prince of Meissen, who thought it expedient to go at once and see how matters stood between them and this man, found an immense throng of people already gathered in the streets leading to Kohlhaas' house when he appeared soon after with a retinue of knights and men. The news of the presence of the avenging angel who chastised the oppressors of the people with fire and sword had aroused all of Dresden, city and suburbs; the door had to be bolted against the pressure of the curious crowd, and boys clambered up to the windows to catch a glimpse of the incendiary at his breakfast.

As soon as the Prince had made his way into the house with the help of a bodyguard that cleared a path for him and had entered Kohlhaas' room, he asked the horse dealer, whom he found standing half undressed at a table, whether he was Kohlhaas the horse dealer; whereupon the latter drew from his belt a wallet with papers in it dealing with his affairs, and, respectfully handing it to the Prince, he said yes, adding that after disbanding his company he had come to Dresden, under protection of the safe-conduct granted him by the sovereign, to press his suit against the Junker Wenzel von Tronka before the court. With a rapid glance the Prince took Kohlhaas in from head to foot, then looked through the papers in the wallet; had him explain the meaning of a certificate from the court at Lützen acknowledging a deposit in favor of the

Electoral treasury; and, after asking him all sorts of questions about his children, his means, and the kind of life he intended to lead in the future, so as to see the kind of man he was, and concluding that they might set their minds at rest about him in all respects, gave him back his papers and said that nothing now stood in the way of his suit, and that all he need do to commence proceedings was to apply directly himself to the Lord High Chancellor of the Tribunal, Count Wrede. "In the meantime," said the Prince after a pause, as he crossed over to the window and looked out in astonishment at the crowd in front of the house, "you must have a guard for the first few days to protect you in your house and when you go out."

Kohlhaas looked down, disconcerted, and said nothing.

"Well then, never mind," said the Prince, coming away from the window. "If anything happens, you have only yourself to blame for it," and he turned to the door to leave. Kohlhaas, who had had some second thoughts, said, "My Lord, do as you like! If you give me your word the guard will be withdrawn whenever I wish it, I have no objection." The Prince replied that that was understood; and after telling the three lansquenets detailed for the duty that the man whose house they were staying in was completely at liberty and that it was merely for his own protection that they were to follow him when he went out, he saluted the horse dealer with an easy wave of the hand and left.

Toward midday, escorted by his three lansquenets and trailed by an immense crowd whom the police had warned against offering him any harm, Kohlhaas went to visit the Lord Chancellor, Count Wrede. The Chancellor received him with great kindness in his antechamber and, after talking with him two whole hours and hearing Kohlhaas' story from beginning to end, he referred him to a celebrated lawyer in the city, one who was a colleague of the court, so that he might have the complaint drawn up and immediately presented. Kohlhaas did not lose a minute in going to the lawyer's house; and after having the suit drawn up exactly like the one which had been quashed—he asked for punishment of the Junker according to the law, restoration of the horses to their previous condition, and compensation for his damages and also for those suffered by his man Herse, who had fallen at Mühlberg, the latter to be paid to the groom's old mother—he returned home, still followed by the gaping crowd, his mind made up never to quit the house again unless his affairs absolutely required it.

Meanwhile, the Junker had been released from his prison in Wittenberg and, after getting over a dangerous attack of erysipelas that had inflamed his foot, he had been peremptorily summoned to appear before the Dresden court to answer the charges made against him by the horse dealer Kohlhaas concerning a pair of black horses that had been unlawfully taken from him and ruined by overwork. The two brothers von Tronka, cousins of the Junker, at whose house he came to stay, received him with the greatest bitterness and contempt; they called him a worthless wretch who had brought shame and disgrace on the whole family, told him he was sure to lose his suit, and to get ready to produce the pair of blacks which he would be condemned to fatten to the accompaniment of the scornful laughter of the world. The Junker answered in a weak and quavering voice that he was the most pitiable man alive. He swore he had known very little about the whole damned business that had brought him so much misfortune, and that the castellan and the steward were to blame for everything, for they had used the horses to get the harvest in without his remotest knowledge or consent and worked them until they were skin and bones, part of the time too in their own fields. Sitting down as he said this, he begged them not to abuse and insult him and bring back the illness from which he had only recently recovered. The next day the lords Hinz and Kunz, who owned property in the vicinity of the ruins of Tronka Castle, wrote, at the urging of their cousin the Junker, since there was nothing else to do, to ask their steward and tenants for information about the two black horses that had disappeared on that unhappy day without being heard of since. But because the castle had been completely destroyed and most of its inhabitants massacred, all they could discover was that a stable boy, beaten with the flat of the incendiary's sword, had rescued them from the burning shed, and that afterwards, when the boy had asked him where to take the horses and what to do with them, the crazy fellow had answered him with a kick. The Junker's gouty old housekeeper, who had fled to Meissen, assured him, in reply to his written inquiry, that on the morning after that terrible night the stable boy had gone off with the horses toward the Brandenburg border; but all the inquiries made there proved vain, and anyhow there seemed to be an error at the bottom of this information, since none of the Junker's people came from Brandenburg or even from somewhere along the road to it. Some men from Dresden who had been in Wilsdruf a few days after the burning of Tronka Castle said that a groom had turned up there about that time leading two horses by the halter, and, since the animals were on their last legs and could not go any further, he had left them with a shepherd who had offered to feed them back to health in his barn. For a variety of reasons, it seemed quite probable that these were the pair of blacks in question; but the shepherd of Wilsdruf, according to the people had just come from there, had already disposed of them again, no one knew to whom; and a third rumor, whose author could not be discovered, had the two horses quite simply dead and buried in the Wilsdruf boneyard.

The lords Hinz and Kunz found this turn of affairs extremely welcome, as can readily be imagined, for it spared them the necessity (since their cousin the Junker no longer had any stables of his own) of fattening the horses in theirs, but they wanted to verify the story so as to be absolutely sure. Consequently Junker Wenzel von Tronka, as lord of the demesne, liege lord, and lord justice, addressed a letter to the magistrates at Wilsdruf minutely describing the horses, which he said had been placed in his care and accidentally lost, and requesting them to be so good as to ascertain their present whereabouts and to urge and admonish their owner, whoever he might be, to deliver them to the stables of the Chamberlain Sir Kunz in Dresden, where he would be generously reimbursed for all his costs. And a few days later the man to whom the shepherd at Wilsdruf had sold the horses did in fact appear with them, cadaverous creatures stumbling at the tail of his cart, and led them to the Dresden market place; but as the bad luck of Sir Wenzel and still more of honest Kohlhaas would have it, he turned out to be the knacker of Döbbeln.

As soon as the rumor reached Sir Wenzel, in the presence of his cousin the Chamberlain, that a man had arrived in the city with the two black horses that had escaped from the Tronka Castle fire, the two of them, after hurriedly rounding up some servants from the house, went down to the palace square where the fellow was, intending, if the animals proved to be Kohlhaas', to pay him the money he had spent on them and take the horses home with them. But the knights were surprised to see a crowd, whom the spectacle had attracted, already gathered around the two-wheeled cart to which the horses were tied and getting bigger by the minute; laughing uproariously, the people shouted to one another that the horses on whose account the foundations of the state were tottering were already in the knacker's hands! The Junker, after walking around the cart and staring at the miserable creatures who looked as if they were going to die any minute, mumbled in embarrassment: they were not the horses he had taken from Kohlhaas; but Sir Kunz the Chamberlain, throwing him a look of speechless rage, which if it had been made of iron would have smashed him to bits, and flinging back his cloak to show his orders and his chain of office, strode over to the knacker and said: were those the black horses that the shepherd of Wilsdruf had got hold of and that the Junker Wenzel von Tronka, to whom they belonged, had commandeered from the magistrate of that place? The knacker, who had a pail of water in his hand and was giving a drink to the fat and sturdy nag that drew his cart, said, "The blacks?" Then, putting down the pail and slipping the bit out of the horse's mouth, he said that the pair of blacks tied to the back of the cart had been sold to him by the swineherd of Hainichen. Where the latter had got them, and whether they came from the shepherd at Wilsdruf, he didn't know. He had been told, he said, taking up the pail again and propping it between the cart shaft and his knee—he had been told by the messenger from the Wilsdruf court to take the horses to the Tronka residence in Dresden; but the Junker he had been told to go to was named Kunz. And, turning away, he emptied the water his animal had left in the pail onto the pavement. The Chamberlain found it impossible to get the fellow, who went about his business with phlegmatic diligence, to look at him, and said, amid the stares of the jeering crowd, that he was the Chamberlain Kunz von Tronka; the pair of blacks he was looking for were the ones belonging to his cousin, the Junker; they had been given to the shepherd at Wilsdruf by a groom who ran away from Tronka Castle at the time it was sacked, and originally they had belonged to the horse dealer Kohlhaas. He asked the fellow, who stood there with his legs astraddle, hitching up his pants, whether he didn't know something about all this. Hadn't the swineherd from Hainichen perhaps bought the horses from the Wilsdruf shepherd—for everything depended on that—or from a third person who had got them from the shepherd?

The knacker, after standing up against the cart and passing water, said he had been told to go to Dresden with the horses where he could get the money for them at the Tronka house. He didn't understand what the Chamberlain was talking about; whether Peter or Paul or the shepherd of Wilsdruf had owned them before the swineherd in Hainichen was all one to him so long as they hadn't been stolen. And, cocking his whip across his broad back, he shambled off toward a public house that stood in the square, with the intention, since he was hungry, of getting himself some breakfast. The Chamberlain, who did not for the

life of him know what to do with the horses the swineherd of
Hainichen had sold to the knacker of Döbbeln, unless they were
the ones the devil himself was galloping around Saxony on, asked
the Junker to say something; but when the latter replied, with
white and quivering lips, that the best thing to do under the circumstances was to buy the blacks whether they were Kohlhaas'
or not, the Chamberlain flung his cloak back and, cursing the
father and mother who had made him, strode out of the crowd,
absolutely at a loss to know what he should do. He called over
Baron von Wenk, a friend of his who happened to be riding along
the street, and asked him to stop by at the house of the Lord
Chancellor Count Wrede and have the latter arrange for Kohlhaas
to come out to examine the pair of blacks; for he was stubbornly
determined not to quit the square just because the mob were
looking at him mockingly, their handkerchiefs crammed into
their mouths, and only waiting for him to leave, it seemed, to
burst out laughing. Now it so happened that Kohlhaas was at the
Lord Chancellor's, where he had been summoned by a court
messenger to explain some matters in connection with the deposit
he had made in Lützen, when the Baron entered the room on
his errand; and when the Chancellor got up from his chair with
a look of annoyance, leaving the horse dealer standing with his
papers to one side, the Baron, who did not know Kohlhaas, explained the difficulty in which the lords von Tronka found themselves. The knacker from Döbbeln, he said, acting on a defective
requisition of the Wilsdruf court, had turned up with a pair of
horses in such hopeless condition that it was no wonder the Junker
Wenzel hesitated to recognize them as Kohlhaas'; but if they
were going to be accepted from the knacker notwithstanding and
an attempt made to put them in shape again in the knights'
stables, an ocular inspection by Kohlhaas was needed so as to
remove all doubt. "Will you therefore be good enough," he concluded, "to have a guard fetch the horse dealer from his house

and conduct him to the market place where the horses are?" The Lord Chancellor took his glasses from his nose and said to the Baron that he was laboring under a double misapprehension: first, in thinking that the question of the horses' ownership could only be decided by an ocular inspection by Kohlhaas; and then in imagining that he, the Chancellor, possessed the authority to have Kohlhaas taken by a guard to wherever the Junker happened to wish. Whereupon he introduced him to the horse dealer standing behind him and asked him, as he sat down and put his glasses back on, to apply to the man himself in the matter.

Kohlhaas, whose expression gave no hint of what was passing in his mind, said that he was ready to follow the Baron to the market place to inspect the knacker's horses. As the latter faced around to him in surprise, Kohlhaas went up to the Chancellor's table again, gave him, with the help of the papers in his wallet, the information he needed about the deposit in Lützen, and said goodbye; the Baron, who with a crimson face had walked over to the window, likewise took his leave; and the two men, escorted by the Prince of Meissen's three lansquenets, made their way, with a crowd of people at their heels, to the palace square. The Chamberlain Sir Kunz, who meanwhile, over the protests of several friends who had joined him, had been standing his ground among the people opposite the knacker of Döbbeln, accosted the horse dealer as soon as he appeared with the Baron and asked him, as he tucked his sword with haughty ostentation under his arm, whether the horses standing at the cart tail were his. The horse dealer, after turning diffidently toward the unknown gentleman who had asked the question and touching his hat, moved over without answering to the knacker's cart, followed by all the knights; and, stopping twelve paces off from where the animals stood on unsteady legs with their heads bowed to the ground, refusing the hay the knacker had pitched out for them, he gave them one look, turned back to the Chamberlain, and said, "My lord, the knacker is quite right: the horses tied to his cart are mine." And then, looking around the circle of knights, he touched his hat again and left the square with his guard.

As soon as he heard this, the Chamberlain went across to the knacker at a jump that set his helmet plume nodding and tossed him a bag of money; and while the latter scraped the hair back from his forehead with a lead comb and stared at the money in his hand, Sir Kunz ordered a servant to untie the horses and lead them home. The man left a group of his family and friends in the crowd at his master's summons and did, in fact, with a red face, step over a large pile of dung at the horses' feet and go up to their heads; but he had hardly taken hold of the halter to untie them when Master Himboldt, his cousin, grabbed him by the arm, and crying: "Don't you touch those knacker's nags!" pulled him away from the cart. Then stepping precariously back over the dung pile, the Master turned to the Chamberlain, who stood there speechless with surprise, and said: he must get a knacker's man to do him a service like that! The Chamberlain, livid with rage, looked at the Master for a second and then turned and shouted over the heads of the knights for the guard; and when, at Baron von Wenk's command, an officer emerged from the castle at the head of some of the Elector's gentlemen-at-arms, he gave him a brief account of the shameful way in which the burghers of the city were inciting to rebellion and called on him to arrest the ringleader, Master Himboldt. Catching the Master by his shirt, he accused him of mistreating the servant he had ordered to untie the black horses and pushing him away from the cart. The Master twisted skillfully out of the Chancellor's grasp and said, "My lord, showing a boy of twenty what he ought to do is not inciting to revolt! Ask him if he wants to go against everything that's customary and decent and meddle with those horses tied to the cart. If after what I've said his answer is yes, it's all right with me, he can start skinning them right now for all I care!"

The Chamberlain turned to the groom and asked him if he had any objection to carrying out his order to untie Kohlhaas' horses and lead them home; when the fellow, retreating into the crowd, timidly replied: the horses must be made decent and respectable again before that could be expected of him, the Chamberlain came right after him, knocked off his hat in which he wore the badge of the Tronka house, trampled it under his feet, and, drawing his sword, drove him from the square and out of his service. Master Himboldt cried, "Down with the murderous tyrant!" And while his fellow citizens, outraged by this scene, pressed shoulder to shoulder and forced back the guard, he knocked the Chamberlain down from behind, ripped his cloak, collar, and helmet off, wrenched the sword from his hand, and with a violent motion sent it clattering across the square. The Junker Wenzel, escaping from the tumult, called to the knights to go to his cousin's aid, but to no avail: before they were able to take a step toward him, they were scattered by the rush of the mob, and the Chamberlain, who had hurt his head in falling, was exposed to their full fury. The only thing that saved him was the appearance of a troop of mounted lansquenets who happened to be crossing the square and whom the officer commanding the Elector's men called over to help him. The officer, after dispersing the crowd, seized the enraged Master and had some troopers lead him off to prison, while two of the Chamberlain's friends lifted the latter's blood-spattered form from the ground and carried him home. Such was the unhappy conclusion of the well-meant and honest attempt to procure the horse dealer satisfaction for the injustice done him. The Döbbeln knacker, as his business was done and he wished to be off, tied the horses to a lamp post when the crowd began to disperse and there they stayed the whole day through, without anybody's bothering about them, objects of ridicule for the ragamuffins and the idlers; but finally the police took charge of them for lack of anybody else, and toward evening they got the knacker of Dresden to carry them off to his yard outside the city until their disposition was decided.

The riot in the palace square, as little as Kohlhaas was to blame for it, nevertheless aroused a feeling throughout the land, even among the more moderate and better class of people, that was highly dangerous to the success of his suit. It was felt the state had got itself into an intolerable position vis-à-vis the horse dealer, and in private houses and public places alike the opinion grew that it would be better to do the man an open wrong and quash the whole proceedings again, than to see that justice, extorted by violence, was done him in so trivial a matter, just to satisfy his crazy obstinacy. To complete poor Kohlhaas' ruin, it was the Lord Chancellor himself, with his rigid honesty and his hatred of the Tronka family which sprang from it, who helped strengthen and spread this sentiment. It was most unlikely that the horses now in the hands of the Dresden knacker would ever be restored to the shape they were in when they left the stables at Kohlhaasenbrück, but even if this were possible through skillful, unremitting care, the disgrace that had fallen on the Junker's family as a result of everything that had happened was so great that nothing seemed fairer and more reasonable to people—seeing the important place the von Tronkas occupied in the government as one of the oldest and noblest houses in the country—than that they should pay Kohlhaas a money amends for the horses. Yet a few days later, when the President, Count Kallheim, acting for the Chamberlain who was laid up with his injuries, sent a letter to the Chancellor making just such a proposal, and even though the Chancellor wrote to Kohlhaas warning him against declining such an offer if one were made to him, he himself wrote the President a curt, barely civil reply asking to be excused from any private commissions in the matter, and advising the Chamberlain to address himself directly to the horse dealer, whom he described as a very reasonable and modest man. The horse dealer, whose iron determination had in fact been weakened by the incident in the market place, was ready, following the advice of the Chancellor, to meet any overture from the Junker or his kinsmen half way, with perfect willingness and forgiveness for everything that had happened; but just such an overture was more than the proud knights could stomach; and highly indignant at the answer they had received from the Lord Chancellor, they showed it to the Elector the next morning when he came to visit the Chamberlain in the room where he was laid up with his wounds. The Chamberlain, in a voice that illness made weak and pathetic, asked the Elector whether, after risking his life to settle the business according to his sovereign's wishes, he must also expose his honor to the censure of the world by going hat in hand to beg indulgence from a man who had already heaped every imaginable shame and disgrace on him and his family. The Elector, after reading the letter, asked Count Kallheim in embarrassment if the court did not have the right, without consulting further with Kohlhaas, to take its stand on the fact that the horses were past recovery and bring in a verdict for a money amends, just as if the horses were already dead.

"Your Highness," the Count replied, "the horses *are* dead, legally dead because they have no value any more, and they will be physically dead before any one can get them from the knacker's yard to the knights' stables"; upon which the Elector tucked the letter in his pocket, said that he would speak to the Lord Chancellor about it himself, spoke reassuringly to the Chamberlain who had raised himself on his elbow and seized his hand in gratitude, and, after recommending him to watch his health, he rose with a benign air from his chair and left the room.

So matters stood in Dresden when poor Kohlhaas found himself the center of another, even more serious storm that came up from the direction of Lützen, and whose lightning the crafty knights were clever enough to draw down on his unlucky head. A man called Johann Nagelschmidt, one of the band whom the horse dealer had

collected and then turned off again after the Electoral amnesty, had
some weeks later rounded up a part of this rabble, which shrank
from nothing, on the Bohemian border, with the intention of carrying on for himself the trade Kohlhaas had taught him. This ruffian
announced, partly to scare the sheriff's officers on his heels, and
partly to get the peasantry to take a hand in his rascalities as they
had done with Kohlhaas, that he was Kohlhaas' lieutenant; had it
spread about, with a cleverness learned from his master, that the
amnesty had been broken in the case of several men who had gone
quietly back to their homes; that Kohlhaas himself, indeed, with a
perfidiousness that cried aloud to heaven, had been arrested on his
arrival in Dresden and placed under guard; the result of this being
that the incendiary crew were able to masquerade, in manifestoes
very much like Kohlhaas' that Nagelschmidt had posted up, as
honest soldiers assembled together for the sole purpose of serving
God and watching over the Elector's amnesty—all this, as has just
been said, done not at all for the glory of God nor out of attachment
to Kohlhaas, whose fate the outlaws did not care a straw about, but
to enable them to burn and plunder with the greater impunity and
ease. When the first word of this reached Dresden, the knights could
not conceal the joy they felt over a development that seemed to put
such a different face on things. With sage displeasure they recalled
what a mistake it had been, in spite of their earnest and repeated
warnings, to grant Kohlhaas an amnesty, going on as if there had
been a deliberate intention to give every scoundrel in the country
the signal to follow in the horse dealer's footsteps; and not content
with accepting Nagelschmidt's claim that he had taken up arms
only to defend his oppressed master, they expressed the certain
opinion that his appearance on the scene was nothing but a plot on
Kohlhaas' part to scare the government and hasten and assure a
verdict that would satisfy his mad obstinacy down to the last detail.
Indeed the Cupbearer, Sir Hinz, went so far as to say to some courtiers and hunting companions who had gathered around him after

dinner in the Elector's antechamber that the disbanding of the brigands in Lützen had been nothing but a damned trick; and, while making fun of the Lord Chancellor's love of justice, he cleverly concatenated various facts to prove that the band was still intact in the forests of the Electorate and only waited for a signal from the horse dealer to burst forth afresh with fire and sword.

Prince Christiern of Meissen, who was highly displeased with this new turn of affairs, which threatened so much damage to his sovereign's reputation, went at once to the palace to see the Elector; and, clearly perceiving how the knights would wish to encompass Kohlhaas' ruin by convicting him of new offenses, he asked permission to question the horse dealer without delay. The horse dealer, not a little surprised at the summons, appeared at the Government House under a constable's escort with his two little boys, Heinrich and Leopold, in his arms—for his five children had arrived the day before with Sternbald from Mecklenburg where they had been staying, and for reasons too numerous to detail here Kohlhaas, when the two burst into childish tears on his getting up to leave and begged to be taken along, had picked them up and carried them to the hearing. The Prince, after looking benevolently at the children whom their father had seated beside him and asking them their names and ages with friendly interest, told Kohlhaas about the liberties that his old follower Nagelschmidt was taking in the valleys of the Erzgebirge; and, handing him the latter's so-called manifestoes, he asked him what he had to say in his own defense. The horse dealer, though indeed he showed extreme dismay when confronted with these treasonable documents, had little difficulty in satisfying a man as upright as the Prince that the accusations leveled against him were baseless. He not only did not see how he needed the help of a third person, as matters stood now, to obtain a judgment in his suit, which was progressing entirely satisfactorily, but he had papers with him which he showed to the Prince that made it appear most unlikely that Nagelschmidt should ever wish to give him such help: for shortly before the disbanding of his band at Lützen he had been on the point of hanging the fellow, for a rape committed in open country and other outrages, when the publication of the Electoral amnesty severed their connection and saved Nagelschmidt's life; the next day they had parted deadly enemies.

With the Prince's approval, Kohlhaas sat down and wrote a letter to Nagelschmidt, in which he called the latter's claim to having taken up arms to enforce the amnesty a shameless and wicked fabrication; on his arrival in Dresden, he told him, he had neither been jailed nor put under guard, also his lawsuit was progressing just as he wished; and he gave him over, because of the acts of arson Nagelschmidt had committed in the Erzgebirge after publication of the amnesty, to the full vengeance of the law, as a warning to the rabble around him. Extracts from Kohlhaas' trial of Nagelschmidt in the castle at Lützen on account of the above-mentioned crimes were appended to the letter, to inform the people about this scoundrel who already at that time was destined for the gallows and owed his life, as we have mentioned, only to the Elector's edict. Upon which the Prince soothed Kohlhaas' resentment over the suspicions that had unavoidably to be expressed at the hearing; promised him that as long as he remained in Dresden the amnesty would not be violated in any way; shook the boys' hands again as he made them a present of some fruit on the table; and said goodbye to Kohlhaas. Nevertheless, the Lord Chancellor recognized the danger hanging over the horse dealer's head and did everything in his power to press the lawsuit to a conclusion before new circumstances arose to complicate and confuse it; but to complicate and confuse the case was exactly what the crafty knights desired and intended. They no longer silently acknowledged the Junker's guilt and limited their efforts to obtaining a milder sentence for their cousin, but instead began to raise all sorts of cunning arguments and quibbling objections, so as to deny his guilt entirely. Sometimes they would pretend that Kohlhaas' horses had been detained at Tronka Castle by the castellan's and the steward's arbitrary action, and that the Junker had known little if anything about it; at other times they claimed the animals had been sick with a violent and dangerous cough when they arrived at the castle, and promised to produce witnesses to confirm the truth of what they said; and when, after lengthy investigations and explanations, they were forced to abandon these arguments, they fell back on an Electoral edict of twelve years' standing that in fact forbade importing horse stock from Brandenburg to Saxony on account of a cattle disease: clear proof that the Junker had not only the right but even the duty to seize the horses Kohlhaas had brought across the border.

Meanwhile Kohlhaas, who had repurchased his farm at Kohlhaassenbrück from the honest bailiff, paying him a small additional sum to reimburse him for the loss he suffered thereby, wished to leave Dresden for a few days and pay a visit to his home, apparently in order to settle the matter legally—in which decision, however, the above-mentioned consideration, pressing as it may actually have been on account of the need to sow the winter crop, undoubtedly played less part than a wish to test his position in the strange and dubious circumstances prevailing; and he may also have been influenced by still other reasons that we shall leave to those who know their own hearts to divine. Accordingly, leaving his guard at home, he went to the Lord Chancellor and, with the bailiff's letters in his hand, explained that if he was not needed in court now, as seemed to be the case, he would like to leave the city and travel to Brandenburg for some eight to twelve days, within which period he promised to return. The Lord Chancellor, looking down with an annoyed and doubtful face, expressed the opinion that Kohlhaas' presence was more necessary than ever just then, as the court required statements and explanations from him on a thousand and one points that might come up, to counter the cunning shifts and dodges of his opponent; but when Kohlhaas referred him to his lawyer, who was thoroughly posted on the case, and pressed his request with modest persistence, promising to limit his absence to a week, the Lord Chancellor, after a pause, only said, as he dismissed him, that he hoped he would apply to Prince Christiern of Meissen for a pass.

Kohlhaas, who could read the Lord Chancellor's face very well, was only strengthened in his determination and, sitting down on the spot and giving no reason, he asked the Prince of Meissen, as Chief of the Government, for a week's pass to Kohlhaasenbrück and back. In reply, he received an order from the Governor of the Palace, Baron Siegfried von Wenk, to the effect that his request to visit Kohlhaasenbrück would be laid before his Serene Highness the Elector, and as soon as the latter's consent was forthcoming the pass would be sent to him. When Kohlhaas asked his lawyer how the order came to be signed by a Baron Siegfried von Wenk and not by Prince Christiern of Meissen, to whom he had addressed his request, he was told that the Prince had left for his estates three days ago and that during his absence the affairs of his office had been turned over to the Governor of the Palace, Baron Siegfried von Wenk, a cousin of the gentleman of the same name whom we have already encountered.

Kohlhaas, whose heart began to pound uneasily amid all these complications, waited several more days for an answer to his request, which had been submitted to the sovereign with such surprising formality; but when a week and more had passed without his either receiving a reply or the court's handing down a judgment in his case even though it had been promised him without fail, he sat down on the twelfth day, his mind made up to force the Government to reveal its intentions toward him, whatever they might be, and earnestly petitioned the Government once again for a pass. But on the evening of the following day, which had likewise passed without his getting the answer he was expecting, going over to the window of his little back room with his mind very much on his present situation and especially the amnesty Dr. Luther had got for him, he was thunderstruck to see no sign, in the little outbuilding in the yard which was their quarters, of the guard assigned him on his arrival by the Prince of Meissen. Thomas, his old servant, whom he called to him and asked the meaning of this, said with a sigh: "Sir, there's something wrong; there were more lansquenets here today than usual and at nightfall they posted themselves around the whole house: two of them, with their shields and pikes, are standing out in the street in front of the house door; two more are at the back door in the garden; and still another pair are stretched out on some straw in the entrance hall where they say they are going to spend the night."

Kohlhaas' face paled; turning away, he said it didn't really matter, seeing that they were there already; when Thomas went down to the hall, he should put a light there so they could see. And, after he had opened the front shutters on the pretext of emptying a pot and convinced himself of the truth of Thomas' words, for just at that moment he saw the guard silently being changed—something no one had ever thought of doing since the arrangement existed—he went to bed, even though he did not feel much like sleeping, with his mind instantly made up about what he would do the next day. For what he disliked most about the regime he had to deal with was the show of justice it put on, at the same time that it went ahead and broke the amnesty which he had been promised; if he was in fact a prisoner, as he could no longer doubt, he was going to make them say so straight out. Accordingly, the next morning he had Sternbald hitch up his wagon and bring it around to the door; he meant, he said, to drive to Lockewitz to see the steward there, an old friend of his who had spoken to him a few days before in Dresden and invited him to pay him a visit with his children. The lansquenets, having watched with huddled heads the stir these preparations made in the household, secretly sent one of their number into town, and a few minutes later an official of the Government marched up at the head of some constables and went into the house across the way as if he had business there. Kohlhaas was busy getting his children's clothes on, but he did not miss these goings-on and purposely kept the wagon wait-

ing in front of the house longer than was really necessary; as soon
as he saw the police had taken up their posts, he came out in front
of the house with his children, told the lansquenets in the doorway
as he went by that they needn't bother to come along, lifted the boys
into the wagon, and kissed and comforted his tearful little girls whom
he had ordered to stay behind with the old servant's daughter. No
sooner had he himself climbed into the wagon than the official with
his following of constables came out of the house across the way
and asked him where he was going. On Kohlhaas' answering that he
was going to Lockewitz to see his friend the steward, who a few days
ago had invited him and his two boys to visit him in the country, the
official said that in that case he must ask Kohlhaas to wait a minute
or so, as he would be accompanied by some mounted lansquenets in
obedience to the Prince of Meissen's orders. Kohlhaas looked down
with a smile from the wagon and asked him if he thought his life
would not be safe in the house of a friend who had invited him to
share his board for the day. The official replied good-humoredly that
the danger was certainly not very great, adding that the soldiers were
not to incommode him in any way. Kohlhaas, now looking grave,
answered that on his coming to Dresden the Prince of Meissen had
left it up to him as to whether he should have the guard or not; when
the official expressed surprise at this, and in carefully chosen words
reminded him that he had been accompanied by the guard all the
time he had been there, the horse dealer described the circumstances
under which the soldiers had been put into his house. The official
assured him that by order of the Governor of the Palace, Baron von
Wenk, who was at the moment chief of police, he must keep an uninterrupted watch over his person; if he would not consent to the
escort, would he be good enough to go to the Government House
himself to clear up the misunderstanding that must certainly exist.
Kohlhaas, giving the man an expressive look, and his mind now
made up to settle the matter once and for all, said that he would do
just that; got down from his wagon with beating heart; gave the

children to the servant to take back into the house; and, leaving the groom waiting in front of the house with the carriage, went off to the Government House with the official and his guard.

When the horse dealer entered with his escort, he found the Governor of the Palace, Baron von Wenk, in the middle of looking over a group of Nagelschmidt's men who had been captured near Leipzig and brought to Dresden the evening before, while the knights with him questioned the fellows about a great many things that information was wanted on. The Baron, as soon as he caught sight of the horse dealer, went up to him in the silence that followed the sudden cessation of the interrogation and asked him what he wanted; and when the horse dealer respectfully explained his intention of going to dine at midday with the steward at Lockewitz, and said he wished to leave the lansquenets behind since he did not need them, the Baron changed color and, seeming to swallow something that he was about to say, told Kohlhaas that he would do well to stay quietly at home and postpone the spread at the Lockewitz steward's for the present. Then, turning to the official and cutting short the colloquy, he told him that the orders he had given him about Kohlhaas still held good and that the latter was not to leave the city unless accompanied by six mounted lansquenets. Kohlhaas asked him if he was a prisoner, and if he was to understand that the amnesty solemnly granted him before the eyes of the whole world was now broken, upon which the Baron wheeled around suddenly, thrust his face, which had flushed a fiery red, up to Kohlhaas', said, "Yes! Yes! Yes!"—turned his back on him again, left him standing where he was, and went back to the Nagelschmidt men. Whereupon Kohlhaas left the room. Although he realized that what he had done had made the only possibility now remaining to him—flight—much more difficult, nevertheless he did not regret it because he now felt released from any further obligation to observe the terms of the amnesty. Arriving home, he had the horses unharnessed and, feeling depressed and upset, went to his room, still accompanied by the official; and while the latter assured the horse dealer, in a way that sickened him, that all the trouble must be due to some misunderstanding which would shortly be cleared up, he signed to the constables to bolt all the doors leading to the courtyard; but the main entrance, he hastened to say, was still open for him to use as he pleased.

Meanwhile Nagelschmidt had been so hard pressed from every side by sheriff's men and lansquenets in the forests of the Erzgebirge that the idea occurred to him, seeing how he lacked all means to carry through the kind of role he had undertaken, of actually getting Kohlhaas to help him; and since a traveler passing that way had given him a fairly accurate notion of how matters stood with Kohlhaas' lawsuit in Dresden, he thought he could persuade the horse dealer, in spite of the open enmity between them, to seal a new alliance with him. He therefore sent one of his fellows to him with a letter, written in almost unreadable German, that said: if he would come to the Altenburg and resume command of the band they had got together there from the remnants of his dispersed troops, he, Nagelschmidt, was ready to help him escape from Dresden by furnishing him with horses, men, and money; at the same time he promised Kohlhaas to be more obedient, indeed better behaved in every respect, in the future than he had been in the past; and to prove his faithfulness and attachment, he pledged himself to come in person to the outskirts of Dresden in order to rescue Kohlhaas from jail. Now the fellow whose job it was to deliver this letter had the bad luck, in a village right near Dresden, to fall down in a violent fit of a kind he was susceptible to from childhood; the letter that he was carrying in his tunic was discovered by the people who came to his aid, while he himself, as soon as he had recovered consciousness, was arrested and, followed by a large crowd, carried to the Government House under guard. As soon as Baron von Wenk had read the letter, he went to see the Elector at the Palace, and there he also found Sir Kunz (who was now recovered from his injuries), Sir Hinz, and the President of the Chancery of State, Count Kallheim. It was these gentlemen's opinion that Kohlhaas should be arrested without delay and tried for secretly conspiring with Nagelschmidt; for they pointed out that such a letter could not have been written unless there had been earlier letters from the horse dealer's side and unless a criminal compact had been concluded by the two for the purpose of hatching fresh iniquities. But the Elector steadfastly refused to violate, on the sole grounds of this letter, the safe-conduct he had solemnly promised Kohlhaas; he himself was inclined to think that Nagelschmidt's letter indicated there had been no previous connection between the two; and all he would consent to do to get to the bottom of the matter, though only after long hesitation, was, following the President's proposal, to let the letter be delivered to Kohlhaas by Nagelschmidt's man, just as if he had never been arrested, and see whether Kohlhaas would answer it. The next morning, accordingly, the fellow, who had been put in jail, was brought to the Government House where the Governor of the Palace gave him back the letter and ordered him to deliver it to the horse dealer as if nothing had happened, in return for which he promised him his freedom and to let him off the punishment he had earned. The fellow lent himself to this base deception forthwith, and in apparently mysterious fashion, on the pretext of selling crabs (which the official supplied him with from the market) he gained admission to Kohlhaas' room. Kohlhaas, who read the letter while the children played with the crabs, in other circumstances would certainly have seized the rascal by the collar and handed him over to the lansquenets at his door; but in the present temper of men's minds even such a step was liable to misconstruction, and anyhow he was fully convinced that nothing in the world could ever rescue him from the business in which he was entangled: so, looking mournfully into the fellow's face which he knew so well, he asked him where he was staying and told him to come back in an hour or so when he would let him know his decision. At his bidding Sternbald, who happened to come in the door of his room, bought some crabs from the man; when this was done, and both men had left without recognizing one another, Kohlhaas sat down and wrote Nagelschmidt as follows: First, that he accepted his offer to take command of the band in Altenburg; that Nagelschmidt should therefore send a wagon with two horses to Neustadt-near-Dresden so that he could make his escape with his five children; that, to get away faster, he would also need another team of two horses on the road to Wittenberg which, though a roundabout way, was the only one he could take to come to him, for reasons it would take too long to explain; that he thought he could bribe the lansquenets who were guarding him, but in case force was necessary he would like to be able to count on finding a pair of stout-hearted, capable, and well-armed fellows in Neustadt; that he was sending him twenty gold crowns by his messenger to pay the cost of all these preparations, and he would settle with him afterwards about the sums actually paid out; and that as for the rest, he requested Nagelschmidt not to come to Dresden to take a personal part in the rescue as it was unnecessary, indeed he explicitly ordered him to stay behind in Altenburg in temperary command of the band, which could not be left without a chief.

When the messenger returned in the evening Kohlhaas gave him the letter, accompanied by a generous tip, and warned him to guard it carefully.

Kohlhaas' intention was to go to Hamburg with his five children and there embark for the Levant or the East Indies or wherever the blue sky looked down on people entirely different from the ones he knew: for quite apart from his reluctance to make common cause with Nagelschmidt, in the despair and anguish of his soul he had given up hope of ever seeing his pair of blacks fattened by the Junker.

No sooner had the fellow delivered the horse dealer's answer to the Governor of the Palace than the Lord Chancellor was deposed, the President, Count Kallheim, was appointed head of the court in his place, and, by an order in council of the Elector, Kohlhaas was arrested, put in chains, and thrown into the Dresden dungeon. On the evidence of the letter, a copy of which was posted at every street corner, he was brought to trial; and when he answered "Yes!" to a councilor who held the letter up in front of him at the bar and asked him if he acknowledged the handwriting as his own, but looked down at the ground and said "No!" when he was asked if he had anything to say in his own defense, Kohlhaas was condemned to be tortured with red-hot pincers by knackers' men, to be drawn and quartered, and his body burned between the wheel and the gallows.

Thus matters stood with poor Kohlhaas in Dresden when the Elector of Brandenburg intervened to pluck him from the fist of arbitrary power; in a note presented to the Chancery of State in Dresden, he claimed him as a subject of Brandenburg. For the honest City Governor, Sir Heinrich von Geusau, during a walk on the banks of the Spree, had told the Elector the story of this strange person who was really not a bad man, and when closely questioned by the astonished sovereign about it he could not avoid indicating the heavy responsibility which his own royal person bore for the improper way in which his Archchancellor, Count Siegfried, had conducted himself. The Elector, extremely angry, called the Archchancellor to account, and, finding that his kinship with the house of Tronka was to blame for it all, he immediately relieved him of his post, with more than one token of his displeasure, and appointed Sir Heinrich von Geusau to his place.

Now just at this time the Polish crown was involved in a dispute with the House of Saxony, over what we do not know, and pressed the Elector of Brandenburg repeatedly to make common cause with them against the Saxons; and in this situation the Archchancellor, Sir Geusau, who did not lack for skill in such matters, saw an opportunity to satisfy his sovereign's desire to see justice done Kohlhaas without imperiling the peace of the whole realm more than consideration for one individual warranted. Accordingly, the Arch-

chancellor not only insisted on Saxony's immediately and uncon-
ditionally surrendering Kohlhaas on account of the arbitrary proceedings used against him, which were an offense against God and
man, so that the horse dealer, if he were guilty of a crime, could
be tried according to the laws of Brandenburg on charges preferred
by the Dresden court through an attorney in Berlin; but Sir Heinrich
even demanded a passport for an attorney whom the Elector of
Brandenburg wished to send to Dresden to see that justice was done
Kohlhaas in the matter of the black horses that the Junker Wenzel
von Tronka took from him on Saxon territory, as well as other
flagrant instances of ill-usage and acts of violence. The Chamberlain,
Sir Kunz, who had been appointed President of the State Chancery
in the change of posts in Saxony, and who in his present hard-pressed
circumstances had a number of reasons for not wishing to offend the
Berlin court, replying in the name of his sovereign, whom the note
from Brandenburg had very much cast down, said: he wondered at
the unfriendliness and the unfairness which Brandenburg showed
in challenging the right of the Dresden court to judge Kohlhaas according to its laws for crimes he had committed on Saxon ground,
since the whole world knew that the horse dealer owned a large piece
of property in the capital and did not himself dispute the fact that he
was a citizen of Saxony. But since the Polish crown was already
assembling an army of five thousand men on the Saxon frontier to
press their claims by arms, and since the Archchancellor, Sir Heinrich von Geusau, announced that Kohlhaasenbrück, the place after
which the horse dealer was named, lay in Brandenburg and they
would consider the execution of the death sentence on him as a
violation of the law of nations, the Elector of Saxony, following the
advice of the Chamberlain Sir Kunz himself (who wanted to withdraw from the whole business), summoned Prince Christiern of
Meissen from his estates and decided, after a few words with this
prudent man, to heed the Berlin court's demand and give Kohlhaas
up. The Prince, little pleased with all the improprieties committed

in the Kohlhaas affair but required by his hardpressed sovereign to take over its direction, asked the Elector on what grounds he now wished to act against the horse dealer in the High Court at Berlin; and since they could not base their case on Kohlhaas' unfortunate letter to Nagelschmidt because of the questionable and obscure circumstances under which it had been written, nor on all of Kohlhaas' earlier acts of depredation and arson for which he had been pardoned by edict, the Elector decided to furnish His Majesty the Emperor in Vienna with an account of Kohlhaas' armed invasion of Saxony, accuse him of breaking the Emperor's peace, and appeal to His Majesty, who was of course not bound by any amnesty, to have Kohlhaas arraigned by the Imperial prosecutor for these crimes before the High Court at Berlin. A week later the horse dealer, still in chains, was packed into a wagon by the Knight Friedrich von Malzahn, whom the Elector of Brandenburg had sent to Dresden with six horsemen, and, reunited with his five children who had been collected at his plea from various foundling homes and orphan asylums, he was carried toward Berlin.

Now just at this time the Elector of Saxony, at the invitation of the High Bailiff, Count Aloysius von Kallheim, who in those days owned broad estates along the Saxon border, had gone to a great stag hunt at Dahme that had been got up for his entertainment, and in his company were the Chamberlain Sir Kunz and his wife Lady Heloise, daughter to the High Bailiff and sister to the President, not to mention other brilliant lords and ladies, hunting pages, and courtiers. Under the shelter of tents streaming pennants that were pitched right across the road on a hill, the entire company, still covered with the dust of the hunt, were seated at table and being served by pages, while lively music sounded from the trunk of an oak tree, when Kohlhaas and his escort of horsemen came riding slowly up the road from Dresden. For the illness of one of his little children, who were quite frail, had made it necessary for the Knight of Malzahn to hold up for three days in Herzberg; a measure which, as he was answerable only to the Prince he served, the Knight had seen no need to inform the Dresden government about. The Elector, with his shirt open at the throat and his feathered hat stuck with sprigs of fir in hunter's fashion, was seated beside the Lady Heloise, who had been the first love of his youth, and the gaiety of the fête having put him in a high good humor, he said, "Let's go and offer this goblet of wine to the unfortunate fellow, whoever he may be." Lady Heloise, giving him a splendid look, immediately got up and levied tribute on the whole table to fill a silver dish handed her by a page with fruit, cakes, and bread; and the entire company had already streamed out of the tent with refreshments of every kind in their hands when the High Bailiff came toward them in evident embarrassment and begged them to stay where they were. When the Elector asked him in surprise what had happened to throw him into such confusion, the Bailiff, looking at the Chamberlain, stammered out that it was Kohlhaas who was in the wagon; at this piece of news, which none could understand, for it was public knowledge that the horse dealer had departed six days ago, the Chamberlain, Sir Kunz, turning back toward the tent, emptied his goblet of wine into the sand. The Elector, flushing violently, set his goblet down on a plate that a page held out to him at a sign from the Chamberlain; and while the Knight Friedrich von Malzahn, respectfully saluting the company whom he did not know, passed slowly through the tent ropes running across the road and continued on his way toward Dahme, the ladies and gentlemen, at the Bailiff's invitation, returned inside the tent. The Bailiff, as soon as the Elector was seated again, secretly sent a messenger to Dahme to tell its magistrate to see to it that the horse dealer was speeded on his way; but as the day was too far gone and the Knight of Malzahn insisted on spending the night there, there was nothing for it but to put Kohlhaas up, very quietly, at one of the magistrate's farmhouses, which lay hidden in the thickets off the main road. Toward evening, when all recollection of the incident had been driven from the lords' and ladies' minds by the

wine and sumptuous desserts, the High Bailiff announced that a herd
of stags had been sighted and proposed that they should take their
stations again, a proposal that the whole company eagerly took up.
Getting guns for themselves, they hurried, in pairs, over ditches and
hedges, into the nearby forest—which was how it happened that the
Elector and the Lady Heloise, who had taken his arm to go and
watch the sport, found to their astonishment that their guide had led
them right into the yard of the house in which Kohlhaas and the
Brandenburg horsemen were lodged. Lady Heloise, when she heard
this, said, "Come, your Highness," playfully tucking the chain that
hung around the Elector's neck inside his silk tunic, "let's slip inside
the farmhouse before the crowd catches up and see what the strange
man spending the night there is like!" The Elector, reddening, caught
hold of her hand and said, "Heloise, what are you saying?" But
when she looked at him in surprise and said there was no fear of his
being recognized in the hunting clothes he was wearing, and pulled
him along, and when at that very moment a pair of hunting pages
who had already satisfied their curiosity came out of the house and
reported that neither the Knight nor the horse dealer, thanks to the
High Bailiff's efforts, knew who the company gathered in the neighborhood of Dahme were, the Elector pulled his hat down over his
eyes with a smile and said, "Folly rules the world, and her throne is a
pretty woman's lips!"

The nobleman and lady entered to find Kohlhaas sitting on a heap
of straw with his back against the wall, in the midst of feeding bread
and milk to the child who had fallen ill at Herzberg. Lady Heloise,
to start a conversation, asked him who he was and what was the
matter with the child, and what he had done, and where were they
taking him with such an escort, to all of which Kohlhaas, doffing his
leather cap, gave short but sufficient answers as he went on feeding
his child. The Elector, who was standing behind the hunters, noticed
a little lead capsule hanging from a silk string around the horse
dealer's neck, and for lack of anything better to say he asked him

what it meant to him and what was in it. "This capsule, your Worship!" Kohlhaas replied, and he slipped it from around his neck, opened it, and drew out a little piece of paper sealed with gum— "There is a very strange story connected with this capsule. Seven months ago, I think it was, the very next day after my wife's funeral— I had left Kohlhaasenbrück, as you perhaps know, to capture the Junker von Tronka, who had done me a very grave injustice—the Elector of Saxony and the Elector of Brandenburg met to discuss some business, though exactly what it was I do not know, in the market town of Jüterbock, through which my expedition led me; and having satisfactorily settled matters between them by evening, they walked along in friendly conversation through the streets of the town to see the merrymaking at the fair, which happened to be taking place just then. In the market square they came upon a gypsy woman sitting on a stool, telling the fortunes of the people standing around her, and they asked her jokingly if she didn't also have something to tell them that they would like to hear. I had just dismounted with my men at an inn and was present in the square when all this happened, but as I was standing at the rear of the crowd, in the entrance to a church, I could not make out what the strange woman said to the two lords; and when the people, whispering laughingly to their neighbors that she did not share her knowledge with everybody, crowded in close to witness the scene about to take place, I got up on a bench behind me that was hewn out of the church entrance, really not so much because I was curious myself as to make room for the curious. No sooner did I catch an interrupted view, from this vantage point, of the two lords and the old woman, who was sitting on the stool in front of them and seemed to be scribbling something, than she stood up suddenly on her crutches and, searching around the crowd, fixed her eye on me, who had never exchanged a word with her nor ever in all my life desired to consult her art; making her way through the dense throng, she said, 'There! If the gentleman wishes to know his fortune he may ask you about it!'

And with these words, Your Worship, she handed me this paper in her shriveled, bony hands. And when I said in astonishment, as all the people turned to look at me, 'Granny, what's this present you are giving me?' she answered, after mumbling a lot of stuff I couldn't make out, in the middle of which, however, I was flabbergasted to hear her say my own name, 'An amulet, Kohlhaas the horse dealer; take good care of it, some day it will save you your life!'—and she vanished. Well," Kohlhaas continued good-naturedly, "to tell the truth, I had a pretty close call in Dresden, but still I got off with my skin. But how I shall make out in Berlin, and whether the charm will come to my rescue there too, the future must show."

At these words the Elector dropped down on a bench; when Lady Heloise asked him anxiously what was the matter with him, he answered, "Nothing, nothing at all," only to collapse unconscious on the floor before she could spring forward and catch him in her arms. The Knight of Malzahn entered the room just then on an errand and said, "Good God, what's wrong with the gentleman?" Lady Heloise cried, "Fetch some water!" The pages lifted the Elector up and laid him on a bed in the next room; and the consternation reached its height when the Chamberlain, who had been summoned by a page, declared, after several vain attempts to restore him to consciousness, that he gave every sign of having suffered a stroke. The Bailiff, while the Cupbearer sent a courier on horseback to Luckau for the doctor, had the Elector, after he had opened his eyes, put in a carriage and carried at a walk to his hunting lodge nearby; but the ride was responsible for his falling into two more fainting fits after he had arrived there, and it was not until late the next morning, after the doctor from Luckau had arrived, that he recovered somewhat, though showing definite symptoms of the onset of a nervous fever. As soon as he was fully conscious again, the Elector raised himself on his elbow and his first question was: where was Kohlhaas? The Chamberlain, misunderstanding the question, took his hand and said he could set his mind at rest about that dreadful man: after that strange and inexplicable occurrence, he himself had given orders for Kohlhaas to remain where he was in the farmhouse at Dahme with his escort from Brandenburg. Assuring the Elector of his warmest sympathy, and protesting how bitterly he had taxed his wife for her irresponsible frivolity in bringing him together with that man, the Chamberlain asked his master what had produced such a strange and awful effect on him in the interview. He had to confess, the Elector replied, that it was the sight of an insignificant piece of paper the man carried about with him inside a lead capsule that was to blame for the whole unpleasant incident. He added a great deal more besides by way of explanation, which the Chamberlain could not understand; suddenly swore to him, as he clasped his hand in his own, that his possessing the paper was of the utmost consequence to him; and begged him to mount that instant, ride to Dahme, and get it for him from the horse dealer at whatever cost. The Chamberlain, who had difficulty in concealing his dismay, assured him that if the piece of paper had the slightest value to him, nothing in the world was more essential than to hide that fact from Kohlhaas: if an indiscreet remark made the latter suspect something, all the Elector's riches would not suffice to buy it from that ferocious fellow with his insatiable vindictiveness. To reassure the Elector, he added that they must think of another way, and since the scoundrel probably did not set much store by the paper for its own sake, perhaps they could trick him into giving it up to some third person who had never had any part in the matter. The Elector, wiping his sweating face, asked if they might not send somebody to Dahme right away to try and do that, and meanwhile they could keep the horse dealer from going on until the paper was got hold of somehow. The Chamberlain, who could hardly believe his ears, answered that unfortunately, by every reckoning, the horse dealer must already have left Dahme and got across the border onto Brandenburg ground, where any attempt to interfere with his going on or to make him turn back would create exceedingly unpleasant and in all

likelihood insurmountable difficulties. As the Elector fell back
mutely on the pillow with a look of utter despair, the Chamberlain
asked him what was in the paper and by what strange and inexplicable chance he had found out that the contents concerned himself. To this, however, the Elector gave no answer, only looking
suspiciously at the Chamberlain, whose obligingness he was beginning to distrust; he lay there rigid, his heart beating nervously, staring
down abstractedly at the corner of the handkerchief he was holding
in his hands, when suddenly he asked the Chamberlain to summon
the Junker von Stein, an energetic, clever young man whom he had
often employed before in affairs of a secret nature, on the pretext
that he had some other business to arrange with him. After explaining the matter to von Stein and impressing upon him the importance
of the paper in Kohlhaas' possession, the Elector asked him if he
wished to acquire an eternal claim on his friendship by getting hold
of the paper for him before the horse dealer reached Berlin; and
when the Junker, as soon as he had somewhat grasped the situation,
which in truth was a very strange one, promised to serve him to the
utmost of his ability, the Elector commanded him to ride after Kohlhaas and, since there was little likelihood of his being got at with
money, to make him a shrewd speech and offer him his life and
liberty in exchange for the paper—indeed, if Kohlhaas insisted on
it, he should help him then and there, with horses, men and money,
albeit prudently, to escape from the Brandenburg horsemen. The
Junker, after requesting a letter of credentials which the Elector
wrote out for him, immediately set out with several men, and, as he
did not spare the horses, he was lucky enough to overtake Kohlhaas
in a border village where the horse dealer, his five children, and the
Knight von Malzahn were eating their midday meal in the open air
before the door of a house. The Knight of Malzahn, on the Junker's
introducing himself as a passing stranger who wished to catch a
glimpse of his extraordinary prisoner, at once made him acquainted
with Kohlhaas and courteously invited him to be seated; and since

the Knight was coming and going continually in his preparations to leave, and the troopers were eating their dinner on the other side of the house, the Junker soon found an opportunity to tell the horse dealer who he was and the special business he came to him on.

The horse dealer already knew the title and name of the man who had swooned in the farmhouse at Dahme at the sight of the lead capsule and all he needed to climax the excitement into which this discovery had thrown him was to open the paper and read its secrets; but this, for various reasons, he was determined not to do for mere curiosity's sake. Replying to the Junker, he said that, in view of the ungenerous and unprincely treatment he had been forced to endure in Dresden despite his entire willingness to make every possible sacrifice, he would keep the paper. When the gentleman asked him why he gave this strange refusal to a proposal involving nothing less than his life and liberty, Kohlhaas said, "Noble sir, if your sovereign should come to me and say, 'I'll destroy myself and the whole pack of those who help me wield the scepter'—destroy himself, mind you, which is the dearest wish of my soul—I would still refuse him the paper, which is worth more to him than his life, and say, 'You can send me to the scaffold, but I can make you suffer, and I mean to.' " And Kohlhaas, with death staring him in the face, called a trooper over and invited him to have the large portion of food left in his dish. And all the rest of the hour that he spent in the place he behaved as if the Junker sitting at the table were not there, only turning to give him a parting glance when he climbed into the wagon.

The Elector's condition took such a turn for the worse on his receiving this news that for three critical days the doctor feared for his life. But thanks to the fundamental soundness of his constitution he recovered at the end of several painful weeks on a sickbed; or at least he was well enough to be placed in a carriage amply supplied with pillows and robes and carried back to Dresden to take up the affairs of government again. No sooner did he arrive in the city than he summoned Prince Christiern of Meissen and inquired how far along the arrangements were for the departure for Vienna of the attorney Eibenmayer, whom the government intended sending there as its legal representative to accuse Kohlhaas before his Imperial Majesty of breach of the peace of the Empire. The Prince replied that, pursuant to the Elector's orders on his departing for Dahme, the attorney had left for Vienna immediately after the arrival in Dresden of the jurist Zäuner, whom the Elector of Brandenburg had commissioned to proceed against the Junker Wenzel von Tronka in the matter of Kohlhaas' black horses.

The Elector, walking over to his desk with a flushed face, expressed surprise at such haste, for he thought he had made it clear that he wanted Eibenmayer's departure postponed until after a consultation they needed to have with Dr. Luther, who had procured the amnesty for Kohlhaas, when he meant to issue a more definitive order. As he said this, he shuffled together some letters and documents lying on his desk with an expression of suppressed annoyance. The Prince, after a pause in which he looked at him in surprise, said that he was sorry if he had displeased him in this matter; however, he could show him the Council of State's decision requiring him to send the attorney off at the aforesaid time. He added that nothing had been said in the Council about a consultation with Dr. Luther; earlier in the affair it might perhaps have served some purpose to give consideration to the churchman's views because of his intercession on Kohlhaas' behalf, but this was no longer the case now that the amnesty had been broken before the eyes of the whole world and the horse dealer had been arrested and handed over to the Brandenburg courts for sentencing and execution. Well, the Elector remarked, the mistake of sending Eibenmayer off was really not too serious; however, for the present, until further orders from himself, he did not wish the man to bring the action against Kohlhaas in Vienna, and he requested the Prince to send a courier to him immediately with instructions to that effect. Unfortunately, the

Prince replied, this order came a day too late, as Eibenmayer, according to a report he had just received, had already gone ahead and presented his complaint to the State Chancery in Vienna. "How was all this possible in so short a time?" the Elector asked in dismay, to which the Prince replied that three weeks had already passed since Eibenmayer's departure and his instructions had been to settle the business with all possible dispatch as soon as he arrived in Vienna. Any delay, the Prince added, would have been all the more unseemly, seeing how the Brandenburg attorney, Zäuner, was pressing his case against the Junker Wenzel von Tronka with stubborn persistence; he had already made a motion for the court to remove the horses from the hands of the knacker for the time being, with a view to their being ultimately restored to health, and, in spite of all his opponent's objections, he had won his point. The Elector rang the bell, saying never mind, it did not matter, and after turning back to the Prince and asking him, with a show of unconcern, how things were going in Dresden otherwise, and what had happened in his absence, he lifted his hand and, unable to conceal his inner distress, signalled him to go. That same day the Elector sent the Prince a note asking for the entire Kohlhaas file, on the pretext that the political importance of the case required him to give it his personal attention; and since he could not bear to think of destroying the one man who could tell him the paper's secrets, he wrote a letter in his own hand to the Emperor beseeching him with all his heart, for weighty reasons that he would perhaps be able to explain at greater length a little later on, to be allowed to withdraw for a time the accusation made against Kohlhaas by Eibenmayer. The Emperor, in a note drawn up by the State Chancery, replied as follows: he was astonished at the Elector's apparently sudden change of mind; the report that Saxony had furnished him on the Kohlhaas case made it a matter for the entire Holy Roman Empire; he consequently felt it his duty as Emperor to appear as Kohlhaas' accuser before the House of Brandenburg; and since the Court Justiciary, Franz Müller, had already gone to Berlin as the Emperor's advocate for the purpose of accusing Kohlhaas of breach of the public peace, retreat was no longer possible and the affair must take its course according to the law.

The Emperor's letter disheartened the Elector completely. When word reached him privately from Berlin a short time after that the action had been commenced before the High Court, and that Kohlhaas would in all probability end on the scaffold, the unhappy prince, resolving on one more effort, wrote a letter in his own hand to the Elector of Brandenburg in which he begged him to spare the horse dealer's life. He gave the pretext that the amnesty granted the man did not, in justice, permit a death sentence to be executed on him; assured the Elector that, in spite of the apparent severity with which Kohlhaas had been treated in Saxony, it had never been his intention to let him die; and described how inconsolable he would feel if the protection Berlin had said it wished to extend to the man should, by an unexpected turn of events, prove worse for him in the end than if he had remained in Dresden and his case had been decided according to Saxon law. The Elector of Brandenburg, to whom much in this account seemed ambiguous and obscure, answered that the vigor with which His Majesty's counsel was proceeding made any departure from the strict letter of the law in order to satisfy his wish absolutely out of the question. The misgivings that he had expressed about the justice of the proceeding were really excessive: for though the Elector of Saxony had granted Kohlhaas an amnesty for the offenses of which he now stood accused before the High Court in Berlin, it was not he who was the accuser but the Supreme Head of the Empire, whom the amnesty in no way bound. At the same time he pointed out how necessary it was, in view of Nagelschmidt's continuing outrages, which the outlaw, with unheard of audacity, had even carried as far as Brandenburg, to make an example of Kohlhaas; and asked him, in case he was not swayed by these considerations, to appeal to the Emperor himself, since an edict of reprieve for Kohlhaas could only be proclaimed by His Majesty.

The Elector fell ill again from chagrin and vexation over all these unsuccessful efforts; and when the Chamberlain visited his bedside one morning, he was moved to show him the letters he had written to Vienna and Berlin in his efforts to obtain a reprieve for Kohlhaas and in that way gain some time in which to try to get hold of the paper in the latter's possession. The Chamberlain fell on his knees in front of him and pleaded in the name of everything he held sacred and precious to tell him what the paper said. The Elector asked him to bolt the door and sit on his bed; and after taking his hand and pressing it to his heart with a sigh, he began as follows: "Your wife, I gather, has already told you how the Elector of Brandenburg and I encountered a gypsy woman on the third day of our meeting in Jüterbock. Now the Elector, who has a very lively spirit, had decided to play a joke on the bizarre old woman and ruin her reputation for soothsaying, which had just been all the talk at dinner, in front of all the people. Walking up to her table with folded arms, he demanded a sign from her, one that could be put to the proof that very day, to confirm the truth of the fortune she should tell him; otherwise, he declared, though she were the Roman Sibyl herself, he would not believe one word she said. The woman, measuring us at a glance from head to foot, said that this was the sign: the big horned roebuck that the gardener's son was raising in the park would come to meet us in the market place where we were standing, before we should have gone away. Now the roebuck, you must understand, was intended for the Dresden kitchen and was kept under lock and key inside an enclosure surrounded by high palings and shaded by the oaks of the park; and since the park as a whole, as well as the garden leading into it, was also kept carefully locked because of the smaller game and the fowl they contained, it was impossible to see how the beast could fulfill the strange prediction and come to meet us in the square. Nevertheless, the Elector was afraid there was some trick in it, and after a short consultation with me, since he was absolutely bent on exposing the ridiculousness of everything she had to say, he sent to the castle and ordered the roebuck slaughtered then and there and the carcass dressed for dinner on one of the next days. Then, turning back to the woman, before whom all this had been openly done, he said, 'Well, now! What kind of fortune have you got to tell me?' The woman studied his palm and said, 'Hail, my Elector and Sovereign! Your Grace shall rule for many years, the house from which you spring shall endure for many years, and your descendents shall be great and glorious and more powerful than all the other princes and sovereigns of the earth!'

"For a brief moment the Elector looked thoughtfully at the woman, then muttered in an undertone, as he took a step toward me, that now he almost regretted sending a messenger to stop the prophecy from coming true; and while the knights who followed him, amid loud rejoicing, showered money into the woman's lap, to which he added a gold piece from his own pocket, he asked her whether the greeting that she had for me had as silvery a sound as his. The woman, after opening a box at her side, very deliberately arranging the money in it according to kind and quantity, and then closing it again, shaded her eyes with her hand as if the sun annoyed her and looked at me; and when I repeated the question to her, and jokingly added to the Elector, while she studied my hand, 'She has nothing very pleasant to say to me, it seems,' she seized her crutches, laboriously raised herself up from the stool by them, and, pressing close to me with her hands held out mysteriously in front of her, she whispered distinctly in my ear, 'No!'

" 'Is that so?' I said in confusion, recoiling a step before her cold and lifeless look, which seemed to come from eyes of marble, as she sat down again on the stool behind her. 'From what direction does the danger to my house come?' Taking charcoal and paper and crossing her knees, she asked whether she should write it down for

me; and when I said, 'Yes, please do,' because I was really at a loss
and there was simply nothing else for me to say under the circumstances, she replied, 'All right. I will write down three things
for you: the name of the last ruler your house shall have, the year
in which he shall lose his throne, and the name of the man who shall
seize it for himself by force of arms.' And having done so under the
eyes of the crowd, she arose, sealed the paper with gum that she
moistened in her wrinkled mouth, and pressed it with a leaden
signet ring that she wore on her middle finger. And when I reached
for the paper, more curious than words can express, as you may
well imagine, she said, 'No, no, no, your Highness!' turned, and
pointed with one of her crutches. 'From that man there, the one
with the feathered bonnet, standing on the bench in the church
entrance, behind all the people—get the paper back from him, if
you like!' And before I could quite understand what she was saying,
she turned around and left me standing speechless with astonishment
in the square; clapping shut the box behind her and slinging it over
her shoulder, she vanished into the crowd, and that was the last I
saw of her. But at that very moment, I confess to my immense relief,
the knight whom the Elector had sent to the castle reappeared and
reported to him, with a broad grin, that two hunters had killed the
roebuck under his very eyes and hauled it off to the kitchen. The
Elector jovially put his arm through mine with the intention of
leading me from the square, and said, 'Well, do you see? Her
prophecy was just an ordinary swindle, not worth the time and money
it cost us!' But what was our surprise when a shout went up, even
before these words were fairly out of his mouth, all around the
square, and everybody turned to see a huge butcher's dog trotting
toward us from the castle yard with the roebuck that he had seized
by the neck in the kitchen as fair game; and, hotly pursued by the
kitchen menials, he let it fall to the ground three paces from us—and
so in fact the woman's prophecy, which had been her pledge for the
truth of everything she said, was fulfilled, and the roebuck, dead

though it was, to be sure, had come to meet us in the market place.

"The lightning that plummets from a winter's sky is no more devastating than this sight was to me, and my first endeavor, as soon as I got free of the people around me, was to discover the whereabouts of the man with the feathered bonnet whom the woman had pointed out to me; but none of my people, though they searched without stop for three days, could discover even the remotest trace of his existence. And then, friend Kunz, a few days ago, in the farmhouse at Dahme, I saw the man with my own eyes!" And letting go the Chamberlain's hand and wiping his sweating face, he fell back on the couch.

The Chamberlain, who thought it a waste of effort to try and convince the Elector of his own very different view of this incident, urged him to use any and every means to get hold of the paper, and afterwards to leave the fellow to his fate; but the Elector said that he saw absolutely no way of doing so, although the thought of having to do without the paper, or perhaps see all knowledge of it perish with the man, nearly drove him out of his mind. When his friend asked him if he had made any attempt to find the gypsy woman, the Elector said that he had ordered the Government to search for her, on some pretext or other, throughout the length and breadth of the Electorate, which they had been doing to this very day without result, but that for reasons he would rather not go into he doubted whether she could ever be found in Saxony. Now it happened that the Chamberlain intended to visit Berlin to see about a number of large properties in Neumark that his wife had inherited from Count Kallheim, whose death had followed upon his dismissal from the Chancellorship; and as he really loved the Elector, he asked him, after a moment's reflection, if he would allow him a free hand with the whole business. When his master pressed his hand warmly to his breast and said, "Be myself in this, and get me the paper!" the Chamberlain turned over his affairs of office, advanced his departure by several days and, leaving his wife behind, set out for Berlin accompanied only by a few servants.

Meanwhile Kohlhaas had arrived in Berlin, as we have said, and by special order of the Elector of Brandenburg was lodged in a knights' jail, where he and his five children were made as comfortable as circumstances permitted. As soon as the Imperial Attorney General from Vienna appeared, he was summoned to the bar of the High Court to answer the charge of breach of the peace of the Empire; and when he pleaded in his own defense that he could not be indicted for his armed invasion of Saxony and the acts of violence accompanying it because of the agreement he had made with the Elector of Saxony at Lützen, he was formally apprised that His Majesty the Emperor, whose Attorney General was the complainant in the case, could not give that any consideration. The matter having been explained to him in detail, however, and on his being assured that on the other hand full satisfaction would be given him in Dresden in his action against the Junker Wenzel von Tronka, he very soon yielded his defense. Thus it fell out that on the very day that the Chamberlain arrived in Berlin, sentence was pronounced and Kohlhaas was condemned to die on the block—a sentence which, in spite of its mercifulness, seeing how complicated the affair was, no one believed would be carried out, which indeed the whole city, knowing the goodwill the Elector bore Kohlhaas, confidently expected to see commuted to a simple, even if long and severe, term of imprisonment. The Chamberlain, who nevertheless understood that there was no time to be lost if he was to execute his master's commission, started out by showing himself to Kohlhaas in his ordinary court costume, clearly and close at hand, one morning when the horse dealer was standing at the window of his prison innocently studying the passers-by; and, concluding from a sudden movement of Kohlhaas' head that he had noticed him, and observing with particular satisfaction how his hand went involuntarily to the part of his chest where the capsule hung, he considered what had passed at that moment in Kohlhaas' soul as sufficient preparation for his going one step further in his attempt to get hold of the paper. He sent for an old woman that hobbled around on crutches selling old clothes, whom he had noticed in a crowd of other ragpickers in the streets of Berlin and who seemed to tally fairly well in her age and dress with the woman described to him by the Elector; and as he felt sure that the old gypsy woman's features had not impressed themselves very sharply on Kohlhaas' memory, since he had had only a fleeting glimpse of her as she handed him the paper, he decided to pass the one woman off as the other and have her masquerade, if possible, as the gypsy with Kohlhaas. To acquaint her with her part, he gave her a detailed account of everything that had taken place between the Elector and the gypsy woman, making sure, as he did not know how much the latter had revealed to Kohlhaas, to lay particular stress on the three mysterious items in the paper; and after explaining how she must mutter an incoherent and incomprehensible speech in which she would let it fall that schemes were afoot to get hold of the paper, on which the Saxon court set great importance, by force or cunning, he instructed her to pretend to Kohlhaas that the paper was no longer safe with him and to ask him to give it into her keeping for a few critical days. The old-clothes woman consented at once to do what was asked of her, provided she received a large reward, a part of which she insisted on the Chamberlain's paying her in advance; and since some months ago she had made the acquaintance of the mother of Herse, the groom that fell at Mühlberg, and this woman had the Government's permission to visit Kohlhaas occasionally, it was an easy matter for her, a few days later, to slip something into the warder's palm and gain admission to the horse dealer.

Kohlhaas, indeed, on the woman's entering and his seeing the signet ring on her hand and a coral chain hanging around her neck, thought he recognized the same old gypsy woman who had handed him the paper in Jüterbock; but probability is not always on the side of truth, and something had happened here which we must perforce record but which those who may wish to question are perfectly free to do: the Chamberlain had committed a most colossal blunder, and in the old-clothes woman whom he had picked up in the streets of Berlin to impersonate the gypsy woman he had stumbled upon that very same mysterious gypsy woman whom he wished to have impersonated. At any rate, the woman told Kohlhaas, as she leaned on her crutches and patted the cheeks of the children, who, scared by her strange appearance, shrank back against their father, that she had returned to Brandenburg from Saxony some time ago, and hearing the Chamberlain incautiously ask in the streets of Berlin about the gypsy woman who had been in Jüterbock in the previous spring, she had immediately pressed forward and offered herself, under a false name, for the business that he wanted done. The horse dealer was so struck by the uncanny likeness he discovered between her and his dead wife that he was inclined to ask the old woman whether she was Lisbeth's grandmother; for not only did the features of her face, as well as her still well-shaped hands and the way she gestured with them as she spoke, remind him vividly of Lisbeth, but he even noticed a mole on her neck just like the one Lisbeth had had. Amid a confusion of thoughts such as he had seldom experienced, the horse dealer invited her to sit down and asked what business of the Chamberlain's she could possibly have with him. The Chamberlain, she said, as Kohlhaas' old dog sniffed around her knees and wagged his tail when she scratched his head, had instructed her to disclose to the horse dealer the three questions that were so important to the Saxon court, the mysterious answers to which were contained in the paper; to warn him of an envoy who was in Berlin for the purpose of obtaining it; and to ask him for the paper on the pretext that it was no longer safe in his bosom where he carried it. But, she said, the real reason for her coming was to tell him that the threat to get the paper away from him by force or cunning was an absurd and empty one; that he need not have the least fear for its safety while he was in the custody of the Elector of Brandenburg; that the paper, indeed, was much safer with him than with her; and that he should take care not to give it up to anybody, regardless of who it was or what the pretext. Nevertheless, she said in conclusion, he would be wise, in her opinion, to use the paper for the purpose she had given it to him at the Jüterbock fair: let him lend a favorable ear to the offer that the Junker von Stein had made him on the frontier and surrender the paper to the Elector of Saxony in return for his life and liberty. Kohlhaas, who exulted in the power given him to wound his enemy mortally in the heel at the very moment that it was treading him in the dust, replied, "Not for the world, Granny, not for the world!" squeezed the old woman's hand, and only wanted to know what the paper's answers were to the awful questions. The old woman lifted the youngest child, who had been squatting at her feet, onto her lap and said, "Not for the world, Kohlhaas the horse dealer, but for this pretty little fair-headed little boy!" and she smiled at the child and petted him as he looked at her wide-eyed, and with her bony hands gave him an apple from her pocket. Kohlhaas, disconcerted, said that the children themselves, when they were grown, would approve his conduct, and that he could do nothing better for them and for their grandchildren than to keep the paper. Besides, he asked, after what had happened to him, who was there to guarantee him against his being deceived a second time, and would he not in the end be fruitlessly sacrificing the paper to the Elector just as he had recently done his band of men at Lützen? "Once a man has broken his word to me, I never trust him again. Only a clear and unmistakable request from you can part me from this bit of writing, through which satisfaction has been given me so wonderfully for all that I have suffered." The old woman, putting the child down again, said that in many respects he was right and he could do just as he pleased. And she took hold of her crutches to leave. Kohlhaas again asked her what was in that marvelous paper; he was eager, he said—as she quickly interjected that of course he could open it, but it would be pure curiosity on his part—to find out about a thousand other things before she left: who she really was, how she had come by the knowledge she possessed, why she had refused to give the paper to the Elector, for whom it had been written, after all, and among so many thousands of people had handed it just to him, Kohlhaas, who had never wanted anything from her skill.

But just at that moment some police officers were heard mounting the stairs and the old woman, alarmed lest she be discovered in the place, said, "Goodbye, Kohlhaas, goodbye till we meet again, when there won't be one of these things you shall not know!" And turning toward the door, she cried, "Farewell, children, farewell!" kissed the little people one after the other, and vanished.

Meanwhile the Elector of Saxony, a prey to his despairing thoughts, had called in two astrologers, named Oldenholm and Olearius, who then enjoyed a considerable reputation in Saxony, to ask their advice about the mysterious piece of paper that was so important to him and his posterity; but when, after an earnest investigation lasting several days that they conducted in the Dresden palace tower, the men could not agree as to whether the prophecy aimed at the centuries to come or at the present time, with perhaps the Polish crown being meant, with whom relations were still very warlike, the uneasiness, not to say despair, in which this unhappy lord found himself, being only intensified by such learned disputes, finally reached a pitch that was more than his spirit could bear. And on top of it all, just at this time the Chamberlain sent word to his wife, who was about to follow him to Berlin, to break the news discreetly to the Elector before she left that after an unsuccessful attempt he had made with the help of an old woman who had not been heard of since, their hopes of ever getting hold of the paper in Kohlhaas' possession seemed very dim, seeing that the death sentence pronounced on the horse dealer had now at last been signed by the Elector of Brandenburg, after a complete review of the file of the case, and the day of execution fixed for the Monday after Palm Sunday—at which news the Elector shut himself up in his room like a lost soul, his heart consumed by grief, but on the third day, after sending a short note to the Government House that he was going to the Prince of Dessau's to hunt, suddenly disappeared from Dresden. Where he actually went, and whether in fact he arrived in Dessau, we shall not attempt to say, as the chronicles which we have compared oddly contradict and cancel one another on this point. This much, however, is certain: that at this very time the Prince of Dessau lay ill in Brunswick at his uncle Duke Heinrich's residence and was hardly in a state to go hunting, and that the next evening Lady Heloise arrived in Berlin to join her husband Sir Kunz the Chamberlain in the company of a certain Count von Königstein, whom she introduced as her cousin.

Meanwhile, at the Elector of Brandenburg's order, the death sentence was read to Kohlhaas, his chains were struck off, and the property deeds taken from him in Dresden were returned; and when the counselors assigned him by the court asked what disposition he wished to make of his possessions, he drew up a will, with the help of a notary, in favor of his children and appointed his honest friend the bailiff of Kohlhaasenbrück to be their guardian. Nothing could match the peace and contentment of his last days; for soon after, a special Electoral decree unlocked the dungeon in which he was kept to all his friends, of whom he had a great many in the city, who were free to visit him day and night. Indeed, he even had the satisfaction, one day, of seeing the theologian Jacob Freising enter his jail with a letter for him from Dr. Luther in the latter's own hand —without doubt a most remarkable missive, all trace of which, however, has been lost; and from the hands of his minister, in the presence of two Brandenburg deans who assisted him, he received the blessing of the Holy Communion.

And now the fateful Monday after Palm Sunday arrived, on which Kohlhaas was to make atonement to the world for his all-too-rash attempt to take its justice into his own hands, amid a general commotion in the city which could not disabuse itself even yet of the hope of seeing him saved by an Electoral pardon. Just as he was passing out of the gate of the jail under a strong escort, with the theologian Jacob Freising leading the way and his two little boys in his arms (for he had expressly asked this favor at the bar of the court), the castellan of the Electoral palace came up to Kohlhaas through the crowd of grieving friends around him who were shaking his hand and saying goodbye, and with a haggard face handed him a paper that he said an old woman had given him. Kohlhaas stared in surprise at the man, whom he hardly knew, and opened the paper; its gum seal bore an impression that instantly recalled the gypsy woman. But who can describe the astonishment that gripped him when he read the following communication: "Kohlhaas, the Elector of Saxony is in Berlin; he has already gone ahead of you to the place of execution and can be recognized, if that is of any interest to you, by the hat with blue and white plumes he has on. I don't have to tell you what his purpose is: as soon as you are buried he is going to dig the capsule up and read the paper inside it. Your Elizabeth."

Kohlhaas, completely dumbfounded, turned to the castellan and asked him if he knew the mysterious woman who had given him the note. But just as the castellan answered: "Kohlhaas, the woman——" and then halted strangely in the middle of his sentence, the procession, starting up again, swept the horse dealer along and he was unable to make out what the man, who seemed to be trembling in every limb, was saying.

When he arrived at the scaffold, he found the Elector of Brandenburg and his suite, which included the Archchancellor Sir Heinrich von Geusau, sitting their horses in the midst of an immense crowd of people; on the Elector's right stood the Imperial Attorney General, Franz Müller, with a copy of the death sentence in his hand; on his left, his own attorney, Anton Zäuner, with the Dresden court's decree; in the center of the half-open circle, which the crowd completed, stood a herald with a bundle of articles in his hand, and the two black horses, sleek with health and pawing the ground with their hooves. For the action that the Archchancellor Sir Heinrich had started at Dresden in his master's name against the Junker Wenzel von Tronka having triumphed in every point, without the slightest reservation, a banner had been waved over the horses' heads to make them honorable again, they had been removed from the knacker's care, fattened by the Junker's men, and handed over, in the Dresden market place, to the horse dealer's attorney in the presence of a specially appointed commission. When Kohlhaas, with his guard, advanced up the knoll to the Elector, the latter said, "Well, Kohlhaas, this is the day on which justice is done you. Look here, I am giving you back everything that was taken from you by force at Tronka Castle, which I as your sovereign was duty bound to restore to you: the two blacks, the neckerchief, gold gulden, laundry —everything down to the money for the doctor's bills for your man Herse who fell at Mühlberg. Now are you satisfied with me?"

At a sign from the Chancellor the decree was handed to Kohlhaas, who set down the two children he was carrying on the ground and read it through with sparkling eyes; and when he found that it contained a clause condemning the Junker Wenzel von Tronka to two years' imprisonment, his feelings overcame him and, crossing his hands on his breast, he knelt down from afar before the Elector. Rising again and putting his hand in his bosom, he joyfully assured the Archchancellor that his dearest wish on earth had been fulfilled; walked over to the horses, examined them and patted their plump necks; and, coming back to the Chancellor, cheerfully announced that he was giving them to his two sons Heinrich and Leopold! The Archchancellor, Sir Heinrich von Geusau, looking down at him kindly from his horse, promised in the name of the Elector that his last wish would be held sacred, and also asked him if he would not dispose as he thought best of the things in the bundle. Kohlhaas thereupon called Herse's old mother, whom he had caught sight of in the square, out of the crowd, and, giving her the things, he said, "Here, Granny, these belong to you!"—adding the sum he had received as damages to the money in the bundle, as a gift to help provide for her in her old age.

The Elector called out, "Kohlhaas the horse dealer, now that satisfaction has been given you in this wise, you on your side prepare to satisfy His Majesty the Emperor, whose attorney stands right here, for breach of the public peace!" Taking off his hat and tossing it on the ground, Kohlhaas said he was ready to do so; he lifted the children from the ground one more time and hugged them tightly; then, giving them to the bailiff of Kohlhaasenbrück, who, weeping silently, led them away from the square with him, he advanced to the block. He had just unknotted his neckerchief and opened his tunic when he gave a quick glance around the circle formed by the crowd and caught sight, a short way off, of the figure that he knew with the blue and white plumes, standing between two knights whose bodies half hid him from view. Kohlhaas, striding up in front of the man with a suddenness that took his guard by surprise, drew out the capsule, removed the paper, unsealed it and read it through; and looking steadily at the man with the blue and white plumes, in whose breast fond hopes were already beginning to spring, he stuck the paper in his mouth and swallowed it. At this sight the man with the blue and white crest was seized by a fit and fell unconscious to the ground. Kohlhaas, however, while his dismayed companions bent over him and raised him from the ground, turned around to the scaffold where his head fell under the executioner's ax.

So ends the story of Kohlhaas. Amid the general lamentation of the people, his body was laid in a coffin; and while the bearers lifted it from the ground to carry it to the graveyard in the outskirts of the city for decent burial, the Elector of Brandenburg called the dead man's sons to him and, instructing the Archchancellor to enroll them in his school for pages, dubbed them knights on the spot. Shortly thereafter the Elector of Saxony returned to Dresden, shattered in body and soul; what happened subsequently there must be sought in history. Some hale and hearty descendants of Kohlhaas, however, were still living in Mecklenburg in the last century.

The Beggarwoman
of Locarno

*A*T the foot of the Alps, near Locarno in northern Italy, stood an ancient castle belonging to a Marquis, which today, coming down the St. Gotthard, one sees in ruins before one—a castle with great, high-ceilinged rooms, in one of which the mistress of the house one day spread a bed of straw out of pity for a sick old woman who had come begging to her door. When the Marquis returned from hunting, he happened to walk into this room, where he kept his shotgun, and irritably ordered the woman to get up out of the corner where she was lying and find herself a place behind the stove. The woman, as she rose, slipped with her crutch on the polished floor and fell, injuring her spine so seriously that it was only with an immense effort that she was able to get up again and cross the room as she had been bidden, but once behind the stove she collapsed, groaning and sighing, and died.

Several years later, when war and bad harvests had brought the Marquis into straitened circumstances, there appeared a Florentine knight who liked the castle's beautiful situation and offered to buy it. The Marquis, who was extremely eager to sell, told his wife to put the stranger up in the unoccupied room mentioned above, which was furnished very splendidly. But imagine the couple's dismay when the knight came downstairs, pale and shaken, in the middle of the night and swore the room was haunted: something invisible to the eye, he said, had got up from the corner with a rustling sound, as if from a bed of straw, quite audibly crossed the room with slow and feeble steps, and collapsed, groaning and sighing, behind the stove.

The Marquis, frightened without knowing why himself, laughed at the knight with forced heartiness, and offered to get up on the spot and pass the night with him in the room, if that would set his mind at rest. But the knight asked him to be good enough to let him spend the rest of the night in an armchair in the Marquis' bedroom, and when morning came he called for his coach, paid his respects, and left.

This incident, which created a great sensation, frightened away several prospective buyers, much to the Marquis' chagrin; and when, oddly and inexplicably, it began to be whispered even among his own people that a ghost walked the room at midnight, he decided to investigate the matter himself, so as to put an end, once and for all, to the rumors. At nightfall, accordingly, he had his bed made up in the room and waited, wide awake, for midnight to come. But imagine his dismay when, at the witching hour, he in fact heard the mysterious noise: it was as if someone got up from a heap of rustling straw, crossed the room, and collapsed, sighing and gasping, behind the stove. The next morning, when he came downstairs, the Marquise asked how his investigation had turned out; and when he looked around him apprehensively and, after bolting the door, assured her there actually was a ghost, she was frightened as never before in her life and begged him not to utter a word about it before he had made another trial of the matter, quite coolly, with her. That night, however, they, as well as the faithful servant who accompanied them, heard the same inexplicable ghostly noise; and only their pressing desire to get rid of the castle at any price enabled them to stifle their terror in the presence of the servant and blame the thing on some petty, accidental cause that would certainly come to light. On the evening of the third day, when the two, with pounding hearts, again climbed the stairs to the guest room, resolved to get to the bottom of the business, they discovered the watchdog, whom somebody had unchained, in front of the door, and, without knowing exactly why, perhaps from an instinctive desire to have the company of some third living creature, they took the dog into the room with them.

Around eleven o'clock, with two candlesticks burning on the table, the couple sat down on separate beds, the Marquise fully clothed, the Marquis with sword and pistols, which he had taken from the closet, at his side; and while they tried as best they could to pass the time in conversation, the dog curled up in the center of the floor and went to sleep. Then, at the stroke of midnight, the dreadful noise was heard again; somebody whom no human eye could see got up on crutches in the corner of the room; there was the sound of straw rustling under him; and at the first step: tap! tap! the dog awakened, started to its feet with its ears pricked up, and backed away to the stove, growling and barking, as if somebody were walking toward it. At this sight the Marquise, her hair standing on end, plunged from the room; and while the Marquis seized his sword and shouted, "Who's there?", slashing the air like a maniac in every direction when there was no answer, she called for her coach, determined to drive to town that instant. But before she had even clattered out of the gate, after snatching up a few belongings, she saw the castle go up in flames all around her. The Marquis, maddened with terror, had caught up a candle and, weary of his life, set fire to every corner of the place, which was paneled in wood throughout. Vainly she sent people in to save the unfortunate man; he had already perished in the most pitiful way, and even today his white bones, which the country people gathered together, rest in the corner of the room from which he had ordered the beggarwoman of Locarno to get up.

The Engagement
In Santo Domingo

$\mathcal{A}$T Port-au-Prince, in the French part of the island of Santo Domingo, on the plantation of M. Guillaume de Villeneuve, there lived at the beginning of this century, in the days when the blacks were killing the whites, a terrible old Negro by the name of Kongo Hoango. This native of the African Gold Coast, who in his youth seemed to possess a loyal and honest disposition, had had countless benefits heaped upon him by his master for having once saved the latter's life during a crossing to Cuba. Not only did M. Guillaume give him his freedom on the spot, and on their return to Santo Domingo set him up in a house and home of his own, but a few years later he also made him, against the custom of the country, overseer of his broad estate and, as Kongo Hoango did not wish to remarry, he gave him instead an old mulatto woman from his plantation named Babekan, to whom the Negro was distantly related by his deceased first wife. Why, when the Negro reached his sixtieth year, M. Guillaume retired him with a large pension and, to cap his kindnesses, he even provided for him in his will; and yet all these proofs of gratitude could not protect M. Villeneuve from the wrath of this ferocious man. In the general frenzy of revenge that flared up in the plantations following the National Convention's ill-considered steps, Kongo Hoango was one of the first to reach for a rifle and, remembering the tyranny that had torn him from his native land, blow his master's brains out. He set fire to the house into which the latter's wife and three children had fled with the other whites of the settlement, laid waste the entire plantation which the heirs who lived in Port-au-Prince might have tried to claim and, after razing every building on the plantation to the ground, he roamed about the region at the head of a band of Negroes he had collected and armed, to help his brothers in the struggle against the whites. Sometimes he would ambush armed companies of travelers crossing the country; at other times, in broad daylight, he would attack the planters barricaded in their settlements and put everyone he found inside to the sword. Indeed, in his inhuman thirst for revenge, he even ordered old Babekan and her daughter, a fifteen-year-old mestizo named Toni, to play a part in this ferocious war which had rejuvenated him completely: seeing that the main building of the plantation, which he now occupied, stood all by itself on the highroad and was often knocked at in his absences by white or Creole refugees seeking food or shelter, he instructed the women to detain these white dogs, as he called them, with help and courtesies until his return. Babekan, who suffered from consumption as the result of a horrible punishment she had received in her youth, used on these occasions to dress up young Toni, whose high-yellow complexion especially suited her for this gruesome deception, in her finest clothes; she encouraged her to refuse none of the strangers' caresses except the ultimate one, which was forbidden her on pain of death; and when Kongo Hoango returned with his Negro band from his forays in the neighborhood, instant death was the fate of the poor fellows who had let themselves be fooled by these tricks.

Now in the year 1803, as everybody knows, General Dessalines advanced on Port-au-Prince with 30,000 Negroes, and all whose skins were white rushed into the place to defend it. For it was the last stronghold of French power in Santo Domingo, and if it fell, every white on the island was lost. It happened that just when old Hoango, who had started out with his following of blacks to carry a load of powder and lead through the French outposts to General Dessalines, was away, somebody knocked at the back door of his house in the darkness and rain of a stormy night. Old Babekan, who was already in bed, got up, opened the window, with just a skirt thrown around her hips, and asked who was there. "In the name of Mary and all the saints," the stranger said in a low voice, as he went over and stood under the window, "before I tell you that, answer just one question!" And, reaching out through the darkness of the night for the old woman's hand, he asked, "Are you a Negress?"

Babekan said, "My goodness, you must certainly be a white man if you would rather face this pitch-black night than a Negress! Come in," she added, "and don't be afraid; it's a mulatto who lives here, and the only other person in the house besides myself is my daughter, a mestizo!" And she shut the window as if she meant to come down to open the door for him; but, pretending that she had trouble finding the key just then, she hastily snatched some clothes from the wardrobe and slipped upstairs into the bedroom to wake her daughter. "Toni!" she said. "Toni!"

"What's the matter, Mother?"

"Quick!" she said. "Get up and get dressed! Here are some clothes, clean linen and stockings. There's a fugitive white man at the door who wants to come in!"

"A white man?" Toni asked, sitting up in bed. She took the clothes the old woman held out to her and said, "Are you sure he is alone, Mother? And is it safe to let him in?"

"There's nothing to worry about," replied the old woman, and lit a candle. "He's unarmed and all alone—he is shaking in every limb, he's so afraid we might attack him!" And while Toni got up and was putting her skirt and stockings on, she lit the large lantern standing in the corner of the room, quickly tied the girl's hair up in a knot on top of her head after the fashion of the country, put a hat on her, and, after lacing up her pinafore, handed her the lantern and told her go down into the yard and bring the stranger in.

Meanwhile the barking of the watchdogs had awakened a boy called Nanky, an illegitimate son of Hoango's by a Negress, who slept with his brother Seppy in one of the outbuildings; and when he saw, by the light of the moon, a solitary figure standing on the back stairs of the house, he ran out at once, as he had been told to do in such cases, to lock the yard gate the man had entered by. The stranger did not understand what these preparations meant and asked the boy, who, he saw with a shudder, was a Negro when he stood near him, who lived in the plantation; and hearing him reply that the estate had passed into Hoango the Negro's hands following the death of M. Villeneuve, the stranger was about to knock him down, snatch the gate key from his hands, and make for the open fields when Toni came out of the house with the lantern in her hand. "Quick," she said, seizing his hand and drawing him toward the door, "in here!" She took care, while saying this, to hold the lantern so that the beam fell full on her face.

"Who are you?" cried the stranger, drawing back as, bewildered for more reasons than one, he stared at her young and charming form. "Who lives in this house where you say I shall find safety?"

"Nobody, by the light of the sun, but my mother and I," said the girl, struggling and straining to draw him along with her.

"What, nobody!" cried the stranger, retreating a step and snatching back his hand. "Didn't the boy just tell me that a Negro called Hoango lives here?"

"No, I say!" said the girl, and stamped her foot in annoyance.

"And even if this house did belong to a madman by that name, he is away right now and ten miles off from here!" And then she drew the stranger into the house with both hands, ordered the boy not to tell a soul who was there, and, taking him by the hand, led him upstairs to her mother's room.

"Now," said the old woman, who had overheard the entire conversation from the window and noticed by the lantern light that he was an officer, "what's the meaning of that sword hanging so ready to hand under your arm? We have offered you a refuge in our home," she continued, putting on her glasses, "and thereby endangered our own lives; did you come in here to repay this kindness with treachery, in the customary fashion of your countrymen?"

"Heaven forbid!" replied the stranger, walking up in front of her chair. He caught hold of the old woman's hand, pressed it to his heart, and said, after a hesitant glance or two around the room as he unbuckled the sword from his hip, "You see the most miserable of men before you, but not an ungrateful or a wicked one."

"Who are you?" asked the old woman, pushing a chair toward him with her foot and ordering the girl to go into the kitchen and prepare him as good a supper as could be got ready on short notice.

"I am an officer with the French forces," the stranger replied, "though not, as you may have already guessed, a Frenchman myself; my native land is Switzerland, and my name is Gustav von der Ried. Oh, if only I had never left it for this unhappy island! I come from Fort Dauphin where, as you know, all the whites were murdered, and I hope to reach Port-au-Prince before General Dessalines is able to surround and besiege the town with his troops."

"From Fort Dauphin!" exclaimed the woman. "With a face the color of yours, you managed to come all this way right through the middle of a nigger country in revolt?"

"God and the saints," replied the stranger, "have protected me! And I'm not alone, Granny; a worthy old gentleman, my uncle, is with me, and his wife and five children, not to speak of several men and women servants belong to the family—twelve people in all, whom I had to lead on unspeakably hard night marches, as we cannot show ourselves on the highroad by day, with only the help of two sorry mules."

"Ei, good heavens!" exclaimed the old woman, shaking her head sympathetically and taking a pinch of tobacco. "Where are your people right now?"

"I am sure," replied the stranger after a moment's hesitation, "I can trust you; the color of your face reflects a gleam of my own. The family is about a mile from here, over near the seagull pond, in the wilderness of the mountain woods bordering it, where hunger and thirst forced us to seek shelter the day before yesterday. Last night we sent our servants out to forage for a little bread and wine among the inhabitants of the country, but with no success; they were too afraid, when it came right down to it, of being caught and killed to dare to speak to anybody, with the result that I had to go out myself today, at the risk of my life, and try my luck. But unless I am completely mistaken," he continued, pressing the old woman's hand, "heaven has led me to merciful people who don't share the terrible and unheard-of madness that has seized all the natives of this island. Be good enough to fill a few baskets with food and refreshment and I will pay you well for it; it is only a five days' journey from here to Port-au-Prince, and if you make it possible for us to reach that city we will be eternally grateful to you for having saved our lives."

"Yes," feigned the old woman, "this raging madness. Isn't it just as though the hands of a body or the teeth in a mouth were furious at each other merely because one wasn't made like the other? What can I, whose father came from Santiago on the island of Cuba, do about the glimmer of light that shines upon my face when day breaks? And what can my daughter, who was conceived and born in Europe, do about the fact that the bright day of that continent is reflected in hers?"

"What?" exclaimed the stranger. "You who, according to your whole physiognomy, are a mulatto and therefore of African origin, and the lovely young mestizo who opened the door to me—you face the same doom as we Europeans?"

"Good heavens!" replied the old woman, taking her glasses off her nose. "Do you think the little property we have worked with our hands to acquire through years of weary labor and sorrow doesn't provoke that ferocious gang of hell-begotten brigands? If we had not known how to protect ourselves against their persecution by every trick and skill that self-preservation teaches the weak, you can be sure the shadow of kinship that lies broad across our faces would not have done it!"

"Impossible!" exclaimed the stranger. "Who is persecuting you on this island?"

"The owner of this house," the old woman replied, "the Negro Kongo Hoango! Since the death of M. Guillaume, the former owner of this place, whom his fierce hand struck down at the very start of the uprising, we who, being his relatives, keep house for him have been at the mercy of all his tyranny and violence. For every piece of bread, every bit of drink that we give out of humanity to one or another of the white fugitives that from time to time pass by here on the highroad, we are repaid with his curses and abuse; and he would like nothing better than whipping the blacks up to revenge themselves on us white and creole half-dogs, as he calls us, partly because he wants in general to get rid of us for disapproving of his ferocity against the whites, and partly because he would like to get hold of the little property we would leave behind."

"You unhappy people!" said the stranger. "You pitiable people! And where is this madman right now?"

"With General Dessalines' army," replied the old woman, "to which he and the other blacks belonging to this plantation are bringing a load of powder and lead that the General needed. Unless he goes off on another expedition, we expect him back within ten or twelve days; and if he should then learn, which God forbid, that we gave shelter and protection to a white man on his way to Port-au-Prince while he himself was putting all his strength and energy into the business of ridding the island of the entire race, you can be sure we will all be death's children."

"Heaven, which loves pity and humaneness," answered the stranger, "will protect you in whatever you do for some one unfortunate! And if he did find out," he added, moving closer to the old woman, "seeing that that would draw the Negro's wrath down on you anyhow, and it would do you no good to go back to obeying him even if you wanted to, couldn't you make up your mind now to shelter my uncle and his family in your house for a day or two, at whatever price you care to ask, so that they could recover a bit from the exhaustion of the journey?"

"Young man!" the old woman said in astonishment, "what are you asking? How could I possibly put a party of travelers as large as yours in a house standing on the main road without its becoming known to the people hereabouts?"

"Why not?" insisted the stranger. "If I myself went out to the seagull pond right now and led the party back here before daybreak, and if we put everybody, masters and servants together, in one room, and perhaps even took the precaution, in case of the worst, of carefully locking all the doors and windows?"

The old woman, after considering his proposal for a while, answered that if he tried to lead his party from their mountain glen into the settlement that night, he would be sure to run into a troop of armed Negroes who were reported by several outposts to be on the main road.

"Very well," answered the stranger, "then let us do nothing more for the moment than send a basket of food to my unfortunate people, and put off the business of bringing them into the settlement to the following night. Would you do that, Granny?"

"All right," said the old woman, while the stranger's lips showered kisses on her bony hand. "For the sake of the European who was my daughter's father, I'll do this favor for you, a countryman of his in distress. Sit down at daybreak tomorrow and write a letter to your people, inviting them to come here to me in the settlement; the boy you saw in the yard can carry the letter to them with some provisions, he can pass the night in the mountains with them for safety's sake, and guide the party here, if the invitation is accepted, at the break of the following day."

Meanwhile Toni had returned with the meal she had prepared in the kitchen, and while setting the table jokingly asked the old woman, with a glance at the stranger, "Mother, tell me, has the gentleman got over the fright that took hold of him at the door? Has he convinced himself that neither poison nor a dagger is awaiting him, and that Hoango the Negro is not home?" The mother said with a sigh, "My dear girl, the burnt child, according to the proverb, shuns the flame. The gentleman would have been foolish to have dared to enter the house without first making sure of its inhabitants' race." The girl, standing in front of her mother, described how she had held the lantern up so that its rays fell full on her face. "But his imagination," she said, "was so full of Moors and Negroes that even if a lady from Paris or Marseilles had opened the door, he would have taken her for a Negress." The stranger, slipping his arm gently around her waist, said with embarrassment that the hat she was wearing had prevented him from seeing her face. "If I had been able," he went on, giving her a hug, "to look into your eyes the way I am doing now, I would have been quite willing, even though everything else about you were black, to drink out of a poisoned cup with you." The mother invited him, as he blushed at his own words, to sit down, and Toni took a seat next to him, her elbows propped on the table, and stared into his face as he ate. The stranger asked her how old she was and where she was born, upon which the mother answered to say that she had conceived and given birth to Toni in Paris fifteen years ago, during a trip to Europe she had taken with M. Villeneuve's wife, her former mistress. She added that the Negro Komar, whom she married later, had adopted Toni as his own child, but that her real father was a rich Marseilles merchant named Bertrand, and so her name was Toni Bertrand.

Toni asked him if he knew of such a gentleman in France. The stranger said no, France was a big country, and during the short time he had spent there before embarking for the West Indies he hadn't met anybody by that name. The old woman remarked that anyway M. Bertrand, according to pretty reliable information she had received, was no longer in France. "His ambitious and aspiring nature," she said, "could find no satisfaction within the limits of a middle-class occupation; at the outbreak of the revolution he went into public affairs, and in 1795 accompanied a French Legation to the Turkish court, from where, as far as I know, he has not returned to this day." The stranger took Toni's hand with a smile and said that in that case she was a girl of rich and distinguished birth. He urged her to take advantage of her connection, and ventured to think she had hopes of one day being introduced on her father's arm to a much more brilliant situation that her present one.

"Hardly," remarked the old woman with suppressed feeling. "M. Bertrand, during my pregnancy in Paris, denied in court that he was the father of this child, because he was ashamed in front of a rich young girl he wanted to marry. I shall never forget the brazenness with which he swore the oath right to my face; the consequence for me was a bilious fever, and right after that sixty lashes at M. Villeneuve's order, the result of which was the consumption I suffer from to this very day."

Toni, who was leaning her head pensively on her hand, asked the stranger who he was, where he came from, and where he was going, to which he replied, after a moment of embarrassment caused by the bitterness of the old woman's speech, that he and Herr Strömli's—his uncle's—family, whom he had left behind in the mountain woods near the seagull pond under the protection of two young cousins, came from Fort Dauphin. At the girl's request, he told some of the details of the uprising that had broken out in that city: how at midnight, when everybody was in bed, the blacks, at a treacherously given signal, had started to massacre the whites; how the leader of the Negroes, a sergeant in the French engineers, had immediately set fire to all the ships in the harbor so as to cut off the whites' escape to Europe; how the family had hardly enough time to snatch up a few belongings and flee through the city gates; and how the simultaneous outbreak of uprisings all along the coast had left them no choice but to strike out, with the help of two mules they had got hold of, straight across the island for Port-au-Prince, which was defended by a strong French army and remained the only place still able to offer resistance to the ever growing power of the Negroes.

Toni asked what the whites in the place had done to make themselves so hated. Taken aback, the stranger replied, "It was their whole conduct, as masters of the island, toward the Negroes, which quite frankly I shouldn't attempt to defend—even though things have gone on here in this way for centuries. The craze for freedom that swept all the plantations led the Negroes and Creoles to strike off the chains that burdened them and revenge themselves on the entire white population for all the terrible ill-usage they had suffered at the hands of a few vicious men among the whites. What in particular," he continued after a brief silence, "struck me as frightful and extraordinary was something a young girl did. When the revolt started, this girl, who was of the Negro race, lay sick with the yellow fever which, to make matters even worse, had broken out in the city. Three years before, she had been the slave of a white planter who, out of chagrin at her refusal to gratify his wishes, had treated her very harshly and afterwards sold her to a Creole planter. On the day of the uprising, when the girl learned that the planter, her old master, had run away from the fury of the Negroes to a nearby woodshed, she remembered how he had mistreated her and sent her brother to him at dusk with an invitation to spend the night with her. The miserable fellow, who did not know what disease she had caught or even that she was sick, came and, full of gratitude—for he thought he was saved—clasped her in his arms; but he had spent barely half an hour in her bed, fondling and caressing her, when she suddenly sat up and said, with an expression of cold and ferocious hatred, 'You have been kissing someone with the plague, some one with death in her breast—that's what you have been kissing! Now go and give the fever to all those who are like you!' "

The officer, while the old woman loudly expressed her abhorrence of all this, asked Toni whether she would be capable of such a deed. "Oh no!" Toni said, looking down confused. The stranger put his napkin down on the table and said that the feeling of his own soul was that no amount of tyranny ever practiced by the whites could justify a treachery so base and dreadful. Heaven's vengeance, he said, rising from the table with a passionate expression, would be disarmed by such a deed: the angels themselves in their outrage would side with the unrighteous and, to uphold the human and the divine order, plead their cause. As he said this, he walked over to the window for a moment and looked out into the night, where storm clouds were driving across the face of the moon and the stars; and because it seemed to him that mother and daughter were exchanging looks, although he could not catch a single sign passing between them, a peevish and annoyed feeling came over him; turning around, he asked if they would show him to the room where he was to sleep.

The mother looked at the clock on the wall and remarked that it was already close to midnight, picked up a candle, and asked the stranger to follow her. She led him down a long corridor to his room; Toni carried his coat and the other things he had taken off; the old woman showed him a bed comfortably heaped with pillows, where he was to sleep, and, after telling Toni to prepare a footbath for the gentleman, she wished him good night and left. The stranger stood his sword in a corner of the room and laid the brace of pistols he wore in his belt on the table. While Toni pulled the bed out and covered it with a white sheet, he surveyed the chamber; and as he quickly concluded from the luxury and good taste of its furnishings that it must have been the old owner's bedroom, a feeling of uneasiness fastened itself in his heart like a vulture and he wished himself back in the woods, hungry and thirsty though he had been, with his own people. Meanwhile the girl had carried in, from the kitchen close by, a basin of hot water smelling of aromatic herbs and invited the officer, who had been leaning against the window, to refresh himself with it. The officer took off his neckerchief and vest in silence and sat down on a chair; he started to pull his shoes and stockings off, and, while the girl crouched down on her knees before him and busied herself with the little arrangements for the bath, he studied her attractive form. Her hair, rippling in dark curls, had tumbled over her young breasts as she knelt down; an expression of extraordinary charm played around her lips and over the long lashes that jutted out from her downcast eyes; if not for her color, which repelled him, he would have sworn that he had never seen anything prettier. At the same time he noticed a faint resemblance to somebody, though exactly to whom he himself could not say, which had struck him on first entering the house and which had won his heart completely. He caught hold of her hand as she stood up at one point in her work, and having decided, quite correctly, that there was only one way to find out whether or not the girl had a heart, he drew her down on his lap and asked her if she was already engaged to a young man. "No!" she murmured, dropping her big black eyes in charming confusion. And then she added, without stirring in his lap, that three months ago a young Negro in the neighborhood by the name of Konelly had asked for her hand; but since she was still too young, she had refused him. The stranger, who held her around her slender waist with his two hands, said that where he came from there was an old saying that when a girl reached the age of fourteen years and seven weeks she was old enough to get married. He asked her, while she examined the little gold cross he wore around his neck, how old she was.

"Fifteen years," Toni replied.

"Well then!" said the stranger. "Doesn't he have enough money to set up housekeeping in the way you want?"

Toni, without lifting her eyes to him, replied, "Oh, it isn't that. On the contrary," she went on, letting go of the cross in her hand, "since the recent changes, Konelly has become a rich man; his father has come into all the property that used to belong to his master the planter."

"Then why did you refuse his offer?" the stranger asked. He pushed her hair gently away from her forehead. "Perhaps you didn't like him?" The girl nodded her head quickly and laughed; and when the stranger jokingly whispered in her ear to ask whether it took a white man to win her favor, she hesitated dreamily for a moment and then, as a charming blush flamed in her sunburned face, suddenly pressed herself against his breast. Touched by her grace and sweetness, the stranger called her his own dear girl and took her in his arms, set free, as if by a divine hand, from all his fears. It was impossible for him to think that all the feelings he sensed in her could merely be the wretched expression of a cold and monstrous treachery. The thoughts that had oppressed him scattered like a flock of obscene birds; he reproached himself for having misjudged her heart even for an instant, and, as he rocked her on his knees and drank in her sweet breath, he pressed a kiss upon her forehead in token, as it were, of reconciliation and forgiveness. But meanwhile the girl had suddenly sat up in his arms, thinking she heard someone coming along the corridor to the door; dreamily she straightened her scarf, which had become disarranged, on her breast; but when she realized she was mistaken she turned back to the stranger with a cheerful look and reminded him that the water would get cold if he did not use it right away. "Well?" she said in perplexity, as the stranger said nothing but kept looking at her thoughtfully. "Why do you stare at me so?" She tried to hide her embarrassment by toying with her pinafore, and then exclaimed with a laugh, "You're a strange man, what strikes you so in my appearance?" The stranger passed his hand across his brow while he suppressed a sigh and, lifting her off his lap, said, "An amazing resemblance between you and a friend of mine!"

Toni, who saw that his good spirits were fled, took his hand sympathetically in hers and asked, "Who is she?" To which he replied, after a brief pause, "Her name was Marianne Congreve and she came from Strasbourg. I had met her in that city, where her father was a merchant, just before the outbreak of the Revolution, and was lucky enough to win her consent to marriage and also the approval of her mother. Oh, she was the most faithful soul under the sun; and when I look at you, the terrible and touching circumstances under which I lost her come back to me so vividly that I can hardly restrain my tears."

"What?" asked Toni, pressing against him tenderly and closely. "She is no longer alive?"

"She died," the stranger replied, "and her death taught me for the first time the meaning of everything good and fine. God knows," he continued, resting his head sadly on her shoulder, "how I could have been so rash as to make remarks one evening in a public place about the terrible revolutionary tribunal that had just been set up. I was informed against, then hunted up and down; cheated of their prey when I was lucky enough to escape into the outskirts, the wild mob of my pursuers, who thirsted for a victim, ran to my fiancée's house and, infuriated by her honest avowal that she didn't know where I was, accused her of being in league with me, and with unspeakable wantonness dragged her off to the scaffold instead of me. No sooner was this terrible news brought to me than I dashed out of my hiding place and raced through the crowd to the place of execution, crying out at the top of my voice, "Here, you monsters, here I am!" But she was already standing on the platform of the guillotine, and in reply to a question by the judges, who unfortunately must not have known who I was, she said, turning away from me with a look that remains indelibly stamped on my soul, "I don't know this man!"—upon which, a few seconds later, to the rolling of the drums and the roar of the rabble, the blade, speeded in its release by the impatience of the bloodhounds, dropped down and severed her head from her torso.—How I was saved I do not know; a quarter of an hour later I found myself in the house of a friend, where I fell out of one fainting fit into another, and in the evening, half insane, I was loaded into a cart and carried across the Rhine." At these words the stranger set the girl down and walked to the window; and when she saw him, deeply agitated, press his face into a handkerchief, a feeling of compassion, awakened by many things, came over her; with an abrupt movement she followed him to the window, threw her arms around his neck, and mingled her tears with his.

There is no need to report what happened next, as any reader who has reached this point in our narrative can supply his own words. When the stranger recovered his self-possession, he had no idea where the act he had just committed would lead; but meanwhile he knew that he had been saved, and that here in this house he had nothing to fear now from the girl. Seeing her crying on the bed with folded arms, he tried to do everything possible to calm her. Taking the little gold cross given him by faithful Marianne, his departed bride, from around his neck, and stooping down over Toni with many caresses, he hung his wedding present, as he called it, around her neck. As she went on crying and paid no heed to what he said, he sat down on the edge of the bed and told her, while alternately stroking and kissing her hand, that in the morning he would ask her mother for her hand. He described the little piece of property he owned, free and clear, on the banks of the Aar: a house that was comfortable and roomy enough to accommodate her and her mother, if the latter's age would allow her to make the voyage there; the fields, gardens, meadows, and vineyards; and his worthy old father who would welcome her with grateful affection for having saved his son. Taking her in his arms when her tears continued to course down her cheeks onto the pillow in an unending stream, and quite overcome himself, he begged her to say what harm he had done her and if she could not forgive him. He swore he would never stop loving her, and that it was only in the delirium of his strangely disordered senses that the mixture of desire and fear she inspired in him could have seduced him into doing such a thing. And, last of all, he reminded her that the morning stars were already shining in the sky and that if she stayed in his bed any longer her mother would surely be along and surprise her there; he implored her, for the sake of her health, to get up and rest for several hours in her own bed; extremely alarmed by the state she was in, he asked permission to lift her up in his arms and carry her to her room. But she said nothing in reply to all his urgings, only huddling motionless amid the tumbled pillows of the bed, her head hidden in her arms and quietly sobbing, and at last he had no choice, with the daylight already glimmering through both windows, but to lift her up without further ado; she hung lifelessly over his shoulder as he bore her upstairs to her room, and after putting her down on the bed and repeating, amid a thousand caresses, everything he had already said to her, he again called her his darling bride, pressed a kiss on her cheeks, and hurried back to his own room.

When day had fully dawned, old Babekan went upstairs to her daughter, sat down on her bed, and disclosed her scheme for dealing with the stranger as well as with his traveling companions. Since the Negro Hoango would not be returning for another two days, everything depended on keeping the stranger in the house until that time, without, however, taking in his family, for the presence of so many people might prove dangerous. Her plan was to pretend to the stranger that they had just heard that General Dessalines and his army were headed in their direction, and, as this would make it too risky to bring his family to the house as he desired, they would have to put it off for three days until the General had passed on. The party itself, she concluded, would meanwhile have to be provided with food to keep them from moving on; at the same time, so that Hoango might lay hold of them later, they must be encouraged to imagine they would find refuge in the house. She observed that the project was an important one, since the family was probably carrying a great many possessions with them, and asked her daughter to do everything in her power to help carry out their plans. Toni, sitting up in bed with an angry flush reddening her face, retorted that it was a shameful and atrocious thing to lure people into one's house and then violate the laws of hospitality in such a way. She thought a fugitive who confided himself to their protection should be doubly safe in their house, and she promised her mother that if she did not give up the bloody plan she had just revealed, she, Toni, would go straight to the stranger and tell him what a den of assassins the house was in which he had thought to find his salvation.

"Toni!" exclaimed her mother, putting her hands on her hips and staring at her, wide-eyed.

"Yes," Toni answered, lowering her voice. "What has this young man, who is not even a Frenchman by birth but, as he told us, a Swiss, done to us that we should want to fall on him like robbers and kill and strip him of everything he owns? Do the grievances we have against the planters here apply to the part of the island he comes from? Doesn't everything indicate, rather, what an honorable, upright person he is, a man who shares none of the blame for the injustices the black people may reproach his race with?"

The old woman, noting the girl's extraordinary vehemence, merely observed with trembling lips how astonished she was. She asked what the young Portuguese whom they had clubbed to the ground a short time ago in the gateway, had done to them? She asked what the two Dutchmen were guilty of, who had been slain three weeks before in the courtyard by the bullets of the Negroes. She wanted to know what they had against the three Frenchmen and all the other fugitives of the white race whom they had put out of the way, since the beginning of the rebellion, in their house with rifles, spears and daggers.

"By the light of the sun," retorted her daughter, starting wildly to her feet, "you are very wrong to remind me of those atrocities! For a long time now I have felt only the deepest loathing for the abominations you force me to take part in; I swear to you that I would rather die ten times over to satisfy the vengeance of the Lord for everything I have done, than suffer even one hair of that young man's head to be touched as long as he is in our house."

"Very well," the old woman said, yielding suddenly, "let the stranger leave then! But when Kongo Hoango returns," she said, getting up to leave the room, "and learns that a white man spent a night in our house, you may answer to him for all those tender feelings which move you to defy his express orders and let the stranger go."

This parting remark, which for all its apparent mildness betrayed the old woman's real anger, left the girl more than a little dismayed. She knew her mother's hatred for the whites too well to believe she would let such an opportunity to satisfy it go by. Fearing that she would send immediately to the neighboring plantations for the Negroes to come and overpower the stranger, the girl threw on her clothes and followed her into the downstairs sitting room. As Toni came in, the old woman started away in confusion from the cupboard, where she seemed to be busy with something, and sat down at a spinning wheel. The girl stopped in front of the door and read the proclamation nailed up there that forbade all black people, on pain of death, to give aid and comfort to a white man; and as if panic-stricken at realizing the crime she had been about to commit, she spun around and fell at her mother's feet who, as she well knew, had been watching her from the back. Hugging her knees, she begged her mother's forgiveness for the mad things she had said in the stranger's defense; pleaded in excuse the fact that she had still been in bed in a half-dreaming, half-waking state when her mother had surprised her with the scheme for tricking the stranger; and announced her perfect readiness to hand him over to the vengeance of the law of the land, which had already decided his destruction. The old woman, after a pause in which she looked steadily at the girl, said, "By heaven, your just saying that has saved him his life for today! His food was already poisoned, since you had threatened to take him under your protection, and Kongo Hoango, in keeping with his orders, would at least have had his dead body." And, getting up, she took a pitcher of milk from the table and emptied it out of the window. Toni, not crediting her own senses, stared in horror at her mother. The old woman sat down again and, lifting the girl, who was still on her knees, up from the floor, asked her what it was that could so have changed her way of thinking in the space of one night. Yesterday, after getting his bath ready, had she stayed with the stranger for any length of time? And had she talked with him a great deal? But Toni, whose breast was heaving violently, said nothing in reply to these questions, or nothing definite; she stood there with her eyes cast down and her head in her hands and blamed a dream she had had; but one look at her unhappy mother's breast, she said, stooping quickly to kiss her hand, had reminded her again of all the inhumanity of the race to which this stranger belonged; and she swore, as she turned away and pressed her face into her apron, that as soon as Hoango the Negro returned her mother would see what kind of a daughter she had.

Babekan was still sitting lost in thought, wondering where the girl's strange passion could have sprung from, when the stranger entered the room with a note he had written in his bedroom summoning his people to spend a few days on the Negro Hoango's plantation. He greeted mother and daughter with great cheerfulness and affability, and, handing the paper to the old woman, he asked her to send someone off to the woods right away, just as she had promised, to provide for his people. Babekan got up and put the note away in the cupboard, and said with an alarmed air, "Sir, we must ask you to return to your room immediately. The road is full of passing Negro soldiers who say that General Dessalines and his army are headed in this direction. This house is open to the whole world, and you won't be safe here unless you hide in your bedroom, which faces the yard, and lock the doors as well as shutters as carefully as possible."

"What!" the stranger exclaimed in surprise, "General Dessalines——"

"Don't ask questions!" interrupted the old woman, and she knocked on the floor with a stick three times. "I'll come after you to your bedroom and explain everything there."

The stranger retreated from the room before the old woman's frightened gesticulations, only turning in the doorway to say, "But my people are waiting for me; shouldn't you at least send a messenger to them to——"

"Everything will be taken care of," the old woman broke in, while in response to her knocking the bastard boy whom we have already met entered the room; whereupon she ordered Toni, who had turned her back to the stranger and walked over to the mirror, to pick up a basket of food standing in the corner; and mother, daughter, the stranger, and the boy went upstairs to the bedroom.

There the old woman settled herself comfortably in a chair and told him how all through the night the glow of General Dessalines' camp fires had been seen upon the mountains on the horizon—which in fact was the case, although not one Negro of his army, which was advancing to the southwest against Port-au-Prince, had appeared in the vicinity so far. With this story she was able to throw the stranger into a fever of anxiety, which she then cleverly assuaged by promising him she would do everything in her power to rescue him, even if worst came to worst and troops were quartered in the house. On the stranger's repeated earnest reminders that under these circumstances his family should at least be provided with some food, she took the basket from her daughter's hand and, giving it to the boy, told him he was to go to the seagull pond in the nearby mountains and deliver it to the foreign officer's family whom he would find there. The officer himself, he was to say, was in good hands; friends of the whites, who had suffered much themselves at the hands of the blacks for their sympathies, had pitied him and taken him into their house. She concluded by saying that, just as soon as the highroad was clear of the armed Negro bands which were expected along at any moment, they would arrange to shelter the family, too, in the house.

"Do you understand?" she asked when she had finished. The boy set the basket on his head and answered that he was well acquainted with the seagull pond she had described to him, for he and his friends used to fish there every once in a while, and that he would deliver the message, just as he was given it, to the foreign gentleman's family spending the night there. The stranger, on the woman's asking if he had anything to add, took a ring from his finger and gave it to the boy to deliver to the head of the family, Herr Strömli, as evidence of the truth of his message. After this the mother busied herself with a number of things whose purpose, she said, was to safeguard the stranger; ordered Toni to close the shutters; and, to dispel the darkness that this made in the room, she herself struck a light, though not without some difficulty, as the tinder would not catch, with the tinder box on the mantelpiece. The stranger took advantage of this moment to slip his arm around Toni's waist, put his lips to her ear, and ask her in a whisper whether she had slept well and if he shouldn't perhaps tell her mother what had happened. Toni, however, said nothing to his first question, and her reply to the other, as she twisted out of his grasp, was, "No, not a word, if you love me!" She suppressed the pangs of fear that all her mother's deceitful preparations awakened in her; and on the pretext of getting breakfast for the stranger, she hurried downstairs to the living room.

Trusting to luck that her mother would not miss it, she took from the cupboard the letter in which the stranger in his innocence had asked his family to follow the boy to the settlement and, resolved, if worst came to worst, to die together with him, she raced down the road after the boy. For in her heart and before God she no longer saw the young man as merely a guest to whom she had given shelter and protection, but as her fiancé and husband, and her mind was made up to tell all this quite openly to her mother as soon as his party was numerous enough in the house, counting on the confusion into which the situation would throw the old woman.

"Nanky," she called when she had overtaken the boy in breathless haste on the highroad, "Mother has changed her plans about Herr Strömli's family. Here, take this letter! It is addressed to Herr Strömli, the old man who is the head of the family, and in it is an invitation to spend a few days with all his people at our plantation. Be smart and do everything you can to get them to agree to this; Kongo Hoango the Negro will reward you for it when he returns!"

"All right, Cousin Toni," replied the boy. He put the carefully folded note into his pocket and asked, "Shall I be guide for the party on the way here?"

"Of course," Toni answered, "that goes without saying, since they don't know the country. But as troops may be marching along the road, be sure you don't start out before midnight; once on your way, however, hurry as fast as you can to get here before daybreak. —Can you be depended on?" she asked.

"Just depend on Nanky!" answered the boy. "I know why you're luring these white fugitives to the plantation, and the Negro Hoango will be satisfied with me!"

Returning to the house, Toni carried breakfast up to the stranger,

after which mother and daughter cleared the dishes away and returned to the front living room to do their household chores. It was inevitable that the mother should go to the cupboard a little while later
where, quite naturally, she missed the letter. Putting her hand to her
head for a moment, for she distrusted her memory, she asked Toni
where she might have put the letter the stranger had given her. Toni,
after a short pause in which she looked at the floor, answered that
the stranger had put the letter back in his pocket, as she must surely
know, and torn it up in his room in the presence of both of them. The
mother stared in astonishment at the girl; she said she distinctly
remembered taking the letter from his hand and putting it in the cupboard; but when she had searched it over and over again and could
find no trace of the letter, and as several such incidents in the past
had made her distrust her own memory, there was nothing for her
in the end but to accept her daughter's explanation. However, she
could not suppress the keen regret its loss gave her and remarked that
it would have been very useful to the Negro Hoango in getting the
family to come to the plantation. At midday and in the evening,
when Toni was serving the stranger his meals, she sat at the corner
of the table talking to him and seized on several occasions to ask
him about the letter; but Toni was skillful enough, whenever the
conversation approached this dangerous subject, to change or confuse it, so that her mother was never quite able to understand the
stranger's explanation of what had actually happened to it. And
so the day went by; after supper her mother took the precaution, as
she described it, of locking the stranger's room; and after discussing
with Toni the tricks she might use to get another such letter from
him the next day, she went to bed and told the girl to do the same.

　　As soon as Toni, who had been longing for this moment, reached
her room and felt sure her mother was asleep, she took down the
portrait of the Holy Virgin that hung near her bed, propped it on
a chair, and knelt before it with clasped hands. She implored the
Savior, her divine Son, in a prayer full of infinite devotion, to give her

the courage and the resolution to confess the crimes weighing on her young soul to the young man she had given herself to. She vowed to conceal nothing from him, whatever it cost her heart, not even the pitiless and terrible purpose with which she had lured him into the house the day before; yet she prayed that, for the sake of all the steps she had already taken to save him, he would forgive her and take her back to Europe with him as his faithful wife. Wonderfully strengthened by this prayer, she stood up, took the master key that unlocked all the rooms in the house, and without a light crept silently along the narrow passage that traversed the building to the stranger's bedroom. Softly she opened the door and went up to the bed where he lay deep in sleep. The moon shone down on his fresh young face, and the night wind, through the open windows, ruffled the hair on his forehead. Gently she bent over him and, inhaling his sweet breath, spoke his name; but he was lost in a dream that seemed to be about herself, at least she heard his ardent, trembling lips whisper the word "Toni!" several times. An indescribable sadness came over her; she could not gather the resolution to pull him down from the blissful heavens of his imagination into the middle of a common and wretched reality; and, feeling sure that sooner or later he would waken by himself, she knelt beside his bed and covered his dear hand with kisses.

But who can describe the terror that gripped her bosom a few moments later when, from inside the courtyard, she suddenly heard a clatter of men, horses, and weapons and distinctly recognized in it the voice of the Negro Kongo Hoango, who had unexpectedly come back from General Dessalines' camp with his crew. Carefully avoiding the moonlight that threatened to betray her, she ran to the window and hid behind the curtain, where she heard her mother already telling the Negro everything that had happened in his absence, and also that there was a European fugitive in the house. In an undertone the Negro commanded his men to be quiet. When he asked the old woman where the stranger was at that moment, she pointed out the room to him and took this opportunity to tell the Negro about the strange conversation she had had with her daughter about the fugitive. She swore the girl was a traitor, and that the entire plot to capture the stranger was in jeopardy. At all events, the little thief had stolen into his bed at nightfall, as she had seen with her own eyes, where she undoubtedly was taking her ease this very moment; and if the stranger hadn't escaped already, very likely he was being warned this very instant and the means for his escape were being decided on. The Negro, who had already tested the girl's loyalty in similar circumstances in the past, answered that this was hardly possible. "Kelly!" he called out in anger, "Omra! Bring your rifles!" And without saying another word, followed by all his men, he climbed the stairs to the stranger's room.

Toni, under whose eyes this whole scene had been enacted within the space of minutes, stood paralyzed in every limb, as though struck by a lightning bolt. Her first thought was to wake the stranger; but, for one thing, the soldiers in the yard made escape impossible, and for another, she foresaw his snatching up his arms and running headlong to his immediate destruction, since the Negroes far outnumbered him. Indeed, the most dreadful possibility she had to consider was that the unfortunate man, when he found her at his bedside at this time, would take her for a traitor and in the madness of this terrible delusion charge senselessly right into the arms of the Negro Hoango instead of heeding her advice. In this moment of unspeakable fear, her eyes lighted on a rope hanging from a nail in the wall, God knows by what chance. The Lord himself, she thought, as she snatched down the rope, had put it there to save her friend and herself. She lashed the young man's hands and feet with the rope and knotted it securely; and after pulling the ends tight without paying any attention to his tossing and turning, she tied them to the bed frame, pressed a kiss upon his lips in joy at having mastered the situation for the moment, and rushed out to meet the Negro Hoango clattering up the stairs.

The Negro, who still did not believe what the old woman had told him about Toni, stood stock-still in the corridor with his following of torchbearers and armed men, dumbfounded at seeing her come out of the room. He shouted, "Traitor! Turncoat!" and, turning to Babekan, who had gone a few steps forward toward the stranger's door, he asked, "Did the stranger escape?" Babekan, seeing the door open, turned around without looking in and came back like a madwoman, crying, "The sneak! She's let him escape! Run and block the exits before he gets out into the open!"

"What's going on?" asked Toni, looking astonished at the old man and the Negroes around him.

"What's going on?" retorted Hoango, and he grabbed her by the front of her dress and dragged her toward the room.

"Are you mad?" cried Toni, pushing the old man away as he stiffened at the sight that met his eyes. "There's the stranger, tied up fast in his bed by me; and, by God, this isn't the worst thing I've managed in my life!" And, turning her back on him, she sat down at a table as if in tears. The old man turned to the mother standing flabbergasted at his side and said, "Oh, Babekan, what kind of stories have you been deceiving me with!"

"Thank heavens!" answered the mother, and in embarrassment examined the ropes with which the stranger was tied. "Here the stranger is, but I can't understand it." The Negro, thrusting his sword back into its sheath, went over to the bed and asked the stranger who he was, where he came from, and where he was going. But as the only thing the latter said amid his violent struggles to free himself was, "Oh, Toni! Oh, Toni!" in a tone of heart-rending anguish, the mother broke in to say that he was a Swiss named Gustav von der Ried, and that he had come from the coastal town of Fort Dauphin with a whole family of European dogs, who were at this moment hiding in the mountain caves near the seagull pond. Hoango, seeing the girl sitting with her head propped dejectedly in her hands, went over to her and called her his darling girl, patted her cheeks, and asked her forgiveness for the hasty suspicion he had voiced. The old woman, who had also gone to the girl, asked her, with hands on hips and much shaking of her head, why she had tied the stranger to his bed when he had had no suspicion of the danger he was in. Toni, actually crying with grief and rage, turned suddenly on her mother and said, "Because you have no eyes and ears! Because he did so realize the danger he was in! Because he was trying to escape; because he had asked me to help him get away; because he had plotted against your own life and would undoubtedly have carried out his plan at daybreak if I hadn't tied him up in his sleep." The old man patted and soothed the girl and ordered Babekan to say no more about the matter. Then he called over a couple of soldiers armed with rifles to carry out on the spot the law by which the stranger stood condemned; but Babekan whispered to him privately, "No, for heaven's sake, Hoango!" She took him aside and explained that the stranger, before being shot, should be got to write the invitation with the help of which his family could be enticed to the plantation, as it was too risky a business to attack them in the woods. Hoango thought it unlikely that the family was unarmed and gave his approval to this suggestion; but, as it was too late to write the letter, he posted two guards over the white fugitive and, after taking the precaution of examining the prisoner's bonds, which he found too slack and summoned a couple of his men to tighten, he and all his crew left the room and silence gradually descended on the household.

But Toni, who had only pretended to say goodnight to the old man and go to bed when he shook her hand again, got up as soon as she saw that everything was quiet in the house, slipped out of a back gate into the open and, the wildest despair in her heart, raced madly down a path that crossed the highroad in the direction from which Herr Strömli's family would have to come. For the look of contempt that the stranger had flung at her from his bed had gone straight to her heart like a knife thrust; a feeling of burning bitterness began to mingle with her love for him, and she exulted at the thought of dying in this attempt to rescue him. She posted herself, for fear of missing the family, near the trunk of a stone pine which they would have to pass if they had accepted the invitation; and hardly had the first rays of dawn shot across the horizon when, just as it had been arranged, the voice of the boy, Nanky, acting as the party's guide, could be heard in the distance among the trees.

The procession consisted of Herr Strömli and his wife, the latter riding one of the mules; their five children, two of whom, Adelbert and Gottfried, young men of eighteen and nineteen, walked alongside the mule; and three menservants and two maids, one of whom, with an infant at her breast, was riding the other mule: twelve people all told. They moved along slowly, over the path laced with tree roots, toward the pine trunk where Toni, as quietly as possible so as not to scare them, emerged from the shadow of the tree and called out, "Stop!" The boy recognized her immediately; and when she asked him which was Herr Strömli, while men, women, and children crowded around her, he was glad to introduce her to the elderly head of the family, Herr Strömli. "Sir!" Toni said, cutting short his greeting with a resolute voice, "Hoango the Negro with all his crew has unexpectedly returned to the settlement. You can't put up there now except at the peril of your lives; indeed, your nephew, who was unlucky enough to find a welcome there, is lost forever unless you take your arms and follow me to the plantation to free him from the captivity in which he is held by Hoango the Negro!"

"My God!" all the members of the family exclaimed in horror; and the ailing mother, exhausted by the journey, fell to the ground from her mule in a dead faint. While the servant girls rushed up at Herr Strömli's call to help their mistress, Toni, bombarded with questions by the youths, led Herr Strömli and the other men aside for fear of being overheard by the boy, Nanky. She told them everything that had happened, without restraining her tears of shame and remorse: how matters stood in the house at the moment when the young man came along; how their conversation in private had miraculously changed everything; what she had done, in her half-demented panic, when the Negro unexpectedly returned, and how she was now determined to stake her own life on the attempt to rescue him from the captivity in which she herself had put him. "My weapons!" shouted Herr Strömli, running over to his wife's mule to get his rifle. While his strapping sons, Adelbert and Gottfried, and the three brave servants were also arming themselves, he said, "Cousin Gustav has saved the life of more than one of us; now it is our turn to perform the same service for him"; then he lifted his wife, who had regained consciousness, back onto the mule; took the precaution of tying up the hands of Nanky, who was a kind of hostage; sent all the women and children back to the seagull pond under the sole protection of his thirteen-year-old son Ferdinand, who was also armed; and, after questioning Toni, who had taken up a helmet and a pike herself, about the numbers and disposition of the Negroes in the courtyard, and promising, if possible, to spare her mother and Hoango too, he bravely placed himself at the head of his little company and, putting his trust in God, set out, with Toni as his guide, for the plantation.

Toni, as soon as the party had slipped through the back gate, pointed out to Herr Strömli the room in which Hoango and Babekan lay asleep; and while Herr Strömli and his men entered the unlocked house without a sound and seized the Negroes' stacked rifles, she slipped away to the shed where Seppy, Nanky's five-year-old brother, slept. For Nanky and Seppy, old Hoango's bastard children, were very dear to him—especially the latter, whose mother had died only a short time ago; and since the retreat to the seagull pond and the flight from there to Port-au-Prince, which she intended to join, would still be exposed to many dangers even if the Negroes did set the young man free, she concluded, not unwisely, that their holding the boys as a sort of pledge might prove very useful in case they were pursued. She was able to pick the boy up out of his bed and carry him, half asleep in her arms, across to the main building without being seen. Meanwhile Herr Strömli and his men had entered the door of Hoango's room as stealthily as they could; but instead of finding him and Babekan in bed as he expected, both of them, awakened by the noise, were standing, half naked and helpless, in the middle of the room. Herr Strömli raised his rifle and commanded them to surrender or be killed on the spot! But Hoango's only answer was to snatch a pistol from the wall and fire it point-blank into the group, grazing Herr Strömli's head. At this signal, Herr Strömli's band fell upon him fiercely; Hoango, after firing a second shot that pierced a servant through the shoulder, was wounded in the hand by a saber stroke and the two of them, Babekan and the Negro, were thrown to the ground and tied with ropes to the pedestal of a large table.

Meanwhile, awakened by the shots, Hoango's Negroes, twenty or more in number, came rushing from their huts and, hearing old Babekan screaming inside the house, they charged forward furiously to try to recapture their weapons. Herr Strömli, whose wound was trifling, posted his men at the windows of the house and commanded them to empty their rifles at the Negroes to drive them back, but in vain; paying no heed to two of their men already sprawled out dead in the yard, the Negroes were about to fetch axes and crowbars and break down the house door, which Herr Strömli had barred, when Toni, trembling and shaking, entered Hoango's room with the boy Seppy in her arms. Herr Strömli was only too pleased to see her; snatching the boy from her arms, he turned to Hoango, drew his cutlass, and swore he would kill the child on the spot if Hoango did not order his Negroes to fall back. Hoango, whose strength was broken from the blow across the three fingers of his hand, and knowing his own life was in jeopardy if he refused, after a moment's reflection, during which he was lifted from the floor, said that he would do it; escorted to the window by Herr Strömli, he took a handkerchief in his left hand and, signaling to the Negroes in the yard, he shouted for them to leave the door alone and go back to their huts, as he didn't need their help to save his life! At this, the struggle quieted down a little; when his men lingered in the court-yard to discuss things, Hoango, on Herr Strömli's demand, sent out a Negro who had been taken prisoner inside the house to repeat his order. The blacks, as little as they understood what was happening, had no choice but to obey the words of so unmistakable a message; and, abandoning their assault, for which everything stood ready, they went back one by one, grumbling and cursing, to their huts. Herr Strömli had Seppy's hands tied up under Hoango's eyes, told the Negro that his only purpose was to free the officer, his nephew, from his imprisonment on the plantation, and that, if no obstacles were put in the way of their flight to Port-au-Prince, he would have nothing to fear for his own, Hoango's, life, or for that of his children, who would be returned to him. Babekan, when Toni came up to her and, in an irrepressible burst of feeling, put her hand out to say goodbye, knocked it violently aside. She called her a villain and a traitor, and, twisting about against the pedestal of the table to which she was tied, said the vengeance of the Lord would overtake her before she had a chance to enjoy her infamy. Toni re-plied, "I did not betray you; I am white and engaged to the young man you are holding prisoner; I belong to the race of those you are waging open war against, and shall know how to account to the Lord for my having sided with them!" Thereupon Herr Strömli had a guard posted over the Negro Hoango, whom he had taken care to tie up again and bind to a doorpost; had the servant who lay un-conscious on the floor with a smashed shoulderblade lifted up and carried away; and, after telling Hoango that he could come and fetch his two children, Nanky as well as Seppy, a few days later in Sainte Luce, where the first French outposts stood, took Toni, who was a prey to all sorts of feelings and could not keep back her tears, by the hand and led her from the bedroom, amid the curses of Babekan and old Hoango.

Meanwhile Herr Strömli's sons, Adelbert and Gottfried, right after the first main skirmish at the windows had ended, ran at their father's command to their cousin Gustav's room where, after meeting a stubborn resistance from the two Negroes guarding him, they were lucky enough to overpower them. One lay dead on the floor; the other, with a bad bullet wound, had crawled out into the corridor. The two brothers, the eldest of whom had also been hit, in the thigh, but lightly, untied their beloved cousin; they hugged and kissed him and, handing him a rifle and sidearms, jubilantly told him to follow them to the front room where Herr Strömli, as the victory had already been decided, was probably getting everything ready for their withdrawal. Cousin Gustav, however, sitting halfway up in bed, only gave their hands a friendly squeeze; otherwise he was silent and distracted, and, instead of taking the pistols they held out to him, he raised his right hand and passed it across his forehead with an indescribable expression of woe. The young men, sitting down beside him, asked what was wrong; and when he put his arm around them and leaned his head silently against the younger brother's shoulder, Adelbert thought he was going to faint and was about to get up and bring him a glass of water when Toni, with the boy Seppy on her arm, entered the room, holding Herr Strömli's hand. Gustav instantly changed color; he clung to his two friends for support as he got up, as though he were about to collapse; and before the young men realized what he meant to do with the pistol that he now snatched from their hands, he had already discharged it, gnashing his teeth in rage, full at Toni. The shot went right through her breast; when, with a stifled cry of pain, she took several steps in his direction and, handing the boy to Herr Strömli, collapsed in front of him, he flung the pistol across her body, kicked her away with his foot and, calling her a whore, threw himself back onto the bed. "Monster!" shouted Herr Strömli and his sons. The two young men flung themselves down beside the girl and, lifting her up, they called for one of the old servants who had served them as doctor in several similarly desperate situations in the past; but the girl, with her hand clutched convulsively to her wound, pushed her friends away and gasped out: "Tell him——!" while pointing to the man who had shot her, and again: "Tell him——!"

"What shall we tell him?" cried Herr Strömli—but the approach of death robbed her of the power of speech. Adelbert and Gottfried stood up and shouted at the murderer if he knew that the girl was the one who had saved him; that she loved him and had sacrificed everything, parents and possessions, in order to flee with him to Port-au-Prince? When he lay insensible on the bed, oblivious to their presence, they thundered "Gustav!" in his ears and asked if he could hear them, and shook him and pulled him by the hair. Gustav sat up. He looked at the girl lying bathed in her own blood, and the rage that had given rise to his deed gave way, by a natural sucession, to a feeling of ordinary compassion. Herr Strömli, shedding burning tears into his handkerchief, asked, "Why, wretch, did you do it?" Cousin Gustav, rising from the bed and looking at the girl while he wiped the sweat from his brow, replied that she had treacherously tied him up during the night and handed him over to the Negro Hoango. "Oh!" cried Toni, and with an indescribable look stretched her hand out to him. "I tied you up, dearest friend, because——!" But she was incapable of speech, nor could her hand reach him, she fell back again, with a sudden flagging of her strength, into Herr Strömli's lap.

"Why did you tie me up?" asked Gustav, white-faced, kneeling beside her. Herr Strömli, after a long pause punctuated only by the rattling in Toni's throat, during which they waited in vain for her to answer, spoke. "Because, after Hoango's return, there was no other way to save you, you unhappy man; because she wanted to avoid the fight you would certainly have started, because she wanted to gain time until we who, thanks to her, were already hurrying here, could free you with our arms."

Gustav covered his face with his hands. "Oh!" he cried, without looking up, and imagined the earth was sinking under his feet. "Are you telling me the truth?" He put his arms around her and looked into her face, his heart pitiably torn.

"Oh!" cried Toni, and these were her last words: "You shouldn't have distrusted me!" And her noble spirit fled.

Gustav tore his hair. "True, true!" he cried, as his cousins dragged him away from the corpse, "I shouldn't have distrusted you; you were engaged to me by an oath, even though we never said a word about it to one another!" Herr Strömli sorrowfully smoothed down the pinafore over the girl's breast. He urged the servant standing beside him with his few inadequate instruments to extract the bullet he was sure he would find lodged in the breastbone; but all his efforts, as we have said, were in vain, the lead had gone clean through her and her soul had already fled to a better star.

Meanwhile Gustav had gone over to the window; and while Herr Strömli and his sons, weeping silently, considered what to do with the body and whether they should call the mother in, Gustav sent the bullet with which the other pistol was loaded through his brain. This last act of horror robbed the kinsmen of their senses. All their efforts were now turned to him; but the poor unfortunate's skull was completely shattered, with fragments of it clinging to the wall, as he had stuck the pistol right into his mouth. Herr Strömli was the first to get command of himself. For with daylight already shining brightly through the windows, and word being brought in that the Negroes were again to be seen in the courtyard, nothing remained but to think immediately of retreat. The two corpses, which they did not wish to leave behind to the unpredictable mercies of the Negroes, were placed upon a plank, and, reloading their rifles, the grieving column of men set out for the seagull pond. Herr Strömli, with the boy Seppy on his arm, took the lead; the two strongest servants, heaving up the bodies on their shoulders, followed next; the wounded man hobbled behind them on a stick, and Adelbert and Gottfried, with their rifles cocked, marched on either side of the slow-moving funeral cortege. When the Negroes saw how weak the little group was, they rushed out of their huts with spears and pitchforks in their hands and seemed on the point of attacking; but Hoango, whom the party had had the foresight to untie, stepped out onto the stairs of the house and signaled the Negroes to keep back.

"At Sainte Luce," he called to Herr Strömli, who was already passing through the gate with the corpses.

"At Sainte Luce," the latter replied, and the column, unpursued, passed into the open and reached the forest. At the seagull pond, where they found the family, a grave was dug, amid tears and weeping, for the bodies; and after the rings Gustav and Toni wore on their fingers were exchanged, the two were lowered, amid hushed prayers, into the abode of eternal peace. Five days later Herr Strömli, with his wife and children, was fortunate enough to reach Sainte Luce, where he left the two Negro boys behind as he had promised. Arriving at Port-au-Prince shortly before the siege began, he fought on its walls in the cause of the whites; and when the city, after a stubborn defense, fell to General Dessalines, he escaped with the French army aboard the British fleet, after which the family took ship for Europe, reaching their native country, Switzerland, without further incident. There Herr Strömli, with the remainder of his small fortune, brought a piece of property near the Rigi; and even in the year 1807 one could still see, amid the shrubbery of his garden, the monument he had erected to the memory of his nephew, Gustav, and the latter's bride, the faithful Toni.

The Foundling

[THE FOUNDLING]

*A*NTONIO PIACHI, a well-to-do real-estate broker of Rome, found it necessary from time to time to go on lengthy business trips. On such occasions he would leave Elvira, his young wife, behind in the care of her relatives. One of these trips took him and his son Paolo, an eleven-year-old boy by his first wife, to Ragusa. It so happened that a pestilential sickness had just broken out in Ragusa that spread panic through the town and its environs. News of the outbreak first reached Piachi's ears after he was already on his way, and he stopped in the outskirts of the city to make inquiries about it. But when he learned that the sickness was getting worse every day and the city gates might be shut at any moment, concern for his son triumphed over all business considerations and he took horse and carriage and drove away.

He noticed, when he gained the open country, a boy alongside his carriage who held out his hands to him imploringly, apparently in great distress. Piachi had the carriage stop; and when he asked him what he wanted, the boy, in his innocence, replied that he had caught the plague; the bailiffs were on his heels to carry him off to the hospital, where his mother and father had already died; he begged Piachi, in the name of all the saints, to take him along and not leave him to perish in the city. And, catching the old man's hand, he squeezed and kissed it and bathed it with his tears. Piachi, in a first reaction of horror, was about to fling the boy from him; but when the latter changed color at this very instant and sank to the ground in a dead faint, the kind old man's pity was aroused; he and his son got out, lifted the boy into the carriage, and drove on, although he did not have the faintest notion what he was going to do with him.

At the first halting place, in the very act of discussing with the innkeeper and his wife what he should do with the boy, he was arrested by the police, who had got wind of the matter, and was carried back, under guard, to Ragusa with his son and Nicolo (as the sick boy was called). All of Piachi's protestations against the cruelty of this order did no good; in Ragusa the three of them, in the custody of a bailiff, were led off to the hospital, where Piachi himself continued in good health and the boy recovered, but where his son, the eleven-year-old Paolo, catching the infection from Nicolo, died within three days.

The city gates were now thrown open again and Piachi, after burying his son, received permission from the police to leave. Overcome with grief, he had just climbed into the carriage and, seeing the empty seat next to him, taken out his handkerchief to give free vent to his tears, when Nicolo came up to the carriage, cap in hand, and wished him a safe journey. Piachi leaned out of the coach door and asked him, in a voice interrupted by violent sobs, if he would like to come along with him. As soon as the boy understood the old man's question, he nodded his head and said, "Oh yes, very much"; and as the wardens of the hospital, upon the broker's asking whether the lad was free to get in, smiled and assured him that Nicolo was a son of God whom nobody would miss, Piachi swung the boy up into the carriage in one motion and took him along to Rome in his son's place.

On the road outside the city gates, the real-estate broker had his first good look at the boy. He was handsome in an odd, rather impassive way, his black hair falling over his forehead in straight bangs and shading a serious, intelligent face that never changed expression. The old man asked the boy a few questions, to which the latter gave only short replies; taciturn and withdrawn, he sat in the corner with his hands thrust into his trousers pockets and stared in shy absorption at the scenery whirling past the carriage. Occasionally, with a noiseless movement, he drew a handful of nuts out of a pouch he carried and, while Piachi was wiping the tears from his eyes, put them between his teeth and cracked them.

In Rome, Piachi introduced the boy to Elvira, his virtuous young wife, and gave her a short recital of what had taken place; although she could not keep from bursting into tears at the thought of Paolo, her little stepson, whom she had dearly loved, she nevertheless embraced Nicolo, as stiff and strange as he stood before her, showed him to the bed in which Paolo used to sleep, and made him a gift of all the dead boy's clothes. Piachi sent Nicolo to school, where he learned to read, write, and reckon; and as, very understandably, he had grown fond of the boy just because he had cost him so dear, in a few weeks' time he adopted him, with the consent of the good Elvira who could no longer expect to have any children by the old man, as his own son. Later on he dismissed a clerk with whom he had grown dissatisfied for various reasons and had the pleasure of seeing Nicolo, whom he installed in his place in the counting house, manage with expertness and profit the complicated transactions in which he was involved. With Nicolo the father, who was the sworn enemy of all bigotry, found fault in one thing only: his friendship with the friars of the Carmelite monastery, who showed the young man great favor on account of the sizable fortune he was one day expected to inherit from the old man; and the mother, for her part, was concerned only about his rather premature, as it seemed to her, inclination toward the female sex. For already in his fifteenth year, during one of his visits to the friars, he had been seduced by a certain Xaviera Tartini, the Bishop's concubine, and, although he had immediately broken off this liaison on the old man's stern insistence, Elvira had more than one reason to believe that his powers of abstinence in this dangerous quarter were not especially great. But when Nicolo, at the age of twenty, married Constanza Parquet, Elvira's niece, an amiable young girl from Genoa who had been educated in Rome under her supervision, this latter vice, at least, seemed to have been nipped in the bud; both parents were united in their satisfaction with him, and by way of showing this they set him up in a splendid establishment, turning over to him a sizable part of their beautiful and spacious residence. And when Piachi reached his sixtieth birthday, he did the utmost he could for Nicolo: he legally made over to him all the property which was the foundation of his real-estate business, keeping back only a small fund for himself, and with his faithful wife Elvira, whose worldly wants were few, withdrew into retirement.

There was a streak of quiet melancholy in Elvira's spirit that had remained with her from a very affecting incident of her childhood. Philippo Parquet, her father, a prosperous dyer of Genoa, lived, as his craft required, in a house whose back gave directly on the stone-walled edge of the sea; set into the house gable were massive beams that extended several yards over the water and on which the dyed cloth was hung. One unfortunate night, when the house caught fire and all its rooms burst in an instant into flame as if made of pitch and sulphur, the thirteen-year-old Elvira, fleeing from stairway to stairway in terror of the fire raging all around her, found herself, without knowing how she had got there, on one of these beams. Suspended between heaven and earth, the poor child had no idea how to save herself; behind her was the burning gable, whose flames, fanned by the wind, had already begun to eat into the beam, and below her the vast, empty, dreadful sea. She was about to commend herself to the saints and, choosing the lesser of the evils, jump into the water, when all of a sudden a young Genoese from a patrician family appeared at the entrance, flung his cloak across the beam, took her in his arms, and with as much courage as skill slid down one of the lengths of wet cloth hanging from the beam into the water. There were gondolas floating in the harbor that picked the pair up and brought them ashore amid the cheers of the watching crowd; however, the young hero had been struck on the head by a falling stone from one of the cornices while making his way through the burning house, and the bad wound he had got soon made him fall unconscious to the ground. His father, the Marquis, into whose hotel he was carried, called in doctors from all over Italy when his son's recovery was slow in taking place, and he was trepanned a number of times and had several bones removed from his skull; but all the doctors' arts, by the unfathomable decree of Heaven, were in vain; he rallied only infrequently under the hand of Elvira, whom his mother had called in to nurse him, and at the end of three tortured years on a sickbed, during all of which time the girl never left his side, he clasped her hand affectionately one last time and died.

Piachi, who had business dealings with the young nobleman's house and met Elvira there while she was nursing him, married her two years later; he took care never to mention the young man's name in her presence or to remind her of him in any way, for he well knew the violent agitation into which it threw her gentle, sensitive spirit. The slightest allusion, no matter how distant, to the time the young man had suffered and died for her brought a rush of tears to her eyes, after which there was no calming or consoling her; wherever she was, she instantly ran off and nobody tried to follow her, since it had been found that there was nothing for it but to let her quietly cry her grief out by herself. None but Piachi knew the reason for these many strange outbursts, for she never allowed a word about that event to cross her lips as long as she lived. People were accustomed to blame her fits of agitation on a strained nervous system, the result of a high fever into which she had fallen shortly after her marriage, and this put a stop to all inquiry into their cause.

Once Nicolo, without his wife's knowledge, on the pretext of having been invited to a friend's house, went to the carnival with Xaviera Tartini, with whom he had never broken completely in spite of his father's prohibition of the connection, and came home late at night, when all the household lay asleep, dressed in the costume of a Genoese knight which he had chosen quite by chance. Now it so happened that the old man had been seized with a sudden indisposition that night and Elvira, who had got up to help him in the absence of the maidservants, went into the dining room to fetch him a bottle of vinegar. She had just opened a cupboard that stood in the corner and was searching among the bottles and decanters while balancing on the edge of a stool when Nicolo, carrying a candle he had lit in the hall, softly opened the door and, dressed in a plumed hat, cape, and sword, crossed the room. All unconscious of Elvira, he approached the door that led to his bedroom and had just realized with dismay that it was locked when Elvira, behind him, with bottles and glasses in her hand, as if struck by an invisible lightning bolt at the sight of him, fell headlong from the stool to the inlaid floor. Pale with fright, Nicolo spun around and was about to rush to the aid of the unfortunate woman; but since the sound of her fall would undoubtedly bring the old man from his bed, his fear of being scolded triumphed over all other considerations; in nervous haste he snatched the bunch of keys that she wore at her waist and, finding one that fitted, tossed the ring back into the room and disappeared. A few minutes later, when Piachi, sick as he was, had jumped out of bed and lifted Elvira from the floor and servingmen and women hurried up with candles in answer to his ringing, Nicolo too put in an appearance, wearing his dressing gown, and asked what had happened;

but as Elvira was dumb with shock and could not reply, and aside from her there was no one but himself who could have answered the question, the whole incident remained shrouded in the deepest mystery; trembling in every limb, Elvira was put to bed, where she lay ill for several days with a raging fever, but, her natural good health triumphing over the effects of the accident, she made a fairly good recovery, except for a strange melancholy that stayed with her.

A year passed and Nicolo's wife, Constanza, was brought to bed with child and died, together with the infant she had borne. It was enough cause for regret that a virtuous and well-bred woman should perish in this way, but Constanza's death was all the more regrettable as it gave free rein to Nicolo's two passions, his bigotry and his penchant for women. He passed entire days in the cells of the Carmelite friars on the excuse of seeking consolation, although everybody knew that when his wife was alive he had shown her only the scantest love and faithfulness. Indeed, Constanza was not yet in the ground when Elvira entered his room one evening to talk over some matters in connection with the funeral and found a girl there who, with her fripperies and rouged face, was only too well known to her as Xaviera Tartini's lady's maid. Seeing her, Elvira lowered her eyes, turned on her heel without a word, and left the room; neither Piachi nor anybody else learned a word about the matter; all she did was kneel with heavy heart beside the corpse of Constanza, who had loved Nicolo dearly, and weep. But Piachi, who had been in the city, happened to meet the girl as he entered the house and, realizing very well what business had brought her there, angrily went up to her and, half by cunning, half by force, got her to give him the letter she was carrying. He went to his room to read it and, just as he had anticipated, found that it contained an urgent plea from Nicolo to Xaviera to name the time and place for a rendezvous, which he ardently desired. Piachi sat down and, disguising his hand, wrote out an answer in Xaviera's name: "At once, before nightfall, in the Church of St. Magdalene"—sealed the note with a different crest, and had it delivered to Nicolo's room just as if it had come from the lady. The ruse worked perfectly; Nicolo immediately reached for his cloak and left the house without a thought for Constanza laid out in her coffin. Whereupon Piachi, feeling deeply disgraced, cancelled the funeral solemnities appointed for the next day, ordered the corpse to be taken up just as it was by bearers, and silently laid it to rest in the vault prepared for it in St. Magdalene's, with Elvira, himself, and a few relatives as the only mourners. Nicolo, standing in the porch of the church wrapped in his cloak, was astonished to see a funeral procession approaching made up of people whom he knew, and he asked the old man walking behind the coffin what this meant and whom they were carrying. But the latter, without lifting his head from the prayerbook in his hand, only answered, "Xaviera Tartini"—and as if Nicolo were not there the body was uncovered once more, blessed by the bystanders, and then lowered and locked in the vault.

This incident, which humiliated Nicolo deeply, awakened a burning hatred for Elvira in his heart, for he thought he had her to thank for the affront the old man had given him before all the world. For several days Piachi did not speak to him, but, as Nicolo needed the old man's favor and support in the matter of Constanza's estate, he saw no choice for himself but to catch hold of his hand one evening and promise him, with a look of contrition, to part from Xaviera once and for all. But he had small intention of keeping his promise; on the contrary, the coldness with which he was met only increased his defiance and schooled him in the art of eluding the honest old man's observation. At the same time, Elvira had never seemed more beautiful to him than at the moment when, to his undoing, she had opened the door to his room and, discovering the girl there, shut it again. The warm blush of indignation that spread over her cheeks had lent an infinite grace to her gentle and generally placid face; it seemed incredible to him that, with all the temptations that offered, she did not herself occasionally stray along the path for the plucking of whose flowers he had just been so ignominiously punished by her. He burned with the desire to serve her with the old man, if this were so, as she had served him, and looked and longed for nothing better than an opportunity to carry out this design.

Once when Piachi happened to be out of the house Nicolo was passing by Elvira's room and was surprised to hear someone speaking inside. Seized with a sudden malicious hope, he stooped down with eyes and ears to the keyhole and—good heavens, what did he see? There she knelt, in an attitude of ecstasy, at someone's feet, and though he could not see who it was he distinctly heard her whisper lovingly the word: "Colino." With a pounding heart he stepped into the corridor window, from where he could observe the entrance to her room without seeming to do so; and he was already thinking, at the faint sound of the unbolting of the door, that the priceless moment had arrived in which he would unmask the hypocritical woman when, instead of the stranger he expected, Elvira herself emerged from the room, quite alone, and looked across the distance at him with a quite indifferent and quiet glance. Under her arm she carried a piece of linen woven by herself; and after locking the door with a key that she took from her waist, she walked calmly down the stairs with her hand on the banister. Such dissimulation, such apparent indifference, seemed to him the height of brazenness and cunning, and, as soon as she was out of sight, he ran to fetch a master key and, after looking furtively around to make sure that nobody was watching, stealthily opened the door to her chamber. But he was flabbergasted to find the room entirely empty, and all his peering into every corner discovered nothing even remotely resembling a man except the life-size portrait of a young knight, illuminated by a candle of its own, behind a red silk curtain in a niche in the wall. Nicolo felt afraid, why he did not know himself, as he stood opposite the portrait with its large eyes staring fixedly at him, and a crowd of thoughts jostled in his mind; but before he was able to put them into some kind of order, he grew alarmed that Elvira would discover him there and punish him, so he locked the door again, feeling more than a little perplexed, and went away.

The more he thought about this strange occurrence, the more important the painting he had discovered seemed to him and the more tormenting and burning grew his curiosity to find out whom the painting was a portrait of. For he had seen her figure, in clear outline, on its knees, and he was convinced that the person she had been kneeling before was the young knight on the canvas. His mind possessed by these restless thoughts, he went to Xaviera Tartini and described to her the astonishing scene he had witnessed. The latter, who shared Nicolo's eagerness to ruin Elvira because she blamed her for all the obstacles in the way of their intercourse, expressed a wish to see the portrait hanging in Elvira's chamber. For she boasted a large acquaintance among the Italian nobility and felt reasonably certain that if the man in question had ever been in Rome and was of any standing at all, she would know him. And soon, as luck would have it, Piachi and his wife, who had occasion to visit a relative, went off to the country on a Sunday; the minute Nicolo knew the coast was clear, he sped to Xaviera and conducted her and her little daughter, whom she had had by the Cardinal, into Elvira's room, pretending she was a strange lady come to admire the paintings and embroidery. But imagine Nicolo's confusion when little Clara (as the daughter was called), as soon as he raised the curtain, exclaimed, "My God! Who else is it but you, Signor Nicolo?" Xaviera was dumbfounded. And, indeed, the more she looked at the portrait, the more striking seemed its likeness to Nicolo, especially when she imagined him, as it was easy for her to do, in the knight's costume he had worn a few months ago when he had secretly escorted her to the carnival. Nicolo tried to cover with a joke the sudden blush that colored his cheeks; kissing the little girl, he said, "Really, my darling Clara, the portrait resembles me as much as you resemble the person who thinks he is your father!" But Xaviera, in whom bitter feelings of jealousy had already begun to stir, looked sharply at him;

walking over to the mirror, she said that, after all, it didn't really matter who the person was; nodded goodbye rather coldly, and left the room.

No sooner was Xaviera gone, than Nicolo fell into a fever of excitement. Exultantly he recalled the violent effect his fantastic appearance had had on Elvira that night. The thought of having awakened the passion of this woman who was regarded as the model of virtue flattered his vanity almost as much as it excited his wish to be revenged on her; and since the prospect was now opened to him of satisfying both his desires at one stroke, he impatiently awaited Elvira's return and the moment when a look into her eyes would crown his supposition with certainty. The ecstasy that possessed him was disturbed only by his distinct recollection of having heard Elvira, that time when he had listened through the keyhole, address the portrait before which she knelt by the name of Colino; but even in the sound of this name, which was an uncommon one for that part of the country, there seemed to echo things that started his heart, he did not know why, to dreaming, and when faced with the alternative of doubting one or the other of his senses, his eyes or his ears, he naturally tended to believe the one most flattering to his desires.

Meanwhile, several more days passed before Elvira returned from the country, and, since she brought back with her from the cousin's house where she had visited, a young kinswoman who wished to see the sights of Rome, her attention was so taken up with civilities toward her guest that she gave Nicolo only a fleeting, meaningless glance when, with the utmost friendliness, he handed her out of the coach. Several weeks devoted entirely to the visitor passed in an excitement unusual for the Piachi house; they visited all the places inside and outside the city that might interest a young and lively girl; and Nicolo, who was never invited to join these little excursions because of his duties in the counting house, fell back again into his evil temper toward Elvira. Again he began to brood, with the bitterest and most tortured feelings, about the stranger she idolized in secret; and these emotions tore at his brutalized heart with particular violence on the evening following the young kinswoman's departure, which he had so longingly awaited, when Elvira, instead of talking to him at last, sat for a whole hour at the dining table, silently absorbed in a piece of delicate feminine handiwork. It so happened that Piachi, a few days earlier, had asked about a box of little ivory letters that had been used for teaching Nicolo when he was a boy, and the old man, now that nobody needed them any longer, had thought of making a present of to a little child in the neighborhood. But the maid who was asked to hunt them out from among a lot of old things had found only the six letters making up Nicolo's name; no doubt the other letters, because they had meant less to the boy, had not been kept so carefully and had been thrown away at one time or another. As Nicolo now picked up the letters, which had been lying on the table for several days, and, with his arm resting on the table top, idly toyed with them, his mind full of gloomy reflections, he discovered—quite by accident for even he was surprised as never before in his life—the combination that spelled the name Colino. Nicolo, who had never known his name possessed this anagrammatic property, was again filled with wild hopes, and darted a hesitant, covert glance at Elvira sitting next to him. The correspondence he had discovered between the two names seemed to him more than a coincidence; with suppressed joy he weighed the implications of this strange discovery and, lowering his hands from the table, he waited with a beating heart for the moment when Elvira would look up and notice the name openly spread on the table top. Nor were his hopes in any way deceived; for no sooner had Elvira paused a moment in her work, noticed the letters arranged upon the table, and bent forward innocently to read them (for she was a little nearsighted), than she swept Nicolo's face, who was looking down at them with apparent indifference, with a strangely troubled glance, picked up her work again with indescribable sadness, while a soft blush spread across her cheeks, and, thinking herself unobserved, let one tear after another fall into her lap. Nicolo, who had watched all this out of the corner of his eye, now felt no doubt at all that it was his own name which lay hidden for her under the transposed letters. He saw her gently push the ivory letters into a heap, and his mad hopes reached the peak of confidence when she stood up, put her work down, and vanished into her bedroom. He was about to get up and follow her there when Piachi came in and asked a housemaid where Elvira was; she answered that she was not feeling well and had lain down on her bed. Piachi, without showing any particular alarm, turned around and went to see how she was getting on; and when he came back a quarter of an hour later and vouchsafed no more than that Elvira would not be coming to the dinner table, Nicolo thought he had at last discovered the key to all the puzzling scenes of this kind that he had witnessed.

Next morning, while he was busy considering, in his unholy elation, how he might hope to take advantage of this discovery, a note arrived from Xaviera asking him to come and see her, as she had something to tell him about Elvira that would interest him. Through the Bishop who kept her, Xaviera had very close connections with the friars of the Carmelite monastery; and since his mother went to confession at this monastery, he felt sure Xaviera had managed to get hold of some information about the secret history of his mother's feelings that would confirm his unnatural hopes. But after being greeted with a strange roguishness by Xaviera, he was most disagreeably tumbled out of his bed of dreams when she drew him down with a smile on the divan where she was sitting and said that she only wanted to tell him that the object of Elvira's adoration was somebody who had been dead and buried for the last twelve years—Aloysius, Marquis of Montferrat (surnamed Collin by an uncle in Paris to whom he had been sent for his education, which name was later jokingly changed to Colino in Italy), was the original of the portrait he had found behind the red silk curtain in the niche in

Elvira's bedroom: the young Genoese knight who had so gallantly rescued her from the fire when she was a child and died from the injuries he had got while doing so. Xaviera added that all she asked of him was that he should not repeat the confidence, as it had been whispered to her in the monastery under the seal of absolute secrecy by someone who himself had no right to divulge it. Nicolo, turning red and white by turns, assured her she had nothing to fear; and, quite unable to hide from Xaviera's teasing looks the embarrassment into which this disclosure had thrown him, he pleaded the excuse of pressing business, picked up his hat with an ugly twitch of his upper lip, said goodbye, and left.

Shame, lust, and the thirst for revenge now joined in hatching the vilest deed ever perpetrated. He felt sure that he could get at Elvira's spotless soul only by a trick; and the instant Piachi went off to the country for a few days and left him a clear field, he set about the execution of the satanic plan he had contrived. He provided himself with the very same costume in which he had appeared to Elvira that night a few months ago when he had come back secretly from the carnival; and wearing the cloak, collar, and plumed hat of Genoese cut just as the portrait showed, he slipped into Elvira's bedroom, covered the picture in the niche with a black cloth, and, taking a staff in his hand and striking the very same pose as that in which the young patrician was portrayed, awaited Elvira's adoration. In the shrewdness of his unholy desire he had calculated quite correctly; for a few minutes later Elvira entered the room, undressed in placid silence, and drew back, as she was accustomed to do, the silk curtain covering the niche—which no sooner had she done and perceived him standing there than she cried, "Colino, my love!" and fell in a dead faint to the floor. Nicolo emerged from the niche; he paused for a moment, absorbed in her charms, and gazed at the fragile figure that was rapidly turning pale under the kiss of death; but, as there was no time to lose, he picked her up in his arms and, snatching the black cloth from the painting, carried her over to the bed in the corner of the room. Then he went to bolt the door, but found it already locked; and feeling sure that even after she came to her senses she would offer no resistance to the phantasmal, apparently supernatural apparition, he went back to the bed and tried to wake her with burning kisses on her bosom and lips. Yet the Nemesis that treads hard on the heels of a wicked deed decreed that Piachi, whom the wretch believed away and gone for several days, should return home unexpectedly at this very minute; thinking Elvira already asleep, he tiptoed softly down the corridor and was able to enter her room, whose key he always carried with him, without a sound. Nicolo stood up thunderstruck; but as there was no way to hide his villainy, he could only throw himself at the old man's feet and, swearing he would never again lift his eyes to his wife, beg his forgiveness. And in fact Piachi, too, was inclined to end the whole thing as quietly as possible; struck speechless by a few words from Elvira, who cast a look of horror at the wretch when she recovered consciousness in the old man's arms, he merely took a whip down from the wall and, drawing shut the curtains of the bed on which she lay, opened the door and gestured to Nicolo to get out that instant. But no sooner did the latter see that nothing was to be gained by a show of contrition than he jumped up from the floor and announced, in a manner that would have done honor to Tartuffe, that the old man was the one who would have to get out of the house: he had documents that showed conclusively that he was the owner, and he would defend his rights against anybody and everybody in the world.

Piachi could not believe his ears; as if disarmed by such unheard-of insolence he put down the whip, took his hat and stick, went directly to his old lawyer friend Dr. Valerio, rang until a maid came and opened the door, and, when he reached his friend's room, before he was able to utter a word, he collapsed unconscious on the bed. The doctor, who took him, and later on Elvira as well, into his house, hurried out the first thing the next morning to have the hellish villain arrested. But the latter had a number of advantages on his side; and while Piachi was straining every nerve in a vain attempt to dispossess him of the property he had made over to him, Nicolo had already flown to his friends, the Carmelite friars, with the deeds and asked them to protect him against the old fool who wanted to turn him out of everything. In short, as Nicolo agreed to marry Xaviera, whom the Bishop wished off his hands, wickedness triumphed and the government, upon the priest's intervention, issued a decree confirming Nicolo in his possession and commanding Piachi to cease from troubling him about it.

Just the day before, Piachi had buried the unfortunate Elvira, who had died from the effects of a high fever brought on by the episode. Maddened by this double grief, he put the decree in his pocket, went to the house, and, with the strength that rage lent him, threw Nicolo, who was the naturally weaker one, to the floor and dashed his brains out against the wall. The deed was done before the people in the house knew he was there; when they found him, he was holding Nicolo between his knees and stuffing the decree down his throat. After which he got up and surrendered all his arms; he was put in jail, tried, and condemned to be hanged by the neck until dead.

In the Papal States there is a law forbidding a criminal to be executed without his first receiving absolution. Piachi, after he was condemned to death, obstinately refused absolution. After every means that religion offers had been tried without success to make him feel the heinousness of his offense, it was hoped that the sight of the death in store for him might frighten him into a feeling of remorse and he was led out to the gallows. On one side stood a priest who, with the voice of the last trumpet, depicted all the terrors of that hell whither his soul was about to depart; on the other side another, with the Body of Christ, the holy means of atonement, in his hand, extolled to him the abode of eternal peace.

"Do you wish to share in the blessings of redemption?" both demanded. "Do you wish to receive the Holy Communion?"

"No," Piachi answered.

"Why not?"

"I don't want to be saved. I want to go down to the lowest pit of hell. I want to find Nicolo again, who won't be in heaven, and take up my revenge again, which I could only satisfy partly here!" And with these words he climbed the ladder and told the hangman to do his duty. In short, they saw nothing for it but to stop the execution and take the unfortunate man, whom the law protected, back to prison. On three successive days the same attempt was made, and always with the same result. When, on the third day, he again had to come down the ladder without having been hanged, he raised his hands up in a fierce gesture and cursed the inhuman law that kept him from going to hell. He summoned all the host of devils to come and fetch him, swore his only wish was to be executed and damned, and promised he would take the first priest that came along by the throat just so he could lay his hands on Nicolo again in hell!

When this was reported to the Pope, he gave orders for him to be executed without absolution; unaccompanied by any priest, he was hanged, very quietly, in the Piazza del Popolo.

The Earthquake in Chile

$\mathcal{I}$N Santiago, the capital of the
kingdom of Chile, at the very moment of the great earthquake
of 1647 in which many thousands of lives were lost, a young
Spaniard by the name of Jeronimo Rugera, who had been locked
up on a criminal charge, was standing against a prison pillar,
about to hang himself. A year or so before, Don Henrico Asteron,
one of the richest noblemen of the city, had turned him out of his
house, where he had been employed as a tutor, for falling in love with
Donna Josepha, Don Henrico's only daughter. A secret rendezvous,
held in defiance of the old man's express warning, and betrayed
through the malevolent watchfulness of his proud son, made Don
Henrico so angry that he sent his daughter away to the Carmelite
convent of Our Lady of the Mountain. But, thanks to a lucky chance,
Jeronimo was able to renew the attachment there and make the con-

251

vent garden, one dark night, the scene of his perfect bliss. It was on
Corpus Christi Day, and the solemn procession of nuns, followed by
the novices, was just starting out when the unfortunate Josepha, as
the bells were pealing all around her, collapsed on the cathedral steps
in the pangs of childbirth. This event caused a great outcry; the young
sinner, without any attention being paid to her condition, was
straightway imprisoned, and no sooner had she got up out of
childbed than the Archbishop ordered her to be put on trial for her
life. The scandal was talked about with such bitterness in the city, and
the convent in which it had occurred was criticized so severely, that
neither the pleas of the Asteron family nor even the wish of the
Abbess herself, who had grown fond of the young girl because of
her otherwise irreproachable behavior, could mitigate the harsh
punishment with which she was threatened by conventual law. The
only thing they could do was to get the Viceroy to commute her
sentence of being burned at the stake to one of beheading, much to
the indignation of the matrons and virgins of Santiago. Windows
were rented out along the route the sinner would follow to her execution, roofs were lifted off, and the pious daughters of the city
invited all their friends to join them in watching the spectacle offered
the divine wrath. Meanwhile Jeronimo, who had been imprisoned
too, nearly went out of his mind when he learned about the monstrous turn events had taken. He racked his brains in vain for a way
to save her; everywhere his most audacious flights of thought bore
him he ran into bolts and walls, and an attempt to file through
the bars of his prison window only got him, when it was discovered, more closely confined. He prostrated himself before an image
of the Holy Mother and with boundless fervor prayed to her from
whom alone salvation now could come. But the dreadful day arrived, and with it the conviction that his situation was utterly hopeless. When he heard the air ring with the bells that accompanied
Josepha's march to the scaffold, despair overwhelmed his soul.
Life now seemed hateful to him and he made up his mind to hang

himself with a rope that he found in his cell. Just as he was standing next to a wall pillar, as we have said, tying the rope that was to snatch him from this wretched world to an iron bracket in the cornice, the greater part of the city suddenly collapsed with a roar, as if the firmament had given way, burying every living thing in its ruins. Jeronimo Rugera went rigid with terror; and, as if all his awareness of things had been destroyed, he now clung to the very pillar on which he had meant to die, to keep himself from falling. The ground swayed under his feet, great cracks suddenly appeared in all the prison walls, and the whole building leaned forward and would have come crashing down into the street if the building opposite had not fallen forward at the same time so that the two met and by a fluke formed a kind of arch over the street that saved it from being completely leveled. Shaking uncontrollably, his hair standing on end and his knees nearly buckling under him, Jeronimo slid down the steeply slanting floor to the hole driven into the prison's front wall by the coming together of the two buildings. No sooner was he in the clear when a second tremor of the earth caused the already shattered street to collapse completely. Unnerved and at a loss as to how to save himself from the general destruction, he scrambled over rubble and beams, while death snatched at him from every side, toward one of the nearest city gates. Here another house crashed down, hurtling wreckage all around, and drove him into a neighboring street; here the flames were licking out of all the gables, flashing brightly through the clouds of smoke, and frightened him into another; here the Mapocho River, heaved out of its bed, bore down upon him in a flood and swept him with a roar into a third street. Here lay a heap of dead bodies, here a voice still groaned beneath the rubble, here people screamed from burning rooftops, here men and animals battled against the waves, here a brave man tried to rescue others; here another man, pale as death, mutely stretched his trembling hands to heaven. When Jeronimo had passed through the gate and climbed a hill outside, he sank to the ground unconscious. He lay there for a quarter of an hour and more, in a deep swoon, before he finally awoke and pushed himself up on his knees, with his back to the city. He felt his forehead and chest, not knowing what to make of the state he was in, and an unutterable feeling of bliss possessed him when a west wind from the sea blew on the life stirring in him again and his eyes looked out on Santiago's flowering countryside. Only the bewildered crowds of people that he noticed everywhere made him feel uneasy; he could not understand what had brought him and them to this place, and only when he turned around and saw the prostrate city behind him did he remember the terrible time that he had just gone through. He stooped so low that his forehead touched the ground and thanked God for his miraculous escape; and just as if the last dreadful experience had effaced the recollection of everything before, he wept for joy that all the sweetness and vivid show of life should still be his. But, catching sight of a ring on his finger, he suddenly remembered Josepha, and, with her, his imprisonment, the bells he had heard in his cell, and the moment just before the collapse of the prison. A deep feeling of grief gripped him again; he began to regret his prayer of gratitude, and terrible to him seemed the being who ruled from above the clouds. Jeronimo went down among the people who, busy saving whatever they could of their possessions, were streaming out of the gates, and ventured to ask them, very fearfully, about Asteron's daughter and whether she had been executed; but nobody was able to tell him anything very definite. A woman who was bent almost to the ground under the immense load of household goods on her neck, as well as the two children she carried at her breast, said as she went by, as if she had seen it with her own eyes, that Josepha had been beheaded. Jeronimo turned back; he could not doubt, when he calculated the time, that the execution had been carried out before the earthquake struck; and he sat down in a solitary wood and gave way to his grief. He hoped that all of nature's destructive force would fall upon him anew. He did not understand why death, which his despairing soul craved, should have eluded him just when it seemed to be offering him deliverance of its own accord from every side. He was determined not to flinch and run if even now the oak trees were uprooted and their tops came crashing down on him. But when the torrent of his grief had at last subsided and hope returned to him amid his burning tears, he got up again and tramped the fields in every direction. He visited every hilltop on which people had gathered; he followed all the roads along which the streams of fugitives were still flowing; wherever a woman's dress blew in the wind, there his trembling limbs carried him, but none covered Asteron's beloved daughter. The sun was already beginning to set, and all his hopes with it, when he came to the edge of a cliff, and a view into a broad valley, with just a soul here and there in it, was disclosed to him. His glance strayed over the solitary groups of figures as he hesitated about what to do next, and he was on the point of turning away when he suddenly noticed a young woman bathing an infant at the spring that watered the ravine. His heart jumped at this sight, he sprang down over the rocks full of hope, crying, "Holy Mother of God!" and recognized Josepha when she looked timidly around at the sound. How they hugged each other, with what bliss, the unhappy pair snatched from destruction by a miracle of heaven! Josepha, on her death march, had almost reached the place of execution when the sudden crashing down of the buildings scattered the entire procession. Her first terrified steps took her toward the nearest gate; but soon recovering herself, she turned and ran back to the convent where she had left her helpless little boy. She found the whole place already in flames, and the Abbess, who during the moments which were to have been Josepha's last ones had promised to take care of the infant, was standing at the door shouting for help to save him. Josepha plunged fearlessly through the smoke billowing out of the already collapsing building and soon afterwards emerged unharmed from the portal again, with the boy in her arms, just as if all the angels of heaven were watching over her. She was about to fall into the arms of the Abbess, who had thrown her hands up in amazement, when the latter, together with almost all her nuns, was killed by a falling gable. Josepha recoiled from the dreadful sight; hurriedly she closed the Abbess's eyes and, full of terror, fled with the precious infant, whom heaven had returned to her arms, to save him from the destruction. She had only gone a few steps when she encountered the battered corpse of the Archbishop, which had just been dragged out from under the wreckage of the cathedral. The Viceroy's palace was a heap of rubble, the courthouse in which she had been sentenced was in flames, and on the spot where her father's house had stood there was now a lake whose boiling waters sent up reddish clouds of steam. Josepha mustered all her strength to hold on. Putting aside her feelings of distress, she walked bravely through street after street with her prize in her arms, and was already nearing the city gate when she came upon the ruins of the prison in which Jeronimo had suffered. She tottered at the sight of it and would have fallen in a corner in a faint; but just then a building that had been rocked to its foundations by the quakes collapsed behind her and drove her on again, terror lending her new strength; she kissed her child, wiped the tears from her eyes and, disregarding the horrors all around her, reached the gate. Once out in the open country, it soon became apparent to her that not everybody who had lived in a wrecked building must inevitably have died in its ruins. At the next crossroads she stopped and waited to see if the one who was dearest to her in the world after her little Philip would come along. But when there was no sign of him, and the press of people grew, she journeyed on, then turned back and waited again; and finally, shedding many tears, she crept into a dusky pine-shaded valley to pray for his soul, which she believed had taken leave of this world; and found him here, her love, in this valley, and such bliss as made it seem like Eden. All this she now told Jeronimo, in a voice choked with emotion, and when her story was done she handed him the boy to kiss.

Jeronimo took him in his arms and petted him with a father's inexpressible delight, and, when his stranger's face made the infant cry, he stopped his mouth with endless kisses. Meanwhile such a night had fallen as only a poet could imagine, rich with a marvelous, mild fragrance, all silvery and still. Everywhere along the valley stream people had dropped down in the shimmering moonlight and were heaping soft beds for themselves of moss and leafy branches, to rest in after their harrowing day. And since the poor unfortunates were still lamenting what they had lost—one his house, another his wife and child, and a third the loss of everything—Jeronimo and Josepha crept away to where the woods were thicker lest the secret jubilation in their souls give pain to anyone. They found a marvelous pomegranate tree, with spreading branches full of fragrant fruit; and in its top the nightingale sang its sensual music. Jeronimo sat down with his back against the trunk, with Josepha in his lap and Philip in hers, and his cloak around them all; and there they sat and rested. The checkered light and shade of the tree danced across them and the moon was already paling in the rosy dawn before they fell asleep. For there was no end of things they had to tell each other, about the convent and the prison and what they had suffered for each other's sake; and they felt it keenly when they thought of how much woe the world must suffer so that they should find their happiness! They made up their minds, as soon as the last quakes were over, to go to Concepción where Josepha had a close friend from whom they might hope to borrow a small sum with which to embark for Spain, where Jeronimo's relatives on his mother's side lived, and there they would live happily to the end of their lives. After this, and after many kisses, they fell asleep.

When they awoke the sun was already high in the sky, and not far off they noticed several families busy around a fire, getting a little breakfast for themselves. Jeronimo was just thinking how to get some food for his own family when a well-dressed young man with an infant in his arms came up to Josepha and diffidently asked her whether she would not give her breast to the poor little thing for a while, as the mother was lying injured under the trees over there. Josepha betrayed some confusion as she recognized him for somebody she knew; but when, misinterpreting her embarrassment, he continued, "It will only be for a little while, Donna Josepha— the child has had nothing since the hour that has made us all un- happy," she said, "I didn't answer for another reason, Don Fer- nando; in times like these no one refuses to share whatever he has with others"; and, taking the little stranger from him, while she handed her own child to its father, she gave him her breast. Don Fernando was very thankful for this kindness and asked them if they would not care to join his people at the fire, where they were just getting a little breakfast ready. Josepha said that she would be delighted to, and as Jeronimo had no objection, she followed Don Fernando to his family, where she was welcomed with the utmost cordiality and affection by his two sisters-in-law, whom she knew for very respectable young ladies. Donna Elvira, Don Fernando's wife, whose feet were badly injured, was lying on the ground; she drew Josepha down beside her with great friendliness when she saw her own drooping boy at her breast. Don Pedro, his father-in-law, who had a shoulder wound, also gave her an amiable nod.

Strange thoughts now began to stir in Jeronimo's and Josepha's breast. When they saw themselves received with so much confidence and kindness, they did not know what to think about the past, the execution block, the prison, and the bells, and whether they had only dreamed it all. A universal reconciliation seemed to have fol- lowed the terrible stroke that had fallen on them all. No one seemed able to go farther back in his memory than to the earthquake. Only Donna Elizabeth, who had been invited by a friend to yesterday morning's spectacle, but had refused, occasionally allowed her glance to rest dreamily on Josepha; but the account of some new hideous misfortune soon recalled her briefly strayed attention to the present. Stories were told of how, immediately after the first main quake, the city had been crowded with women who gave birth right under the eyes of all the men; how monks with crucifixes in their hands had rushed wildly up and down screaming that the end of the world had come, and how a guard who had commanded everybody to leave a church at the Viceroy's order, got for answer the shout that there was no Viceroy in Chile any more; how the Viceroy, when the disorder was at its height, had had to put up a gallows to stop the looting; and how an innocent man, escaping out of the back of a burning building, had been seized by the owner, who did not stop to ask any questions, and immediately lynched. Donna Elvira, whose wounds Josepha was busy tending, used a moment when the stories were flying back and forth at their quickest to ask her what had happened to her on that terrible day. And when Josepha, with a heavy heart, told her some of the most important things, she was intensely pleased to see tears start into the lady's eyes; Donna Elvira caught hold of her hand and squeezed it, and signed to her to say no more. Josepha felt as if she were among the blessed. Try as she might, she could not help thinking that the preceding day, in spite of all the woe it had brought into the world, had been a blessing such as heaven had never vouchsafed her before. And indeed, at the very moment when all of men's earthly possessions had perished and even nature was threatened with being overwhelmed, the human spirit itself seemed to spring up like a lovely flower. In the fields, as far as the eye could see, people of all classes were jumbled together, princes and paupers, gentlewomen and peasant girls, state officials and day laborers, monks and nuns, commiserating with one another, helping one another, gladly sharing whatever they might have saved to keep themselves alive, as if the general disaster had united all the survivors into a single family.

Instead of the empty chatter for which the world of tea tables used to furnish the subject matter, examples of prodigious deeds were now related: people whom one had hardly noticed in society had displayed a Roman virtue; examples without number of fearlessness, of cheerful contempt for danger, of self-denial and godlike self-sacrifice, of lives being thrown away, like some paltry little possession one could pick up again a few steps later on, without an instant's hesitation. Indeed, since there was not a soul on that day to whom something heart-stirring had not happened or who had not himself done some generous deed, the anguish in everybody's breast was mixed with so much sweet delight that it was impossible to decide, as she thought, whether the sum of general happiness had not increased on one side by as much as it had declined on the other. Taking Josepha by the arm after they had both exhausted this theme in silent reflection, Jeronimo walked up and down with her, in a mood of inexpressible elation, in the shade of the pomegranate trees. He told her that the generous temper of mind that they saw everywhere, together with the revolution in social relations, had persuaded him to give up his purpose of sailing for Europe, that he would take the chance of going to see the Viceroy (if he were still alive) and throwing himself at his feet, for he had always been favorably disposed toward his case, and that he hoped (and here he gave her a kiss) to remain with her in Chile. Josepha said that she had been having similar thoughts; that if her father still lived she no longer doubted her becoming reconciled with him; but that she felt it would be better for them to go to Concepción and from there appeal in writing to the Viceroy, rather than for Jeronimo to go and throw himself at his feet, since they would have the harbor near them at Concepción if worst came to worst, but that if all went well and their case took the direction they wished it to, they could easily return to Santiago. After a moment's reflection, Jeronimo applauded her prudence, strolled with her about the paths a little more while looking forward to their future happiness, and rejoined their friends.

Meanwhile the afternoon had arrived bringing an abatement of the earth shocks, so that the swarming refugees were a little easier in their minds, when the news spread that the Abbot of the monastery himself was going to read a solemn Mass in the Church of the Dominicans, the only one the earthquake had spared, imploring heaven to shield them against further calamities. From every region people were setting out and streaming into the city as fast as possible. In Don Fernando's group the question came up as to whether they should not join the throng, too, and attend the ceremony. Donna Elizabeth reminded them with some uneasiness of the trouble there had been in the church the day before; that many more such thanksgiving celebrations would be held; and that when the danger had receded more into the past, they would be able to give gladder and serener expression to their gratitude. Josepha leaped enthusiastically to her feet and said that the wish to bow her face in the dust before her Maker had never been so strong in her as now, when He had given such proof of His unfathomable and supernal power. Donna Elvira emphatically endorsed Josepha's view. She absolutely insisted on their hearing the Mass, and called on Don Fernando to lead them to the church, whereupon everybody, not excepting Donna Elizabeth, rose from his seat. But seeing how violently her breast was heaving and how hesitant she was about getting ready to go, they asked her what was wrong; she could not understand why, she said, she had such a deep foreboding of disaster. Donna Elizabeth then suggested that she should stay behind with her sick father and herself, and spoke reassuringly to her. Josepha said, "Since you are staying here, Donna Elizabeth, perhaps you will take this little darling off my hands, who, as you see, has crept back into my bosom again."

"Gladly," Donna Elizabeth answered and put her arms out for him; but when the infant wailed plaintively at the wrong being done to him and refused to be handed over, Josepha smiled and said that it looked as if she would have to keep him, and hushed him with kisses. Don Fernando, who was charmed by the dignity and grace of her demeanor, offered her his arm; Jeronimo, carrying little Philip, conducted Donna Constanza; the other members of the company followed after; and in this order they set off toward the city. They had hardly gone fifty steps when they heard Donna Elizabeth, who meanwhile had been speaking aside to Donna Elvira with great concentration, call out, "Don Fernando!" and saw her hurry after them with anxious steps. Don Fernando halted and turned; waited for her without letting go of Josepha's arm; and, when she stopped some ways off as if expecting him to come to her, asked her what she wanted. Donna Elizabeth then came closer, although apparently with some reluctance, and murmured in his ear so that Josepha could not hear her. "Well," said Don Fernando, "and where would be the harm in that?" Donna Elizabeth continued to whisper in his ear with a distraught look on her face. Don Fernando reddened with displeasure and said that that would do! Donna Elvira could put her mind at rest; and he went on with Josepha.

When they reached the Church of the Dominicans, the sonorous splendor of the organ could already be heard and a huge multitude swayed beneath the roof. The crowd overflowed the portal of the church far out into the square, and high up on the cathedral walls boys were clinging to the picture frames and squeezing their caps in their hands with looks of intense expectation. The chandeliers shed a brilliant light, the pillars cast mysterious shadows in the falling dusk, the great rose window of stained glass at the far end of the church glowed like the very evening sun by which it was illuminated; and when the organ left off playing, silence fell upon the whole assembly, as if no one there could make a sound. Never did the flame of devotion leap more brightly toward heaven from a Christian cathedral than from the Dominican church of Santiago that day; and nobody's breast fed it with warmer fervor than Jeronimo's and

Josepha's! The solemnity began with a sermon preached from the pulpit by one of the oldest canons of the church, attired in all his regalia. His trembling hands reaching toward heaven out of the flowing sleeves of his surplice, he began by giving praise and thanks that there were still men in this part of the world, which was collapsing into ruins, who were capable of lifting up their stammering voices to God. He described what, at a signal from the Almighty, had happened; Judgment Day could not be more fearful; and when he pointed to a crack in the cathedral wall and called yesterday's earthquake a mere herald of that coming time, a shudder ran through the entire congregation. His flow of priestly eloquence carried him on to the moral corruption of the city; he castigated it for abominations such as Sodom and Gomorrah had never known; and he ascribed it only to God's infinite forbearance that the city had not been wiped off the face of the earth. But the hearts of our two unfortunates, already lacerated by this sermon, were stabbed as if by a sword when the canon seized the occasion to describe in detail the outrage that had been perpetrated in the convent garden of the Carmelites; called the tolerant attitude the world took toward it a piece of godlessness; and in an aside loaded with maledictions against the two miscreants, whom he named aloud, he consigned their souls to all the princes of hell! Donna Constanza tugged Jeronimo's arm and cried, "Don Fernando!" The latter, however, putting as much emphasis as could be combined with stealth into his reply, said, "Keep absolutely quiet, Donna, don't even blink your eyes, and make believe you have fainted; then we'll leave the church." But before Donna Constanza could carry out this clever ruse, a voice broke loudly into the canon's discourse: "Stand back, citizens of Santiago, the godless creatures are right here!"

"Where?" cried another voice, full of fear, a circle of dread spreading around it; a third man answered, "Here!" and, full of pious brutality, pulled Josepha by the hair, so that she would have fallen to the ground with Don Fernando's son if the latter had not held her up.

"Are you out of your mind?" the young man cried, putting his arm around Josepha. "I am Don Fernando Ormez, son of the Commandant of the city, whom you all know."

"Don Fernando Ormez?" a shoemaker standing right in front of him called out, a man who had done work for Josepha and knew her at least as well as he knew her tiny feet. "Who is this child's father?" and he turned with insolent defiance to Asteron's daughter. Don Fernando turned pale at this question. First he looked hesitantly at Jeronimo, then around the congregation to see if there were anybody there who knew him. The terrible situation that had arisen forced Josepha to call out, "This isn't my child, Master Pedrillo, as you imagine," and she looked at Don Fernando with immense fear in her soul. "This young man is Don Fernando Ormez, son of the Commandant of the city, whom you all know!"

The shoemaker asked, "Citizens, who among you knows this young man?" And several of those standing nearby repeated, "Who here knows Jeronimo Rugera? Let him come forward!" Now just at this moment little Juan, frightened by the noise, leaned out of Josepha's arms and stretched his hands toward Don Fernando. "He is too the father!" a voice yelled; "He is Jeronimo Rugera!" screamed another; "These are the blaspheming sinners!" a third—"Stone them! Stone them!" all the Christians assembled in the temple of Jesus roared.

Upon which Jeronimo: "Stop, you monsters! If you are looking for Jeronimo Rugera, here he is! Let that man go, he is innocent!" The enraged mob, confused by what Jeronimo had shouted, did not know what to do; several hands fell away from Don Fernando; and when a naval officer of high rank came running up at that moment, calling out, "Don Fernando Ormez! What has happened to you?" as he pressed through the tumultous crowd, Don Fernando, now entirely set free, responded with truly heroic presence of mind,

"Just look at them, those murderers, Don Alonzo! I would have been lost if this good man here had not pretended to be Jeronimo Rugera, to quiet the raging mob. Would you be good enough to arrest him, and also this young lady, for their own safety; and also this wretch here," and he seized Master Pedrillo, "who started the whole commotion!"

The shoemaker called out, "Don Alonzo Onoreja, I ask you on your conscience, isn't this girl Josepha Asteron?" When Don Alonzo, who knew Josepha quite well, hesitated in replying, and several voices, incensed anew by this, cried, "It's she, it's she!" and "Kill her!" Josepha put little Philip, who Jeronimo had been carrying till then, in Don Fernando's arms, together with little Juan, and said, "Go on, Don Fernando, save your two children and leave us to our fate!" Don Fernando took both children and said he would sooner die on the spot than suffer anything to happen to his friends. After asking the naval officer for his sword, he gave Josepha his arm and called to the couple behind to follow. And they did indeed manage to leave the church, for the crowd gave way with grudging respect before them, and thought themselves saved. But no sooner were they in the square, which was just as tightly packed with people, when a voice rang out of the frenzied mob that had pursued them: "Citizens, this is Jeronimo Rugera, for I am his own father!" and with a tremendous blow of his club, he struck him down at Donna Constanza's side. "Jesus Maria!" Donna Constanza screamed, running toward her brother-in-law; but already there was a cry of "Convent whore!" and a second blow, from another side, felled her lifeless to the ground beside Jeronimo.

"Monster!" a stranger cried out, "that was Donna Constanza Xares!"

"Then why did they lie to us!" the shoemaker retorted. "Find the right one and kill her!"

Don Fernando, when he caught sight of Donna Constanza's corpse, was maddened with rage; drawing his sword, he brandished it over his head and struck a blow that would have split the fanatical murderer who was the instigator of all these horrors in half if the shoemaker had not dodged out of its way. But since it was impossible for him to overcome the mob pressing in on him, Josepha cried out, "Farewell, Don Fernando and the children!"—and: "Here, murder me, you bloodthirsty tigers!" and plunged into their midst, to put an end to the struggle. Master Pedrillo felled her with his club. Then, spattered with her blood, he yelled, "Send the bastard to hell right after her!" and pressed forward afresh with still unsatisfied blood lust. Don Fernando now stood, heroic as a god, with his back to the church; his left hand held the children, his right his sword. With every lightning stroke he toppled somebody to the ground; a lion does not fight better. Seven of the bloodhounds lay dead in front of him, the leader of the satanic pack himself was wounded. But Master Pedrillo would not rest until he had pulled one of the children from Fernando's breast by the legs and, whirling it in the air, smashed it against the edge of a church pillar. Then silence fell upon the square and the crowd drew back. When Don Fernando saw his little Juan lying there with his brains oozing out, he lifted his eyes, full of inexpressible woe, to heaven. The naval officer reappeared and tried to comfort him, and told him how sorry he felt about his own inaction, although there were several circumstances to explain it; but Don Fernando said he had nothing to reproach himself for, and only asked him to help remove the bodies. These were now carried through the darkness of the falling night to Don Alonzo's house, whither Don Fernando followed, raining tears on little Philip's face. He passed the night at Don Alonzo's, and for quite some time hid the full extent of the misfortune from his wife under a trumped-up story: for one thing, because she was ill, and then, too, because he did not know how she would judge his own behavior; but shortly after, learning the whole story by accident from a visitor, this good lady cried her maternal grief out in silence, and then one morning, throwing her arms around his neck, with a teardrop shining in her eye, she kissed him. Don Fernando and Donna Elvira took the little stranger for their own child; and when Don Fernando compared Philip with Juan, and the different ways the two had come to him, it almost seemed to him that he had reason to feel glad.

St. Cecilia, or the Power of Music

[A LEGEND]

$\mathcal{T}$OWARD the end of the six-
teenth century, when the iconoclastic riots were raging in the Netherlands, three young brothers, who were students at Wittenberg, met
a fourth brother, who was a predicant in Antwerp, in the city of
Aachen. They had to come there to collect an inheritance left them
by an old uncle whom none of them had ever seen, and, as there
was nobody in Aachen who might have put them up, they took
lodgings at an inn. After passing several days in listening to the
predicant tell about the remarkable events that had occurred in
the Netherlands, it reached their ears that the sisters of the Convent
of Saint Cecilia, which at that time lay just outside the city gates,
were going to perform a solemn Corpus Christi celebration; and,
inflamed by fanaticism, youth, and the example of the Netherlanders,

271

the four brothers decided to provide the city of Aachen, too, with the spectacle of a religious riot. The predicant, who had led more than one such enterprise in the past, got together, on the evening before the festival, a number of young men, merchants' sons and students devoted to the new doctrine, who spent the night at the inn in eating and drinking and damning the papacy; and, when dawn rose above the spires of the city, they provided themselves with axes and every other kind of instrument of destruction, in preparation for their wanton work. Jubilantly they agreed on the signal at which to start smashing the stained-glass windows with their pictures of Biblical scenes; and, confident of finding a large following among the people, they marched off to the cathedral at the hour the bells began to ring, resolved to leave not one stone upon another. The Abbess, whom a friend had already warned at dawn about the threat hanging over the convent, in vain appealed several times to the Imperial Commandant of the city for the posting of a guard to protect the cloister; the officer—who was himself an enemy of the papacy, and therefore inclined to sympathize, at least covertly, with the new doctrine—refused her the guard, on the politic grounds that she must be seeing ghosts, for there was not the shadow of a threat to her convent. Meanwhile the hour had struck for the solemnities to begin, and the sisters, amid fear and prayers and pitiable anticipations of what was to come, got ready for the Mass. Except for a seventy-year-old beadle, who posted himself with a few armed servants at the entrance to the church, there was no one to protect them.

In convents, as we know, the nuns, who are trained to play every kind of instrument, provide their own music, which is often of a precision, an understanding, and a depth of feeling that one misses in male orchestras (perhaps because of the feminine character of this mysterious art). Now, to make matters doubly distressing, it so happened that the regular conductor of the orchestra, Sister Antonia, had been taken violently ill several days before with a nervous fever;

and so, in addition to having to reckon with the four blasphemous brothers, who could already be seen behind the pillars of the church closely wrapped in their cloaks, the nuns found themselves completely at a loss for a suitable piece of music to perform. The Abbess, who the night before had ordered the orchestra to play a very ancient Italian Mass, the composition of an unknown master, which they had performed several times already with overwhelming effect thanks to its special sanctity and splendor, sent again, for she was more than ever determined to have her way, to ask how Sister Antonia was feeling; but the nun who went on this errand returned with the news that Sister Antonia was stretched out completely unconscious and that it was out of the question that she should conduct the Mass. Meanwhile several very ominous incidents had already occurred in the cathedral, where more than a hundred rioters of every class and age, armed with axes and crowbars, had gradually assembled: several servants standing at the doors had been baited in the most indecent way and the rioters had permitted themselves to call out the most impudent and shameless things to the lone sisters who now and then, in the course of their pious tasks, showed themselves in the aisles. The situation got so bad that the beadle hurried into the vestry and implored the Abbess on his knees to cancel the celebration and place herself under the protection of the Commandant in the city. But the Abbess steadfastly insisted that the celebration in honor of the Almighty God must take place; she reminded the beadle that it was his duty to lay down his life, if need be, to protect the Mass and the solemn procession that would be held in the church; and, just as the bell began to peal, she ordered the sisters, who were standing around her in a circle, trembling and shivering, to choose any oratorio, never mind who wrote it or how good it was, and start the performance right away.

The nuns in the organ gallery were just getting ready to do so; they had passed out the score of a composition they had already performed many times; the violins, hautboys, and contrabasses were tried and tuned, when Sister Antonia, looking fresh and healthy even if her face was rather pale, suddenly appeared at the top of the stairs; under her arm she carried the music of the ancient Italian Mass which the Abbess had been so insistent that they should play. When the nuns asked her in astonishment where she had come from and how she had recovered so suddenly, she replied, "Never mind, friends, never mind," passed out the score she had brought, and, radiant with enthusiasm, sat down at the organ to direct the splendid music. A wonderful feeling of heavenly comfort seemed to fill the hearts of the pious women; with their instruments they instantly took their places at the music stands; the very oppression which had weighed upon them helped to lift their souls, as if on wings, through all the heavens of harmony; the oratoria was played with surpassing splendor; not a breath stirred in the aisles or along the benches throughout the entire performance; during the *Salve regina* especially, and even more so during the *Gloria in excelsis,* the audience in the church seemed struck dead; and so, in spite of the four god-forsaken brothers and their followers, not even the dust on the pavement of the church was stirred and the convent stood untouched to the end of the Thirty Years' War, when, however, by a provision of the Peace of Westphalia, it was secularized.

Six years later, when this incident was already long forgotten, the unhappy mother of the four young men arrived from The Hague saying that all her sons had vanished, and instituted a legal inquiry with the magistrate of Aachen, to determine what road they might have taken when leaving the place. The last word received from them in the Netherlands, which was their real home, had been a letter, the mother reported, from the predicant to his friend, a schoolteacher in Antwerp, written on the eve of Corpus Christi, just before their disappearance, in which the predicant, with a great deal of merriment, or rather boisterousness, had informed his friend in four closely written pages of a forthcoming attempt on the Convent of St. Cecilia, the details of which the mother did not care, however, to reveal. After many fruitless attempts to discover the whereabouts of the grieving woman's sons, somebody finally remembered that for a number of years, which roughly coincided with the period of her sons' disappearance, four young men of undetermined nationality and origin had been lodged in the madhouse with which the Emperor's care had provided the city not so long ago. But since these men were suffering from a religious mania, and were, according to vague reports the magistrate recalled hearing, extremely despondent and melancholy in their behavior—all of which little resembled the character of her sons, with which she was unfortunately only too familiar—the mother was not inclined to set much store by this information, especially as it was fairly certain that the men were Catholics. Yet, finding herself strangely moved by the description of their various identifying marks, she visited the madhouse one day, in the company of an usher of the court, and asked the wardens' permission to go in and examine the four unfortunate lunatics they were keeping there. But who can describe the poor woman's horror when, upon entering the door, her first glance showed her her sons: they wore long black robes and sat around a table with their clasped hands silently resting on the top, apparently addressing prayers to a cross that stood in the center. Her strength forsook her and she sank into a chair; to her question as to what they were doing, the wardens replied that they were only worshiping the Savior, whom they believed they saw for the true Son of the only God better than anyone else. They added that the young men had been leading this spectral existence for six years; that they ate and slept very little; that no word ever crossed their lips; and that they would only get up from their seats at midnight, to intone, in voices that shattered the windows of the house, the *Gloria in excelsis*. The wardens concluded by assuring her that, in spite of everything, the young men's health was excellent; that there was even a certain cheerfulness about them, though of a stern and solemn kind; that the four shrugged their soulders pityingly when anyone

called them insane; and that more than once already they had remarked that, if the good city of Aachen only knew what they knew,
it, too, would lay aside its affairs and gather around the crucifix of
the Lord to sing the *Gloria*.

The woman, who could not bear the terrible sight of her unfortunate sons and soon had herself, her knees shaking, escorted home,
next morning went to see Veit Gotthelf, the famous cloth merchant
of Aachen, to find out what he knew about the awful happening; for
this man had been mentioned in the predicant's letter, and it was
apparent that he himself had been actively involved in the plan to
destroy the Convent of Saint Cecilia on Corpus Christi Day. Veit
Gotthelf, the cloth merchant, who meanwhile had married, begotten
several children, and taken over his father's considerable business,
greeted the stranger cordially; and, when he learned why she had
come to him, he bolted the door and, after inviting her to sit down,
addressed her as follows: "My dear woman, if you won't get me mixed
up in any investigations because I was closely associated with your
sons six years ago, I will be frank and open with you: yes, our
scheme was just as the letter says! Why it failed, after we had
planned things down to the last detail with truly godless ingenuity, I
can't understand; Heaven herself must have taken the convent of
pious women under her protecting wing. For your sons, you know,
had already indulged in a number of rowdy tricks that interrupted
the service, so as to set the stage for the more climactic scenes to
follow; more than three hundred rascals armed with axes and torches
who had sallied out of the walls of our then misguided city were only
waiting for the predicant's signal to raze the cathedral to the ground.
Yet when the music began, all of a sudden your sons snatched off
their hats, as if in one motion, in a way that impressed us all; slowly,
as if overwhelmed by a deep, unspeakable emotion, they put their
hands in front of their bowed faces, and the predicant, after a
thrilling pause, turned around abruptly and called to us in a ringing,
awful voice to uncover our heads too! Several comrades vainly

nudged him with their elbows and urged him in a whisper to give the agreed-on signal; instead of answering, the predicant fell to his knees without a word and, with his hands crossed upon his chest and his forehead fervently pressed into the dust, he and his brothers began to murmur all those series of prayers which they had made fun of only a moment ago. Completely unnerved by this sight, and deprived of their ringleaders, the pitiable fanatics stood about irresolutely in knots until the marvelous strains of the oratorio's peroration came pouring down from the gallery; and, as a number of arrests were now being made on the Commandant's orders, with several of the culprits who had figured in the disturbances being seized and led away by the guard, the wretched crew had no choice but to slink hurriedly out of the church under cover of the milling crowd. That evening, after inquiring repeatedly at the inn, without success, about your sons, who had not returned, I felt a terrible uneasiness and, returning with a few friends to the convent, I asked the doorkeepers, who had assisted the Imperial guard, what had become of them. But how describe to you, dear lady, the shock I felt when I saw those four men still prostrated in utter devotion before the altar, their clasped hands stretched out in front of them and their breasts and foreheads kissing the ground, as if turned to stone! The beadle went up to them at that very moment and tugged at their cloaks and jogged their elbows, vainly pleading with them to leave the church, which was already dark and quite deserted; half rising as if in a trance, they paid no attention to him till he ordered some of his servants to catch them under the arms and lead them out of the door, where at last they followed us to the city, though not without repeated sighs and many heart-rending backward glances at the church sparkling gloriously in the setting sun. Over and over again on the way back, my friends and I begged them tenderly and lovingly to tell us what dreadful thing it was that could have caused such a revolution in their souls; but they shook our hands with a friendly smile, stared thoughtfully at the ground, and from time to time, with oh!

such an expression as even now breaks my heart, wiped the tears from their eyes. Once back in their lodgings, they cleverly fashioned birch twigs into a little cross, which they stood on the large table in the middle of the room, with the base pressed into a small mound of wax, between two candles fetched in by a servant girl; and while the crowd of their friends, whose number hourly increased, stood to one side in scattered groups and wrung their hands, watching the brothers' ghostly actions in speechless sorrow, they sat down around the table as if their senses were completely closed to anything else, clasped their hands together, and quietly began to pray. They had no desire to taste the food that the servant girl, following their instructions of the morning, carried in for their friends, nor to lie down on the bed that their weary appearance led her to make up for them later on, at nightfall, in the adjoining room. To mollify the innkeeper, whom these proceedings had unpleasantly surprised, their friends were obliged to sit down to one side at a board that groaned under the weight of provisions for a large party and eat food seasoned with the salt of their own tears. Now the hour of midnight suddenly struck; your four sons, after listening for a moment to the hollow sound of the bell, rose up in a body from their seats; and, while we put down our napkins and stared across the room at them, anxiously waiting for what might follow so untoward a beginning, they began to intone, in dreadful, ear-splitting voices, the *Gloria in excelsis*. Leopards and wolves must make such sounds when they howl at the sky on an icy winter's night; the pillars of the house, believe me, trembled, and the windows, under the visible impact of their breath, rattled and shook as if bombarded with fistfuls of heavy sand and threatened to smash to bits. At this fearful spectacle all of us started up madly and fled, our hair standing on end; leaving hats and coats behind, we scattered through the neighboring streets, which the next moment were filled with more than a hundred people who had been frightened out of their sleep; bursting through the front door of the inn, the crowd pressed up the stairs

to discover where this appalling outcry was coming from, which
seemed to rise up, like the shrieks of eternally damned sinners, from
the nethermost depths of fiery hell and piteously beseech the ear of
God for mercy. Finally, at the stroke of one, without having paid
the slightest attention to the angry protests of the innkeeper or the
shocked exclamations of the people crowding around them, they
fell silent; with a kerchief they mopped the sweat which trickled in
great drops down their chins and onto their chests, from their brows
and, spreading their cloaks upon the parquet floor, lay down to rest
an hour from their agonizing exertions. The innkeeper, who did not
attempt to interfere, made the sign of the cross over them as soon
as he saw them fall asleep; happy to have gained a moment's respite,
he assured the crowd of bystanders, who were whispering furtively
among themselves, that the men would be much better in the morning and persuaded them to leave the room. But, alas, at the first
crowing of the cock the unhappy men got up again and, facing the
cross on the table, recommenced the same spectral monastic routine
which they had been forced to interrupt for a while only because of
sheer exhaustion. The innkeeper's heart melted at the pitiful sight
they presented, but none of his urgings, none of his offers of help
had any effect; they asked him to give a polite refusal to their friends
who used to gather regularly every morning in their room; they
wanted nothing from him but bread and water and a bit of straw, if
possible, for the night; the upshot being that the man who had once
got so much money from their carousing saw himself obliged to
report the whole incident to the authorities and to request the removal from his house of the four men, whom an evil spirit doubtless
possessed. At the magistrate's orders, they were held for medical
examination and, upon being adjudged insane, they were lodged, as
you know, in the madhouse which the benevolence of our late Emperor founded inside the walls of our city for the benefit of such
unfortunates." All this Veit Gotthelf, the cloth merchant, told the
mother, and much more, which we shall omit here, as we believe

we have said enough already to explain the inner circumstances of the matter; and again he begged the woman not to involve him in any way if there should be a judicial inquiry into the affair.

Three days afterwards, when the mother, who had been deeply moved by the merchant's story, took advantage of the fine weather to stroll out to the cloister on the arm of a friend with the melancholy intention of viewing the fearful place where God had struck her sons down as if by invisible lightning bolts, the two women found the entrance to the cathedral boarded up, as there was building going on, and could see nothing of the interior, when they laboriously got up to peer through the chinks between the boards, except the rose window sparkling gorgeously at the rear of the cathedral. On an intricate maze of slender scaffolds, several hundred gaily singing workmen were busy raising the height of the towers by a good third and replacing the slate that covered the roofs and pinnacles with strong, bright copper that sparkled in the rays of the sun. Just then a dark thundercloud with gilded edges was seen towering in the air behind the building; it had already spent its force over the neighborhood of Aachen and, after hurling a few last feeble lightning bolts in the direction of the cathedral, passed off eastwards, murmuring disgruntledly, and dissolved into mist. While the two women were gazing at this double spectacle from the steps of the extensive cathedral residence, their minds engrossed by all sorts of thoughts, a passing nun accidentally discovered who the woman standing under the portal was and informed the Abbess; the latter, who had heard about a letter concerning the Corpus Christi celebration which the mother of the four sons had in her possession, immediately sent the nun downstairs with a request to see the Dutchwoman. Though taken aback momentarily, she was nevertheless ready to obey the order that had been sent her; and while the nun invited the friend to step aside into a room hard by the entrance, the folding doors to the Abbess's own beautiful balcony room, which was reached by a flight of stairs, were thrown open to the stranger. She found the superior of the convent, a noblewoman of a serene and regal appearance, sitting in a chair, her foot propped upon a stool that stood on dragon's-feet; next to her, on a stand, lay a music score. The Abbess, after having ordered a chair to be brought for the stranger, told her that the Burgermeister had already informed her of her arrival in the city; and, after inquiring with great kindness how her unfortunate sons were, and encouraging her to reconcile herself as far as possible to the fate that had befallen them since there was no changing it anyhow, she expressed a wish to see the letter that the predicant had written to his friend the schoolteacher in Antwerp. The woman knew the world well enough to appreciate the consequences such a disclosure might have and felt a momentary embarrasssment; but, as the Abbess's venerable face inspired absolute confidence, and it was unthinkable that she intended to make public use of its contents, she took the letter from her bosom, after this short hesitation, and gave it to the princely lady, at the same time pressing a fervent kiss on her hand. While the Abbess read the letter, the woman stole a glance at the score lying carelessly open on the stand; and as the cloth merchant's story had made her think that it might have been the power of music which had deranged and destroyed the minds of her poor sons that dreadful day, she turned shyly to the nun who stood behind her chair and asked if this was the piece of music that had been played in the cathedral on the morning of that remarkable Corpus Christi celebration six years ago. When the young nun answered yes, she remembered having heard so, adding that ever since, when not in use, the score was kept in the room of the Reverend Mother, the woman rose up in a turmoil of emotion and stood in front of the music stand, while all sorts of thoughts raced through her head. She stared at the unknown magical signs by which a terrible spirit seemed mysteriously to mark out its sphere, and thought she would sink into the earth when she found the pages opened just at the *Gloria in excelsis*. It was as if all that terrible power of music which had destroyed her sons were raging around her head; she thought the mere sight of the score would make her lose her mind, and, after hastily pressing the page to her lips in an access of boundless humility and submissiveness to the Divine Omnipotence, she sat down again in her chair. The Abbess had meanwhile finished reading the letter and, as she folded it up, said, "God Himself protected the convent on that miraculous day against the insolence of your greatly erring sons. What means He used to do this couldn't possibly be of any interest to you who are a Protestant; and even if I should tell you, you would hardly understand. For you must realize that not a soul really knows who it was that sat down calmly at the organ bench, in the tense and dreadful hour when the storm was about to break over us, and conducted the work you see lying open over there. Testimony taken the next morning in the presence of the beadle and several other men, and deposited in the archives, proves that Sister Antonia, the only person who could have conducted the work, lay prostrate in the corner of her cell throughout the entire performance, sick, unconscious, and absolutely incapable of moving a limb; a nun who was a blood relation and had been assigned to look after her did not stir from her bedside during the entire morning of the Corpus Christi celebration in the cathedral. Indeed, Sister Antonia herself would have unfailingly sworn to the fact that it was not she who made so strange and surprising an appearance in the organ gallery if her unconscious state had permitted any questioning, and if she had not died that very same evening as a result of the nervous fever (which had not seemed serious at first) that she was suffering from. The Archbishop of Trier, who was informed of what happened, has already given the only possible explanation of the whole affair, namely, that Saint Cecilia herself performed this terrible and at the same time glorious miracle; and I have just received a Papal brief confirming this." And with these words she handed the woman back the letter, which she had asked to see simply to learn more about a matter with which she was already well acquainted, promising her at the same time that she would make no use of it; and after asking the woman whether there was any hope for her sons' recovery, and whether she could help her with money or anything else to bring it about—to all of which the woman answered tearfully in the negative, while kissing the hem of the Abbess's gown—she gave her a friendly handshake and let her go.

So ends this legend. As the woman's presence in Aachen served no purpose, she deposited a small sum of money with the magistrate for the benefit of her poor sons and went back to the Hague, where a year later, deeply moved by everything that had happened, she returned to the bosom of the Catholic church; her sons, however, lived to a ripe old age, dying a serene and cheerful death after they had once more sung, as was their custom, the *Gloria in excelsis*.

The Duel

[THE DUEL]

$\mathcal{D}$UKE Wilhelm von Breysach, who after his clandestine marriage to a lady of ostensibly inferior rank, the Countess Katharina von Heersbruck of the house of Alt-Hüningen, had been at daggers drawn with his half-brother, Count Jacob the Redbeard, returned home one St. Remigius' night toward the end of the fourteenth century from an audience with the German Emperor in Worms, whose consent he had won—seeing that all his legitimate children had died—to legitimize his natural son, Count Philip von Hüningen, whom his wife had borne him before their marriage. Looking toward the future with an easier mind than he had ever been able to enjoy before in his reign, Duke Wilhelm had already reached the park in the rear of his castle when suddenly an arrow flashed out of the darkness of the shrubbery and pierced him just beneath the breastbone. Sir Friedrich von Trota, his chamberlain,

utterly dumbfounded by this, had several knights help him carry the
Duke into the castle, where the latter had just enough strength, as
his distraught wife supported him in her arms, to read out the Imperial act of legitimation to the assembled vassals of the realm, whom
the Duchess had hastily convoked; and after the vassals had complied
with his last wish and recognized Count Philip as heir to the throne
(his mother, however, becoming Regent and guardian, since Philip
was under age), though not without first putting up a lively resistance
and insisting on the Emperor's approval being obtained, for the
crown should by law have passed to his half-brother Count Jacob
the Redbeard, the Duke lay back and died.

The Dutchess now mounted the throne without further ado,
merely dispatching several envoys to her brother-in-law, Count
Jacob the Redbeard, to inform him of the fact; and what several
knights at court, who were convinced they could penetrate the
latter's close reserve, had predicted, happened, or so at least it
seemed: shrewdly gauging the situation, Jacob the Redbeard chose
to ignore the injustice done him by his brother, or at least he refrained
from taking any kind of action to set aside the Duke's last testament,
and heartily congratulated his young nephew on his elevation to the
throne. To the envoys, whom he cheerfully invited to dine with him,
he described the free and independent life he led in his castle since
the death of his wife, who had left him a king's fortune; how he enjoyed the society of the wives of the neighboring nobility, his own
wine and, in the company of boon companions, the chase; and how
the only project he still looked forward to at the end of his life was a
crusade to Palestine, by which means he hoped to atone for the sins
of his turbulent youth, and unfortunately, too, as he confessed, for
those of his riper years. His two sons, who had been brought up in
the settled expectation of succeeding to the throne, reproached him
bitterly for the callousness and indifference with which he had
acquiesced, so unexpectedly, in this irreparable injury to their claims,
but in vain; with a few short, sarcastic words he peremptorily ordered

the still beardless youths to hold their tongues, on the day of the old Duke's solemn funeral he made them accompany him to the town, there at his side, as was fitting, to lay their uncle to rest in the vault; and, after paying homage, like the rest of the nobility at court, to the young prince, his nephew, in the throne room of the Ducal palace, with the Regent-Mother standing by, and refusing all the offices and honors the latter offered him, he returned to his castle accompanied by the blessings of the people, who revered him all the more for this display of magnanimity and moderation.

The Duchess, finding her first concern disposed of in this unexpectedly auspicious way, now set about fulfilling her second duty as Regent: to search out her husband's murderers, who, it was said, had been seen in a large troop in the park, and with this purpose in mind she herself, together with her chancellor, Sir Godwin von Herrthal, examined the arrow that had taken her husband's life. But there was nothing about it that might have betrayed its owner, except perhaps its remarkably fine and careful workmanship. Large, stiff, shiny feathers were set in a strong and slender shaft of finely turned dark walnut; the fore part was sheathed in shining brass and only the very tip, sharp as a fishbone, was made of steel. The arrow seemed to have been made for the armory of some rich gentleman of rank who was either involved in feuds or was an ardent huntsman; and as the date engraved on its head indicated that it had been made quite recently, the Dutchess, on her chancellor's advice, sent it around, under the seal of the crown, to all the workshops of Germany to find out the master who had turned it and, if he were discovered, to learn from him the name of the man who had commissioned its manufacture.

Five months after, Sir Godwin, the Chancellor, to whom the Duchess had turned over the entire inquiry, received word from an arrowsmith in Strasbourg that three years previously he had made three score such arrows, as well as a quiver to hold them, for Count Jacob the Redbeard. The Chancellor was staggered by this news and for several weeks kept the letter under lock and key; for one thing, he thought he knew the Count for too high-minded a man, in spite of his libertine and dissolute life, to consider him capable of so abominable a deed as the murder of a brother; and for another, in spite of the Regent's many other excellent qualities, he was too little acquainted with the disinterestedness of her justice to proceed without the greatest circumspection in a matter that involved the life of her worst enemy. Meanwhile he began to make private inquiries along the lines indicated by the extraordinary communication he had received, and when, quite by accident, he learned from the officers of the town dungeon that the Count, who never or rarely left his castle, had been away from home on the very night of the Duke's murder, he felt it his duty to lay aside all secrecy and tell the Duchess in detail, at an early session of the Privy Council, about the two pieces of information which cast so strange and surprising a suspicion on her brother-in-law, Count Jacob the Redbeard.

The Duchess, who counted herself lucky to be on such a friendly footing with her brother-in-law, the Count, and feared nothing more than offending him by some ill-considered action, surprised the Chancellor by showing not the slightest sign of satisfaction on receiving this suspicious disclosure; on the contrary, after carefully reading through the documents twice, she expressed her lively displeasure at so dubious and delicate a matter's being broached in the Privy Council. She was convinced that either malice or a mistake was at the root of it, and gave orders that under no circumstances was a notification to be made to the courts. Indeed, considering the extraordinary, almost fanatical reverence in which the people, by an understandable turn of events, held the Count after his exclusion from the throne, even this mere mention of the matter in the Privy Council seemed a dangerous thing to her; and, as she anticipated that the gossip of the town would reach his ears, she sent him a copy of the two points of accusation, which she blamed on some kind of misunderstanding, together with the supporting evidence, accompanying all this with a truly magnanimous letter from herself asking him to spare her all denial, as she was convinced of his innocence in advance.

The Count, who was seated at table with a party of friends when the knight with the Duchess' message entered the room, courteously got up from his chair; but hardly had he read the letter through in the arch of the window, while his friends looked at the knight who ceremoniously declined a seat, than he changed color and handed the papers to his friends, saying, "Brothers, see what a shameful accusation they have concocted against me about the murder of my brother!" With flashing eyes he took the arrow from the knight's hand and, hiding the havoc in his breast, he added, as his friends crowded around him in commotion, that the arrow was indeed his, and that it was quite true that he had been absent from his castle on St. Remigius' Night! His companions cursed such malignant and mean-spirited cunning; they threw the suspicion of murder back upon the wicked accuser herself, and were about to heap insults on the envoy, who had sprung to the defense of his mistress, the Duchess, when the Count, who had read the documents through a second time, advanced suddenly into their midst and called out; "Easy, my friends!"—and, reaching for his sword that stood in a corner, he gave it to the knight and announced that he was his prisoner! When the dumbfounded knight asked him whether he had heard him correctly, and whether the Count in fact acknowledged the two charges that the Chancellor had drawn up, he replied, "Yes, I do, yes!" Meanwhile, he trusted it would not be necessary for him to prove his innocence anywhere but at the bar of a court formally convened by the Duchess. His knights heard all this with great discontent and vainly pleaded with him that in that case he was accountable to no one but the Emperor; but the Count, having thus suddenly and strangly changed his mind and appealed to the Regent's justice, insisted on appearing before a Ducal court, and wrenching himself loose from their hands, he was already shouting out of the window for his horses, ready, as he said, to follow the envoy into custody right away, when his comrades-in-arms barred the way by force and offered a suggestion that he had finally to accept. They all drew up a letter to the Duchess demanding the right of safe-conduct for him that is every knight's in such circumstances, and offering 20,000 silver marks as bail for his standing trial before a court of her appointment, and also for his accepting whatever verdict that might be passed on him.

The Duchess, upon receiving this unexpected and inexplicable declaration, deemed it politic, in view of the nasty rumors already circulating among the people as to the motives behind the accusation, to withdraw from the case herself and lay the whole matter before the Emperor. At her Chancellor's recommendation, she sent all the documents in the case to the Emperor and requested him, as the supreme authority in the realm, to relieve her of the investigation of a matter in which she herself was an interested party. The Emperor, who was in Basel just then negotiating with the Swiss Confederation, granted her request; he appointed a court of three counts, twelve knights, and two assistant judges to sit in that city; and, after granting a safe-conduct to Count Jacob the Redbeard, in accordance with his friends' request, upon a security of 20,000 silver marks, he commanded him to appear before the said tribunal and make reply to the counts of the indictment: how the arrow, which according to his own admission belonged to him, had got into the hands of the murderer, and also: where he had been on the night of St. Remigius.

It was on the Monday after Trinity Sunday that Count Jacob the Redbeard, with a brilliant retinue of knights, stood at the bar of the court in Basel as he had been commanded and, after passing over the first point, which he confessed he was helpless to explain, replied as follows to the second and decisive one: "Noble lords!" he said, leaning with his hands upon the rail and looking at the assembly out of his tiny flashing eyes shaded by reddish lashes. "You accuse me, who has given ample proof of his indifference to crown and scepter, of the most fearful crime anyone can commit, the murder of my brother, a man who had little liking for me, it is true, but who was not any the less dear to me for that reason; and one of the grounds on which you base your accusation is my absence from my castle, contrary to the custom of many years, on the night of St. Remigius, when the outrage was committed. Now I know very well what a knight owes to the reputation of a lady whose favor he has secretly enjoyed; and on my word, if this strange fatality had not fallen on me right out of the blue sky, the secret locked inside my breast should have died with me, turned to dust, and only risen up again, to stand with me before God, when the last trumpet had burst open the graves. But as you must doubtless see yourself, the question that his Imperial Majesty asks my conscience through your mouth makes all scruples and considerations vain. Very well then: since you wish to know why it was not likely or even possible for me to have taken part, either personally or indirectly, in the murder of my brother, let me tell you that on Saint Remigius' Night, which is to say the night of the murder, I was secretly visiting the High Bailiff Winfried von Breda's beautiful daughter, Wittib Littegarde von Auerstein, whose love and devotion I enjoy."

Now the reader should know that Wittib Littegarde von Auerstein was considered not only the most beautiful but also, up to the moment of this slanderous accusation, the most irreproachable and spotless lady in the land. After the death of her husband, the Palace Governor von Auerstein, from a contagious fever caught a few months after their marriage, she had lived in quiet seclusion in her father's castle; and it was only at the urging of the elderly bailiff, who would have liked to see her married again, that she consented to put in an appearance now and then at the hunts and banquets given by the knights of the neighborhood, especially Count Jacob the Redbeard. On such occasions the lords and heirs of the country's noblest and richest families assiduously courted her hand, the dearest one of all in her eyes being Sir Friedrich von Trota, the Chamberlain, who once during a hunt had courageously snatched her from the path of a wounded boar; but as she did not wish to displease her two brothers, who were counting on inheriting her fortune, she hesitated to make up her mind, in spite of her father's repeated exhortations, to give him her hand. Indeed, when Rudolph, the elder of the two brothers, married a rich young woman of the neighborhood, who after three childless years presented him with a son and heir, to the family's great delight, Lady Littegarde, yielding to their many direct and indirect promptings, wrote a tear-stained letter of farewell to her friend Sir Friedrich, and, to keep peace in the family, she agreed to her brother's suggestion that she should become the Abbess of a convent situated not far from her father's castle on the banks of the Rhine.

At the very moment when this plan was being urged on the Archbishop of Strasbourg and seemed in a fair way of succeeding, the High Bailiff Sir Winfried von Breda received a communication from the court appointed by the Emperor, informing him of his daughter Littegarde's disgrace and ordering him to have her appear in Basel to answer Count Jacob's accusation against her. The letter named the exact time and place in which the Count testified to having secretly visited Lady Littegarde, and even enclosed a ring of her late husband's that the Count swore to having received from her hand as a souvenir of the night the two had passed together. Now on the very day this letter arrived, Sir Winfried was suffering from a serious and painful ailment of old age; he tottered around his room, in a state of intense irritability, on his daughter's arm, his eyes already fixed upon that limit which is set for everything that breathes; and when he read the terrible accusation against her, he had a stroke on the spot, the letter dropped from his hand, and he collapsed on the floor with paralyzed limbs. The brothers, who were present, in consternation lifted him up from the floor and called for the doctor living in a side-wing who looked after the old man; but every effort to bring him back to life proved futile, he gave up the ghost while Lady Littegarde lay senseless in the lap of her women, and, when the latter regained consciousness, she did not even have the last bitter-sweet consolation of having been able to utter a word in defense of her honor which her father might have carried with him into eternity. The horror of the two brothers at their father's death, and the anger they felt at the shameful act their sister was accused of, unfortunately only too plausibly, which had caused it, were indescribable. For they knew only too well that Count Jacob the Redbeard had in fact paid her ardent court throughout the previous summer; he had held several tournaments and banquets in her sole honor, and had preferred her, in a manner that even then bordered on the scandalous, to all the other ladies of the company. Indeed, they remembered Littegarde's saying, just about the time of the Saint Remigius day in question, how she had lost the ring her husband had given her while out walking, this selfsame ring which now had turned up so strangely in Count Jacob's hands; and so they did not doubt for a second the truthfulness of what the Count had testified before the court. While her father's body was borne away amid the lamenting of the servants, she vainly clasped her brothers around the knees and begged them to listen to her for just one moment; Rudolph, livid with rage, turned on her and demanded whether she could produce a witness to disprove the accusation, and when she tremblingly replied that unfortunately she had only the blamelessness of her past life to offer in her defense, as her waiting woman had been absent from her bedroom on the night in question visiting her parents, Rudolph kicked her away from him, snatched a sword from a scabbard hanging on the wall and, in a monstrous fury, while he shouted for the dogs and servants, ordered her out of the house and castle that very moment. Littegarde got up from the floor, white as chalk; suffering his abuse in silence, she asked him to give her at least time enough to arrange for her departure; but Rudolph, beside himself with rage, only shouted, "Out, get out of the castle!" He would not even listen to his own wife when she came between them and begged him to show some pity and humanity, but flung her madly aside with a blow with the hilt of his sword that made her bleed, upon which the unfortunate Littegarde, more dead than alive, left the room and tottered across the courtyard, under the stares of the common people, to the castle gate, where Rudolph ordered a bundle of clothing thrust into her hands, to which he added some money, and, cursing and swearing, he himself slammed the gates shut behind her.

This sudden fall from a state of serene and almost unmarred happiness into the bottomless depths of helplessness and distress was more than the poor woman could bear. Not knowing where to turn, she stumbled down the rock path, clutching the railing for support, to find shelter for herself at least for the coming night; but before she even reached the entrance to the village, which lay scattered through the valley, she sank to the ground, utterly worn out. She must have lain there in this way about an hour, beyond the reach of all earthly cares, and darkness had descended all around, when she woke to find herself inside a ring of pitying villagers. A boy playing on the rocky slope had caught sight of her there and run home to tell his parents about the strange apparition he had seen, upon which the good people, horrified at hearing that Littegarde, who had shown them many kindnesses in the past, should be in such a plight, had at once hurried out to give her all the help they could. Thanks to their efforts, she soon came around, the sight of the castle standing barred behind her also helping to recall her to her senses; but when two of the women offered to take her back up to the castle, she refused and asked only if they would be good enough to provide her with a guide so that she could continue on her way. They tried without success to persuade her that she was in no condition to travel; Littegarde, on the pretext that her life was in danger, insisted on immediately getting beyond the limits of the castle district; indeed, as the crowd around her grew bigger all the time without her getting help from anyone, she started to push her way through the throng and, in spite of the gathering night, strike out along the road alone; at which point the villagers finally gave in, for fear their masters would hold them responsible if she should come to harm, and fetched out a wagon which, after she had been repeatedly asked where it was she wanted to go, started off with her toward Basel.

But before they had even reached the village, she changed her mind, after a more careful consideration of her circumstances, and told the driver to turn around and take her to Trota Castle only a few miles away. For she realized that without help there was no chance of her prevailing before the court at Basel against an adversary like Count Jacob the Redbeard; and no one seemed to her more worthy of being entrusted with the defense of her honor than her gallant friend, the noble Chamberlain, Sir Friedrich von Trota, who, as she well knew, still loved her devotedly. It must have been about midnight and the lights in the castle were still shining when she drove up in the wagon, utterly exhausted by the journey. She sent a servant of the house, who had run out to welcome her, upstairs to notify the family of her arrival; but even before he had done so, the ladies Berta and Kunigunde, Sir Friedrich's sisters, who happened to be downstairs in the entrance hall about a household chore, came out of the door. Her two young friends, who knew Littegarde very well, lifted her out of the wagon with delighted greetings and brought her upstairs to their brother (though not without a certain apprehension) whom they found sitting at a table immersed in the documents which a lawsuit had showered upon him. Sir Friedrich's surprise was indescribable when he turned his head on hearing the noise behind him and saw Lady Littegarde, pale and distraught, a veritable picture of despair, sinking to her knees before him. "Dearest Littegarde!" he cried, jumping up and raising her from the floor. "What has happened to you?" Littegarde, after sinking into a chair, told him her story: how Count Jacob the Redbeard had slandered her before the court at Basel, to clear himself of the suspicion of having murdered the Duke; how the news of this gave her old father, who was just then in the throes of his affliction, a stroke from which he died a few minutes later in the arms of his sons; and how the latter, maddened with rage, allowed her no chance to defend herself but overwhelmed her with terrible abuse and then drove her from the house like a criminal. She begged Sir Friedrich to send her to Basel with a proper escort, and to get her an advocate to stand at her side and advise her, when she appeared before the Emperor's court to defend herself against the Count's foul accusation. She swore to him that such an accusation could not have surprised her more if it had come from the lips of some Parthian or Persian whom she had never laid eyes on than from those of Count Jacob the Redbeard, for she always hated him from the bottom of her heart on account of his unsavory reputation as well as his physical appearance, and had steadily rejected with cold contempt the compliments he had allowed himself to pay her from time to time during the banquets of the past summer. "That's enough, my dearest Littegarde!" Sir Friendrich cried, seizing her hand with noble fervor and pressing it to his lips. "Not another word to defend and justify your innocence! There is a voice in my heart that pleads for you more vigorously and convincingly than all your protestations, or even all the legal points and proofs that you will be able to marshal in your defense before the court in Basel. Since your brothers have shown themselves unjust and ungenerous by forsaking you, let me be your brother and your friend, and grant me the glory of defending you at the trial; I will restore the brightness of your honor before the court in Basel and before the eyes of the whole world!" Then he escorted Littegarde, whom these generous words had moved to tears of gratitude, upstairs to Lady Helena, his mother, who had already retired to her bedroom; he told the worthy old lady, who had always held Littegarde in special affection, that she had come to stay with them for a while because of a quarrel that had arisen in her own family; then and there one whole wing of the sprawling castle was placed at her disposal, with its closets generously stocked with clothes and linen from his sisters' stores; she was also provided, as befitted her rank, with a considerable, even splendid, servant body; and the third day found Sir Friedrich von Trota already on the road to Basel with a numerous retinue of troopers and esquires, without his having breathed a word about how he intended to prove her innocence.

Meanwhile the court at Basel received a letter from the lords of Breda, Littegarde's brothers, that described what had happened at the castle and gave the poor woman up, as one whose guilt was already proven, to the full rigors of the law, either because they really believed her guilty or else because they may have had some other reason for wishing to undo her. At any rate, they lied shamefully when they called her ejection from the castle a voluntary flight; as they described it, when a few angry remarks escaped their lips she was unable to say a single word in defense of her innocence and immediately fled from the castle; and since all their efforts to find her, they assured the court, had proved fruitless, they had come to the conclusion that she was in all likelihood now wandering about the world at the side of some third adventurer and completing the measure of her disgrace. To redeem the honor of their family, they proposed that her name should be blotted from the family tree of the house of Breda, and offered far-fetched legal arguments to support their wish to have all her claims on their noble father's estate, whom her disgrace had driven to his grave, declared null and void as punishment for her shocking transgression. Now the judges at Basel were far from approving this request, which it lay outside their competence to hear in any case, and as meanwhile Count Jacob, on receiving this news, had given the most unequivocal and definite proof of his sympathy for Littegarde in her present plight by secretly sending horsemen out, as they had learned, to discover her whereabouts and offer her asylum in his castle, the court no longer doubted the truthfulness of his testimony and decided to dismiss forthwith the charge of murder hanging over him. Indeed, the sympathy he showed the unfortunate woman in her hour of need had a very favorable influence on the people's good opinion of him, which lately had been wavering; they now excused what before they had strongly condemned—the way he had exposed a woman who loved him to the world's contempt—and found that under such extraordinary and terrible circumstances, when nothing less than life and honor were at stake, he had had no choice but to lay aside all scruples and reveal his St. Remigius' Night's adventure. Accordingly, at the Emperor's command, Count Jacob the Redbeard was summoned before the court once more, to be formally absolved, while all the doors stood wide, of any suspicion of having taken part in the murder of the Duke. The herald in the gallery of the great courtroom had just read the letter from the lords of Breda, and the court, in accordance with the Emperor's verdict, was about to pronounce the formal exoneration of the accused, who stood beside the herald, when Sir Friedrich von Trota approached the bar and asked permission, as was the right of every disinterested onlooker, to examine the letter for a moment. His wish, as everybody's eyes turned toward him, was granted; but no sooner had Sir Friedrich received the letter from the herald's hands and given it a cursory glance than he ripped it from top to bottom and, rolling up the pieces in his glove, flung it in Count Jacob the Redbeard's face, saying that he was a shameless, dirty-minded liar, and that in a trial by combat he would prove Lady Littegarde innocent before the whole world of the offense she had been accused of.

Count Jacob the Redbeard, after picking up the gauntlet with a pale face, said, "As surely as God judges justly in a judgment by arms, so surely will I prove the truth, in honorable combat, of what I have been forced to reveal about Lady Littegarde! My lords," he continued, turning to the judges, "let His Imperial Majesty be informed of Sir Friedrich's challenge, and entreat him to fix the time and place in which we may meet with sword in hand to settle this dispute!" Accordingly, the judges suspended the session of the court and sent a deputation to the Emperor with an account of what had happened; and as Sir Friedrich's coming forward as Littegarde's champion had shaken the Emperor more than a little in his belief in the Count's innocence, he summoned Lady Littegarde, as the code of honor required, to Basel to witness the duel, and appointed Saint Marguerite's Day as the time, and the palace square in Basel as the place, in which the mystery surrounding the matter would finally be cleared up by the encounter of Sir Friedrich von Trota with Count Jacob the Redbeard.

The midday sun stood just above the towers of Basel on St. Marguerite's Day, and a huge crowd, for whom benches and stands had been put up, were gathered in the palace square, when Sir Friedrich and Count Jacob, both clad from head to foot in shining mail, advanced into the lists at the triple summons of the herald standing in front of the umpire's platform, to fight their quarrel to a conclusion. Almost the entire chivalry of Suabia and Switzerland were present on the palace ramp in the background; and in the balcony, surrounded by his court, sat the Emperor himself, with his wife and the princes and princesses, his sons and daughters. Just before the start of the encounter, as the judges were dividing up the light and shade between the antagonists, Lady Helena and her two daughters, Berta and Kunigunde, who had accompanied Littegarde to Basel, approached the gates of the square and asked permission of the guards standing there to enter and speak to Lady Littegarde, who, according to ancient custom, sat upon a stage within the lists. For even though her past conduct seemed to entitle her to their fullest respect and to justify unqualified faith in the truthfulness of her assurances, yet the ring that Count Jacob the Redbeard had been able to show, and even more the fact that on the night of St. Remigius Littegarde had sent away her waiting woman, the only person who might have been a witness for her, stirred the keenest apprehensions in their minds; they decided to test again, under the stress of this crucial moment, the firmness of the accused woman's conscience, and to explain to her the futility, indeed blasphemousness, of trying to clear herself, if there was indeed any burden of guilt on her conscience, by appealing to the sacred verdict of arms which unfailingly brought the truth to light. And indeed Littegarde had every reason to weigh carefully the step that Sir Friedrich was about to venture for her: the stake awaited her and her champion if God, by the verdict of steel, decided not for Sir Friedrich von Trota but for Count Jacob the Redbeard and the truth of what he had deposed before the court. Lady Littegarde, seeing Sir Friedrich's mother and sisters enter from the side, rose from her chair with characteristic dignity, which her evident suffering made even more touching, and, advancing to meet them, asked what brought them to her at such a fateful moment. "My dear little daughter," Lady Helena said, taking her aside, "will you spare a mother, whose only comfort in her lonely old age is her son, the pain of having to weep at his grave? Even now, before the duel begins, will you get into a carriage and accept the gift of one of our estates across the Rhine, where you will receive a suitable and cordial welcome?" Littegarde, suddenly turning pale, stared in her face for a moment and, after grasping the full import of these words, knelt in front of her on one knee. "Most noble and worthy lady," she said, "does your fear that God will decide against my innocence in this fateful hour have its source in your gallant son's heart?"

"Why do you ask?" Lady Helena said.

"Because in that case I would entreat him solemnly not to draw his sword without a confident hand to wield it, but to yield the field to his opponent on some pretext or another and leave me to my fate, which I entrust to God, rather than give ear so inopportunely to feelings of pity, to which I will be indebted for nothing!"

"No," said Lady Helena in confusion, "my son knows nothing about this. It would do him little credit, after pledging his word before the court to defend your cause, to make such a proposal to you now that the hour of decision has struck. There he stands opposite the Count your enemy, firmly convinced of your innocence and already armed for the fight, as you can see; it was something my daughters and I thought of in the distress of the moment, as a way to make the best and avoid the worst of this situation."

"Very well then," said Lady Littegarde, wetting the old lady's hand with her tears as she gave it a fervent kiss, "let him honor his word! My conscience is not stained by any guilt; even if he went into battle without helmet or harness, God and all his angels would protect him!" And with these words, she got up and showed Lady Helena and her daughters to some seats upon the stage that were placed just behind the chair draped in red in which she herself sat down.

Now the herald, at a nod from the Emperor, sounded the signal for the combat, and the two knights, with sword and shield in hand, lunged at one another. Sir Friedrich wounded the Count with his very first blow, slashing him with the tip of his sword, which was not especially long, just at the point between arm and hand where his armor was linked together; the Count, who leaped back in dismay at the pain and examined the wound, found that, though the blood flowed freely, it was only a scratch, and when the knights on the ramp grumbled at his clumsy performance, he pressed forward again and resumed the contest with renewed vigor, like a perfectly whole man. Back and forth the struggle now surged, the two foemen colliding like tempests in midair, like two clashing thunderclouds that dart lightning bolts from their midst and whose towering bulks swirl around each other without mingling amid the continual rattling of thunder. Sir Friedrich stood his ground, his sword and shield extended before him, as if determined to take root there; he dug himself into the loose earth (the paving stones had been purposely removed) up to his spurs, up to his ankles and calves, shielding his head and breast against the cunning thrusts of the nimble, small-statured Count, who attacked almost simultaneously from every side. The fight had already lasted close to an hour, including the pauses both antagonists needed in order to catch their breath, when a fresh murmur of disapproval arose from the audience in the stands. This time, it would seem, it was aimed not at Count Jacob, who did not lack for zeal in trying to press the combat to a conclusion, but at Sir Friedrich's entrenching himself in the selfsame spot and his strange, apparently almost fearful, or at least stubborn, reluctance to do more than counter his opponent's blows. Sir Friedrich, although he perhaps had good reasons for these tactics, was nevertheless too sensitive not to abandon them immediately upon the demand of those who at this moment were the judges of his honor; sallying boldly from the spot he had chosen to defend at the outset of the combat, with its sort of natural entrenchment around his feet, he delivered a succession of lusty blows with undiminished vigor at the head of his adversary, whose strength had already begun to flag, but which the latter managed to parry skillfully with his shield. But in the very first moments of this new phase of the combat Sir Friedrich was the victim of a piece of ill luck that did not, however, necessarily indicate the presence of a higher power swaying the struggle: catching his foot in his own spur he stumbled and fell, and as he sank to his knees under the weight of the helmet and armor encumbering the upper part of his body, his hand stretched out in the dust to support himself, Count Jacob the Redbeard, in not exactly the most magnanimous and chivalrous fashion, thrust his sword into his exposed side. Sir Friedrich, with an cry of momentary pain, sprang up from the ground. Settling his helmet in place and wheeling quickly to confront his adversary again, he prepared to continue the battle, but as he leaned for a moment on his sword, his body doubled up in pain and darkness overspreading his eyes, the Count thrust his battle sword twice more into his breast, just under the heart; whereupon he crashed to the ground in a clatter of armor, his sword and shield dropping at his side. The Count, after tossing his weapons over the barrier, set his foot on his foeman's chest as the trumpets sounded a triple flourish; and while all the spectators, led by the Emperor himself, started up from their seats with stifled outcries of horror and pity, Lady Helena, followed by her two daughters, threw herself upon her darling son who lay in the dust weltering in his own blood. "My Friedrich!" she cried, kneeling grief-stricken at his head, while two bailiffs lifted Lady Littegarde, limp and unconscious, from the floor of the platform where she had collapsed and carried her off to prison. "The wretch!" Lady Helena said, "the abandoned creature, to dare to come here, knowing her own guilt full well, and force weapons into the hand of the truest and most chivalrous of friends so that he might try to win God's verdict for her in an unrighteous duel!" And wailing and raising her beloved son from the ground, while her daughters freed him of his armor, she tried to staunch the blood welling from the wounds in his breast. But bailiffs came up on the Emperor's orders and arrested him as one whose life was also forfeit to the law; with the help of doctors he was laid upon a litter and carried, at the head of a large crowd, straight off to prison, where Lady Helena and her daughters, however, were given permission to attend him until his death, about which no one had any doubts.

But it soon appeared that Sir Friedrich's wounds, as sensitive and vital as were the affected parts, were not, by a special heavenly dispensation, mortal; on the contrary, the doctors in whose care he was placed were able in a few days to assure the family positively that he would live, that, indeed, he would be completely recovered in a few weeks' time, without suffering any mutilation of the body, thanks to the strength of his constitution. No sooner had he recovered consciousness, after having fainted from the pain for a long spell, than Sir Friedrich began to ask his mother over and over again how Lady Littegarde was. He could not keep back his tears when he thought of her alone in prison, a prey to the most dreadful despair, and he begged his sisters, as he affectionately stroked their chins, to visit and comfort her. Lady Helena, dismayed by these words, implored him to forget the infamous woman; one could forgive her the offense Count Jacob had mentioned before the court, she said, which the outcome of the duel had now exposed to the light of day, but not her shamelessness and insolence in appealing like any innocent person to the sacred verdict of God, even though she had been well aware of her own guilt and of the destruction she was bringing down on her gallant friend.

"Oh, Mother," said the Chamberlain, "show me the man who, even if he possessed the wisdom of the ages, would dare to interpret the mysterious verdict God has rendered in this duel!"

"What?" Lady Helena exclaimed. "The meaning of the divine verdict is obscure to you? Isn't it only too plain and unambiguous, alas, that you were beaten by your opponent's sword?"

"All right," answered Sir Friedrich, "I was beaten by him, for a moment. But did the Count really triumph over me? Am I not alive? Do I not thrive again miraculously, as if under the breath of heaven, ready in perhaps a few days, with redoubled or tripled strength, to resume the battle that a silly accident interrupted?"

"Fool!" cried his mother. "Don't you know there is a law that says a duel, once the umpires' verdict has ended it, can't be fought again over the same cause before the bar of divine justice?"

"Never mind!" retorted the Chamberlain angrily. "What do I care about these arbitrary laws of human beings? How can a combat that hasn't ended in the death of one or the other of the contestants be considered fought to a finish in any reasonable view of things; mayn't I hope that, if I am allowed to resume the fight, I could repair the accident that befell me and with my sword compel an altogether different verdict of God than the one that is now so narrowly and shortsightedly taken as such?"

"Nevertheless," rejoined his mother thoughtfully, "the laws you say you don't care anything about are the ones that hold sway; reasonable or not, they enforce the authority of the divine statutes and deliver you and her up, like a pair of detestable sinners, to the full rigors of criminal justice."

"Oh," exclaimed Sir Friedrich, "that is just what fills me with such despair! She has been condemned to death exactly as if she were a convicted criminal; and I who wanted to prove her virtue and innocence to the world, I am the one who has brought all this on her: one disastrous stumble in the straps of my spurs—perhaps God meant by that to punish me for my own sins, it had nothing to do with Lady

Littegarde's cause—consigns her budding limbs to the flames and her memory to eternal disgrace." At these words his eyes filled with tears; taking out his handkerchief, he turned to the wall, while Lady Helena and her daughters, greatly moved, knelt down wordlessly beside the bed to kiss his hands and mingled their tears with his. Meanwhile the warder of the tower had come in with food for the prisoner and his people, and when Sir Friedrich asked him how Lady Littegarde was, he gathered from the man's abrupt and offhand words that she lay upon a heap of straw and had not spoken a word since the day of her confinement. This news alarmed Sir Friedrich extremely; he instructed the warder to tell the lady, so as to ease her mind, that by a strange decree of heaven he was on the way to full recovery, and that he asked her permission, once he was fully restored to health, to pay her a visit in her cell with the castellan's approval. But the answer the warder said she gave him, after he had shaken her arm repeatedly as she lay on the straw like a madwoman, seeing and hearing nothing, was no: she did not want to see another soul again as long as she was on this earth—indeed, it transpired that on this very day she had given orders to the castellan, in a note by her own hand, to allow absolutely no one, Chamberlain von Trota least of all, to visit her. But moved by his extreme concern for her, Sir Friedrich got up one day when he felt an access of his old strength, obtained the castellan's permission, and feeling sure of her forgiveness, without any warning, accompanied by his mother and two sisters, went to her cell.

How describe the unfortunate Littegarde's horror when she got up, on hearing the noise at the door, from the straw that had been put down for her, her bosom half exposed and her hair disheveled, and instead of the expected warder saw her noble friend, the Chamberlain, enter her cell on Berta's and Kunigunde's arm, a melancholy and touching figure on whom the traces of his recent sufferings plainly showed. "Go away!" she cried, throwing herself backward on the covers of her pallet in despair and hiding her face in her hands. "If there is a spark of pity in your bosom, go away!"

"But why, dear Littegarde?" Sir Friedrich said. Leaning on his mother, he crossed the room and bent down, with inexpressible feeling, to take her hand.

"Go away!" she cried, recoiling from him on her knees across the straw. "If you don't want me to go mad, don't touch me! You are an abomination to me; the hottest flames are less dreadful to me than you!"

"Abomination?" Sir Friedrich said in bewilderment. "What has your Friedrich done, my generous-hearted Littegarde, to deserve this greeting?" Here Kunigunde, at a signal from her mother, drew up a chair for him and asked him to remember how weak he was.

"Oh, Jesus!" Littegarde cried, flinging herself down in a frenzy of terror at his feet and pressing her face to the floor. "Leave the room, my darling, and forget me! Let me hug your knees, let me wash your feet with my tears, let me writhe like a worm in the dust before you, only I beseech you to grant me this one merciful favor: leave the room, my lord and master, leave it this instant and forget me!"

Sir Friedrich stood in front of her, shaken through and through. "Do you find the sight of me so unpleasant, Littegarde?" he asked, looking earnestly down at her.

"Dreadful, unbearable, crushing!" she answered, bending forward despairingly on her hands and hiding her face between his feet. "All the horrors of hell are pleasanter for me to look at than the love and kindness beaming at me out of the springtime of your face!"

"Good heavens!" exclaimed the Chamberlain. "What am I to think of such violent remorse? Did the ordeal tell the truth, unhappy woman, after all, and are you guilty of the crime the Count accused you of before the court?"

"Guilty, convicted, and condemned—damned and doomed through time and eternity!" exclaimed Littegarde, beating her breast like a madwoman. "God is truthful and never errs; go, my

mind is leaving me and I'm at the end of my strength. Leave me
alone with my misery and despair!"

At these words Sir Friedrich fainted away; and while Littegarde
covered her head with a veil and lay back upon her bed as though
taking leave of the world forever, Berta and Kunigunde, with
exclamations of pity, knelt down beside their unconscious brother
to revive him. "A curse on you!" cried Lady Helena as the Chamberlain's eyes fluttered open again. "May you suffer eternal remorse
this side of the grave, and eternal damnation on the other, not for
the guilty deed you now confess to, but for your pitilessness and
cruelty in admitting to it only after having dragged my innocent son
down with you to destruction! What a fool I am!" she went on,
turning contemptuously away from Littegarde. "If I had only
believed what the prior of the Augustinian cloister in this place
confided to me just before the duel began, right after the Count,
who was preparing his soul for the fateful hour ahead, had come to
him for confession! He swore on the Sacred Host to the truth of what
he had testified before the court about this wretched woman; he
described the garden gate where they had agreed to meet at nightfall; the room, an out-of-the-way one in the uninhabited castle tower,
to which she led him without attracting the notice of the guards;
the comfortable couch, with its heaped-up cushions and splendid
canopy, in which she went to bed with him in secret, shameless
debauchery. A solemn oath, sworn at such a time, is no lie; if only
I had not been so deluded and had given my son some hint of this,
even at the moment the duel began, I should have opened his eyes
to the truth and he would have drawn away from the abyss's edge!
But come," called Lady Helena, gently embracing Sir Friedrich
and pressing a kiss on his forehead, "telling her our indignation only
does her honor; let her look at our backs and despair, crushed by
our unspoken accusations!"

"The wretch!" retorted Littegarde, stung by these words and
sitting up. Resting her head in her grief on her knee, and shedding

hot tears in her handkerchief, she said, "I remember when my brothers and I visited his castle three days before St. Remigius's Night; he had arranged a banquet in my honor, as he often used to do, and my father, who enjoyed seeing the charms of my blossoming youth fêted, had persuaded me to accept the invitation and attend the banquet in the company of my brothers. Late in the evening, when the dancing had ended, I entered my bedroom and found a note upon the table, written in an unfamiliar hand and without a signature, that contained an open declaration of love. It so happened that my two brothers had come in with me to discuss our departure the next day; in silent astonishment I handed them the strange communication I had found, for there were never any secrets between us. Immediately recognizing the Count's hand, they boiled with rage, and my elder brother was ready to burst into the Count's room with the paper in his hand; but my younger brother pointed out how risky such a step would be in view of the fact that the Count had been shrewd enough not to sign the note; whereupon both of them, outraged at such offensive behaviour, got into the carriage with me that very night, and swearing never to honor his castle with their presence again, returned home.—This," she added, "is the only thing I have ever had to do with that scoundrel!"

"What?" exclaimed the Chamberlain, turning his tear-stained face to her. "These words are music to my ears! Let me hear them again!" he said after a pause, getting down on his knees to her and clasping his hands. "Is it true that you haven't been false to me with that wretch, and you are innocent of what he accused you of before the court?"

"Dearest!" whispered Littegarde, pressing his hand to her lips.

"Are you?" shouted the Chamberlain, "Are you?"

"As innocent as a newborn baby's breast, as the conscience of a man who has just come from confession, as the corpse of a nun that died in the vestry while taking the veil."

"Oh merciful God!" exclaimed Sir Friedrich, hugging her knees,

"Your words make me live again; death has no terror for me any longer, and eternity, which just a moment ago stretched before me like a sea of endless misery, now looms up bright as a country with a thousand suns!"

"Oh, you unhappy man!" said Littegarde, recoiling from him. "How can you believe a single word that comes from my mouth?"

"Why shouldn't I?" asked Sir Friedrich impetuously.

"Madman! Maniac!" cried Littegarde. "Hasn't God's sacred judgment gone against me? Weren't you beaten by the Count in that fatal duel? Hasn't he vindicated with his arms the truth of what he accused me of before the court?"

"My dearest Littegarde," exclaimed the Chamberlain, "don't let despair get the better of you; rear up the conviction that you have within you like a tower of rock; cling to it and never waver, even if the earth below and the heavens above should founder. Let us believe the more intelligible and reasonable of the two ideas that baffle the understanding here, and, rather than thinking you guilty, let us think I won the duel I fought for you.—God, Lord of my life," he added at this point, pressing his face into his hands, "keep my own soul from distraction! As truly as I hope to be saved, I believe that my enemy's sword hasn't triumphed over me, seeing that I have arisen from under the dust of his heel to live again. Why must divine wisdom be expected to announce and proclaim the truth the very instant it is invoked? Oh Littegarde," he concluded, pressing her hand between his own, "in life let us look forward to death, and in death to eternity, and hold fast now to our unshakable conviction that your innocence will at last be revealed in the clear light of day, and through this very duel I fought for you." Just then the castellan came in; and when he reminded Lady Helena, who sat crying at a table, that so much agitation might do her son harm, Sir Friedrich was prevailed upon by his family to return to his cell, not without a feeling that he had given and received some consolation.

Meanwhile an indictment was presented to the Emperor's court in Basel, charging Sir Friedrich von Trota and his friend Lady Littegarde von Auerstein with having culpably invoked the verdict of God, and the pair were condemned, according to the law, to die ignominiously at the stake on the very spot on which the duel had been fought. A deputation of councilors was sent to inform the prisoners of this, and the verdict would have been carried out as soon as the Chamberlain's health was restored if the Emperor had not secretly decided that he must have an opportunity to observe how Count Jacob the Redbeard, against whom he could not suppress a kind of suspicion, behaved at the scene of the execution. But the latter, quite unaccountably and strangely, was still sick from the small and apparently trifling wound that Sir Friedrich had given him at the beginning of the duel; an extremely dangerous condition of his bodily fluids had for days, and then for weeks, prevented the wound's healing, and all the skill of the doctors who were called in, one after the other, from Suabia and Switzerland did not avail to close it. Indeed, a malignant pus unknown to the entire medical science of that day ate its way, cancerlike, through the whole hand down to the bone, so that it proved necessary, to the horror of all his friends, to amputate it and—when this did not halt the infection —the arm itself. Yet even this remedy, which was recommended as a radical way of dealing with the infection, only made matters worse, as could have easily been foreseen today; and when his entire body began gradually to fester and rot away, the doctors announced that there was no way to save him—he would be dead before the week was out. The Prior of the Augustinian cloister, who thought he saw the dread hand of God in this unexpected turn of events, vainly exhorted him to tell the truth about his quarrel with the Regent-Duchess; the Count, who was completely unnerved, again took holy sacrament upon the truthfulness of his testimony, and giving every indication of the most terrible fear, wished his soul eternally damned if he should have falsely accused Lady Littegarde. Now despite the looseness of his life, there were two good reasons for believing in the essential honesty of this assurance: first, the sick man as a matter of fact possessed a certain piety that made it seem unlikely he would swear a false oath at such a time; and secondly, an interrogation of the warder of the tower of Breda Castle, whom the Count claimed to have bribed to let him in, bore out his words, thus proving conclusively that he had been inside Breda Castle on the night of St. Remigius. Such being the case, hardly anything else remained for the Prior but to conclude that the Count himself had been deceived by some unknown third person; and the wretched man, to whom this same terrible thought occurred when he heard of the Chamberlain's miraculous recovery, had still not reached the end of his life when this suspicion was, to his despair, completely confirmed. Now the reader should know that long before the Count's desire fixed on Lady Littegarde, he had been enjoying illicit relations with her waiting woman, Rosalie; on almost every one of her mistress' visits to his castle he was accustomed to taking the girl, who was a thoughtless, loose creature, to his room in the middle of the night. When Littegarde, on the last visit she and her brothers paid his castle, received the tender note in which he announced his passion for her, the anger and jealousy of the girl, whom the Count had been neglecting for months, was aroused; she had to accompany Littegarde when the latter made her hasty departure from the castle, but she left behind a note, signed with her lady's name, in which she told the Count that because her brothers were so outraged at what he had done it would be impossible for her to see him immediately, but that he was invited to visit her in an apartment of her father's castle on the night of St. Remigius. The Count was overjoyed at the success of his venture, and immediately wrote a second letter to Littegarde to say that he would certainly be there on that night, and he only asked her, so as to avoid any mistakes, to send a trustworthy person to guide him to her rooms; and since the waiting woman, who was a practiced hand at every kind of intrigue, had expected

such a letter from him, she was able to intercept it and send him
a second forged note saying that she herself would meet him at the
garden gate. Then on St. Remigius' day, on the excuse of wishing
to visit a sister who was ill, she asked Littegarde's permission to go
into the country; when this was granted, she did in fact leave the
castle, late in the afternoon, with a bundle of laundry under her
arm, and in full view of everybody took the road leading to her
sister's. But instead of actually going there, she came back to the
castle at nightfall, on the pretext that a storm was coming up; since
she would be making an early start in the morning, she said, and
did not want to disturb her mistress, she arranged to spend the
night in one of the vacant rooms in the solitary and seldom visited
castle tower. The Count, who got into the castle by bribing the
warder and was met at midnight, as agreed, by a veiled figure at the
garden gate, had no suspicion, as one may easily imagine, of the
trick being played on him; the girl gave him a hasty kiss on the
mouth and led him up and down several stairways and corridors in
the deserted wing until they came to one of the most splendid rooms
in the castle, the windows of which she had carefully locked beforehand. Here, after stealthily listening at the doors while holding his
hand and whispering to him to be quiet on the pretense that her
brothers' bedroom was close by, she sank down with him on the bed
standing in the corner; the Count, deceived by her shape and stature,
swam in transports of pleasure at having made such a conquest at
his age; and when she sent him away at the first glimmering of dawn,
placing on his finger, as a souvenir of the night they had passed together, a ring given Littegarde by her husband, which she had pilfered
from her the evening before for just this purpose, he promised, as
soon as he reached home, to send her one in return which his late
wife had given him on their wedding day. Three days later he kept
his word and secretly sent the ring, which Rosalie was again clever
enough to intercept; but perhaps fearing that this adventure might
go too far, he made no further advances and on all sorts of pretexts

avoided a second meeting. Afterwards the girl was dismissed because of a theft that she was suspected almost certainly of having committed and was sent back to her parents' home on the Rhine; and nine months later, when the consequences of her debauched life came to light and she was sternly questioned by her mother, she named Count Jacob the Redbeard as the father of her child and revealed the whole story of her secret intrigue with him. Luckily she had been quite timid about offering the Count's ring for sale, for fear she would be suspected of having stolen it, and also because she had found nobody ready to pay its great price; and as there could be no doubt about the truth of her story, her parents, relying on this piece of visual evidence, sued the Count for support of the child. The court in which the suit was brought had heard of the strange case being tried in Basel and was eager to bring the discovery, which had a vital bearing on the latter's outcome, to the attention of the tribunal there; and as an alderman was just then leaving for that city on public business, they gave him a letter, to solve the terrible riddle that had all of Suabia and Switzerland on tenterhooks, to Count Jacob the Redbeard which contained the girl's official testimony as well as the ring.

It was on the very day appointed for the execution of Sir Friedrich and Lady Littegarde, which the Emperor, unaware of the doubts that had sprung up in the Count's own breast, felt he could postpone no longer, that the alderman bearing this letter entered the sick man's room and found him twisting and turning on his bed in terrible despair. "Enough!" he cried after reading the letter and receiving the ring, "I am tired of seeing the sunlight! Fetch me a litter," he said, turning to the Prior, "and carry this wretch that I am, whose strength is crumbling to dust, to the place of execution, I will not die until I've done an act of justice!" The Prior, deeply moved, immediately had four servants lift him up on a litter as he wished; and together with the immense crowd summoned by the pealing of the bells, he arrived with the unhappy man, who was clutching a crucifix in his hand, at the stake to which Sir Friedrich and Littegarde were already bound.

"Stop!" shouted the Prior, as he had the litter set down opposite the Emperor's balcony. "Before you light that pyre, hear what this sinner's mouth has to say to you!"

"What?" called the Emperor, rising pale as a corpse from his chair. "Has the sacred verdict of God gone against him after all, and is it conceivable, after all that has happened, that Littegarde is innocent of the offense he accused her of?" With these words he stepped down in astonishment from the balcony; and more than a thousand knights, whom the populace followed across the benches and barriers, crowded around the sick man's bier. "Innocent," he replied, raising himself up part way with the Prior's support—"such was the judgment Almighty God pronounced upon that fateful day before the eyes of all the assembled citizens of Basel! For the one of us who got three wounds in the duel, each of them a mortal injury, now flourishes, as you can see, in all the fullness of his strength and vigor; while a blow from his hand that scarcely seemed to scratch the husk and surface of my life has eaten its way with terrible patience into the kernel of my being and toppled my strength like the tempest does the oak. But in case there is some skeptic still harboring any doubts, here are the proofs: it was Rosalie, her waiting woman, who received me on that St. Remigius' Night while I imagined in the blindness of my senses that I was holding in my arms the one who had always contemptuously rejected my advances!" The Emperor, at these words, stood as if turned to stone. Turning toward the pyre, he ordered a knight to climb the ladder himself, untie the Chamberlain and Lady Littegarde, who had already fainted in Lady Helena's arms, and bring them to him. "See now, an angel watches over every hair on your head!" he exclaimed, when Littegarde, with half-bared bosom and loosened hair, leaning on the arm of her friend Sir Friedrich, whose own knees shook under the emotions of this miraculous deliverance, advanced toward him through the ring of people who made way for them in awe and wonder. He kissed both of them on the forehead as they knelt before him; and after asking his wife for the ermine she wore and hanging it around Littegarde's shoulders, he took her arm before the eyes of all the assembled knights and was about to lead her into the Imperial palace himself. But turning back to the Count, who was writhing pitiably on his litter, while the Chamberlain was exchanging his condemned man's shirt for a plumed hat and knight's cloak, and feeling compassion for the dying man, who had not after all entered into the duel that had destroyed him in any wanton or sacrilegious spirit, he asked the doctor standing at his side whether there was any hope for him.

"No hope!" answered Jacob the Redbeard, while he supported himself, amid terrible convulsions, in his physician's lap. "And I deserve to die. Since the arm of worldly justice cannot reach me now, let me tell you that I am the one who murdered my brother, the noble Duke Wilhelm von Breysach; six weeks before, hoping to gain the crown, I hired the villain who struck him down with the arrow from my armory." And with this explanation he fell back on the litter and breathed out his black soul.

"Ha, just as my husband suspected!" cried the Regent, who had come down to the square from the palace balcony in the wake of the Empress and stood next to the Emperor. "When he was dying he gasped out as much to me, though I did not quite understand him at the time!"

The Emperor retorted angrily, "The arm of justice shall at least reach your corpse! Take him," he cried, turning to the bailiffs, "and hand him over to the executioners as a convicted murderer; to brand his memory forever, let him be destroyed on the same pyre on which we were just about to sacrifice two innocent people for his sake!" And while the poor wretch's body crackled in the ruddy flames and the north wind blew his ashes all around, the Emperor, attended by all his knights, led Lady Littegarde into the castle. By Imperial decree he gave her back her inheritance from her father, which her brothers in their ignoble greed had already appropriated; and in three weeks' time the marriage of the noble couple was celebrated at the castle at Breysach, where the Regent-Duchess, very pleased at the turn events had taken, made Littegarde a wedding present of a large part of the Count's estates, which had been forfeited to the law. After the wedding the Emperor hung a chain of honor around Sir Friedrich's neck; and no sooner had he returned to Worms after winding up his affairs in Switzerland, than he had the statutes governing the holy trial by combat, wherever it was assumed that guilt was immediately revealed, amended to read: ". . . if it should be the will of God."